I0612286

The Offenses

Of

Jonce Nash

The Offenses

Of

Jonce Nash

Book three of the Walter Pigg trilogy

Carl Purdon

Copyright © 2023 Carl Purdon

All rights reserved, including the right to reproduce this book or portions thereof in any form without the written consent of the author. For information, email:

Carl.purdon@gmail.com

Or visit

CarlPurdon.com

ISBN-13: 978-1-7350027-4-3 (Paperback)
ISBN-13: 978-1-7350027-3-6 (E-book)

Cover by Damonza

This novel is a work of fiction. Any similarities to actual persons or events is unintentional.

Dedication

This book is dedicated to Nelda Leann Goodin. She was a loyal fan and good friend. She is greatly missed.

(April 4, 1964 - April 4, 2023)

Acknowledgements

I would not be able to do this without the love and support of my beautiful wife, Sharon. Thank you for being my editor, beta reader, and lifelong companion.

Also By Carl Purdon

THE NIGHT TRAIN

NORTON ROAD

BLINDERS

RED EYES

TEMPLE'S GHOST

THE DECONSTRUCTION OF WALTER PIGG

THE RECONSTRUCTION OF WALTER PIGG

Chapter One

J once Nash didn't believe in God. Even as a boy he had shunned religion. He never bought into the idea that God cared very much what a dirt-poor Mississippi boy did, and he couldn't imagine burning in hell for very long without getting used to it. Adaptability had always been his superpower, but now that death seemed imminent, he recalled an old saying about foxholes and atheists and mumbled his first prayer since childhood.

"Bet you're too smart to fall for that old saw," he said, looking up toward the roof of his pickup. "I ain't promising nothing in return." His head bobbed forward and struck the steering wheel with a thud. When he raised it again the sun had breached the horizon. It would be dark enough to move soon. Twenty minutes. Half hour at the most. Time stuck like a fly in molasses. Survival meant living one more second, then another. Reaching his apartment alive would be like winning the lottery.

The pain in his left bicep reminded him of stepping barefoot on a rusty nail when he was ten, except that he couldn't jerk his arm away from the bullet the way he could his foot off the nail.

His apartment was across the street and down two blocks. A short drive if he could keep his wits about him. Getting up the single flight of stairs without attracting attention would be the trick. He had the sort of neighbors who didn't call the cops but they might remember seeing something if they got pinched. A good number of them were Mexicans. Undocumented, probably, not that Jonce cared. His neighbor at the top of the stairs was married but her husband stayed away during the week. He had the strut of a construction worker. Their weekends were evenly split between loud fighting and louder lovemaking. The old woman on the other side was either a recluse or dead. Jonce hadn't smelled her rotting so he assumed recluse.

It was Friday and the husband would be home soon if not already. Sometimes he came home on a bender and the fireworks really went off. She cursed him for drinking and he cursed her for smoking pot and something inevitably hit the wall before the fighting stopped and the lovemaking began. She wasn't much to look at but she had energy. Jonce had always been drawn to women with energy, not that they were necessarily drawn to him because he wasn't much to look at either. He wasn't fat, though. He could say that much about himself.

The sun sank fast now. A man should die in his own bed instead of cowering behind the burned-out shell of a gas station like a stray dog cringing in the shadow of a boot. He checked his arm again. The sleeve of his shirt was slick with blood that had begun to congeal so that it stuck to his fingers instead of dripping off. The wad of shirt he had poked into the hole with his finger had stopped the gushing, though if it started again he didn't know if he could stand repeating the process. It might be easier to bleed out and be done with it. Get it over with. Bleeding out is like going to sleep, right? Hadn't he heard that someplace? Not by anybody who knew for sure, though. All those guys were dead.

Jonce opened his eyes and saw a woman standing over him. Her hair was black with blond highlights and it fell across her left shoulder when she leaned down and asked if he was awake. Her eyes were brown with the whites streaked red. She reeked of marijuana and he didn't know if she was going through his pockets or trying to help.

"You ain't no angel so I guess I'm alive," he said. She was too plain in the face to be a heavenly being. She wore a gray sweatshirt with a frayed collar, so she wasn't a hospital nurse. He moved his head and recognized his bedroom. "You live next door," he said, remembering her now that his eyes had adjusted to seeing. He gritted his teeth against the searing pain in his arm. He wasn't too proud to cry out, he just lacked the strength.

"Bobbie," she said. "You're heavier than you look."

She was smaller than he remembered from the few times he had seen her. Too small to carry him.

"Where'd you find me?"

"Half in and half out," she said.

"Half in and half out what?"

"Your door, stupid."

"You call anybody?"

"Not yet. Just got you put down."

"Who helped you?"

"You did," she said, "babbling out of your head about some woman named Ellie."

"Don't call nobody."

"Figured as much. You rob a bank or something?"

"No."

"I guess I would've heard about a bank getting robbed. Want me to call Ellie for you?"

"She's dead."

"You kill her?"

"She died on her own."

Bobbie pressed the back of her hand against his forehead. "You've got a terrible fever."

"Can you get this bullet out of my arm?"

"Sure, let me run next door and get my medical license," she said.

"I can't do it myself."

"I sew cushions for a living. I don't do surgery."

"I'll die if you don't."

"You'll die quicker if I start digging around in that arm," she said. "Best I call an ambulance."

"No!" Jonce grabbed her arm. "Don't call nobody!"

"You'll die."

"I ain't going back to prison."

She pulled her arm away. "If I was smart I would've looked the other way and left you laying."

"Well now you're in the thick of it so you gotta help me," he said. He squeezed his eyes shut to stave off the surge of pain that radiated up his arm and into his shoulder with hellacious fury. "If you won't do that then go away and let me die on my own. I don't like being watched."

"My husband'll be home soon. His name's Don and he wouldn't like me being over here. I can come back Sunday after he leaves if you want me to. He works construction. He sleeps around on me but he thinks I don't know. I got a nose, though, and I know what I don't smell like. Did you ever cheat on Ellie? Before she died I mean."

"You got any whiskey?"

"I've got some pot."

"Whiskey," Jonce said. "I'll pay." He grabbed her arm again and squeezed tighter this time. She tried to pull away but he summoned the strength to hold her. Desperation gives a man that little something extra. "There's a liquor store on the corner. There's money in my right front pocket."

"I can't. Don might come home." She jerked her arm free and stood.

"Is Don the kind of man who'd let somebody die?"

"He's the kind who'll call the cops on you then give me a black eye when they leave."

"Take the hundred and keep the change," Jonce said. "Two bottles of whatever's cheap."

"I might have a wine cooler in my fridge. Whiskey tears my stomach up and Don drinks beer."

"It has to be whiskey," he said. "And bring me a joint."

She reached down and stuck her fingers into his pocket. "I know who you are," she said. "Your name's Jonce Nash and you're just out of prison for robbing a place. Maybe I'll keep the money and call the cops. It's probably not your money anyway. Is it marked?"

"You call the cops and they'll take me to a hospital and I'll live," Jonce said. "You'll never sleep with both eyes closed again wondering when they'll let me out."

She laughed. "You don't scare me." She held the hundred up to the light and examined both sides, then she stuffed it into her pocket. "Maybe I won't call the cops. You'll be dead by morning if that fever don't break."

Jonce closed his eyes. When he opened them again she was gone.

Jonce awoke hungry. Famished, as if he hadn't eaten in days. His head hurt and his mouth felt dry and fluffy like cotton. He was incredibly thirsty. His entire body felt as dry as a cracked sponge. He didn't remember being shot until he moved. The pain was dull and achy now instead of sharp and piercing. His bedroom was mostly dark but it was *his* bedroom and not a hospital. She hadn't called the cops. He turned his head and tucked his chin into his collarbone and tried to see his arm. The bandage looked fresh, with a dark spot the size of a half dollar over the wound. She had wrapped it at least, and she hadn't called the cops.

His tongue stuck to every part of his mouth that it touched. He closed his eyes and imagined himself lying in a cold stream with water flowing in one end and out the other, mouth to ass, refreshing everything in between with its coolness. The room spun when he raised his head, so he relaxed back into his pillow and took three deep breaths. Three seemed to be the exact number of breaths for all occasions. When he was fifteen and dislocated his shoulder the coach told him to take three deep breaths before he jerked it back into place. When the prison doctor inserted that huge needle into his right knee to drain off the fluid after he got knocked down a flight of stairs he told him to take three deep breaths. So three it was.

It didn't help.

The nearest water was the bathroom sink. Walk, crawl, or drag, he had to have water. He could do it with proper girding, he told himself. The human body can endure almost anything provided the brain gets advance warning.

He squeezed his eyes shut and took three deep breaths again. Habits are hard to break. The place was quiet. Too quiet. Weekends were when his neighbors let off steam. Don and Bobbie should either be arguing or screwing, or recovering from one or the other with the television blaring through the wall. His bedroom had the one small window so he knew it was light outside, though he had no idea what time of day it was.

He dropped his right leg off the mattress and felt his foot touch the floor. Raising himself took more effort but he soon sat on the edge of the bed with his eyes fixed on the bathroom door and his mind on the water he could get from the sink. She had given him some pills. He remembered that part now. She left with his money then she came back and poked three pills into his mouth and told him to swallow. He didn't remember anything else. The pills were worth the hundred dollars she took. He wished he had three more. Three breaths and three pills.

With a Herculean effort, he stood, then he steadied himself and took a step, then another, until he reached the bathroom sink and drank greedily from the faucet. Had it not given him water he would have drank from the toilet. The effect was immediate. When he raised himself again his head didn't spin and his knees didn't wobble, so he stepped out into the bedroom with his sights set on reaching the kitchen. His refrigerator was never crowded but he remembered there being a pack of sliced ham and a jar of pickles. There were other things too, such as cheese and mayo and milk, but it was the ham and pickles he wanted. A pile of ham slices between two pieces of bread, loaded with pickles, smeared with mayonnaise. His stomach grabbed his backbone and shook him. His wiry frame didn't have a fat store.

He rode the wall to the living room. His apartment was small and dirty. Every stick of furniture had belonged to the previous tenants. A single mother with two small boys, according to the pasty landlord and the crayon drawings on the bedroom wall. Not much of a cleaner upper. If cleanliness is next to godliness, the woman must have had one foot in hell because the place still had a stink to it. A dankness. Filth underneath a superficial layer of things wiped down with a rag every now and then. Floors swept but never mopped. Appliances that probably hadn't been pulled out from the wall and cleaned behind in forever. It hadn't bothered him much until that moment. Pain puts the senses on alert.

By the time he reached the kitchen he felt feverish again. For all he knew gangrene was eating away at the soft tissues of his arm beneath the bandage. Maybe that was what he smelled instead of the apartment. It might already be too late to save the arm. He should have given himself up. A man can get out of prison but he can't grow back his arm. He would be a sitting duck in Parchman. May as well drop his drawers and grab his ankles. Damned perverts. That was the part that took the most getting used to.

He pushed off the wall and staggered into the kitchen without falling, then he threw open the refrigerator door and devoured three ham slices straight out of the pack, then he grabbed the mayonnaise and pickles and cheese and dumped them on the table along with a loaf of bread and a knife from the drawer by the stove. Two sandwiches later he went to the cabinet and opened a bag of potato chips and grabbed a Coke from the refrigerator. There was beer, but he needed to get his head clear. The stove clock said 2:13 in big green digits. Strange for it to be so quiet next door at that time on a Saturday.

He nodded off at the table then awoke with a jerk. The stove clock said 2:21. The small rectangular table had three chairs instead of four, which didn't matter unless the manager tried to deduct the missing one from his deposit when he left the place.

It was time to take a serious look at his arm. She had wrapped the gauze in neat spirals like a real professional. He poked the bloody spot with his finger and grimaced. Whatever was underneath still hurt. Maybe it wasn't time to look yet. Not on a full stomach. He raised himself from the table and stumbled toward the sofa and collapsed. Dying wasn't such a terrible thing. Being dead didn't take any kind of special talent. As he drifted in and out of consciousness he visualized his funeral and tried to come up with names of the people who might attend. Outside of his parents he couldn't think of anyone, and even they might not make the trip up from Florida just to see a dead body.

He jumped awake, ready to fight or run, whichever option made the most sense, then he saw her standing over him and closed his eyes again. "If you've come for the bullet you'll have to wait," he said. "I feel like I've been pulled through the crack underneath the bathroom door. I can't stand no more pain right now."

She pressed the back of her hand to his forehead. "You're still burning up." She fumbled her purse and produced a small brown bottle. "I got something that might help." She dumped a small pill into her hand and offered it to him. "A friend of mine at work had these. She's allergic to penicillin. Are you? No? Well it's a good thing because antibiotics are harder to get than pain pills. Almost impossible. Funny, ain't it?"

He stared up at her. "Nothing's funny to me right now."

She went to the kitchen and ran a glass of water from the faucet. "I didn't expect you to be up. Looks like you ate something judging by this mess you left on the table. If you're still hungry I can fix something."

"Won't Don mind?"

"You remembered his name. I'm surprised you remember anything." She returned with the water and stuck the glass toward him. "He won't be back for four days," she said. "Sometimes I don't mind him being gone so much. Too much of anything is too much. You ever get tired of your wife? What was her name again?"

"Ellie."

"Yeah, Ellie. I probably shouldn't be asking, her being dead."

Four days. Jonce did the math in his head. "What day is this?"

7

"Monday."

"Monday! You mean I've been out all weekend?"

"Lucky thing for both of us, too," she said. "Don stuck to me like a tick this weekend. I only managed to get over here twice. Both times I expected to find you dead. Don't know what I would've done if you had been. What I would've told the cops, I mean. Don't go getting the idea I would've missed you. Are the cops watching this place? I expect they are. I've been real careful."

Jonce gently placed his hand on his arm and squeezed. The pain wasn't what he expected. "You sure that pill you gave me was an antibiotic?"

"Penicillin," she said. "It says something I can't pronounce on the bottle but my friend swore it was penicillin. You ain't feeling allergic are you?"

"Arm's going numb. I probably got gangrene."

"I washed the knife with alcohol," she said. "Rubbing, not drinking. And I poured some in the hole after I got the bullet out. You was out cold. Good thing I reckon."

Jonce squeezed the bandage again. "You got the bullet out?"

"It practically came out on it own. Lucky for you Don hit the bars before he came home or you'd probably be dead by now. When I came back with the whiskey you were out of your head. You spilled more than you drank."

"I remember you gave me some pills. After that I don't remember anything."

She smiled. "Good ain't they? I could've sold 'em on the street for a small fortune but lucky for you I don't deal. They were expired but I guess they still had some kick."

Jonce squeezed his forehead and tried to focus the room. "I'll say they did. Are you sure this is Monday?"

"Well if it ain't I went to work today for nothing," she said. "The bottle said one but I figured you needed two. It wouldn't hurt you to thank me, you know. I saved your life."

"How'd you get in here?"

"Your key," she said, producing his key from her purse and holding it up. "You left it in the door that night I found you passed out on the floor. Good thing it was me who found you and not the Mexicans."

"Mexicans ain't so bad," he said, remembering a few who had done him a good turn.

"Don says they're taking all the jobs."

"Mexicans gotta eat too," Jonce said. "Are you sure it's Monday?"

"It's Monday. Stop asking. Don tells me all the time to keep the door locked or they'll steal everything not nailed down."

"No more than anybody else," Jonce said. "Anybody else know about this?"

"Sure, I went and told everybody," she said. "Are you going to thank me or not? I could put the bullet back in you know."

Jonce sank back into the sofa and took a deep breath to clear his head. He had been in and out of some scrapes before but this one took the cake. The guys back on his old cell block wouldn't believe it, and he hoped he never got the chance to tell them.

"Unwrap it so I can see what it looks like."

"Unwrap it yourself. Your other arm ain't hurt."

"Okay, thank you," Jonce said. "Thank you very much for helping me."

"That's better."

"Now unwrap the damned thing and let me see it."

She leaned forward with a tortured sigh and unwrapped his arm one slow spiral at a time. She smelled harsh, the way a woman does when she perfumes herself then sweats.

"They must keep it hot inside that factory where you work," he said.

"How'd you know? You didn't follow me did you?"

"Never mind."

The blood stain grew larger with each layer removed, until the entire width of the gauze was colored red.

"There," she said, exposing the wound. "Happy?"

He twisted his arm upward trying to see the full extent of his condition. The hole was closed but he didn't see any stitches. "How'd you close it up like that?"

"Superglue."

"How'd you get the bullet out?"

"Like I said, it practically fell out on its own," she said. "It was all the way on the back side of your arm. Good thing for you I felt it before I started digging. All I had to do was make a little cut and squeeze it out. Just like popping a pimple."

He reached around and explored the backside of his bicep with his fingers. "How come you didn't glue that hole?"

"I did," she said. "It was big enough to put my thumb in. I thought maybe it needed to drain so I left a little bit of it open."

Jonce was impressed. "Not bad for a girl who sews cushions."

"I watch Chicago Med," she said. She picked up on his lack of understanding and told him it was a TV show. A medical drama.

"Are there any red streaks coming out if it?"

"No."

"Any yellow pus?"

"It's not infected," she said. "You owe me for a bottle of rubbing alcohol."

Jonce relaxed his head back into the cushion and breathed a sigh of relief. Maybe he wasn't going to lose his arm after all. "You can't tell nobody about this."

"It ain't the sort of thing I want getting back to my husband," she said. "Or to whoever shot you. Who did shoot you anyway?"

"Never you mind," Jonce said. He knew Tipton Palo wouldn't talk. He had every reason in the world to keep his mouth shut unless he got pinched and thought he could weasel his way into a deal. Throw Jonce under the bus and hide behind his stellar reputation that wasn't so stellar anymore.

"Did I talk while I was out of my head?"

"Besides calling for your wife?"

"Besides that."

"You didn't tell any secrets if that's what you're asking. Who's Jayrod?"

"None of your business."

"Well whoever he is I hope you don't find him."

"I'm not looking for him," he said. "But if I was I'd find him. How long have I been on the couch?"

"You were in bed this morning when I went to work."

That explained why he wasn't hungry. Instead of eating Saturday, he had eaten a few hours ago. The entire weekend was lost. "You seen anybody snooping around?"

"If you mean cops, no."

"I mean anybody."

"You afraid of somebody?"

"Did I say I was afraid of somebody?"

"Maybe whoever shot you'll come around to finish the job," she said. "Maybe I shouldn't be here when he comes." She went to the kitchen and rinsed the glass in the sink, then she rinsed out the plate he had left on the table. Jonce watched her, wondering what her angle was. Everybody has an angle. She looked better from behind than straight on. The kind of woman a man sees and gets his hopes up, then she turns around. She wasn't ugly, just plain. Ellie had been plain that way. More plain, now that he thought about it. Plain from all directions.

Bobbie finished the dishes and returned. "Want me to help you back to bed?"

"No."

"Want the TV on?"

"No."

"Want another pill for the pain?"

"No."

"Good. If you need anything just knock on the wall."

Jonce studied her. "Why are you doing this?"

She shrugged. "I don't know. Nothing much ever happens around here. Maybe I'm just bored."

She turned to leave but he stopped her. "How did you know I was in prison?"

"Internet," she said. "You looked the type. You're lucky you're not a rapist or a murderer or I would've let you die. Maybe not for murder but for rape I would. A man can have a reason for killing somebody but not for raping."

"I'm just a petty thief," Jonce said. He was more than that now, of course, but she didn't need to know any of that. "Can you wrap my arm again before you leave?"

"As long as you don't start thinking I'm a nurse."

"Just until I can do it myself," he said.

She fetched a roll of gauze and some antibiotic salve from the bedroom then sat beside him on the edge of the sofa. "You know any child molesters in prison?"

"I knew all sorts of men in prison," Jonce said. "It's not an easy place."

She began dabbing on some salve with a finger he hoped was clean. "Is it true what they say about men like that in there? What happens to them?"

"Sometimes. Not everybody in prison is guilty you know."

She laughed.

"It's true. Take me, I've done all sorts of criminal acts in my life but the one they sent me to prison for was the one I didn't do."

She finished with the salve and started with the gauze.

"I was framed by my own kid."

11

She hesitated, then continued. "I don't believe you."

"It's true. You and Don got any kids?"

"Don's sterile," she said. "He tried to blame it on me after we'd been trying for a while but I checked out good so they tested him. Turns out his little swimmers don't swim."

"Kinda puts you in a tight spot if you turn up pregnant, don't it?"

She pulled the gauze tight and made him squirm. "Just what exactly are you trying to say?"

"Nothing," he said, exhaling the pain away. "I was just making an observation about him being out of town so much and you being, well —."

"Me being what? Don't get any ideas, tiger. My Don would break you in half."

Jonce grinned. "These walls are so thin I can't help but hear things."

She blushed. The color in her cheeks made her look a bit more appealing. He looked at his arm. The job was finished except for tying the ends so it wouldn't come loose.

"I'm sure you press your ear to the wall," she said, tying the ends with a bit too much force. He grimaced. "What? Too tight?." She stood. "I'll bring you some supper over in a little while if you want. Just supper, mind you. Don't get no ideas."

"No," he said. "I think I'll sleep."

Chapter Two

T he upper half of the sign in front of the only motel in Hayes had been taken off by a storm or by rot. Jackie couldn't tell which and she couldn't afford to be choosy. For the first time in a long time money was an issue, and every transaction had to be strictly cash. No credit cards. No personal checks. She had to live completely off the financial grid if she wanted to survive.

Jordan carried the bags from the car to the room without the complaining one might expect from a boy his age. Fifteen going on twenty. The past few days had matured him at the expense of his innocence. Every mother wants to think her son is innocent, but in Jordan's case it was true. Had been true.

"See, it's not so bad," she said, standing between two queen beds looking around the dull interior that could have been a movie set from 1970. The carpet was worn almost to the backing along a narrow trail from the door to the bathroom, then along an arc to the bed.

"Smells like feet," Jordan said with a sniff. "Stanky ole truck driver feet."

"What do you know about truck driver feet? Get those bags on the bed so I can unpack." She looked around, hoping the place didn't have bedbugs. "We passed a Walmart on the way in," she said. "I'll run down and get some cleaning supplies and pick us up a pizza." His face brightened at the mention of pizza.

Half an hour later she returned with a large pepperoni and two Cokes in plastic bottles and ate lunch with her son, then she showed him the cleaning supplies and told him to be sure to clean the toilet seat before sitting on it. He grumbled as she stripped the covers and sheets from both beds and told him she would be back soon. "You know I've got that job interview and you like to eat so stop

13

complaining." She scooped up the pile of linens and told him to get the door. "Lock it behind me and don't go out," she said. "You don't know this neighborhood." It had been a long time since she had traveled south of the Mason Dixon. Old memories die hard.

The Hayes police department was housed in a small building on Main Street not far from City Hall. The white brick front begged for a fresh coat of paint. She had lied to her son about having a job interview, but she had faxed the police chief her resume before leaving Detroit so it wasn't a completely cold call. Hayes needed a detective and she needed a job.

"I'd like to speak to Chief Ball," she said to the only person she saw upon entering. The woman sat at a desk behind a thick glass barrier that she probably thought was bulletproof. Awkward seconds passed without the woman acknowledging her.

"Excuse me. I'd like to speak to Chief Ball."

The woman raised her eyes. "And you are?"

"Detective Jackie Deen," she said with all the confidence she could muster. "Detroit Police Department."

The woman's eyes widened. "*Detroit?*"

"Yes, I —."

"Michigan?"

"Yes," Jackie said. "I'm here about —."

The woman tapped on her computer keyboard. "No," she said, slowly shaking her head side to side. "We don't have any extraditions to Detroit." She leaned forward and looked past Jackie. "Not expecting anyone either."

"I'm alone," Jackie said. "If I can speak to the chief I'll —."

The woman raised a finger to shush her, then she lifted the handset of a black desk phone and spoke with her hand cupped around the mouthpiece. Three seconds later she returned the phone to its cradle and forced a smile. "Have a seat over there," she said, pointing toward a row of plastic chairs along the far wall.

Jackie surrendered herself to the row of chairs and selected the least dirty of the bunch, a red one near the center that had a crack in the seat that she didn't notice until she sat down. The woman at the desk stood and disappeared through a door behind her.

Minutes passed. Ten, then fifteen, until finally a reasonably handsome man about her age or slightly older appeared from a hallway and looked in her direction. He looked too young to be a chief. Realizing she was about to be brushed off by an underling, she forced a smile as he approached.

"I'm Assistant Chief Andrew Gant," he said, offering his hand. His manner was pleasant but he wasn't the chief. At least he wasn't a sergeant. It had been silly of her to expect to go straight to the top without an appointment. "What brings you all the way from Detroit, Detective --?"

"Deen," she said, coming so close to giving her real name that it scared her. So much depended on her being careful. She stood and shook the assistant chief's hand. "Jackie Deen. I'm here about the job."

"Oh, that," he said. "I'm afraid we've had to put that position on hold. I wish you had called before coming all this way."

Jackie glanced at the woman who had returned to her position behind the glass. The woman looked away. "I was in the area," Jackie said, "and I thought it was worth shot to stop by."

Gant glanced back over his left shoulder at the woman. "Perhaps we should talk in my office."

Jackie followed with reluctance, wondering why if there was no job there should be a conversation. Her gut told her the job was still open, just not to her. Not to any woman, probably. Not to a black woman especially. She felt within her rights to think it.

The office was small and in need of fresh paint but was meticulously tidy. Assistant Chief Gant was no slob. He waited for her to sit before taking his place behind his nondescript steel desk. Her desk in Detroit had been identical except for the color. Hers had been dark gray where his was cream.

"I'm surprised our little ad reached your neck of the woods," he said.

"I'm originally from Birmingham."

Gant nodded as though she had just solved a riddle. Hayes wasn't very far off the beaten path between Birmingham and Detroit. He looked around his office. "You've probably already guessed we get by on a shoestring budget."

"Salary isn't the reason I came," she said.

"It's our pleasant summers then," he said. He had a warming smile. Very cordial. Almost attractive.

"No, I remember the summers too well," she said. "My father moved back to Birmingham ten years ago. He was recently diagnosed with lung cancer."

"I'm very sorry."

"I want to be closer to him."

"It's three hours to Birmingham."

"That's better than seventeen."

Jackie's lie was well-baked. She had rehearsed it during the fourteen-hour drive south. Fourteen hours broken up over the course of three days. Two other departments had already turned her down. One in South Bend, Indiana and one in West Memphis, Arkansas. Hayes was the last town on her list and she was getting desperate. "Three hours is close enough," she said. "It's complicated." She dropped her eyes for dramatic effect. Most people won't push if they think you're on the brink of tears. "I faxed my resume to Chief Ball."

"Did he offer you the job?"

"Not exactly." The truth was that the chief had given her no response at all.

"I see."

"You need a detective and I need a job. I'm a very good detective, Chief Gant."

"Assistant Chief," he corrected her. "And I'm afraid it's not my decision. The board approved the hiring but we've, well, some other things have popped up. Fires to put out you might say."

What little money she had would be gone soon, but she refused to appear desperate. "If I can ask without offending you," she said, watching his face for any red flags before continuing. "Is it possible for me to speak to Chief Ball? I really need this job." She pulled out a paper with the name and number of her former boss. He was one of two people in the world she still trusted. "I have references." Her former partner was the second name but she would hold it in reserve until asked, thinking if she forced them to ask for a second they might not press her for a third.

"I'm afraid that's not possible right now," he said, hiding something.

"If you're trying to tell me I'm not *right* for the job then just say it outright," she said, thinking not *white* enough, or not *male* enough, suppressing the anger because anger rarely makes any situation better.

"I'm sure you're qualified," he said. "Probably too qualified."

"There's no such thing as too qualified."

"More qualified than our little town can afford is what I meant."

"I wouldn't expect to make what I made in Detroit."

He nodded again. "Are you staying in town?"

"I have a room at the motel. I was hoping to get an interview before going on to Birmingham."

"And if you got that interview ... would you still be going to Birmingham?"

"If you're asking me when I could start, immediately."

"We had a murder last week," he said. "And we've got state investigators crawling all over the place right now. Until recently, I was the detective."

"The? As in you only have one?"

"Had one," he said. "I guess you could say I'm pulling double duty."

Her hopes rose. They were almost as desperate as she was. "I've solved my share of murders."

"Well I haven't. Until recently we didn't have much crime here."

"Recently?"

"You might say our crime rate exploded overnight. Take some time this afternoon and read last week's newspaper if you can find a copy," he said. "If not, the new edition comes out tomorrow."

"Am I looking for something in particular?"

"You'll know what I mean when you see it," he said. "I'm not trying to be evasive, but things are up in the air right now and I'm not sure when we'll be able to fill the job. I'm sorry."

"I'll read your newspaper," she said. "And I'll be in town a few more days if you change your mind about that interview."

"Email me your resume and I'll talk to the mayor," He handed her a card with his contact information. "There's a nice restaurant just down the street from the motel if you like southern cooking."

"The mayor?"

"Our chief is on suspension," he said. "I may as well tell you since you'll read it in the paper anyway."

"Is he a suspect in the murder?"

"No."

She decided not to press. A good detective knows when to back off.

Jonce heard a noise at the door and scrambled up off the sofa with hopes of reaching the back window before whoever was on the other side broke through, then he considered the two-story drop and decided to hold his ground. If it was the cops he had nowhere to hide.

If it was Palo's men he figured his chances were better without two broken legs. Then he figured Palo didn't have men or he wouldn't have handled the dirty business of shooting him himself.

The door swung open and there stood Bobbie. She was a pretty sight even if she wasn't pretty.

"What the hell's wrong with you?"

It was Tuesday afternoon. One day since he had last seen her.

"You owe me forty-three dollars," she said, kicking the door closed with her foot. Plastic grocery bags hung from both hands as she lugged her way to the kitchen and deposited her load onto the table. She wore loose shorts and a little tube top that exposed her shoulders. An open invitation had he been interested. He wasn't.

"I can eat a month on forty-three dollars," he said. "Bring me a beer while you've got your head in my refrigerator."

She finished unpacking and putting away. "You can't drink alcohol with antibiotics."

"Who says I can't?"

She left the kitchen and felt his forehead. "No fever," she said. "Want me to fix you something to eat?"

"You trying to nurse me or bed me?"

"Don't flatter yourself. If you die I won't be able to tell anybody until you stink up the whole upper floor. Did you take your antibiotic?"

"Twice."

She frowned. "One in the morning and one before bed. It won't work if you don't take it right." She grabbed his arm and checked the dressing.

"I didn't know you were coming so I changed it myself."

She poked at the bandage and shook her head in a disapproving fashion. "I told my friend I had a yeast infection to get those antibiotics. If I get one now it'll be your fault."

He slapped her on the ass and said she might be right. She recoiled and told him to keep his hands to himself. Her face told him she meant it. All the better, because Jonce liked a good fight. Suddenly he was interested.

"There's talk in town," she said.

"What sort of talk?"

"About the police chief, mostly, and that man who got killed last week. They're saying his throat was cut. Have you heard about that?"

"No."

"They say everybody in town is scared to death who'll be next. I'm not scared though. Should I be scared?"

"What about the police chief?"

She shrugged as she stepped back within reach and removed the bandage. "That he's crooked."

"What cop ain't?"

"They're being all hush hush about suspects. One of our truck drivers is second cousins with the dispatcher and he said they think it was somebody he knew because there was no sign of a struggle. You know why I'm not scared?"

"Tell me."

"Because it was a man who got killed so it ain't no serial killing rapist who gets his jollies slicing up women. Let the men be scared for a change. Are you scared?"

"No, I ain't scared." Perry Stubbs had screwed over a lot of people. The suspect list had to be a mile long.

"I never understood that show," she said, tilting her head toward the television. "Is he the bad guy or the good guy?" Jonce had been watching a Breaking Bad marathon since noon. All the episodes were new to him because he had never seen the series.

He shrugged. "Never seen it before today."

"I can't remember if he's a good guy doing something bad, or a bad guy doing something good."

"Why does it have to be either? Why can't it just be a man doing something he wants to do?"

"Is that how you got that bullet in your arm? Doing something you wanted to do?" She finished with the bandage and plopped down on the far end of the sofa, sitting on one foot so that the leg of her shorts flared open in his direction either on purpose or by accident. If he'd had a flashlight he could have seen her business. Plain or not, a man can't resist an open shot.

"Is that really what you wore to work?"

Her hand dropped and pushed the peephole closed. "Well look who's feeling better all of a sudden."

"I wasn't thinking nothing," he said.

"Sure you wasn't. I bet you've got AIDS or something worse. I've heard what men do in prison."

"My self is unharmed in that regard," Jonce said. "And I wasn't locked up long enough to turn. There's more than one way to skin a cat, you know."

19

She rolled her eyes and tried to frown. "Well you can keep right on skinning your cat because you ain't skinning mine."

"Loosen up this bandage," he said. "My arm can't breathe."

She scooted toward him to check.

"You smell nice."

"I showered," she said. "You might consider it yourself."

She had him curious about the investigation so he switched to a local station to check the news that was conveniently in progress. A familiar face splashed on the screen. "Well I'll be damned."

"Somebody you know?"

Tipton Palo was being perp-walked across a parking lot and into the jail. The police chief was nowhere to be seen, and it didn't look like city boys doing the escorting because they all wore suits. The mustached reporter said multiple felony charges but he didn't say what felonies. Jonce would never get his money now. He pushed her hand away from his arm and told her to go home.

Jackie checked her hair in the glass door before pulling it open and stepping into City Hall. Nerves and the fact that she had overdressed for the mild southern February morning had her fearing a visible sweat as she stepped into the modest lobby and heard the lonely echo of her dress heals against the tile floor. Her nose caught a faint scent of bleach as she walked toward a sign with a right-pointing arrow that read MAYOR'S OFFICE. She turned down the hallway already feeling clammy underneath her two layers of clothing, the outer layer being a gray fleece and the inner being a silk undershirt she had purchased before money became a problem.

The hallway was narrow enough to kill the echo and judging by the spacing of the doors, the offices behind them were small. Each door was solid wood and differed from the others only in the lettering on the nameplate which identified the department its space contained. At the end, straight ahead, she saw the door she was looking for: MAYOR.

An hour ago she had received a call from a very polite lady who asked if she could drop by at her convenience to speak to the mayor. Prior to that she had taken the assistant chief's advice and read the fresh release of the Hayes Beacon as much as time had allowed. A man had been murdered and the mayor's name had been mentioned. It was the second death Mayor Pigg could be tied to the article stated. On top of that the town was in turmoil due to the mayor's incompetence. The police chief was fighting for his career. State investigators were combing through mountains of evidence against countless city and county officials. The assistant chief, according to one article, was the mayor's only ally and would be dealt with once the mayor was unseated.

So why had the mayor summoned her? More importantly, if he offered her a job, did she really want to align herself with the losing team? The answer to the first question lay beyond the next door. She paused to check herself one last time, then pushed open the door. Immediately she saw two desks and two women. To her left sat a woman she guessed to be mid-fifties, to her right sat a much younger woman with red and purple hair. And odd styling for a mayor's office, she thought, it being so deep in the South. If a mayor allowed purple hair in his office then maybe he would be open to a black woman on his police force, unless the young woman was his daughter, which threw the entire argument out the window. Rules don't apply to daughters the way they apply to everyone else, especially strangers, and it had been her experience that rules don't apply to mayors at all. The simple fact that she was about to speak to a mayor flew in the face of everything she thought she knew about politics.

She announced herself to the older lady and immediately recognized her voice as the person she had spoken to on the phone. The nameplate on her desk read Mildred Pigg. Without knowing the mayor's age, she guessed the woman to be his wife. Nepotism in any regard. Pigg was an uncommon name so they had to be related.

"You may go right in."

"Just like that?"

The lady smiled. "Unless you need a moment to prepare yourself."

Jackie hesitated. Should she take a moment to prepare herself? She didn't think so, but the offer caused her to second-guess herself. Her exposure to politicians had been through her marriage more than through her job. The rank of detective hadn't given her access to the mayor, but her marriage to Kelton Mulvaney had.

"He's not very busy this morning," Mildred Pigg said with sort of a laugh that immediately put Jackie at ease. She glanced at the girl with purple hair and caught her staring with an inquisitive look that one had to forgive a woman her age. Her nameplate was turned so that Jackie couldn't make out the name, not that it mattered because she was old enough to be married and first names mean nothing. She bore no resemblance to Mildred, but she had not yet seen the mayor.

The mayor's door stood open and Jackie very quickly saw what appeared to be a meek little man sitting behind a tidy desk. She had met two mayors in her life and both of them had been dreadful liars. Politicians, she firmly believed, have no capacity for telling the truth.

He looked up and waved her in. Too gentle, she thought as she entered the room and formulated her first impression. Kindness is a common camouflage for brutality. It was a lesson she had learned the hard way, and she had no intention of learning it again. Not ever.

The sweat beneath her sweater had reached the saturation point. "Should I close the door?"

"If you prefer," he said, rising with visible effort to greet her. Almost immediately she noticed a cane propped against the wall behind him and guessed that he had suffered an injury because he was much too young to need it otherwise. He bore no resemblance to either of the women she had just met.

She closed the door more from habit than a want of privacy. Good manners prevented him from offering his hand to a woman so she made the gesture herself and found his handshake to be warm and gentle. Could he be authentic? The newspaper had called him incompetent, not evil. Perhaps he was simply a man in over his head. Jimmy Carter came to mind.

She introduced herself as Jackie Deen — a lie she had created out of necessity — but stopped short of presuming the nature of the meeting aloud.

She glanced once more at the cane as she sat.

"My doctors told me I'd never walk again," he said as he lowered himself back into his chair with the same effort it had taken him to stand. "Now they take all the credit for my recovery. Doctors. They make a man hesitate to get sick."

"Was the accident recent?"

"Two years give or take," he said. "My wife marks the day I took my first step as though it were George Washington crossing the Delaware." He winked, then said, "I don't have the heart to tell her she has the date wrong. I'd been secretly walking for the better part of a month before I tried it in front of her. If she had seen how many times I fell, well, I'd probably still be chair-bound." He laughed in a gentle way that made him immediately likable. "You won't tell her, I trust."

"Is Mildred your wife?"

"Yes, and before you charge me with nepotism, she was here first. I had to beg her to stay on after the people of this town saddled me with this wretched position. In all honesty, she should be in here and me out there. On second thought, I'm even less qualified to do her job than I am mine. I'm an engineer by training and education. Mechanical, not that electrical nonsense. I like to work with things I can touch without getting knocked on my backside."

"She seems like a wonderful woman," Jackie said, meaning the mayor's wife. "And the younger woman, is she your daughter?"

"She came with the office. My first impression of her was quite different than it is now, though. Don't let the hippie hair fool you. She's bright as a sunspot and almost as disruptive." He laughed again. "She's loyal, too. You can't put too high a price on loyalty in this business."

"In any business," Jackie said. "Especially when it comes to your police force."

He grinned and nodded. "Well played," he said. "You're quick. I like that." He opened a thin folder that contained two pages she immediately recognized. "Assistant Chief Gant sent this over yesterday. Your captain spoke very highly of you when I called him this morning."

The effect on her was immediate. This was a serious interview. Then the mayor frowned and sent her hopes spiraling. "Unfortunately, he also told me what they were paying you in Detroit and I'm afraid —."

"I don't expect you to match my salary in Detroit," she said a bit too anxiously. "This being a small town, naturally there'll be a pay cut."

"I'm afraid the word *cut* doesn't do justice," the mayor said. "Obliteration might be the better descriptor. I'm the mayor and I don't make enough to pay your rent up there." He closed the folder. "We do need a detective, though."

"I'm a very good detective."

"According to your captain you're among the best he's seen. That's quite a recommendation, but I don't see it working. You'd be bored here. Our crime rate, ordinarily, consists of traffic violations and drunk drivers. We get an occasional break-in, and once in a very blue moon there's a murder. Most of those have been domestic. Husband gets tired of wife, or wife gets tired of husband."

"You have an open murder now I believe."

"Open, yes," he said in a queer manner. "If ever a man deserved killing it was Perry Stubbs."

"Surely you aren't condoning —."

He waved her off. "No, I'm not condoning it. Murder is murder and killing is wrong in the eyes of the Lord. We're a God-fearing community by and large. It's just that sometimes, well, sometimes a man takes upon himself the burden of fixing what our justice system can't ... or won't. We'll catch him, probably. Very likely if we bring you aboard, I imagine, if you're half the detective your captain says you are. We'll catch him and send him to prison knowing in our hearts he did what needed to be done."

"I won't take the job if you're asking me to look the other way."

"I haven't offered the job," he said. "But no, I'd never ask you to compromise your values. You're a cog in the wheel same as I am. We all have our role to play in grinding the public corn."

"I would like very much the honor of helping Hayes grind its corn," Jackie said. "And again, salary is unimportant. Like I told your assistant chief, I was raised in Birmingham, and I'm moving back to —."

"I'm very sorry about your father," the mayor said. "Have you —?"

"Birmingham isn't hiring," she said. She felt the opportunity slipping through her fingers and grappled with her emotions. "Mayor Pigg, I loved being a detective in a large city, but I've reached a point in my life where I want to slow down and enjoy the things that really matter. I think this job would be perfect for me and I think I have a lot to offer." She watched his eyes stroke her face. She had rehearsed a generic version of the pitch hundreds of times during the drive down from Detroit. Between the motel and city hall she had adapted it to Hayes and rehearsed it a dozen times more.

He flipped open the folder and scanned the page again, then raised his eyes to meet hers. "Thirty-five is a bit young to start slowing down, don't you think?"

"My father's cancer has put things in perspective for me."

He closed the folder. "I'll tell Mildred to pray for your father. I'll say one for him too, of course, but it's my wife's prayer you'll want said." He winked. "She's got more clout upstairs than I do."

"Thank you."

"Now let's get down to business," he said. "Is it Miss Deen or Mrs. Deen?"

"It's Jackie," she said. She would lie if forced to, but omission seemed the better course. The mayor's eyes narrowed at her obvious dodge but he seemed too much of a gentleman to press her.

"Well, like Chief Gant told you, we haven't begun the interviews yet. I'm sure we'll have a few patrol officers eager to move up, not that any of them are qualified. Most of them shouldn't even be allowed to drive."

Jackie stopped hearing after the fourth word. "Did you say *Chief* Gant? He told me —."

"A slip of the tongue," he said. "If you're the detective I think you are then you've read our newspaper."

"I have."

"So you know I'm a prime suspect in our little murder."

She nodded.

"You're probably wondering how much of what you read about me is true."

"My first impression says not very much," she said. "Your paper wasn't very kind to the assistant chief either."

"What did you think of Gant? First impression I mean."

She floundered. "I only spoke to him for a few minutes. He seemed very nice."

"Professionally speaking," the mayor said. "You're a cop. Do you think he could lead my police department?"

"It's impossible for me to say, but —."

"I'm not so incompetent that I don't know when I'm out of my depth," Pigg said. "There's no one in the department who hasn't already taken a side. You're a detective so you must know how to read people. I hope you're not timid."

"He was very professional during our meeting," she said. "If you hire me I can give you a more complete answer."

Mayor Pigg smiled. "I like you, Detective Deen. Gant likes you too or he wouldn't have sent your file over."

"Does this mean you're giving me a chance?"

"Slow down," he said. "We haven't started interviewing yet. There's a process we're supposed to follow." He laughed. "The board keeps reminding me of that. They have a process for everything. How long were you planning on being in town?"

"For a very long time," she said, "but of course that depends on me getting this job."

He leaned forward and propped on his elbows. "Tell you what I'll do. I've already called a special meeting of the board to discuss our police chief. I'll throw your name out and see how they react."

"Thank you."

"Don't expect too much. They're all hoping it was me who killed Perry Stubbs so they can get rid of me. They've tried every other way."

"I got that impression from the newspaper," she said.

"My stock is way up with the people, though," he said. "The board can't figure out what to make of it. Politics is a strange business. I don't recommend it to honest folk. Of course there's those who think I manufactured all the evidence I turned over. Others say I did it to hide my own guilt."

"Did you?"

"No, and I don't mind if you consider me a suspect. Assuming you get the job."

"The mayors I've worked for in the past wouldn't see it that way."

"I'm too incompetent to be compared to other mayors."

"For what it's worth you don't strike me as incompetent, or a murderer."

"I *have* killed a man," he said with shocking frankness. "Don't worry, they called me a hero. I was all the rage for fifteen minutes. Now I'm just a cripple."

"No one is *just* a cripple."

"No one is *just* anything," he said. "We're all complex animals with enough secrets to fill a novel. Take you for example. You're running from something. Take my advice and face it. You'll have to sooner or later. Running only wears you down." His perception sent a chill up her spine. He couldn't know, of course. She had been too careful.

She stood and thanked him for the interview.

"If I have as much clout as I think I do Gant will be chief in a few days. If you think you can work for him, and you're serious about the salary not being a factor, well, no promises, but I'll see what I can do."

She thanked him again.

"In the meantime go shopping. That's a beautiful sweater but our winters can't support it and our summers are downright inhumane."

By Wednesday afternoon Jonce felt bored and in need of fresh air, so he put on a bulky coat and drove down to the convenience store on the corner and bought a can of Skoal. While waiting for his change, he noticed a stack of newspapers beside a gallon glass jar of pickled eggs floating in a piss-green solution. The headline caught his attention.

MURDER ROCKS HAYES

"Something ain't it?" said the kid behind the counter who looked like he'd been shot in the face with an acne gun. "People say it was a hired job."

"What people?"

"Just people. You from around here?"

"You taking a census?"

"Just asking, mister. Didn't mean no offense."

Jonce pulled a paper from the stack and handed the boy a dollar. "Newspapers used to be fifty cents." The boy shrugged and put the dollar in the cash drawer. Jonce unfolded the paper and dumped the inserts onto the counter, decreasing its thickness by half. The boy eyed him but kept the thought behind his eyes to himself.

"A man in here this morning said all these black SUVs in town are state investigators," the boy said. "Not FBI like everybody's been saying. And they ain't here about that murder, neither."

Jonce knew a little something about why the MBI was in town but he didn't feel like sharing it with a pimple-faced kid who overcharged for newspapers, so he tucked his paper underneath his arm and left. Back at his apartment he opened a beer and spread the newspaper out on his kitchen table and immediately recognized the name on the byline. Dexter Mann was Tipton Palo's stooge in addition to being editor of the Hayes Beacon. Stubbs hadn't liked him much but then Stubbs wasn't much for liking people.

The article was full of lies and half-truths. The victim's hands weren't tied and he wasn't tortured, though having his throat cut slow might be viewed as such by some. Jonce had never been much of a deer hunter so he had never cut a throat before. It was harder than it looked on the ISIS video he found on the internet. Maybe if Stubbs had had more hair, or if Jonce had tied his hands the way Dexter Man misreported. There was a lot of blood — the article had that part right. A tremendous amount of blood. Enough blood to fill a kiddie pool almost. The article didn't state it that way but that's how it was. Jonce could still smell the blood on his hands sometimes. He didn't enjoy killing but he wasn't one to shrink from responsibility.

He pushed the newspaper away and finished his beer. Sometimes cops give out wrong information on purpose. They say his hands were tied and wait for somebody to say they weren't and bam! Jonce grinned as he took another sip of beer. He was too wily a fox to trot into an open henhouse. His only concern was that Tipton Palo keep his mouth shut, and there were ways to make sure he did.

Chapter Three

J once awoke Friday morning to someone pounding on his front door. Exactly one week ago Tipton Palo shot him in the arm. Two days ago the cops arrested Palo on felonies related to the documents Jonce stole from Palo's safe on orders from Perry Stubbs. The mayor was in the process of taking down more than the handful of local officials mentioned in the paper. Half the city department heads and at least two judges were in his crosshairs, but that information hadn't been released to the public yet. Dexter Mann wasn't as smart as he thought he was. Jonce had read hundreds of documents before turning the cache over to Stubbs, and he had siphoned off a little something for himself as insurance.

Why should the mayor have all the fun?

He rolled out of bed and made for the living room naked, then he remembered his arm and trotted back to pull on a shirt to cover his wound. "Keep your britches on! I'm coming," he yelled as the pounding continued. The cops would've broken it down already, and Palo was still in jail as far as he knew. Bobbie — the girl next door — didn't have his key anymore but she would be at work.

He reached the door and put his eye to the peephole and cursed under his breath as he recognized the police chief's ugly mug. Maybe Palo hadn't kept his mouth shut after all. Being a lawyer gave Palo the advantage over Jonce when it came to navigating the minefield of legal deal-making. Being rich put him even higher up the pole because justice is only blind in one eye.

He jerked open the door. "Well run me up a tree and call me a coon," he said in his best backwoods drawl. "If it ain't Deputy Dawg."

Police Chief Ball opened his mouth to say something clever then his eyes snagged Jonce's lower region exposed. "Put some damned clothes on!"

Jonce looked down at himself and grinned. "I sleep raw, boss."

"You're wearing a shirt!"

"My upper self gets cold," Jonce said, making no effort to cover himself. He enjoyed the chief's discomfort. "I was that way as a boy, too." He grinned, showing his perfectly white teeth. "Course I weren't big down there like I am now."

The chief's eyes dropped down then bounced back like an over-inflated ball, probably comparing himself and coming up short. "Put on some pants," he said with less authority.

"Feeling outmanned are you?"

"Now!"

Jonce laughed as he turned and quick-stepped it back to the bedroom and pulled on the pants he had worn the day before. When he returned to the living room he found the chief standing two feet from his coffee table. "Is this a sit down talk or a stand up talk?"

"I got some questions and you'd better not give me any lip," Ball said, trying to sound more confident than his body language said he was.

"Must be important questions if they sent the chief."

"I sent myself," Ball said. "Now sit down and shut up."

Jonce sat. Being on parole hamstrung him when it came to basic human rights. Cops could harass him for the pure fun of it, but Glenn Ball wasn't no ordinary cop. Jonce remembered seeing his name in some of the papers he stole from Palo and gave to Stubbs. The chief was paid for something, though Jonce hadn't taken the time to dig through the numbers. His interests lay elsewhere at the time. A mistake, perhaps.

"I know what kind of work you did for Stubbs," Ball said.

"Deliveries," Jonce said. "Pawn shop stuff. Perfectly legal."

"I think you know who killed him," the chief said.

"Nope."

"Where's Corey Pickle?"

"The last pickle I saw was in a jar swimming in vinegar."

Ball clenched his teeth and balled his fists. "So help me Jonce Nash if I have to run you in I will!"

"On what charge?"

"On whatever charge I make up on the way, and it'll be a good one too! Now tell me where Corey Pickle is."

Jonce shrugged. "Last I heard he was in Texas."

"Texas?"

"Stubbs said he sent him away for being stupid. Said he wouldn't stand out in Texas for being stupid."

"Don't badmouth Texas," Ball said.

"Texas special to you?"

"Shut up and answer my questions."

"I just answered it," Jonce said. "I said Texas. Now it's your move."

"Stubbs say why he sent him away? Other than being stupid?"

"Something about him framing the mayor's brother instead of the mayor," Jonce said. "Stubbs told him to git and he got. Is that why you're after him? Afraid he'll talk?" He grinned at the chief's discomfort. "Don't sleep in the henhouse if you can't face the fox." The chief's face throbbed red. Jonce was enjoying himself very much. Glenn Ball was so crooked water wouldn't run off him, and the mayor had the goods. His clock was ticking.

"One call to Prichard and you'll be riding the van back to Parchman so lose the attitude."

"Prichard's hard," Jonce said, feigning concern. "He strikes a terrible fear in me. Makes my whole body tremble and shake." He quivered head to toe and grinned. Nobody alive knew what happened to Corey Pickle except himself, and there was no way they would ever find the body. When Jonce Nash hides something, it's hid.

"Pickle broke into Palo's safe then he killed Stubbs," Ball said. "Don't play dumb with me or I'll pin it all on you."

Jonce almost swallowed his tongue. So Palo was sending the chief down a rabbit hole after a man neither one of them knew was dead. "I overheard him and Stubbs talking about some papers but that's all I know."

"Heard who and Stubbs?"

"Pickle."

"What exactly did you hear?"

Jonce's brain raced ninety to nothing trying not to trip itself. Play his cards right and he could put the cops on the wrong trail and forever be in the clear. He knew that once they set their sights on a man they go after him with blinders on. "Some kind of argument about money," Jonce said. He pretended to remember something important, then pretended not to want to say what it was. Ball threatened to put him in handcuffs and throw his carcass under the jail if he didn't talk. After the appropriate amount of mental wrangling, Jonce sighed and said he guessed it didn't matter anymore since they knew it was Pickle. "He told me Stubbs stiffed him and he was gonna get even." Jonce summoned all the sadness he could muster. "I guess he meant it."

Ball looked satisfied. "Is he really in Texas?"

Jonce frowned. "No telling. My guess is he won't show himself again."

Waiting was the hardest part. Not knowing if she had the job or if the mayor was trying to brush her off with feigned interest meant to insulate the town from a discrimination lawsuit. She was, after all, a double threat. Black in Mississippi and female anywhere. It was true that not a single person had harassed her because of her color or her sex, but she had no way of knowing what they were thinking. Even in Detroit she had felt she had to work twice as hard to be viewed equally as good as other cops, especially since making detective. Above all else she hated being patronized. It was a narrow ledge to walk.

"What's wrong, Momma?"

They were hunkered down in their dingy motel room and it had been two days since her meeting with Mayor Pigg. Mildred, the mayor's wife, had called twice with leads on more permanent living arrangements. First an apartment that cost too much, then a three-bedroom brick house with a pool. She seemed nice enough, and was probably trying to be helpful, but the places she suggested were impossible given her sudden financial situation.

"Nothing," she said to her son. She had refused to give Jordan a name that would disqualify him on paper before he had a chance to prove himself. Whatever Jordan grew up to be, he would not be hampered by a name that was too black.

"Don't look like nothing."

"Doesn't look like nothing," she corrected him, causing him to frown. The public education system had failed him. It was failing a lot of kids, and if Detroit was bad Hayes, Mississippi had to be ten times worse. She had done her research and had decided to give homeschooling a try, which was fine by Jordan because he had some mistaken notion that it would be easy having her for a teacher. He didn't yet know the real reason she couldn't enroll him in public school, and she certainly couldn't afford a private academy.

"Well, what is it then?"

She waved him in for a hug. Reluctant, he moved from the chair and plopped down beside her on the foot of her bed and allowed her to squeeze him tight before squirming away.

"Geez, mom, don't crush me."

"I'm just nervous about this job," she said.

"Nervous you'll get it, or nervous you won't?"

"Both," she said, just then realizing how true it was. If she got the job she would have to prove herself in a new place, to new people. If she didn't get the job they would have to move on to another town and pitch her story all over again. Escaping her husband had become more complicated than she had imagined.

"How long do we have to keep using the name Deen?"

"Until we're safe," she said.

"When will that be?"

"Soon."

"You said that last week."

The past few weeks had been as hard on him as it had been on her, and she knew it would get harder before getting better. Kelton Mulvaney wasn't a man who gave up easily. He would have to be defeated. It was a hard thing to tell a boy about his father.

Gain Prichard kept an office off the court square in a tiny storefront jammed between a dentist office and a boutique. He had room for a desk and two chairs, and when he needed to relieve himself he had to walk around the corner to the courthouse. Running herd on parolees didn't require much space, Jonce surmised, standing inside looking out the window at the Civil War monument in the center of the square, waiting for Prichard to acknowledge his existence. Be one minute late and he hits the ceiling, but come five minutes early and he's struck blind.

Just as well. Jonce had no place to be. "Guess they'll be coming for your statue soon," he said without looking back at the man who was pretending he didn't exist. "Who's that supposed to be perched up there anyway?"

"Shut your yap until I tell you to talk," Prichard said.

"Must've been kin to somebody important to get put up on the square like that."

Papers shuffled behind him. Jonce turned. Prichard sat looking at him as though he were the dumbest animal on earth, which was exactly what Jonce wanted him to think. The dumber they think you are the less they expect from you. "I bet somebody posed," he said. "Imagine posing long enough for that much concrete to set and not getting your name carved on in."

"It's not concrete you idiot, it's granite. Granite don't set. They chisel it into whatever shape they want it to be so shut up about the statue and hand over your paperwork."

Jonce turned up both hands in mock confusion. "What paperwork?" He had paperwork but not the kind Prichard was talking about. The paperwork Jonce had would shoot Prichard right out of his chair, but it wasn't time for that yet. "Nobody told me there was homework."

Prichard folded his hands across his desk and sighed. "How many job interviews have you had this week?"

"Including that furniture plant out by the feed store?"

"Including every place you've gone to and applied for a job."

"None."

Prichard's face turned red as a blister. "Maybe you don't like it on the outside," he said. "And stop looking at me like that!"

"Like what?"

"Like — like a damned retard!"

Jonce stiffened his back and squinted his face. "I seen my daddy punch a man in the face one time for calling his brother Bo — my uncle — that word."

"Are you threatening me?"

"No, just telling. Retard ain't no kind of word to be calling a man, especially when a close uncle of his had special needs."

"I don't give a rat's ass about your Uncle Bo," Prichard said. He breathed hard for a few cycles then calmed himself. The natural pasty white color reclaimed his face and he made some marks on the paper in front of him. Without looking up he said, "You'd better have a job by next Friday or I'll slap you back in Parchman."

"What's got you so mad?"

"I'm not mad," he said, "and if I was it wouldn't be none of your business." He exhaled, then he cut his eyes up at Jonce with a defeated look. "I'm sorry about using that word. I didn't know about your uncle."

Jonce didn't have an Uncle Bo, and he wasn't scared of Prichard. Instead of barrel-chested he was barrel-bellied, and his hair was shoe polish black and slick with a cream that made it shine. "That man daddy punched in the face beat his ass so bad momma had to pay a black man ten dollars to put him in the truck so we could get him home."

Prichard grinned then frowned it away. He looked down and jotted something else in Jonce's file, then he looked up again. "Next Friday," he said. "Now beat it."

Jackie pulled Jordan away from his video games Friday afternoon and hauled him to Sonic for chocolate milkshakes and burgers. The place was mostly empty but she parked near the back in case the mayor or assistant chief happened by. She hadn't told them she had a son for fear it might further hamper her chance of getting the job. It wasn't exactly a lie because they hadn't asked.

"This town is lame," Jordan said after slurping his milkshake. "There's nothing to do here."

"You're fifteen," she said. "Everything looks lame to you."

They finished their lunch and pulled back out into the street. Pretty soon their roles would be reversed and he would be driving. Where had the time gone?

"In six months you can get your permit," she said, thinking it might cheer him up.

"Why get a permit when there's nowhere to go?"

Main Street was bumper to bumper with cars and pickup trucks and every now and then a UPS or FedEx delivery truck. Most of the vehicles were late model, and the people she saw out and about could have been plucked out of any other middle-class neighborhood she had ever seen. None of them had a third arm, or an extra leg. She saw no mullets and no shotguns and there wasn't a single white hood in sight. So much for the stereotypical Mississippi small town.

"Look at that," Jordan said, pointing at a white man and black woman walking together on the sidewalk. The woman carried a small child with skin lighter than hers and darker than his. "Ain't they afraid of getting lynched?"

"Aren't they afraid," she said, "and no, I don't suppose they are. It's twenty-nineteen. I don't think they lynch people anymore."

"That's not what you said three days ago."

Sometimes she allowed the stories from her youth to taint reality.

Racism still existed. It was real. Tangible, and she wanted her son to be aware that to some people the color of his skin made him a target, but she didn't want him to carry it on his shoulder like a chip to be knocked off. "Mothers can be wrong too," she said.

"Whoa! Did you just say what I heard? I'm writing that down."

"Don't be smart."

He wrote a pretend note in the palm of his hand with his finger as he mumbled, "mothers can be wrong."

"So can teenage boys," she said. "As long as you're taking notes."

Something up ahead caught her eye. A commotion of some kind outside the police station. Her trained eye noticed a car with a news logo emblazoned on the door, then another. A wad of people, some holding what appeared to be microphones, stood halfway between the sidewalk and the building. There were two news cameras clearly visible now. Something newsworthy was unfolding and she wanted desperately to know what it was. To be a part of whatever it was. Being a cop is more than carrying a badge and bringing home a paycheck.

"Looks like a wreck or something," Jordan said.

"That's no wreck." She knew from social media and the local news that a prominent attorney had been arrested and released, with more in the pipes. The buzz had half the town in the crosshairs of state police. How much was true she couldn't know, but she hoped the young assistant chief wasn't caught in the net, or the mayor. Like it or not she had picked sides.

She found an empty parking spot in front of a cosmetics store and punched up the website of the television station whose logo she saw on a car door. Their live feed showed the front of the police station and a young female reporter adjusting her pose while looking into a camera she didn't know was live. Seconds later she snapped to attention and told her viewers the mayor was expected to come out and speak any moment now. Good. The mayor speaking meant he wasn't in custody, which meant she might still have a shot at the job.

The live feed buffered, then pixelated, then started again. The young reporter said suspicion had been swirling around Police Chief Ball for days. Since Mayor Pigg handed over incriminating evidence to Assistant Chief Gant a week ago. Filling time, she said prominent attorney Tipton Palo had been arrested earlier in the week then released on an unspecified bond. Suddenly her face brightened and the camera swung away from her and focused on the mayor walking slowly toward the crowd without his cane. Optics is everything in politics.

"There's the mayor," Jackie said aloud. Jordan was playing a game on his phone and paid her no attention.

There was no podium and no official microphone, and the mayor had nothing in his hands to read from. He looked more than a little uncomfortable when he stopped a few feet from the reporters. He cleared his throat and addressed them. "Earlier this morning, Police Chief Glenn Ball was indicted on conspiracy charges in connection with evidence that disappeared while in police custody. He has also been charged with witness tampering and conspiracy in at least three other ongoing investigations, two of which involve Tipton Palo, all of which involved Perry Stubbs."

"Is Chief Ball the only officer involved?" The question came from an unseen female.

"As far as we know, yes."

A male voice rang out. "Is his arrest a product of the documents you turned over last week?"

"I can't go into that," he said. "The Mississippi Bureau of Investigations is handling the case." He seemed less nervous now.

"Has the board made a decision on a new chief?" Two reporters shouted the same question almost in lockstep.

The mayor smiled. "Assistant Chief Gant will fill that position effective immediately."

"Is his position interim?"

"No."

"Who will fill Gant's former position?"

"We haven't made a decision on that yet," the mayor said.

"With Chief Benson's suicide and Ball's arrest, are you concerned at all about the ability of the police department to protect the public?"

"The Hayes Police Department has a sufficient patrol force," Mayor Pigg said. "The community is completely safe." He slipped a wry smile. "And with so many local officials behind bars, our pocketbooks are safer than ever before."

Jackie heard a spattering of laughter from the pool of unseen reporters. Mayor Pigg had a raw honesty about him that she liked.

"Will Chief Gant be working the Stubbs murder?" a reporter shouted.

"We've hired a new detective," the mayor said. Jackie's heart sank. The position was filled.

"Can you give us his name?"

"I've given you too much already," the mayor said. He turned and started back toward the building with questions bouncing off his back. Jackie flipped off her phone.

"Well, kiddo, it looks like we'll be moving on."

Chapter Four

Bobbie's grunts and groans pierced the wall like the wails of a wounded animal. Jonce pulled the pillow over his head and kicked the sheet off the bed. The Booths sounded like a low-budget porn flick with the volume too high.

It was Saturday morning, day nine. His arm only hurt when he worked the muscle. The threat of amputation had passed. Pain was old hat for Jonce. Pain doesn't have to be emotional to build character. Physical pain teaches a man patience.

He swung his legs off the bed and sat on the edge. "Tear it up Donnie Boy," he said to the room. "She's plain but she's feisty." Palo's wife screamed too at first, then she just cried a lot. Palo didn't shoot him for raping his wife, though, he shot him to keep from paying what he owed. That's the trouble with men who have plenty — they never have enough.

Jonce went to the kitchen and poured Rice Krispies into a bowl and floated them in milk. *Snap! Crackle! Pop!* The trick to eating Rice Krispies is to finish off the bowl before the noise stops else they lose their crunch. Halfway through the bowl, the little hellcat next door let out a string of obscenities that signaled the end of festivities.

Jonce left his stool and went to the wall and clapped. "Well done! Bravo! Let's have an encore!"

"Shut the hell up or I'll come over and kick your ass!" It was Donnie, not Bobbie.

Jonce returned to the table and finished his breakfast. Dirty dishes rose from the sink like a leaning tower. He had washed enough dishes in prison to last him a lifetime. Housework and no sex were the only drawbacks to Ellie being dead. She was mediocre in both regards, but she tried.

It didn't take long for the bickering beyond the wall to start. Don's suitcase smelled like a whorehouse and Bobbie sucked at keeping house. Same argument as last weekend. Men drink and chase skirts; women forget to clean behind the refrigerator. The breaking point for Don was the roach he saw last night in the kitchen. A man expects his woman to keep the house clean, so if Jonce was judge and jury, sitting there in his boxers with milk dribbling down his chin as he was, he'd say the smack he'd just heard delivered was a fair sentence carried out. Case closed. Don said he was going out and Bobbie asked where to, then the door slammed and all was quiet again. Then came the doorbell.

"Go away."

She rang the bell again. When he opened the door to tell her to beat it, she ducked underneath his arm and shot the gap like a greased pig. He spun and grabbed her arm and snapped her back. "Not so fast, girlie," he said. "Donnie's a big boy and I got a bad wing."

She jerked her arm free. "Don could stomp you into the ground with both hands tied behind his back. He will, too, if he hears you calling him Donnie."

Jonce laughed. "He's quite a man, I'll give him that." He winked and hitched his head toward the shared wall. "Paper thin."

"Did you really have to clap?"

"For that performance? Yes, ma'am." He whistled. "That was some top notch acting."

"I wasn't acting."

"Just a little bit?"

She raised her face and he saw the shiner forming around her right eye. He closed the door. "I ain't never had me a screamer."

"Ever asked yourself why?"

"Maybe I'll black the other eye."

"You don't scare me." She looked around herself. "I don't have anybody else to talk to."

"Then you ain't got nobody," he said. "I ain't no psychiatrist so beat it."

"He'll find a pool hall somewhere and lose the rest of his paycheck. What he didn't drink up last night before he came home."

Bobbie wasn't wearing a bra underneath the long white sleeping shirt. Might not be wearing anything at all, and those legs. Jonce sported boxers and no shirt because he hadn't expected visitors. How could a woman with such a plain face have such nice legs? Face of a store clerk and legs of a stripper. No wonder Don drank.

She looked around herself again. "You ever clean this place?"

"You gonna black my eye?"

"If there was a roach in my kitchen it rode home on him." She moved to the sink and transferred the dirty dishes to the counter, then she started filling the sink with water. "Got any dishwashing liquid?"

"Might be some under the sink," he said, knowing it was in the overhead cabinet but he wanted to see how high the tail of her shirt rode up when she bent over. It rode up far enough.

"There's nothing under here but a bottle of Lysol," she said. "And more dirt." She withdrew her head and straightened herself.

"Try that cabinet overhead," he said. She had to stand on her tiptoes to reach the bottle of Dawn. "You gonna wash my dishes?"

"Somebody has to."

"When you get through in here the bedroom could use some tidying," he said.

She twisted at the waist and rolled her eyes. "I'm washing your dishes because mine are all clean," she said, then she dropped the cup she was holding and spun around with her hands planted on her hips. "Do you think I'm pretty?"

"Ten seconds ago I did."

She frowned. "I know I'm ugly. You're no prize yourself, you know. Stop staring at my tits."

"I'm helpless in that regard," he said. "You ain't wearing no bra and I was locked up a long time."

"Well you don't have to be so obvious about it. Didn't anybody ever teach you any manners?"

"That rascal's got a mind of his own," he said. Her eyes dropped to his boxers. They were powder blue. "He seen them pink panties when you bent over and now he's wide awake."

"Well he can go right back to sleep because I'm married." She turned back to the dishes. "Don used to say I could've been a leg model."

"What's a leg model?"

She laughed. "Don't you know anything?"

"Teach me."

"You're incorrigible."

"Not anymore," he said. "I'm paroled."

"Ha ha. Very funny. The old lady in twenty-three said a cop came to see you yesterday morning."

"Tell her to mind her own business." He studied the back of her head as she scrubbed a plate. "You ain't been talking to the cops have you?"

"Last time I talked to a cop he was putting Don in the back of his patrol car."

"Good. Keep it that way. They come around asking you questions about me you don't say nothing."

"What kind of questions would they be asking?"

"Any kind of questions," he said. "I'll slap you sideways from Sunday if you say anything about that bullet you took out of my arm."

"I've been slapped before."

"Not by me you ain't," Jonce said. "I'll slap you inside out."

She laughed without turning around. "You don't scare me."

"They'll put you in jail too, you know. Aiding and abetting."

"Exactly what did I aid and abet?"

"Never mind," he said. "Just keep your mouth shut and you won't have to worry about it."

"I wish I had me a college educated man. A man with a degree in something smart. One that comes home in the evening smelling the same way he did when he left that morning."

"Smelling like his secretary you mean," Jonce said. "Being a man ain't something they cure in college."

"Did you go to college?"

Jonce laughed. "Do I look like I went to college?"

"How many times did you hit your wife?"

"Whenever she deserved it."

"You talked about her when I was digging the bullet out, you know."

"You told me that already. Do you always repeat yourself?"

"You talked about your son, too."

"Another thing you already told me."

"You miss them don't you? I know you do by the way you were talking."

He watched her ass shake against the tail of her long shirt as her upper body had a go at the dishes. From the back she was quite a looker. "Ain't but one thing I miss," he said, stepping toward her with his mind made up. "And I'm about to fill my bucket."

❖

Saturday morning found Jackie packing her bags again. She felt angry as she folded their clothes and stuffed them into a suitcase. The least the mayor could've done was call her and let her know he had filled the job. Next stop, Petal, Mississippi, which was a small town in Forrest County on the Leaf River. It had a population barely in excess of ten thousand and they had advertised for a detective. Jackie had found the ad the night before after an exhaustive online search. If Petal didn't pan out, she would move into Alabama and keep trying. If something didn't break soon she would have to resort to answering security guard ads.

Jordan loaded the suitcase into the back of their white Hyundai Tucson while she settled up at the desk and collected her receipt. The car had been a last minute cash purchase before leaving Detroit. An out of work detective driving a Mercedes might raise too many eyebrows. In hindsight she should have saved the cash and traded the Mercedes, but the title was in her husband's name. Everything was in his name.

On the way out of town she drove up Main Street and past City Hall which was closed, and the police station which wasn't. She thought she would have liked Hayes. What a shame.

Fifteen minutes out of town her phone rang with an unknown number. A chill went up her spine as she stared at the Mississippi area code knowing how easy it was to spoof a phone number. Had he tracked her so soon? She had a new phone and a new number that only one other person knew besides her son. Three, she corrected herself. She had given the number to the assistant police chief who was now the chief, and he gave it to the mayor. The possibility tempted her, but her fear of the alternative kept her from answering.

Jordan watched from the passenger seat with the inquisitive nature of a teenage boy who just realized his mother is from another planet. "Aren't you going to answer it?"

"No," she said. "If it's important they'll leave a message."

"A message? Who does that?" He rolled his eyes and went back to his game as the ringing stopped. Ten seconds later a tone alerted her to the voicemail. Jordan glanced at the phone, then at her and shrugged. "Boomers."

She raised the phone to her ear expecting to hear her husband's voice warning her to come home. Instead she heard the police chief telling her if she was still interested in the job to give him a call.

"Good or bad?" Jordan asked without looking up from his phone.

She pulled to the shoulder of the road and stopped the car. Had she heard the message correctly? She put the phone on speaker and played it again. Jordan frowned. "Does this mean we have to go back to that crummy motel?"

"Just for a few more days," she said. "I promise." She didn't like making promises she might not be able to keep but if the job panned out she could begin a serious search for an apartment immediately. Not the apartment the mayor's wife had recommended, but something better than the motel.

Police Chief Gant answered his own phone. "You start Monday morning," he said. "We'll put you in my old office. It's small and has no windows and you'll probably want to invest in an air freshener, but I grew to like it."

"But I heard the mayor say at his press conference the position had been filled," she said.

"He was talking about you," Gant said. "Sometimes he gets ahead of himself."

She thanked him and promised to see him Monday.

"You haven't asked about your salary," he said.

"Tell me Monday," she said, not wanting to spoil the moment. The mayor had already told her it would be significantly less than she had made in Detroit, but less was more than nothing, and having a job would give her the stability she so badly needed.

Bobbie gathered the sheet around herself and slipped out of bed, then she plucked her clothes from the floor and disappeared into the bathroom wrapped in the sheet as though modesty mattered at that point. Jonce lay on his back with his hands behind his head staring up at the ceiling, lost in thoughts that didn't involve her. Worrisome thoughts, such as how his future hinged on people not finding out certain things. When he was fifteen he stole a bicycle off the porch of a house down the street and he spent the night in jail because his father insisted the sheriff teach him a lesson. The law had been trying to teach him lessons ever since, locking him up for weeks at a time, months sometimes, but nothing ever stuck, then they upped the ante and sent him to prison for something he didn't do, and that lesson taught him how the system really works. Guilt and innocence mean about as much to judges and lawyers as promises mean to politicians. They all talk a big game then they deal dirty and slap each other on the backs and go home to their big houses and pretty lives. There's big money in meting out justice. Tipton Palo was a rich lawyer so the fix was in from both directions with him, unless of course they decided to make an example out of him. Every now and then the system had to sacrifice one of its own to keep the herd from stampeding, and Palo had pissed a lot of people off lately. Powerful, important people. Tipton Palo and Mayor Pigg were probably the two most hated men in Hayes amongst people who mattered. The power structure was crumbling at a rapid rate thanks to Palo's accurate bookkeeping and the mayor's inability to keep sensitive information to himself. Mayor Pigg was taking all the credit but it was Jonce who made it happen. His skill at making a woman talk and his ability to blow open a safe with a torch gave the mayor the ammunition he needed to blow the system to hell and back. Jonce prided himself on that — helping take down the kind of people who sent him to prison, though that hadn't been his plan when he cracked the safe. Prison was tougher than jail. Parchman wrung every day of his sentence out of him like water from a dishrag. Almost every day. They released him early so they could own him on the outside too. So they could slap him around like a cat bats a mouse. Toying with him. Prodding him. Daring him to run. Hoping he does. Gain Prichard was a big tough cat that was about to be declawed. The mouse was about to rear up on its hind legs and take a great big chunk out of his nose and the cat was too dumb to see it coming.

The bathroom door opened and spat out Bobbie, dressed and properly dour because of the indignity she had suffered. She looked no worse for the wear as she strode past the foot of the bed and disappeared through the door without so much as a glance in his direction. No better for the wear, but no worse. All she had to do now was pick up the phone and say some things and the cops would come kick down his door and haul him away and teach him another lesson. He heard his mamma's voice almost as if she were standing next to his bed. *Stop taking what ain't yorn, Jonce.*

Jonce had always been drawn to shiny things that hung from other people's pockets.

His front door closed but didn't slam, then he heard another door close the same way. Palo's wife had walked upstairs that same way, like a zombie without a thought in her head. Mrs. Palo hadn't called the cops. She hadn't even told her husband. Time would tell with Bobbie.

She had dug quite a hole for herself.

Jackie and Jordan looked at three apartments Saturday afternoon. One was a rat infested dump with mold inside one of the bedroom closets, one was newly remodeled and outside her price range, and the third required a two year lease agreement. Exasperated, she returned to the motel and paid in advance for three more days. If they stayed beyond Monday she could pay on a per-day basis. The chance that the motel would fill up and leave them homeless didn't exist. The place probably hadn't been full in years.

The room had a different number but looked exactly the same. Two beds with a table and a lamp between them and a television atop a chest of drawers against the opposite wall. Multi-colored carpet that stuck to their feet if they walked without socks. The bathroom was cramped and the towels had frayed edges. Like their last room, it smelled heavy with cigarette smoke despite the No Smoking sign on the door. Burn spots dotted the carpet between the beds, and the nightstand had a permanent ashtray ring.

"This room stinks worse than the other one," Jordan complained as his mother transferred their clothes from the suitcase to the drawers. In addition to looking at apartments, she had stopped by a laundromat and washed their clothes. Had she not been exhausted she might have stripped the beds and laundered the sheets and blankets before climbing in, but it was already dark out and the laundromat was probably closed.

"Do you think dad knows where we are?"

She opened her eyes. The conversation she dreaded most had begun. Kelton was an abusive husband and an indifferent father. He beat Jackie and didn't care if their son witnessed it or not. Jordan was terrified of him.

"No."

"That's what you said last time."

"This time is different," she said. They had changed their names and moved far away. Kelton might think to look in Birmingham but he had no reason to know Hayes, Mississippi existed.

"I won't go back," he said.

Her heart broke. "You won't have to." She wanted it to be true but the truth was more complicated than that. Fathers have rights. The law might side with him because she had left the state under the cover of darkness, but sometimes the law gets it wrong. She thought of all the times she had enforced the law even when she knew it was wrong. Domestic disturbance calls were the worst, especially with kids involved. If cops started doing what they felt was right instead of what the law demanded, pretty soon there would be no law. There's no easy answer.

"I hate him," Jordan said.

"He's your father."

"I still hate him."

"Hate hurts the bearer more than the target," she said.

He looked at her sideways. "Did you read that in a book?"

"Maybe." She didn't press him. A boy shouldn't hate his father, but sometimes he has to figure it out for himself.

Chapter Five

J once made it a point to be on the elevated walkway outside his room when Don headed out Sunday afternoon. Saturday night had passed in virtual silence, and the Booths had spent a good portion of the morning bickering in a non-violent manner. No dishes or lamps crashed against the wall, and no threats were made that one might kill the other. Violent behavior and lovemaking seemed to go hand-in-hand with those two, as though one couldn't occur without the other.

It was a very mild afternoon for February. Blue sky and a breeze so light it barely moved the hairs on Jonce's arm. He leaned against the railing on his right elbow and nursed a beer to the point of having to pretend something touched his lips when he tilted the can. He didn't dare make another trip to the refrigerator and risk missing Don's exodus. A man gets curious about the husband of the woman he's spending time with, especially when the husband is such an imposing physical specimen. If Jonce had an ass whipping coming he meant to face it head on.

At long last he heard their muted voices near the door. She spoke, he spoke, then they talked over each other without Jonce picking out a single word. When the door opened he cut his eyes leftward and made brief contact with her, then him. "Some weather ain't it?"

Don stopped with one foot out and the other in and eyed Jonce the way one dog might eye another, ready to defend his yard for no other reason than because it's his. "Who the hell are you?"

"I ain't nobody," Jonce said, hitching his head toward the open door behind him. "I live in twenty-two."

A black suitcase dangled from Don's left hand and a large Igloo cooler hung from the right. Something to wear and something to consume. What more could a working man want except for his woman to wrap herself around his arm the way Bobbie did as soon as she sensed trouble. They both stared at Jonce for their own reasons. Clearly she hadn't told him.

Don stepped out with Bobbie clinging to his elbow. "Maybe you should stand in front of your door and not ours," he said.

Jonce looked about himself then laughed. "I ain't learnt yet what's mine and what ain't." His eyes stroked Bobbie from head to toe. Don pulled his arm free and snapped at her to get back inside. She retreated and slammed the door.

"She minds good," Jonce said, then he shifted his empty beer can from his right hand to his left and stood straight. "Jonce Nash," he said, sticking out his paw. "It's nice to finally meet a neighbor who speaks English." Don made no effort to free up a hand. "What kind of work do you do, Don?"

"How do you know my name?"

Jonce cleared his throat and pulled back his hand. "Thin walls. It was me who gave you the standing ovation last week."

"So that was you," Don said, twisting his face into a scowl. "I oughta kick your ass for that."

"No need to get violent."

"Stop grinning at me."

Jonce reset his face. "Come on, Don. I could've beat my old lady with a belt and she wouldn't've screamed like that."

Don's biceps tightened against his short sleeves but he didn't drop his cargo.

"Don't take me wrong," Jonce said. "I don't mean nothing. Just making conversation. What kind of work did you say you do?"

"I didn't." Don's grip on the suitcase and the Igloo cooler turned his knuckles white. He took a step toward the stairs. "From now on lean on the rail in front of your door instead of mine," he said. "And stay away from my wife."

"A man ort not be ashamed of his work," Jonce said. "I've looked high and low and can't find a job. Maybe you could get me on with you. I can do most near anything with my hands and I ain't scared of heights."

Don stopped and turned. "I'm a welder if it's any of your business."

Jonce nodded. "You don't say." He cocked his head to one side and said he bet Don could weld underwater. Don frowned and shook his head and said he wasn't trained in that but if he was he wouldn't

49

be living in this dump. "One man's dump is another man's pleasure palace," Jonce said. "Same thing applies to women," he said with a wink. "Know what I mean?"

Don clearly didn't know what he meant, which was a really good thing for Jonce, considering. He hoped Bobbie had her ear to the door. Of course she did. Females are full to the neck with curiosity.

"Mine's a real ball buster," Don said, probably thinking his voice wouldn't carry through the two inches of wood.

"Ain't they all," Jonce said. "Ain't. They. All."

Don walked to the rail and dropped his suitcase and sat his cooler down easy, then he fished a pack of generic cigarettes from his shirt pocket and offered one to Jonce, who never declined anything free. They lit up like two old pals. Don leaned against his forearms on the rail so that he overlooked the parking lot below. Jonce kept his elbow on the rail and his foot raised against the iron, staring intently at the peephole knowing Bobbie's eye was glued to the other side.

"So what'd you do time for," Don asked as he blew smoke at the world.

"Can't nobody keep a secret," Jonce said, shaking his head at the blabby wife beyond the peephole. "Well, if you must know, I done this last stretch for burglary." He raised his finger. "Innocent, mind you."

Don laughed.

"I ever get my hands on that son-of-a-bitching Farley Milo I'll break his neck. That boy of mine too. It was him started it all." He inhaled his nicotine then exhausted it. "I tell ya, Don, most people in this world today ain't worth two pennies rubbed together."

Don grunted as if he understood exactly what Jonce meant. "We got this Mexican on our crew ... and I ain't got nothing against Mexicans ... they some hard working little devils, but this guy, geez, you'd think he used to own the whole damned continent."

"You better watch them little brown bastards," Jonce said. "Ain't their fault, really. It was the Spaniards who came over and bred all that nonsense into 'em." He laughed. "Them Spaniards left this continent with horses and a bunch of pissed off Mexicans."

"He comes in every Monday morning all hyped up on cable news, cussing Donald Trump and Sam Houston." He turned his head to look at Jonce, who was still staring at the peephole. "Trump I know, but I had to google Sam Houston."

"Remember the Alamo," Jonce said. "I've seen the movie a dozen times."

"Sam Houston wasn't at the Alamo."

"Well if he had been we might not've lost and nobody would remembered it," Jonce said. "But hey, we took their land, right?" He slapped Don on the shoulder. "Ain't that what matters?"

"Maybe," Don said. "I just wish the guy would quit watching the news. I'm tired of hearing it."

"I like the way you think," Jonce said. "Yes sir, I bet we share a lot of things." He winked at the peephole, then he turned and thumped the spent cigarette over the rail and watched it bounce off the hood of a blue Toyota. "Bet you get into some shit out on the road." He grinned and poked Don in the arm with a finger. "Am I right? After work? Bunch of guys with nothing to do but blow off steam? Bet you got a girl in every town."

Don chuckled. "We've tore up a hotel room or two." He dropped his cigarette to the ground below. "I quit all that when I married Bobbie." He glanced back at the door. "Can't make her believe it though."

Jonce poked him again. "I bet you got one waiting on you right now. Maybe two. You ever had two at the same time?"

"Nah, I work with a guy who claims he has though. Don't know if I believe him."

"Bet you always wanted to, right? Right? I know I have — wanted to that is. I'm too ugly to fire up two women at one time, but man, I've always wanted to. You know any girls like that?"

Don shrugged. Jonce poked him again. The poking was starting to agitate Don. "I bet you do. I bet you know plenty of girls like that. Big guy like you."

"I better get going. The guys'll be waiting on me."

"Girls too I bet," Jonce said, poking him again. He un-propped himself from the railing and stood straight, still having to look up at Don because he had a good three inches on him. "Well Don, for what it's worth that little gal of yours is home every night watching television so you don't have to worry about her."

A look came across Don's face.

"Thin walls," Jonce said, grinning. "Hell, I farted the other night and they beat on the walls three doors down."

Don laughed, then he picked up his bags and told Jonce it was nice meeting him, then he marched himself down the stairs and across the parking lot and left in his truck. Jonce turned back and put his face close to the door and told Bobbie she could come over later if she felt so inclined.

Bobbie went a mighty long time without feeling inclined. The afternoon expired and the sun went down and still she hadn't come over. Her television blared the same movies through the wall that Ellie used to watch until she got so saturated with estrogen that she began to hate all men in general and Jonce in particular. Jonce had saturated himself with beer until he had to climb something or die.

He left the couch and staggered to the wall and pounded until she muted the television.

"What?"

"Get your ass over here."

"Why?"

"Because I said so."

"You're drunk."

"So what if I am?"

"Your buddy Don wouldn't approve."

"Get over here or I'll kick a hole through this wall and drag you through it."

Silence, then the random noise of her moving around. A woman has no choice but to make herself presentable when she goes to meet a man. It's in their DNA, presentable being whatever it could be. After several minutes his unlocked door opened and she came in without knocking and caught him leaned against the shared wall.

"That how you snoop?"

"Since when don't you knock?"

She glared at him, then she closed the door and helped herself to a beer from the fridge. When she bent over, the thin fabric of her black yoga pants pulled tight against her features and gave him a sensation. It was her best side. Too bad she had to back out of the refrigerator and turn around. Her top was less impressive, not having much to pull tight against. It was white with pink stripes and tied across her belly button.

"You raped me you son-of-a-bitch."

"Now that ain't fair," he said, stepping away from the wall. "I don't remember you screaming for help." He reached toward her face and tried to touch her cheek with his finger but she jerked away. "You had all day to call the cops."

"I still might."

He reached again. This time she let him touch her. "You could've told Don."

"He would've killed us both," she said.

Jonce grinned as he stroked her soft cheek. She could be presentable if she changed her hair and wore more makeup. "I knew you was watching through the peephole."

"I heard what he called me. If I was a ballbreaker he wouldn't come home with lipstick on his collar."

Jonce traced her jawbone with his finger to the center of her chin, then along her Adam's apple all the way down to the first button. She twisted her face into a pout to conceal the smile he knew was coming. "You could've asked, you know," she said. "I would've done it without you having to be mean about it."

He hooked the button with his finger and pulled her into the bedroom. Being mean was half the fun.

Jackie picked up breakfast and ate with her son, then warned him not to leave the room while she was gone. She promised to come back for lunch, then she drove to the police station to start her new job.

Chief Gant gave her the grand tour personally, then spent the better part of an hour in her new office going over the cases she had inherited. Foremost among them was the murder of Perry Stubbs. The state was technically leading the investigation but Stubbs was low on their list of priorities. Hayes was awash with charges of corruption and the state had limited resources. As one investigator put it, chasing down all the leads dumped into their laps by the mayor's trove of documents was like trying to beat back a forest fire with a gasoline-soaked shirt.

Of course there was a laundry list of ordinary crimes, most of them drug related. They, too, had dropped in importance. The next several months, perhaps years, would be a busy time for all involved.

Jackie asked the obvious question: is the mayor a legitimate suspect? Gant was emphatic that Mayor Pigg was the most honest person he had ever met, which to Jackie was in and of itself a red flag. No one is completely honest, and she held a firm belief that too much honesty is often a mask for dishonesty, especially when it came to politicians.

She passed the morning plowing through case files, particularly the Stubbs murder. The victim's throat was cut, meaning there would be an enormous amount of blood. It would have been impossible for the killer to escape the room without leaving at least one footprint. She dug deeper but didn't find a detailed report from the state crime lab. Gant had told her to feel free to come to him with any questions, but she wanted to be independent so she called the state investigator instead.

Sergeant John Timms sounded old on the phone. Jackie visualized a man bumping up against retirement without rising above the rank of sergeant, assigned to a high-profile murder case only because all the better agents were busy. Making snap judgments was a bad habit she had, but her instincts were rarely wrong. She asked about evidence and he regurgitated the usual excuse of waiting on the state crime lab. He didn't seem at all concerned that it had been twelve days. When pressed about the presence of footprints, he admitted he had not actually seen the crime scene before it was cleaned up. At first it had been a local matter, then the mayor dropped what amounted to a nuclear bomb on the town in the form of a thick manila envelope and a thumb drive.

"I haven't worked a murder in five years," Timms said. "And to be perfectly honest, whoever killed this son-of-a-bitch did the world a favor."

Jonce awoke at the crack of dawn and lit a cigarette, took a long draw, then blew smoke toward the ceiling. Bobbie lay with her back to him, exposed from the waist up. Her snores reminded him of the way a cat rattles when it's happy, which irritated him without him bothering to wonder why.

He slapped her on the ass and told her to beat it but she didn't stir, so he nudged her with his knee. She squirmed. "Stop it." Her groggy voice barely escaped her pillow.

The end of his cigarette glowed orange, then faded. Bobbie's snores rattled in her throat again. He thumped the growing ash to the floor and glared at her naked back, his irritation growing with each rise and fall of her ribcage until he couldn't help but snuff out the cigarette on her shoulder. She screamed to the top of her lungs, then called him every filthy name in the English language as she rolled off the bed and into the floor with the sheet twisting around her like a mummy rolling itself up for burial. She hit the floor with a thud and stopped yelling. For a handful of seconds he heard nothing except the angry sounds of her breathing. Then, "what the hell?"

Jonce rolled onto his elbow and thumped the spent cigarette toward the sound of her voice. "Next time I say git you git."

"Next time? Next time!" He heard a mighty struggle then her head popped up above the mattress, then her shoulders. She rose to her knees and glared at him with her hair all over the place and her mouth twisted into a snarl, like a rabid dog blown out of a cyclone. "Who the hell do you think you are?"

He sank back into his pillow and closed his eyes, making a point of showing her he wasn't afraid of what she might do. She had spunk, but she wasn't stupid.

"I'll have you know that hurt," she said, still mad. The direction of her voice told him she was standing.

He didn't respond. With his eyes still closed he heard the heavy in and out of her breathing.

"I hope you die," she said, then she stomped away, slamming the doors to both their apartments. He knew now what it took to make her mad.

Chapter Six

J ackie left the station and drove to the pawn shop in her own car, not yet having been assigned a police vehicle. No mention had been made in that regard. The chief was busy and she was in no hurry to inherit someone else's discarded smells.

The burly man at the counter stroked her with his eyes as she approached, probably thinking she enjoyed being ogled by a white man. He was ugly and put considerable effort into passing himself off as a badass with his shaved head and scraggly beard. She knew the type and wasn't impressed.

His smile vanished when she flashed her badge. It had been Detective Gant's badge before he moved up. "Point me toward the room where your boss was murdered," she said with calm authority.

"I'll have to ask Miss Nelly about that," he said. Nelly Stubbs was the widow who now owned the place.

"Is she here?"

Some type of laughing snort escaped him. "I didn't know she existed until all this happened."

"You didn't know your boss was married?"

He shrugged. "Not to say I ain't glad. At least she's keeping the place open. It don't pay much but it beats slinging furniture."

Jackie looked past the counter and saw a door on the back wall. There was no other door so it had to be the one.

"She had a crew come in and clean it up," the man said. "Ball said it was okay."

"You mean former Chief Ball?"

"Our warehouse is back there too so he said it was okay to clean it up."

"A big man like you shouldn't be afraid of a little blood."

"That was more than a little blood, ma'am. I ain't never seen so much blood in my life. And the smell was awful. Still is sometimes."

He uttered the obligatory protest when she started around the counter but made no physical attempt to stop her. No doubt he knew more than he had told the police. They always do. Pressing him would do no good. Sooner or later he would drink too much and brag to the wrong person. Justice could be a sloppy business.

After a quick shower and shave, Jonce decided it was time to play his hold card. Gain Prichard was probably sweating bullets, wondering when his time to be frog-marched in front of the news cameras would come. The mayor had unleashed hellfire on the town and people in high places were nervous. Jonce didn't consider himself a snitch for his role in the operation because he had done a simple job for Stubbs. Stubbs was the snitch, then Palo snitched back, then the mayor out-snitched them both. No telling how many suicides were about to hit. The high and mighty don't fall well. Hayes might have to build itself a tall building for the guilty to jump from.

He got dressed and drove across town and parked directly in front of Prichard's pitiful little office. Behind the plate glass he saw the cumbersome frame of his parole officer hunched over his desk, pecking at his keyboard, probably searching how to stay alive in prison on the World Wide Web.

Prichard looked up when the door opened. In a split second his face went from victim to bully. One second he was a basket of nerves, the next he was puffed up like a blowfish. "This ain't your day," he said, returning his attention to his computer screen. "Beat it."

Jonce ignored the rebuff and stepped inside. "I got me a job, Mister Prichard, sir."

"Good, now get lost. I'm busy."

"It's a real good job."

Prichard looked up. "What part of get lost don't you understand?"

"I'm the new CEO of my own protection business," Jonce said. "Jonce Nash, protector of important men with sticky fingers." He laughed. "I made that title up on the spot. Catchy ain't it?"

Prichard glared at him, then he kicked up one corner of his mouth and shook his head. "You ain't got the brains of a toilet brush, Nash," he said, pecking his keyboard again. "In two seconds I'm calling the sheriff and having you locked up for vagrancy." He looked up again. "Come to think of it, I ain't had you drug tested in a while." He opened a side drawer and pulled out a form and jabbed it toward Jonce. "Take this down to the hospital and piss in a cup."

Jonce ignored the piece of paper suspended at the end of Prichard's baseball glove of a hand. "I don't blame you for being nervous, Mister Prichard," he said with mock concern. "That damned mayor's like a born again whore hell-bent on shutting down the whorehouse." He winked at Prichard, who was now focused intently on Jonce's face. "You been with a few of them whores, ain't you Mister Prichard? Ain't you? Come on, admit it now."

Prichard's face took color. "What the hell's wrong with you? Take this and get out!"

"No sir, I won't," Jonce said. "Every time I piss in a cup the nurses fight over which one gets to peek at me through that little sliding door in the wall. I'm telling you it's downright humiliating being ogled like a piece of meat. No sir, I won't do it no more."

Prichard shot to his feet. He was agile for his size. Big enough to hurt a man without meaning to. His chair rolled back against the wall with a thud. "Now look here you little bastard!"

"I'm offering you my protection, Mister Prichard, just like the title of my new business says."

"Your protection? Your protection!" He wadded the paper into a ball and flung it against Jonce's chest. His cheeks trembled and his eyes strained against their sockets.

"Maybe you ain't heard they arrested Chief Ball," Jonce said, puffing up his chest and throwing back his shoulders. "That make you nervous?"

"Why should that make *me* nervous?"

"Ain't you wondering why they ain't come for you yet?"

Prichard showed a moment of weakness then flashed hot again. "Get out!" He slung his arm toward the door with such a fury that Jonce stepped back, thinking he had been swung at, then he collected himself and told Prichard to sit down.

"Don't tell me to sit down you little —."

"Sit DOWN, Mister Prichard!"

Prichard dropped his arm to his side. His face took on the confused curiosity of a cat watching a red dot bounce between its paws.

"Since you're too dumb to put two and two together and come up with four," Jonce said, "I'll spell it out in plain ordinary English. I took them papers."

"What papers?"

"Your papers."

Prichard glanced down at his desk in absolute confusion.

"The mayor is shaking the rafters of this town and rats are falling everywhere. Ain't you been wondering why he ain't shook you loose yet?"

"Shook me loose? What are you —?" It hit him like a brick between the eyes. He lowered himself into his chair as though he had aged ten years in two seconds. "Are you saying?"

Jonce nodded. "I'm saying."

"You?"

"Me."

Prichard's face went pale as he considered the things a man like Tipton Palo might have written down about him. Records he might have kept, knowing from the fallout around him that he was an unscrupulous note-taker.

"How did you —?"

"Them papers the mayor's got is my doing," Jonce said. "Without admitting to any lawbreaking on my part, them papers came from Tipton Palo's wall safe." He hesitated. Waited, then, "you starting to get the picture?"

"I —."

"They got enough on Palo to put his grandkids in jail. Too bad, too, because that little woman of his ain't bad company." He snickered. "Glenn Ball might snitch and get a slap on the wrist. He's that type you know. They probably had to sedate him just to shut him up long enough to read him his rights."

Prichard's discomfort visibly eased.

"I know certain things, Mister Prichard. Maybe Glenn Ball don't know as much as you're afraid he knows, but I know."

"There's nothing to know. You're —."

"Bluffing?" He grinned. "I don't bluff, Mister Prichard. Not even a little tiny bit."

"Go away," Prichard said without the authority he had previously commanded. "I need time to think."

"I ain't told you what to think about yet," Jonce said. "We ain't reached our understanding."

Prichard raised his eyes but his mind was a million miles away, thinking about things Jonce could only guess. The humiliation of getting arrested, probably, or prison.

"You've sent a lot of men back to prison," Jonce said. "Hard men. You stomp around like top goose. Name-taker and ass-kicker all rolled up into one big ole mean sonofa —."

"What is it you want?"

"A lot, Mister Prichard. I ain't one for reaching low."

"I'm not rich."

"Money never crossed my mind with you, Mister Prichard. No sir. First day I came in here I knew you was the kind of man who couldn't hold money. I bet you owe fifty cents against your first dollar."

Prichard perked up and held Jonce's gaze. "What exactly is it you think you have on me?"

"It's not what I think," Jonce said. "It's what I know."

"Meaning what?"

"Meaning I went through them papers before I gave 'em to Stubbs. Everything with your name on it I kept."

"Everything?"

"Every last one."

"Are you sure? I mean —."

"Stop wagging your tail," Jonce said. "The only thing you have to worry about is me. I own you lock, stock, and barrel. Butthole and eyeballs."

The color returned to Prichard's face. He relaxed back into his chair and locked his fingers behind his head, elbows up. "Of course I'll need proof," he said, regaining some of his bluster.

"I can send copies to the mayor."

"But you won't," Prichard said. "You won't because then you wouldn't have anything to hold over my head." Prichard grew taller in his chair. The weight was lifted. A moment ago he had been drowning and now he could feel the bottom with his toes. "What exactly is it you want?"

Jonce grinned. "Me and you is gonna get along just fine, Mister Prichard. Just fine."

The small room where Stubbs was murdered had been sanitized. Not only was the blood gone, but so was everything else. Not a shred of paper remained. There were no pictures on the walls. The desk was bare inside and out. The smell of bleach was overwhelming and threatened to give Jackie a migraine.

She killed an hour poking around the warehouse outside the little office, hoping but not expecting to find something that had been overlooked. Dozens of cluttered shelves arranged in three rows held every type of item imaginable. Small tags affixed by various methods identified the owner's name, the amount owed, and the forfeit date of each item. There were a lot of musical instruments. Guitars, horns, a drum set. There were stereos and televisions and computers too numerous to count. One item that stood out in particular was a little girl's bicycle with a pink basket and tassels hanging from the handlebar grips. A little girl's happiness had been traded for ten dollars, but it wasn't the child Jackie felt sorry for, it was the mother. She knew all too well what it felt like to be desperate. She jotted the woman's name and phone number in her notepad, then left to keep a lunch date with her son.

On the way home she passed an apartment complex that looked to be something she might afford. It was a single building with two levels. All the doors looked identical and opened to the outside. The parking lot was empty except for a handful of cheap cars. She called the number on the sign out front and inquired.

"Maybe I've found us a place," she told Jordan over hamburgers. His face lit up at the prospect of getting out of the fleabag motel. "Don't get too excited though," she said. "It's not what you're used to." They had lived well in Detroit, financially speaking, but they had already had that discussion. Her son knew they would have to make sacrifices.

"Apartment or house?"

"Apartment."

He pushed a fry into his mouth. "Does it have a pool?"

"I doubt it."

"Will I have my own room?"

"Of course."

He smiled. "Wi-Fi?"

"Maybe. We can look at it this afternoon when I get off work. The lady seemed really nice on the phone."

When she returned to the station, the woman at the front desk pointed toward Chief Gant's office and raised her eyebrows as if to say you've really done it now. She had expected to have to explain her visit to the pawn shop but not so soon.

Gant told her to close the door and sit. "Nelly Stubbs called."

"That was fast," Jackie said. "I usually don't get into trouble until the second day." She tried to smile to hide her nerves. She really needed the job.

"You're not in trouble," Gant said. "Quite the contrary. I'm glad to see you take the initiative."

Relief overwhelmed her. "I should have run it by you first but I —"

He raised his hand and stopped her. "It's your case. Work it. You'll find I don't micromanage."

She felt herself beaming. "I was hoping you'd see it that way. I spoke with Sergeant Timms about the lack of evidence and got the feeling he isn't putting much effort into the case."

Gant frowned. "Don't blame him too much. I'm afraid our former chief hamstrung the investigation before it got off the ground."

"How so?"

"He took charge and released the crime scene back to the widow before anyone else had a chance to collect any meaningful evidence."

The revelation stunned her. "So there's nothing?"

"Not much," Gant said. "He took pictures, and he collected blood samples which we know will belong to the victim. We have a few things from the victim's desk that are splattered with blood. No murder weapon."

"What about fingerprints?"

"Hundreds," he said. "Half the people in the county had been in there at one time or another."

"What about footprints? With all the blood there had to be at least one."

"Ball allowed the medics and a few volunteer firemen who didn't know any better to trample the scene before they took pictures. Any footprints the killer left were destroyed."

Jackie sat back in disbelief. "What kind of first responder tramples a crime scene?"

"It's not entirely their fault," Gant said. "We don't get many murders around here and most of our first responders are volunteers who had never seen anything like this before."

"But still, it was a crime scene."

"And they'll never make that mistake again, I can promise you that. They're good men and they were trying to help. It was Ball's job to secure the scene."

"How could he be so incompetent?"

"That's not the word I would use," Gant said. He sighed, clearly taking no joy in what he was about to say. "I suspected him of being corrupt. So did Mayor Pigg, but unfortunately we proved it too late."

"So you think he compromised the crime scene on purpose?"

"I'm certain of it. I've seen him work cases before. He knew the basics. He knew enough to secure the scene and let the state boys handle it."

"Then why didn't he?"

"It's your job to find out, Detective Deen." He pulled open a desk drawer and slid a set of keys and a 9mm handgun across the desk. "The black Ford Mustang out back is yours. It'll smoke the tires in third gear so be careful. We seized it in a drug bust last month and everybody's been chomping at the bit to claim it. The other keys are to the front door and your office." He grinned as though he knew what she was thinking. "We hardly ever lock the place, but it *is* a small town and sometimes we're understaffed."

Jonce reclined back on his living room sofa with a beer in one hand and a cigarette in the other. Gain Prichard was his for the taking. No more threats of prison. No drug tests. No job interviews. Just smooth sailing from here on out. His only concern was that if he pushed too hard Prichard might take the coward's way out and shoot himself in the head, but Jonce wasn't going to push that hard.

According to Prichard, Stubbs had known nothing about his little side gig with Palo. Stubbs didn't approve of running dope. Jonce had heard him say it himself. Running dope is asking to be caught. It's only a matter of time before some junkie gets busted and squeals on his dealer, then the dominoes start falling upward. Stubbs had gone so far as to warn Jonce that if he caught him running drugs he would chop off his hands. Jonce had believed him, but now Stubbs was gone so everything was on the table.

Personally, Jonce didn't consume, but he had no problem making it available to those who did. People will always find a way to destroy themselves. Ellie had destroyed herself that way. The woman never so much as took a sip of alcohol the entire time they were married but for some reason she turned to drugs and overdosed while he was in Parchman. It saddened him a little. Ellie hadn't been a bad woman, just dumb. She performed all her duties in and out of bed with the same obedient attention to detail, then with nobody around to beat sense into her she self-destructed.

The little hellcat next door was proving to be a conundrum. She had tricks up her sleeve Ellie never dreamed of but he couldn't figure her out. He regretted burning her with the cigarette because maybe now she wouldn't come back. She wouldn't tell Don, not that it mattered if she did. There wasn't a man alive Jonce was afraid of that way. Sure, cops scared him. Judges and prosecutors and prison guards scared him, but that was different. You can't fight cops and judges and prosecutors and win, but a man like Don you can beat. Any man can be whipped given the right circumstances.

He pulled a puff from his cigarette and told himself to get off the girl and back onto business. His deal with Prichard was not set in stone. Dollar amounts had not been discussed, nor had duties and responsibilities. Of course Prichard would think he was running the show. It was, after all, his operation. Palo had dropped him like a hot potato as soon as the mayor dropped all those documents in the DA's lap. Palo was the kind who liked to puff himself up until shit starts hitting the fan, then he runs and hides behind his ivy education.

It occurred to Jonce as he lay there that Palo might offer Prichard up in exchange for something. Lawyers are always looking for some way to screw somebody over. Maybe Palo was even wondering why Prichard was still free. Maybe he thought Prichard had served him up first.

He laughed. High and mighty people sure do kick when they fall.

Chapter Seven

Chief Gant added a cell phone and a permanent badge to Jackie's arsenal. She was official now, ninety day probationary period aside. For three months she had to be on her best behavior but she was a cop again. Gainfully employed and far away from her husband.

"Did you see the paper this morning?"

She picked up the phone and dropped it into her purse, then she picked up the badge. It would take some looking at. It was gold and shiny with the number 235 in black letters set inside a white rectangle near the bottom. She rubbed her thumb over the number. Last night she and Jordan had moved into their new apartment. It had been an easy haul because they had nothing to move except two suitcases packed tight with clothes and a PlayStation gaming console with all the extras. "I forgot today was Wednesday," she said. "Should I go out and get a copy?"

The chief laughed. "Not if you want news. The headline's another hit piece on Mayor Pigg. I don't remember if I told you or not, but the editor's a cheerleader for Tipton Palo. If he calls you for comment on anything, tell him no comment."

"Is that advice or an order?"

"Both."

"Won't that give him an excuse to print whatever he wants?"

"He'll do that anyway," Gant said. "And he'll twist anything you say to make you or the department look bad, and if you call him on it he'll say it was a mistake and bury a correction in next week's classifieds."

"Is that experience speaking?"

"Not so much personal experience as seeing what they've tried to do to our mayor."

"You really like him, don't you?"

"Mayor Pigg? He's about the finest mayor this town's ever had."

"Does that mean he's off limits?"

Gant looked surprised by the question. "Off limits for what?"

"He told me himself he had trouble with our murder victim," she said, not that she suspected the mayor. She was used to certain people being off limits. It had been a long time since she believed no one was above the law.

"If you find evidence leading you to Mayor Pigg then you follow it, but you'd better be sure it's legitimate and not something planted by his enemies."

"I was only asking in a hypothetical nature," Jackie said. "I have no reason to suspect your mayor."

"*Our* mayor," the chief said. "You work for him too." He looked somewhat relieved. "That man's been through the ringer since he got elected."

She remembered Gant's question about the paper. "Was there something in the newspaper you wanted me to see?"

"Just a lot of disinformation about the murder," he said. "It could work to our advantage, maybe, if you find a suspect and he slips up and divulges information not known to the public. It's a long shot, but there's a decent chance that whoever did this is as unused to murder as we are." He paused, then said he didn't suppose his logic applied to her. He was right in that regard. She had investigated a lot of murders.

Throughout the course of the morning, the name Corey Pickle came up as a person of interest in the Stubbs murder. She was plowing through case files looking for anything that linked anyone to the victim. The more she learned of Stubbs, the harder it was to apply that label to him — victim — but there was no legal way around it. Someone murdered him, and in her book that made that someone worse than the man he murdered.

Undoubtedly the killer was male. Every ounce of police instinct screamed it. Certainly there were women physically capable of cutting an old man's throat, but were they mentally capable? In some realms, yes, probably, but the odds were minuscule. Besides, nothing she had seen led her to believe Stubbs was feeble. Old doesn't necessarily mean weak.

Sergeant Timms answered on the third ring. He was polite as

always. Affable to a fault. He told her that Corey Pickle had worked for Stubbs for a few years and had kept his nose clean until recently.

"He cut the head off a horse and hung it on the mayor's back porch," Timms said with an odd chuckle. "The guy's for sure not right in the head. He also framed the mayor's brother for drug possession."

She had seen the file on Roger Pigg.

"He disappeared around the time of the murder."

"They both did," Jackie corrected him. "Do you think they were involved?"

"Roger Pigg? No, not likely. He's got a list of misdemeanor arrests a mile long but nothing criminal and certainly nothing violent. Do you remember Jimmy Carter?"

"President Jimmy Carter?"

"Yeah, the peanut picker. Remember his brother Billy?"

"No, not really," she said. Carter had been before her time.

"Well, Carter got himself elected president then his brother Billy came crawling out of the woodwork and showed the world what a bunch of hicks they were. He even came out with his own beer. Billy Beer." Timms laughed as though his monologue pertained to the case. "Break that down to the local level and you might say Roger Pigg is the mayor's Billy."

"I see," she said, though she didn't really.

"Corey Pickle planted those drugs in the mayor's car not knowing his brother had borrowed it. They found Pickle's fingerprint on the floorboard of the car next to the dope. Long story short, the former chief — Ball — destroyed the evidence and that's about the time Pickle skipped town."

"The former chief seems to have made a habit of destroying evidence," she said. "Are we sure Pickle skipped?"

"Whatever he did he's gone. Roger Pigg hung around a little while after that then skipped out too. Three days ago he was in New Mexico with a sister who swears he was there on the day Stubbs was murdered."

"Why did I not see any of that in the files?"

Timms sighed. "There's things you put in the record and things you don't."

"So the question is did Pickle skip town before Stubbs was murdered or after," Jackie said. Working with Timms was going to be more of a chore than she had hoped. Interdepartmental investigations are never without wrinkles, but Timms wasn't hiding records, he was failing to create them.

"After would be my guess," Timms said. "Otherwise he couldn't have killed him."

"And his motive?"

"Stubbs was pissed at him for being sloppy so he let him sit in jail too long. When Pickle got out he cut his throat and skipped town. It don't take much with these low types."

"And that's how you think it happened?"

"Yeah," Timms said, "until somebody proves he's not, Pickle's our man."

Jonce made her for a cop the moment he saw her exit the vehicle. Clean cut black female driving a souped up black Mustang with windows so dark he couldn't see past the steering wheel looking down from the elevated walkway with the sun bright against her. She disappeared underneath the slab of concrete on which he stood, beer in hand, wearing a shirt only because he still needed to cover the wound on his left bicep that had not yet fully healed. If she came to question his neighbors then she had picked the wrong floor. He leaned over the railing in a failed attempt to see which room she went into so he could pay the occupant a visit after she left.

Most of his neighbors had somewhere else to be during weekdays but he had seen a few old people milling about, and every apartment complex has its welfare queens. She had been carrying two white bags and two drinks in white Styrofoam cups so maybe she was visiting a relative. An out of towner, maybe, visiting her mother so she could show off.

He walked downstairs and made a wide circle around the parking lot and positioned himself behind a white service van that hadn't moved since he'd moved in. From his vantage point he could see every door downstairs and up, but he wasn't concerned about up. The Mustang had a government tag like every other cop car in town so he still didn't know if she was local or passing through.

It occurred to him that the van he was leaning against was exactly the kind of generic vehicle the cops might set up in if they wanted to surveil the place. He put his ear to the side and listened. Nothing. He gently tried the side door but it was locked, so he put his shoulder against it and rocked it a couple of times. Still nothing. Probably just a van. Nothing he could do about it if it wasn't. He hadn't stepped outside without a shirt on since the shooting, and if they had bugged his place they wouldn't need to sit in the parking lot.

Twenty minutes after she went in, she came out again and went straight to her car without looking around. For a cop she wasn't very curious about her surroundings, but then maybe she had everything she needed. The number on the door was too far away to read but he counted from the far end and knew it had to be number 15. After she left he waited ten minutes then walked straight up to the door and pounded with the side of his fist. "Manager! Open up!"

The door opened and a young black boy stared back at him with an indignation all too common to boys his age. "You're not the manager," he said, then he tried to close the door.

"Get your momma out here," Jonce barked, catching the door with his left hand. The boy jerked back as Jonce's hand struck the door.

"She just left."

The kid pushed against the door and Jonce let it close, then he looked back toward the spot where the fancy Mustang had been, knowing he had just outplayed himself. Instead of going straight back to his room, he went the other way, past 16, 17, 18, all the way to the end and around. He kept walking until he was in back of the place where no one could see him from any direction. He had never been behind the building before and it looked to be the perfect place for addicts to shoot up. Completely secluded with woods close enough to hit with a rock. Trash scattered everywhere. Beer bottles and cans and paper bags from every fast food joint in town. He hugged the back wall all the way to the far end, ducking windows and dodging air conditioners, glad none of the downstairs apartments had back doors. Next to one of the air conditioners he saw a pair of white boxer shorts, soiled, and a condom. He quickened his pace. Just being caught near a discarded syringe or discolored spoon might be enough to violate his parole with or without Prichard's input. When he reached the corner he turned and trotted toward the stairs then up and into his apartment where there was nothing to do but stare out the window and wait.

Several minutes passed, then half an hour. Maybe the boy hadn't been as spooked as he seemed. After a full hour he abandoned the window and settled into the sofa with a cold beer and a ham sandwich. He had a new neighbor and Hayes had a new cop.

69

"A man came today," Jordan said over dinner his mother had brought home in a sack.

A chill shot up Jackie's spine. She studied him as she chewed and swallowed. He didn't seem the least bit frightened. "You didn't open the door did you?"

"He said he was the manager."

"Jordan! We've talked about this. How many times have I told you not to open the door for anyone?"

He ducked his head and pushed another fry into his mouth. "He said he was the manager."

"It doesn't matter who he says he is," she said, trying to restrain her emotions. She didn't want to scare him but he had to understand the danger. "From now on you don't open the door, period. Got it?"

He nodded as he chewed. "I got it."

She folded the wrapper back over her half-eaten burger and pushed it back. Jordan cut his eyes up at her then dropped them back to his burger.

"He said he had the wrong apartment. It was no big deal."

"What did he look like?"

Jordan shrugged instinctively as was his wont when she interrogated him. "About your age. A little taller than me. Kind of skinny."

"What color was his hair?"

"Brown, I think."

"Light or dark?"

"Medium."

"Long or short?"

"Short ... I think. Kind of messy, like he hadn't combed it."

"Did he have facial hair?"

"Yes, a mustache and a little patch on his chin."

"A goatee?"

"Yeah, that's what it was. A goatee."

"What was he wearing?"

"I don't remember, Mom. He was only here for a few seconds. I told him you weren't home and he left. That's all there was to it."

"Wait, he asked for me?"

"Yeah, he said where's your momma."

"Is that exactly what he said?"

"I think so," he said. "No, wait, he said *get your momma out here*."

"Why didn't you close the door?"

Jordan dropped his eyes again. "I tried to. He held it."

A bolt of anger sank into her chest like a dagger, not at her son but at the man. Her brain spun up a list of potential charges. Simple assault; assault on a minor; forced entry. "Would you recognize him if you saw him again?"

He shrugged again. "Maybe. I don't know."

She folded her hands and took a cooling breath. "You could've been hurt you know, opening the door for a stranger that way."

"It won't happen again."

"This isn't a gated community, Jordan. We don't know who our neighbors are."

"I know."

"Anyone can walk up off the street and knock."

"I'm sorry."

"And for your information, the manager is a woman, and she's old enough to be your grandmother."

"You didn't tell me that," he said as though that bit of missing information cleared him of any wrongdoing.

"I didn't think I had to," she said. "I thought *don't open the door for anyone for any reason* covered it."

"I said I'm sorry."

She reached across the table and took his hand. She didn't want him to live in fear, but the danger was real. The longer they stayed in one place the greater that danger would become. Living as Jackie Deen instead of Jackie Mulvaney was a decent firewall, but they still had to be careful. The simple act of using cash for everything made life more difficult. Buying gas for her car was a hassle, made less so now that she had the Mustang and a city-issued gas card. She would never use it for her personal vehicle, though she felt certain at least some of the other officers did. She hated dishonesty, which made her current condition all the more unpleasant.

She looked at her son as he stuffed his mouth with fries. She was teaching him to run from his problems. To lie. To hide out like a hunted animal. Or was she teaching him to survive? The coin had two sides.

He looked up again. "What?"

"Nothing," she said, then went through the motions of picking at her own food again. "You know why we're doing this, right?"

"Yeah."

"So you know why it scared me that a strange man came to our door?"

He nodded. "Does it mean we have to move again?"

"No. Not if you promise to be more careful." She had a job now. It wasn't a good job, not where money was concerned, but it would keep them afloat until something better came along, and Hayes was practically in the middle of nowhere. Kelton couldn't possible find them, not unless one of them made a mistake.

Thursday morning hit Jonce hard. His head pounded and his mouth felt like the leavings on the floor of a cotton gin. He remembered pounding on the wall late and telling Bobbie to come over, and he had the faintest recollection of her telling him to go do to himself what he meant to do to her.

His head spun when he sat up and swung his legs over the side of the bed. The fermented contents of his stomach gurgled, forcing him to concentrate to keep it down. A vow never to drink again crossed his lips and fell impotently to the floor. If broken vows were gold, Jonce would live on a hill in a fine house with servants and clingers.

As he uncoiled his left fist and braced his forehead against the palm, his eyes caught on the ugly scar still visible on his bicep. Two weeks of healing had restored the use of his arm but it wouldn't be safe for him to go shirtless again for a long time. As far as he knew, the cops didn't suspect him and he wanted to keep it that way. They thought Corey Pickle killed Stubbs and Pickle was the one person he didn't have to worry about talking. Not so with the little hellcat next door. Maybe she was a liability now. A scornful woman was more dangerous than a cornered bobcat. She knew nothing about Stubbs, but she knew about the bullet. Sure, he had a story cooked up. He was peeking in a woman's bedroom window and got careless. She saw him, screamed, and next thing he knew he was shot in the arm. Beyond that he would clam up and they couldn't prove anything one way or the other. Come to think of it, maybe he would plant the story in Bobbie's brain and let her tell it for him. That way he could keep his mouth shut and they would fall for it hook line and sinker.

He grinned, proud of himself for thinking it through with his body in full revolt. Too bad she wasn't home. He had worked in his share of factories and he knew what went on. Men and women acting like dogs thrown together in a pen. It wasn't proper for a married woman.

He staggered to the kitchen in his underwear and pulled open the fridge. The shelves were bare except for one egg, a slice of bologna, two beers, and a few odds and ends such as mustard, ketchup, and butter. He fried the egg and bologna in the same pan and drank one of the beers at the table with his head drooping. Afterwards he went to the bedroom closet and pulled down the duffle bag and took out fifty dollars for groceries and aspirin.

Chapter Eight

Tipton Palo had built himself a war chest. A cache of evidence to be used against the powers that be once he became mayor. Implicating himself had been a controllable risk since no one would ever see the evidence except the guilty. Had things gone according to plan, Mayor Palo could have ruled Hayes, Mississippi with impunity. But things didn't go as planned. There never was and never would be a Mayor Palo. His opponent defeated him and threw back the curtain and exposed him. Mayor Pigg had exposed them all. The question foremost in Jackie's mind was how did Mayor Pigg get his hands on the evidence and what, if anything, did he destroy?

Jackie left her desk and went to the tiny room down the hall where coffee was always hot and waiting but not always fresh. Chief Gant stood at the counter with his back to her, topping off his mug.

"The harder I look at Palo the more I see the mayor," she said to Gant's back. No one else was in the room.

"Palo's not your case," the chief said.

"You've seen the evidence," she said. "The overlap is undeniable. Give me two hours alone with him and I'll save us all a lot of time."

"Two hours with Palo or two hours with the mayor?" Gant turned with a Styrofoam cup in each hand. "I don't doubt your interrogation skills, detective." He offered her a cup and she accepted. "But first you'd have to get through Palo's wall of lawyers. They'll smell a fishing expedition before you get your boat wet. Of course if you're talking about Mayor Pigg, be my guest."

"I understand men like Palo," Jackie said. "They're sloppy because they think they're above the law. They have incredible egos."

"And Mayor Pigg?"

"He's an iceberg," she said.

Gant laughed. "An upside down iceberg," he said. "The harder you look below the surface the more of his good side you'll see."

"You sound sure of that."

"I am sure of that," Gant said. "Mayor Pigg didn't kill Stubbs. I'd bet my badge on that."

"So he's off limits?"

"Like I said before, no. If you find evidence to the contrary, follow it."

"But?"

Gant frowned. "But be careful and don't get ahead of your skis."

"Because he's the mayor?"

"Because he's a good man," the chief said. "And because he's got a lot of powerful enemies, including the local newspaper. Don't give them ammunition unless you're absolutely sure."

Jackie was used to police chiefs protecting mayors, but Gant's loyalty came with a twist — he actually believed he was doing the right thing. Perhaps he was. She had stopped by the Hayes Beacon and purchased archived copies of the paper all the way back to the week before Stubbs was murdered. The paper's treatment of Mayor Pigg bordered on parody.

"I won't overstep," she said. "I think Palo's involved though."

"Of course he is," Gant said. "But don't forget the state's heading up that case too. Keep Timms apprised. Convince him you need to interview Palo and you'll stand a chance."

Sergeant Timms had done next to nothing to move the case. Jackie couldn't tell if he was as clueless as he seemed or if he was just leaving her out of the loop. Either way he was an impediment.

"At what point do I stop letting Timms stand in the way?"

"That's a loaded question," Gant said.

"It's a cold hard fact," she said. "I can't tell if he's incompetent or just lazy." She blew across the hot liquid. "Or if it's something more sinister than that."

"Be careful," the chief said. "We need the state's resources. They don't need ours."

"I'm simply expressing a concern to my boss," Jackie said. "It won't go any further than that."

"Work the case," he said. "Keep Timms in the loop. If he can't or won't keep up then that's on him. I'll keep the state off your back as much as I can, but I'm just the police chief of a tiny dot on a big map."

Jackie tested the coffee with a sip. "What's your take on the Corey

Pickle angle?"

"That Pickle killed Stubbs?"

"Yes."

"He had motive," Gant said. "Stubbs hung him out to dry after his screw-up with the mayor's brother."

"That's one angle," she said. "But Pickle disappeared before Stubbs was murdered."

"Or he dropped off radar."

"There's no evidence that he ever turned on Stubbs," she said. "Not even to get out of jail."

"He probably knew what would happen if he did."

"Maybe it did happen," she said. "Stubbs seemed the cautious type."

"Pickle killed a horse," Gant said. "Cut off its head and hung it on the mayor's porch."

"I'd give a week's salary to find him."

"He'll turn up sooner or later."

"Unless he's dead."

Gant nodded. "Too bad our former police chief scrubbed the crime scene. Don't forget that angle."

"Is he off limits too?"

"That's up to the state boys. They've got him under wraps. My guess is he's singing like a bird."

She wondered if that possibility bothered her boss but she wasn't dumb enough to ask. He seemed honest enough, and he was right about the state being in control. Looking at it from their vantage point she wouldn't share any information either.

"Do you believe the mayor's story about Stubbs giving him those documents?"

"Yes."

"You didn't hesitate."

"You asked what I believe and I answered," Gant said. "You're free to investigate a different angle if you choose."

"As long as I'm careful?"

"Respectful," he said.

"Stubbs had to know Palo would react the way he did."

"Do you mean the murder or the evidence he countered with?"

"The evidence," she said. "He couldn't believe Palo would go down without returning fire."

"Unless he didn't know about the other documents," Gant said.

"Could be Stubbs thought he had it all."

"Do you think Pickle double-crossed him? Was that his revenge?"

Gant's face told her he hadn't considered that angle. "We know someone cut open Palo's safe. We assume it contained the documents Stubbs gave the mayor. Stubbs wouldn't have cracked the safe himself, so it had to be Pickle."

"What about the other guy Stubbs hired?"

"Jonce Nash? We can't even prove he worked for Stubbs. Besides, I doubt Stubbs would have trusted a new hire to pull off a job that delicate."

"Would he have trusted Pickle after the way he bungled framing the mayor's brother?"

Gant smiled again. "I'm beginning to see why the mayor insisted on hiring you." He studied her face, reading her surprise. "You didn't know it was the mayor?"

"I assumed it was you," she said.

"I advised against it," the chief said. "Does that give you some idea of how headstrong he is?"

"Can I ask why?"

"Why I was against hiring you?"

"Yes."

"Because I thought you were hiding something," he said. "A detective with your credentials doesn't leave a big city to come to nowhere Mississippi and work for peanuts without a reason."

"I told you my reason. My father —."

"I know what you told me, and I know what you told the mayor."

She felt herself beginning to sweat. "Should I clean out my desk?"

"Not on my account," he said. "Whatever you're hiding is your business as long as it doesn't affect your performance."

"Are you satisfied with my performance?"

"So far."

"Fair enough," she said.

Gant's face softened. "Whenever you're ready to come clean —."

"I haven't admitted to hiding anything."

His smile deepened. "Whenever you're ready to come clean, you may find that I'm not as judgmental as you think I am."

"I'll keep that in mind," she said, wanting desperately to steer the conversation back to official business. Her body language screamed guilt but she was helpless to control it. That's why body language is such a powerful tool in the right hands.

"I'm surprised you haven't asked about the mayor's daughter," Gant said, challenging her to push her theory that he was involved. It wasn't a theory, exactly. She simply wasn't ready to rule him out as a suspect. She didn't know about the mayor's daughter.

"Is there something I should know?"

"She's in prison in California for murder. She killed her husband."

It was a shocking revelation and she felt embarrassed for not knowing.

"You didn't know?"

"It's not relevant to my case so no, I didn't know."

"Her husband beat her until she couldn't take it anymore and left. He sent two of his goons to take her back and kidnap her parents and her son — his stepson — and when he told her he was going to have them executed, she killed him."

"Why did she go to prison?"

"Because she dumped the body and scrubbed the house and the rat bastard who helped her made a plea deal and walked. It was national news for a day or two."

Jackie felt her insides churn. He had just described her life exactly, and she wondered how many goons her husband would send after her. One of them may have already knocked on her apartment door.

"That must be difficult for him," she said, not knowing what to say but feeling the need to say something.

"He walks with a cane because he saved his wife and grandson from one of those goons. It's quite a story. You should google it."

"I will."

"Even the Hayes Beacon praised him as a hero. Of course that was before he threatened their inner circle by becoming mayor."

"You don't care much for rich people do you?"

"I've got nothing against rich people," he said. "Until they use their influence to hurt my town."

Jonce juggled the half dozen plastic bags hanging from both hands and fished his keys from his pocket, then he unlocked the door and bumped it open with a knee. The effect was immediate. The place had been tossed. He stood frozen, struggling to process what lay before him. The door had not been forced. Cops love breaking doors but it might be hard to justify kicking in a door to an empty apartment with a key downstairs in the manager's office.

He cocked his ear and listened. Nothing. Then he glanced over both shoulders to be sure he wasn't being rushed from behind. Whoever had broken in was either gone or hiding. If they were hiding they would want him to rush to the money, then he remembered the documents he had implicating Gain Prichard and the money became secondary. His mind drifted toward Prichard. Any man in his right mind would want to clear himself. It was Prichard's only chance. If the cops found the money and documents in his closet they would link him to the robbery of Palo's safe, then it would all come unraveled. He pushed the door closed with his foot and carried the bags into the kitchen and deposited them on the table, then he locked the door and set the deadbolt — something he had not made a habit of doing, not that a deadbolt would keep the cops out.

He crept down the hall, ready to pounce. Past the overturned couch and scattered cushions. The bedroom was a mess. The bed was overturned and all the drawers had been dumped on the floor. The closet was untouched except for the bag. He had made no real attempt to hide it. Too bad they hadn't looked there first and saved him the trouble of putting the place back together.

Careless.

He braced himself for the assault that didn't come. No one kicked open his door. No one yelled over a bullhorn for him to come out with his hands up. There could be no doubt about it now. He had been robbed.

Fear became anger. Except for fifteen dollars and change in his pocket, he was completely broke. The irony of being mad about it eluded him. Over the years he had broken into more houses than he could put a number to. He had stolen everything from money and jewelry to lawnmowers and bicycles and ATVs. Once he had stolen a calf. Another time he stole a pig. If he thought he could move it, he would steal it. Now the shoe was on the other foot and he didn't like it so much.

He left the bedroom and returned to the kitchen and snatched a beer from the refrigerator. His back was up now and his brain spun at warp speed. Someone got in without breaking the door so either they had a key or they knew how to pick a lock and wasn't afraid to do it in broad daylight. The lock was easy enough to defeat with a credit card or a pocketknife, anything slender enough to slide through the crack and strong enough to push back the bolt. Prichard probably had a dozen cons under his thumb who could do the job easy. All the big plans he had were down the crapper. Prichard was free to go about his business of being a dick. Meanwhile Jonce was broke and without a source of income. Worse, he had made a very powerful enemy.

Prichard sat perched behind his desk in his cramped little office looking like a buzzard on a limb. Jonce waltzed in as if nothing had happened and plopped down in the chair across from him without waiting to be told. When Prichard ignored him, he thumped the metal skirt of the desk with his boot.

Prichard looked up. "What the hell?"

Jonce pretended to study something invisible he was turning between the tips of his thumb and forefinger. "People is stupid, Mister Prichard. Real stupid."

"About time you realized it," Prichard said. "Now get out of here."

"Is that any way to talk to a man who holds your freedom in his hands?"

Prichard laughed. "Hit the bricks, stooge."

"Not until I get my piece of the action," Jonce said. He stood. "Want me to strip to prove I ain't wired?"

"Sit down."

"Remember them papers I got."

"Sit down!" He eyed Jonce as one might a beggar with a plausible story. "There's not going to be a cut. I'm shutting the operation down." He lowered his eyes then raised them again. "Temporarily. Until all this other business blows over."

"I don't believe you."

"Believe what you wanna believe," Prichard said. "These state boys are looking up everybody's skirts and sooner or later they'll get around to mine … if they haven't already. For all I know they've got this place bugged. Every time I see a delivery truck parked on the street I get nervous."

"The drug business ain't something you just quit," Jonce said. "Them people's funny that way."

"You let me worry about *them people*."

Jonce couldn't read him. The man seemed too nervous to be back in control. A tired kind of nervous. Exhausted from worry. He had probably gone to jail a thousand times in his head. "Okay then, I'll take my first cut retroactive."

"Get out."

"You can start with the ten grand you took from my apartment." He mentioned the money and not the documents just in case Prichard wasn't the guilty party. One wasn't necessarily tied to the other. Prichard's lack of surprise or confusion told Jonce all he needed to know. Prichard was behind it all right, but why wasn't he crowing? Why wasn't he filling out the paperwork to bust him back to Parchman?

"Easy come easy go," Prichard said. He frowned and dropped his eyes. "I don't have your money."

What a ridiculous statement. Jonce studied him as Prichard busied himself trying to look busy. He moved the same paper from one place to another for the third time. The man was a wreck. "I got copies, you know," Jonce said, bluffing. "I just ain't got no copies of my ten grand so I want that back pronto."

"You've got nothing," Prichard said. "Neither do I. We've both been outplayed. You by me and me by ..." He sighed with a lot of noise and left the *who* to Jonce's imagination. Certainly not Corey Pickle. Who else did he have on his payroll? Some con for sure, but who?

"Finish that name," Jonce said. "Who's got my money?"

"Why? So you can join up with him and shake me down as a team?"

"Like I said, I got copies."

Prichard spat a sorrowful laugh. "You're too dumb to make copies." The man's eyes kept dropping to the desk, seeing something that wasn't there. Maybe he had a gun in that wide top drawer and he was psyching himself up for one final act of cowardice. He looked the type. Strong on the outside but eat up with yellow underneath. The last thing Jonce wanted was for him to blow his brains out and they send someone else to take his place. The law had no shortage of men willing to ride herd on a bunch of outcasts for a paycheck and a title.

"Now you look here, Mister Prichard, whoever took your papers took my money, and I ain't got two dimes to rub together. Tell me who it is and I'll put everything back the way it's supposed to be."

A split-second of hope flashed across Prichard's face as he looked up, then he frowned it away and dropped his eyes again. "You mean with you blackmailing me instead of him? What difference does that make to me?"

"And you call me dumb," Jonce said. He looked up at the cheap gold picture frame on the wall above Prichard's head. Inside was a diploma from the University of Mississippi. The name of the degree was too small to read from where Jonce sat but it didn't matter. Prichard was proud of it or it wouldn't be hung. "That paper up there says you're smart, but you're dumber than me and that's saying something." He laughed. "What's to keep this other man from turning them papers over to the cops?"

Prichard shrugged.

"Meanwhile if I turned them over it'd be the same as putting a needle in my arm."

Prichard raised his eyes. He was listening.

"You think I didn't know I had myself in a box? I may be dumb like you say but I ain't stupid. I had me an insurance policy against you sending me back, and I had me a little money to eat on. Now we're both stuck."

"It's too late," Prichard said. "Even if you get the documents back he can still talk."

Jonce laughed. "Mister Prichard, after I get them papers back ain't nobody gonna be able to talk."

Prichard looked hopeful again. "How do I know I can trust you?"

"You can't. The first time the cops come down on me I'll shove this so far up your ass you'll taste the ink." He grinned. "Of course you'll get the chance to clear me first."

"With you it's only a matter of time," Prichard said. "You've got a record as long as my arm."

"Them's just the times I was caught," Jonce said. "The times I weren't would paper this room."

Prichard hesitated too long not to be sniffing the bait. "If you double-cross me I'll nail your hide to the wall."

"You're a fair man, Mister Prichard. Now give me that weasel's name."

Jackie found Gain Prichard's office on Main Street after driving past it twice. It was a nondescript storefront stuck between two businesses that probably didn't approve of the clientele he attracted. Half an hour earlier she had visited the pawn shop again armed with information that the big man at the counter was seriously behind on child support and she may have exaggerated her ability to make his life miserable if he didn't cooperate. She left with a new lead.

At first glance, Gain Prichard struck her as a brute. The kind of man who enjoys having power over people who can't fight back. She had dealt with his kind before, assuming of course that he was indeed that kind. They had not yet exchanged words.

She flashed her badge and saw the flight reflex in his eyes. "Tell me about Jonce Nash," she said, deciding on the spur of the moment to sidestep the niceties she would normally afford a fellow officer of the law.

"Nash," he muttered, pretending not to place the name right off. More odd behavior. "Oh yes, he was in here a little while ago. Jonce Nash." He tried very hard to act bored. "What's he done this time?"

"I was hoping you could tell me," she said. "What's he been up to since he got out?"

Prichard pecked on the keyboard in front of him and called up something on his screen that Jackie couldn't see from where she stood. He invited her to sit and she did.

"I assume you've already seen his file?"

She nodded that she had. "I'm more interested in what's not in his file."

"You mean do I think he killed Perry Stubbs?"

"What made you think of Stubbs?"

"Because you're a detective and Stubbs was murdered and Jonce Nash worked for him," Prichard said. "I may not have your training but I've been around the block a few times."

"So do you think he killed him?"

"No."

"That was quick."

"Nash is a petty thief and a con man, not a murderer. He might kick a dog for the fun of it but he wouldn't kill a man. Doesn't have the stomach for it."

A moment ago he had pretended not to know the man's name, now he was vouching for him. "How can you be sure?"

"It's my business to be sure," he said. "Innocent lives depend on me being sure."

She wondered if he was trying to protect Nash or his own reputation. "Maybe something happened between them."

"Perry Stubbs is the reason Nash got out of prison."

"How so?"

"Nothing I know officially, mind you, but the way I heard it Stubbs pulled some strings and got Nash's parole approved."

"Why?"

He shrugged. "I have no idea."

"Weren't you curious?"

"They don't pay me to be curious," he said. "They release 'em and I ride herd until they mess up, then I send 'em back. It's that simple."

"And if they don't mess up?"

"Most of them do."

"What kind of work did he do for Stubbs?"

"Errands I suppose. Deliveries. Stuff like that."

"Did you ever ask?"

Prichard pecked at his keyboard again. "Yes, it says here that he made general deliveries and swept up the place. Grunt work."

"Did you ever drop in and check on him?"

"I'm not paid to babysit."

"Isn't that exactly what you're paid to do?"

Prichard sighed heavily. "Look Miss, if —"

"Detective."

He glared at her. "If I had the time I'd check, but it's just me here and I've got a mountain of paperwork. That's what this job is ninety percent of the time — paperwork. Somebody offends, paperwork. Somebody makes a complaint, paperwork. Somebody —."

"I get it," she said. "We've both got jobs to do. To be honest I'm new here and I've got this murder on my hands and Nash's name keeps popping up."

Prichard smiled. Suddenly amicable. "Take my advice, little lady, and —"

"It's Detective."

"No offense, Detective," he said. "You're barking up the wrong tree with Nash. He's harmless."

"A moment ago you had trouble placing the name," she said.

Prichard leaned back in his chair and peered at her. No more fake smiles. "If you think he killed Stubbs then you have my full cooperation," he said. "I'd like nothing better than to reduce my caseload."

"But?"

"Jonce Nash is one of the most incorrigible thieves I've ever encountered. He's probably stealing something at this very minute, but I don't think he killed Stubbs. He owed his freedom to the man. Corey Pickle's the man you need to be looking into."

"Oh?"

"Find Pickle and you'll find your killer."

"Can you prove that?"

"No ma'am. That's your job."

Chapter Nine

J once stood beside the dumpster behind Cluck's Wing Empire in the predawn hours Friday morning watching the rear door like a hunter watches a food plot. Waz Wazenski's car sat empty behind him along with half a dozen other clunkers that had hauled in the morning shift workers all grumpy and slouched as they entered. Watching them filter in reminded Jonce why he had never held a job for more than a few months at a time. There are easier ways for a resourceful man to make a living.

The crisp smell of chicken and biscuits eventually overcame the dumpster stink and made his stomach growl. Soon the doors would open and the breakfast crowd would fill the place. Wazenski was a smoker according to Prichard, and he had been inside for almost half an hour. That's days in smoker time. The question was not if he would come out back for a puff, but when, and how many people he would bring with him. Two upturned five-gallon buckets and a shipping crate sat near the back door amid a carpet of spent butts. Jonce had arrived early enough to case the place, thinking in the back of his mind that if his money ran out, the back door wouldn't be that hard to defeat.

He rubbed his arms through his light jacket and shuddered against the chill that had settled deep into the marrow of his bones. A single incandescent bulb hung over the back door. Wood, not steel, and no security camera in sight. The back lot had no permanent lighting. All it lacked was a black cat to set the scene for a Humphrey Bogart movie. He shuddered again. Why did February have to pick that particular morning to blow cold?

At ten minutes past six the back door cracked open and a small man slipped out. Jonce couldn't see his face but he moved like a man well into his fifties. Prichard's description, verbatim, was dirty little Polack bastard with bushy eyebrows and thick black hair. He plopped down on the crate and fished a pack of cigarettes from the side pocket of his jacket, jabbed one into his mouth, then cupped his hands around his lighter and lit the end. Jonce saw the bushy eyebrows and moved in slowly.

Wazenski looked up and scratched his nose as Jonce approached but he made no show of alarm. Why should he? The two men had never met. He probably wouldn't know Jonce if he was tattooed on his face. Or maybe Prichard had showed him a mugshot so he knew who to look out for coming and going from his apartment.

"Wazenski?"

"Who wants to know?"

His accent wasn't as thick as Jonce expected. He stopped half an arm's reach from the man, towering over him because Wazenski was sitting on the crate. "If I kick your teeth out you'll think who wants to know."

The little man looked up with no show of fear. Jonce had a mind to slap him off the crate just for the fun of it but he considered how the racket might draw out the others.

"I wondered when you'd show up," Wazenski said, dropping his head so that Jonce could no longer see his face. A spot of pink scalp about the size of a half dollar peeked out from the mop of hair toward the back. "You're wasting your time. I spent the money already."

Jonce reached down and grabbed him by the scruff of the neck and jerked him to his feet. Wazenski flayed his arms and tried to land a blow but Jonce had him pressed against the wall before he could get his bearings. "You better be lying you little Polack bastard!" He leaned into his face until their noses almost touched.

"I — I."

His breath stunk of tobacco and neglected teeth. Jonce pressed his shirt-wrapped fist hard against the little man's breastbone and kept him pinned to the wall. Wazenski's eyes flitted back and forth, up and down. He worked his shoulders and chewed at his lip. Scared shitless all of a sudden.

"Before the sun goes down tonight I'll have my papers back and my money back or you'll be —." The door moved and Jonce saw a face through the crack. "Back inside!" The door snapped shut.

"I have some of the money," Wazenski stammered.

"How much some?"

"Two thousand. Maybe a hundred more. The papers, too, I have those."

Jonce shoved hard enough to leave a bruise then let him drop. "Sundown tonight," he said, stepping back. "And you'd better get to shit'n eight thousand more dollars."

Dillon Keyes had been a police detective in Detroit for seven years, the past three years as Jackie's partner and mentor. She trusted him with her life, literally. Besides her captain, Dillon was the only person in Detroit who knew where she was.

Jackie called Dillon's cell phone from her desk, not afraid of exposing her tracks because a phone call from one police department to another was commonplace, regardless of location. Criminals travel. They migrate. They flee jurisdictions and hide out, then they reoffend. They always reoffend.

Hearing Dillon's voice was like water to a dry sponge. There was no romance between them. Nothing like that. In some ways their relationship transcended romance. There was no one she would rather be in a foxhole with than Dillon. Hayes, for now, was her foxhole.

"I was beginning to worry," Dillon said. "Why haven't you called?"

"Is he still in town?"

"Like nothing ever happened. He goes to work every morning then goes home every night."

"What about his phone?"

"Nothing suspicious."

The phone surveillance was illegal and she hadn't asked him to do it. Being cops gave them tools ordinary people don't have. Most battered women are at the mercy of a system that talks a good game but doesn't deliver, like anti-bullying policies in public schools. She thought of all the women she had wanted to help but couldn't because the law tied her hands, then she thought of Mayor Pigg's daughter. Were it up to her, once a man beats a woman she would have the right to kill him in his sleep, or at whatever time she summoned the courage, or her brother could do it, or her father, or any other male relative worth his salt.

"Lay off his phone," she said, knowing he would dismiss her request the way she would his had their roles been reversed. "I don't want you to lose your job." She knew as the words crossed her lips that she was only trying to relieve herself of guilt should something go wrong. The hard truth was she needed him to stick his neck out for her.

"You let me worry about my job," Dillon said. "You worry about keeping yourself and that boy of yours safe. Just because ole Kelton hasn't strayed from his routine doesn't mean he hasn't got one of his goons out looking for you."

Her husband had a couple of men who would do anything he said and they didn't mind getting their hands dirty. Kelton Mulvaney was a businessman who manufactured aftermarket automobile parts and distributed them worldwide. The only thing that made him more dangerous than the hundreds of other low-life thugs who beat their wives was that he had the resources to fund his revenge after she summoned the courage to leave.

"No one else knows where I am," she said. "I haven't even told my family yet."

"Don't worry, Osama Bin Laden couldn't beat it out of me."

"Bin Laden's dead."

"Yeah, well, if you believe that." he said.

She filled him in on her new job. Kelton didn't have the connections it takes to eavesdrop on private phone conversations so she wasn't worried they were being listened to.

"Any trouble with your paperwork?"

"None," she said. "Your friend with the FBI's a genius." One of Dillon's old girlfriends worked for the FBI and helped make people who testify against gangsters disappear. Again, a resource most battered women don't have. She felt almost guilty. "I'll never be able to repay you for all —."

"Stop. We've been down that road enough already," he said. "You'll repay me by getting through this."

Wazenski showed up at Jonce's door with the documents he had stolen and just over two-thousand in cash. His hands were steady as he passed the large Manila envelope to Jonce but his eyes gave him away. He was scared out of his skin. Jonce had not yet decided what to do with him. He wasn't a killer by nature, meaning it wasn't his go-to response to trouble.

"Come in," Jonce said, pulling the door fully open as he stepped back.

"No thanks," Wazenski said. "I'd better be getting home."

"It weren't no invitation," Jonce said. "Get your ass in here." The little man hesitated, looked as if he might bolt, then complied. Good thing, too, because in his haste Jonce might well have thrown him over the railing and cracked him against the sidewalk below like an egg. Thinking fast didn't always mean thinking smart.

"I told you I don't have the rest of the money."

Jonce closed the door and locked it. "You say *the* money like it's community property." He strode into the kitchen and tossed the envelope onto the table, not bothering to check the contents because the little Polack was too scared to double-cross him. Besides, not checking gave him leverage. "Sit down." He pushed a chair out with his foot and waited. Wazenski sat without taking his eyes off Jonce's face. "You think my money's community property?"

"No."

"Then say whose money it is."

"It's your money."

Jonce grinned. "That's more like it." He pulled out the chair opposite the little man and sat, slouching as though he hadn't a care in the world. "Now about that other eight." He propped a foot in the empty chair. "I know you're running dope for Prichard."

"He shut that down," Wazenski said. "Too many state cops around. Besides, he hardly pays me anything at all."

"You're lying."

"I swear it. I do it because I have to. He'll violate my parole if I don't."

Jonce believed him. A PO may as well be God for all the good it did a con to complain. He looked at the envelope. "Did you make copies?"

"No, I swear."

Dumb Polack. He should've made copies. He didn't though. Jonce saw it in his eyes. "How much do you know about me?"

"Nothing. I swear."

"You had to know something to break into my apartment."

"Just what he told me."

"Didn't I just ask you that?"

"He said you stole something that belongs to him and he wanted it back. Said he'd give me a thousand dollars to bring it to him."

"What else?"

"That you was a killer and I'd better be careful."

"He tell you who I killed?"

"No."

Prichard might suspect but he couldn't know unless Palo told him and Palo probably wasn't stupid enough to admit to knowing. Jonce pondered what to do with him. He could knock him in the head and roll him up in a blanket and take him out after midnight but there was a cop living downstairs.

"I only took the stuff because I thought I could get Prichard off my back," Wazenski said. "After you've been out a while you'll know what I mean."

"I knowed what he was first time I laid eyes on him," Jonce said. "Damned fascist." He eyed Wazenski and enjoyed the way he squirmed. "Suppose I don't kill you?"

The Polack's eyes grew big as quarters and he jerked his back straight. "Kill me? Why would you kill me? I gave your papers back. I didn't make copies."

"I can think of eight thousand reasons."

"Give me time. I'll come up with it."

"How?"

"I'll steal it."

"You're a terrible thief."

Wazenski's fear abated and he smiled. "I stole from you all right."

"You got caught."

"Prichard ratted me out. That's not the same as getting caught fair and square."

Jonce laughed. Maybe the Polack wasn't so bad after all. "How secure is the wing joint?"

Wazenski frowned and shook his head. "If they kept any money there I would've robbed it myself already. The manager makes a deposit every night and he carries a forty-five."

"How much of a deposit?"

"He dreams of being robbed so he can shoot somebody," Wazenski said. "How much money I don't know. Nobody gets close to it but him."

"I bet it's a lot," Jonce said. "Get lost."

Wazenski scampered to his feet and broke for the door.

"Prichard thinks I'm gonna kill you so if you wanna disappear now's the time," Jonce said.

Wazenski turned and looked at Jonce with big sad dog eyes. "How can I leave when I owe you so much money?"

Jackie had a very unproductive day, owing to her focusing more on her personal problems than on the problems of her job, namely, who killed Perry Stubbs. It was her only case and she had yet to uncover a single lead. So far her boss hadn't pressured her, probably because it was her first week on the job and he had made the comment himself that it might take a while for the locals to get used to her. He clarified that it was due to her being a stranger, but she had dealt with bigots in every job she had ever held. The locals in Detroit didn't like cops either.

Jordan sat on the sofa with headphones covering his ears and a game controller in his hands. His focus was on the television. She disapproved of the violent games he played but the boy needed something to take his mind off things. It was the times she caught him staring off into space that concerned her most. Those are the times when a boy can lose his way.

She finished clearing the table and loading the dishwasher, then she went into the living room and settled into the armchair with a quarter-inch thick folder Prichard had given her on Jonce Nash. Disinterest had kept her from reading it last night but now she felt restless and needed something to occupy her thoughts.

Nash had a laundry list of petty offenses. Lawnmowers and small engine equipment seemed to have been his specialty prior to the robbery that sent him to prison. He wasn't very bright to have kept the money wrapped in the shirt he had worn in the robbery. The evidence against him had been airtight. A detective's dream, and that made her suspicious.

He had been arrested twice for domestic battery but his wife had dropped the charges. They so often do, and no one understood why better than Jackie. On paper Nash had been a model prisoner, but so much of what goes on inside prison is undocumented. She had her own theories but they were just that — theories. The totality of her experience inside the prison system had come from interviewing inmates and testifying on occasion at parole hearings.

Something on the last page made her blood run cold. Jonce's address. He lived in her building. Above her several doors down. He had probably watched her come and go all week. She flipped back to the first page and stared at his mugshot. Was he the man who had come to her apartment and talked to her son?

"Jordan?"

She had to call him three times to get his attention.

"Turn that off a minute and come here."

"No, please, I'm right in the middle —."

"Now!"

Being fifteen, her raised voice didn't frighten him, but he still respected her enough to put down the controller and leave the sofa.

"Is this the man who came to the door?"

Jordan shrugged. "Maybe."

"Look harder."

"It could be. Yeah, sure, that's him."

"Are you sure?"

"No, but it looks like him. The eyes, yeah, I think it's him."

She pulled in a deep breath to steady herself. The man who possibly killed Perry Stubbs was living in her apartment complex and he had knocked on her door and terrorized her son.

"What's wrong, Momma?"

She closed the folder and sat with both hands pressed against it and drew another deep breath. Jonce Nash had not exactly terrorized her son. He could have simply knocked on the wrong door. There was an attractive Hispanic woman who lived in the apartment next to her. She could have been Nash's target, either with consent or without. His record didn't include sexual assault but a man who beats his wife doesn't concern himself with yes and no. She considered warning the woman, but what right did she have?

Jordan stood looking down at her with worried eyes. They made contact and held. "It's nothing for you to worry about," she said. "Just don't answer the door again and stay inside when I'm not home."

"Stay inside all day?"

"Yes all day. I know it sucks but it's temporary. I promise."

He turned away and sulked back to the sofa and dropped. "I think I liked it better in Detroit."

Chapter Ten

Like a dutiful servant of the government he served, Gain Prichard was in his office Saturday morning guzzling coffee from a stained mug and pushing papers around his cluttered desk. Jonce stood on the sidewalk and peered at him through the glass for almost two minutes before Prichard looked up and waved him in with the face of a man about to receive an enema.

"Does the whole town have to see you standing out there gawking at me?"

Jonce stepped all the way in and let the heavy glass door close behind him. Prichard was nervous. Good. The meaner a man is the more he sweats when the tables get turned on him, and Jonce was a born and bred table-turner.

Prichard sat motionless as Jonce moved toward him at a gait that would have frustrated a turtle. His right hand held the short fat pen he used to send men like Jonce back to prison, or to stack minor infractions against them like cordwood until he had enough to build a fire. His left hand lay atop the desk like a paperweight, keeping the paper on which he scribbled from moving. There was no detectable rise and fall of Prichard's chest as Jonce closed the gap.

"Well?"

Jonce absorbed the question and stopped behind the chair Prichard kept for the discomfort of his clients. Fear emanated from the big man like a stink. Like the dull odor of sweat after a day of toil. Jonce could smell it. He breathed it in and savored the taste of it the way one might a fresh-baked apple pie. It's important to begin a conversation with the upper hand.

"Your little Polack friend has been defanged," Jonce said.

Prichard tightened his jaw and visibly breathed for the first time. "Sit down. I don't like people standing over me."

"Of course there's still the issue of eight thousand dollars," Jonce said, still standing. "He ain't likely to make that kind of cash slinging chicken wings so he may come crawling to you for a loan."

Prichard's eyes tightened with disappointment. "You mean he's —."

"In need of money, yes sir."

"I thought you were going to take care of him."

"Like I said, he owes me eight grand," Jonce said.

"And you expect me —."

"To help him get it. Right again."

"How?"

"That's your business," Jonce said. "Surely a resourceful man such as yourself can figure it out."

"And if I refuse?"

"You won't."

Prichard summoned his courage then lost it. It's hard for a bully to hand over his lunch money. "Sit down," he said without demanding it. "Let's talk about this like two grown men."

"Like two men all growed up," Jonce said. "Me the slave and you the master, except I'm holding the whip and you're the one tied to the post. Ain't that how it is, Mister Prichard? You done got yourself tied to your own post?"

Prichard worked his neck and shoulders. "There's no need to be adversarial," he said. "The way I see it we've got a mutual problem. We both want the same outcome."

"Spider and fly," Jonce said with a grin. "That's me and you and I promise you we ain't after the same outcome." He plopped down in the chair and slouched. "Until now you was the spider."

"Don't make the mistake of underestimating me."

"Or what?"

"I could send you back to prison with the stroke of a pen."

"And I can send you to prison with the stroke of my jaws," Jonce said. "And them papers I got hid away somewhere that's not in my apartment. No sir I won't make that mistake again."

Prichard's eyes swung toward the upper left-hand drawer of his desk. Jonce had never seen inside the drawer but instinct told him it was where Prichard kept his gun.

"Them state boys bagged 'em a road supervisor yesterday. Did you hear about it?"

"What's that got to do with anything?"

"A whole lot if you was a road supervisor," Jonce said. "But you being a parole officer maybe you think they wouldn't be interested in what I got."

"We've got an agreement," Prichard said. "Just make sure nobody else finds those papers."

"Your more important worry is whether or not I want somebody to find them papers."

Prichard's eyes stroked the drawer again. His tongue wet his lips.

"Stop thinking about that gun, Mister Prichard, because I got myself an insurance policy. Anything happens to me you're done." He was making it up on the fly but it sounded good. Prichard looked away from the drawer.

"What's that supposed to mean?"

"It means if something happens to me them papers goes to the law."

"I thought no one else knows where they are."

"My arrangements is my arrangements," Jonce said. "All you gotta worry about is me staying alive and happy."

He saw Prichard's Adam's apple stroke his throat. "All right, but you'll still have to keep up appearances. That new female detective was here asking questions about you. She's suspicious. If she finds out you're not working she'll know something's up."

"Then you'd better make sure she don't find out."

Prichard scribbled something on a piece of paper and pushed it across the desk. "My cousin's got a landscaping business. Go to that address and —."

"I ain't mowing nobody's yard."

"He'll say you work for him," Prichard said. "At least go meet him so he'll know what you look like in case someone asks."

"Evergreen Landscaping," Jonce read from the note. "How much do I get paid?"

"You don't get paid unless you work."

"Suppose somebody asks to see my paystub?"

"Don't push your luck."

A big man answered the door. He was shirtless and had a nice build.

Jackie guessed him to be mid-thirties. Right away she noticed the half-moon scar underneath his right eye. It was faded and looked to be years old. Any number of things could've caused it but his size and overall demeanor suggested bar fight.

She flashed her badge and introduced herself as Detective Deen. "I have a few questions about the man who lives in twenty-two," she said, hitching her head toward the apartment next door.

"We don't know him." He tried to close the door but Jackie stopped it.

"Five minutes," she said in a tone both polite and firm, holding eye contact.

He mumbled something unintelligible under his breath as he stepped aside. The smell of bacon frying hit Jackie's nose as soon as she crossed the threshold. It had been a long time since she had allowed herself to have bacon.

"We were just about to have breakfast," the big man said after closing the door and trailing her into the living room. The kitchen lay to Jackie's right instead of her left as it did in her own apartment. The man's wife stood at the stove wearing a football jersey that hung just low enough to cover her hips. She had not yet acknowledged Jackie's presence.

"I promise to be brief," Jackie said, looking at the woman's back. The jersey was white and had the number 12 in red. The appliances looked identical to her own, but the living room had been refurnished. The leather recliner had hardly any wear at all, and the sofa looked new except for a small cigarette burn on one arm. Jackie contemplated offering to come back after breakfast but she knew they would never open the door to her again.

Her trained eye caught the man's nervous attention towards an open door that she supposed led to the bedroom, given that their apartments appeared to have mirrored floor plans.

"Turn that off and get over here," he barked to his wife. "She's got questions about that weirdo next door."

"Don't know him," the woman said as she switched off the stove and moved the frying pan off the hot eye. She avoided eye contact when she turned and joined them on the living room side of the bar.

"I'm Detective Deen," Jackie said to the woman, expecting a name in return that didn't come.

"Detective from where?"

"From here," Jackie said. "I've recently joined —."

"You don't sound from around here," the woman said.

"I'm recently from Detroit."

"Oh," she said, looking Jackie in the eyes for the first time. "I thought you sounded northern. I had a friend at work who came from Ohio and she sounded like you."

"She don't care about your friend from Ohio," her husband said. "She's asking about the jailbird."

"So you know he's been in prison?"

The husband bobbed his head toward his wife. "She looked him up on the internet when he moved in."

"He looked like the type," the woman said. "My name's Bobbie and this is my husband Don. He works out of town during the week and I'm home alone and I like to know who's living next door."

"And next door to that, and three doors down," he said. "All the way to the end and back around on the bottom."

"You make me sound nosey."

"I'm only interested in the man next door," Jackie said.

The husband asked what he had done and the wife seemed terribly nervous.

"Have the two of you had any problems with him?"

"I ain't laid a hand on him," Don said, "but if you ask me somebody needs to. Last Sunday I'm leaving for work and he's standing outside our apartment leaning over the rail like he's just waiting for me to leave so he can break in here and rape my wife."

Jackie looked at Bobbie. "Has he bothered you?"

"Don's jealous of everybody." She cut her eyes up at her husband and frowned. "Ask him what he comes home smelling like half the time."

"Don't start with me this early," Don said.

"Have either of you had any interaction with him?"

"Other than last Sunday at the rail, no," Don said. "If you ask me they shouldn't let people like that out of prison."

The wife avoided eye contact.

"Has he made any threats against either of you?"

"Not in exact words," Don said. "But he was up to something all right. The way he kept peering toward the door like he was trying to see inside. She ain't no beauty queen but who can tell what goes through a man's mind when he's been locked up for a long time?"

Bobbie frowned and folded her arms across her chest. "He thinks he's still captain of the high school football team."

Don ignored her. "So what's he done? We've got a right to know."

"It's just a routine check," Jackie said. "His parole officer was concerned he might be making a nuisance of himself." It was a lie but it sounded good. "Is he home now?" She knew the answer already because she had watched his place until he left.

Don shrugged. "You're the detective. Detect."

"My husband. Mister personality. You'll have to ignore him. He gets testy when you get between him and breakfast."

Jackie apologized for the interruption and thanked them for their time. Don asked if he was dangerous.

"He doesn't have a record of violence," Jackie said.

"That's not what I asked."

"He's not dangerous," Bobbie said to her husband. "He's a thief who steels valuables. We got nothing to worry about because nothing we've got is worth a shit, and like you said, I'm too ugly to rape."

Don rolled his eyes. "I have to listen to this crap every weekend when I come home."

As she turned to leave, Jackie noticed the taint of marijuana in the air, which explained the husband's nervous glances toward the bedroom. What they did in their own apartment was their business as far as she was concerned, but she made a mental note of it in case she needed to use it as leverage later. Something told her Bobbie was holding something back.

Her next stop was the apartment flanking Nash on the other side. The woman who answered the door to apartment twenty-three was elderly and frail and stooped at the shoulders so that she couldn't straighten to her full height. She wore a light blue gown that almost matched the color of her hair.

Jackie flashed her badge and introduced herself.

"Well you may as well come in and sit down," the woman said.

Jackie followed her into an apartment with the exact floor plan as the one she had just left. The odor of menthol hit her nose like a fist.

"I don't get many visitors since my son moved to Memphis," the woman said as she hobbled to a padded rocking chair with a flowered sheet covering the upholstery. A small table to the right was piled with newspapers and magazines atop which lay a crinkled tube of arthritis cream.

Jackie took the near end of the sofa. "I wanted to ask you about the man who lives next door," she said, pointing toward the Nash apartment.

"He took a job with a big outfit up there," the woman said, still talking about her son as though she hadn't heard. "They send him all over the world on important work."

"That must be exciting."

"They don't send him to Hayes much though." Her eyes flashed scared. "Is he in some kind of trouble?"

"Your son? No ma'am, that's not why I'm here," Jackie said. "I wanted to ask you about the man who lives next to you." She was careful to keep her voice down in case Nash came home.

The woman frowned. "You can have him for all I care."

Jackie wasn't sure if she meant her son or Jonce Nash. "Can you tell me anything about him? The man who lives next door I mean."

The woman fiddled with something in her ear. "I keep this thing turned down except when I'm watching the TV," she said. "The apartment manager told me I had to keep the TV turned down or she'd throw me out."

"I'm here about the man who lives in apartment twenty-two. Can you tell me anything about him?"

The woman pondered the question. "Well, he's home all the time."

"Have you had any interaction with him?"

She fiddled with her hearing aid again. "Any what?"

"Interaction. Contact. Have the two of you met?"

"No, we haven't met. I don't get out except to go to the doctor. They send a girl around once a week to check on me since Frank moved to Memphis."

"Frank is your son?"

"No, Frank's not my son. Frank's dead."

"Oh, I thought you said he moved to Memphis."

"No, Frank didn't move to Memphis. George moved to Memphis. He's got an important job."

"Yes ma'am."

"They send him all over the world. Last month he went all the way to China."

"Was Frank your husband?"

"Frank died twenty years ago. That's when I moved in here. We had a house over on Fillmore. You know where Fillmore is?"

"No ma'am, I'm new in town." It occurred to her that she had made a slip when she told the Booths she had moved from Detroit. She would have to be more careful.

"It had three bedrooms and a big yard," the woman said. "And two great big pecan trees out back that Frank hated." She laughed. "Every time he mowed he slung a pecan and broke something. We lived one entire winter with plastic stretched over our bedroom window because Frank slung a pecan. Do you like pecans?"

"Yes ma'am."

"I can take 'em or leave 'em myself." She frowned. "I do miss that yard though."

Jackie made another attempt at steering the conversation toward Jonce Nash, not that she expected to learn anything. The woman was practically deaf and probably had dementia.

"I've seen him come and go," the woman said. "Didn't know his name though. Nash did you say it was?"

"Jonce Nash," Jackie said. "If there's nothing you can tell me about him I'll leave you alone."

"Most people think they named it after the president," the old woman said. "Millard Fillmore, but they didn't. They named it after Ralph Fillmore. He was mayor here during the war. Where did you say you was from?"

"Boston," Jackie said, naming the first city that popped into her head that wasn't Detroit.

"No, you're not from Boston," the woman said. "I know a Massachusetts accent when I hear it. President Kennedy was from Massachusetts."

Thinking on her feet, Jackie said she was originally from Chicago, which seemed to satisfy the woman's curiosity. She rose to make her exit. "I'm sorry I bothered you and I hope your son comes home for a visit very soon."

The woman stopped rocking and looked up at her. "Do you know George?"

Jackie said she didn't.

"Oh," the woman said, then rocked again. "He used to come eat dinner with me every Sunday. They've got him working up in Memphis now."

"Yes, ma'am. I hope you see him again real soon." She started toward the door.

"You didn't ask me if he has any visitors," the woman said. Jackie stopped and turned, not knowing if she meant Jonce Nash or her son George.

"Does he?"

"Sometimes," she said. "When her husband's away. That hussy in twenty-one. More than talk goes on between them two. You should ask her about him."

"I will," Jackie said. "Thank you very much."

The woman struggled up out of her rocker. "I'll lock the door when you leave. I always keep it locked in case of hoodlums."

Jackie told her it was a good practice.

"You ever been over to St. Louis?"

Jackie said she hadn't.

"You should get over there sometime," the woman said. "Frank took me to see Chuck Berry back in sixty-one."

"That must've been nice," Jackie said. Her musical interests were more modern.

"It was right before they put him in prison for carrying on with that white girl. Last I heard he ran a juke joint. You should get over that way and hear him sing sometime."

"Chuck Berry died two years ago," Jackie said.

The woman frowned. "Well, he sure could sing."

Jackie felt sorry for the woman being alone. "Do you need anything," she asked. "Groceries? Toilet paper? Anything?"

"No, they send a girl over once a week. She takes good care of me."

Jackie's heart broke for the old woman as she left. She thought of her own mother and how long it had been since they had sat in the same room together, then she wondered how long it would be before Jordan only came to see her on Sundays.

Jonce crawled out of bed at the crack of noon Sunday, kept from sleeping most of the night by activities beyond the wall. Bobbie cursed almost as much when making love as when throwing objects against the wall. It was hard to imagine anything breakable still unbroken in her apartment. For the life of him he couldn't understand why Don didn't punch her in the face and be done with it, except that toning down one emotion might quell the other.

He skipped brushing his teeth and went straight to the kitchen and fixed himself a peanut butter and mustard sandwich. Donnie Boy would be heading out soon, but soon was dragging its feet. It was quiet. Too quiet. Either they were sleeping it off next door or they had killed each other. The noise had abated just before sunup.

He finished off his sandwich and downed his Coke. It was a very mild February afternoon with a cloudless sky so blue it looked like an upside down ocean. Two Mexican men stood talking beside a car in the parking lot below. Their chatter rose and fell as they laughed and swigged beer from bottles. Jonce felt no animosity toward the Mexicans for sneaking into his country considering how Mexico was basically a shit hole. America was built by immigrants fleeing their own corners of hell. Misery makes the world go around.

He stepped outside his apartment and checked the parking lot in case he had slept through Don's departure. His truck still sat in the parking lot. Bobbie's car was there too. He propped himself against the rail on his forearms and smoked a cigarette halfway to the butt before he noticed the lady cop with her kid in tow walking toward the white Hyundai she drove when she was off duty. She didn't have a man that he had seen, which gave him ideas that he eventually pushed to the darker portions of his brain. No sense getting shot over something he could get hassle-free once Don left. When she reached her car she turned to open the door then looked up. It was too far away to see her eyes but she saw him, no doubt about that. The hesitation before she opened the door gave her away.

"That's him," Jordan said as soon as the car doors shut them in. "That's the man who came to the door." He sounded a little breathless, as though he were running from the man grinning down at them from the second floor instead of being watched by him.

Jackie felt anger and relief at the same time. Anger that Nash dared come anywhere near her son, relief that the man Jordan had seen was not one of her husband's henchmen. Jonce Nash was the kind of threat she could handle. Put him behind bars and he becomes instantly harmless. She believed him to be a dangerous man but he wasn't part of anything bigger than himself. At least she didn't believe him to be. Her investigation hadn't turned up any ties to anyone other than her murder victim.

The problem was she didn't have anything on him yet. She forced her eyes not to look up again. Nash was the kind of man who craved attention for himself "Stop looking at him," she said to her son.

"Aren't you going to arrest him?"

She pulled the car into reverse and rolled backward out of the spot. "Arrest him for what? Knocking on our door?" She put the car in drive and felt Nash's eyes on her as she pulled away. "From now on you don't open the door for anyone. Got it? And you stay inside unless I'm home. No exceptions."

"You've told me that a hundred times already."

"And if he shows up again you call me immediately." She looked over at him as they turned into the empty street. Fifteen going on twenty. At a glance he had his father's features — prominent forehead, small nose, piercing eyes. It was Kelton's eyes that had attracted her first. When he focused on someone he made them feel they were the only person in the world who mattered to him. She had seen him hypnotize others in the same manner. He knew it, too, though he pretended not to. Grown men — strong men — fell victim to the intensity of his eyes and more often than not entered into business arrangements that put them at a disadvantage. They all realized it at some later point. They all hated him, though they pretended not to. Money and power attracts men as well as women, though for very different reasons.

"Who is he?"

"A very bad man," she said. "He may have killed someone."

"He doesn't scare me," Jordan said the way a boy trying to be a man says things. She couldn't afford to move them into a safer place yet. Soon though.

"Did dad send him?"

"No. This has nothing to do with your father."

"Do you think he knows where we are yet?"

It was the way he said *yet* that broke her heart.

Chapter Eleven

Bobbie's stubbornness had Jonce in a foul mood. It was Monday morning and he had just finished off a fried bologna sandwich with black coffee. Bobbie was still knocking around her apartment getting ready for work. At least half a dozen times last night he had banged on the wall and invited her over. The first few times she had refused with words, thereafter she had refused with silence. It was the silence that infuriated him.

Her front door opened then closed. Jonce slammed his mug down hard enough to wet the table. Quick as a cat he left his chair and jerked open his door. Bobbie was halfway to the stairs when he grabbed her arm and spun her.

"What the hell?"

"I'll make you think what the hell," he said. He was naked except for a pair of white briefs with yellow stains dotting the front. His injured arm was of no consequence to him at the moment.

She jerked free and raked him head to toe with her eyes. "Touch me again and I'll scream."

"You'll scream all right," he said, reaching for her but stopping short when she recoiled. On second thought he didn't need a public altercation with a cop living downstairs. Without warning Bobbie began to laugh. "What the hell's so funny?"

"You," she said, looking him up and down again. "The least you could do is wear clean underwear." She laughed hard enough to bring tears to her eyes.

Jonce balled his hands into fists and struggled not to knock her on her ass. He looked down at himself and saw the piss stains and a grin spread across his face. At least she was looking in the right place.

"How come you didn't come over last night?"

She stopped laughing and frowned. "Because I'm married."

"You was married last Sunday," he said. "And all them times before that."

"It wasn't that many times," she said. "You make it sound like a fling." Her face hardened again. "And don't forget you forced me," she said in a hushed voice. "I could have you arrested for that you know."

"Your word against mine."

She spun on her heels and started for the stairs again. "Next time ask nice."

Jonce watched her all the way down the stairs and across the parking lot to where her car was parked three rows from the front. Not one time did she look back to see if he was watching. All of a sudden he heard a shriek behind him. He turned and saw the old woman who lived in twenty-three standing outside her door with both hands clutching her face. Her eyes were big as quarters. Jonce dropped his bare foot off the rail and turned. "What are you looking at?"

The old woman stood frozen, her eyes alternating between his face and his underwear. Jonce threw out his arms like wings and screeched, sending her backward through the opening at a stumble. The door slammed and he heard the deadbolt engage. He laughed and went back inside, mindful now that at least one other person knew he had an injured arm, supposing she could see that far, but satisfied that it didn't matter. Palo hadn't talked or the cops would have come for him by now, and without Palo talking there wasn't anything to tie his arm to Stubbs.

He fried another piece of bologna and slapped it between two pieces of bread without bothering to sop off the grease. The old woman wouldn't talk. Who was she going to tell anyway? She was cooped up all alone like a bird in a cage nobody ever bothered to uncover. It was the female cop downstairs he needed to worry about. She had talked to Prichard about him and no telling who else. Maybe she needed to be put in her place just in case Gain Prichard wasn't the steadfast Jonce-defender he made himself out to be. Maybe Prichard had dropped a few hints. Breadcrumbs for the little bird to gobble up then suddenly one day her eyes pop open and she sees Jonce standing at the end of the trail with a bloody knife in his hand.

He ate the sandwich in three bites, thinking maybe he should have disposed of Stubbs the same way he had Pickle. No body no crime, but that was hindsight, and Jonce wasn't one to lay up and lick his wounds. He was a doer. A get-things-doner. Forward was his only gear. Besides, Prichard didn't know what Prichard didn't know. He was used to getting his way for so long that he had become dull and stupid. Sending the Polack to ransack his apartment had been sloppy. Two seconds of clear thought would have told him exactly what Wazenski would do once he got his hands on the papers. Two seconds more would have told him how Jonce would react. Two cons against a bull who's been out to pasture too long. Now Jonce had a Polack to deal with on top of all his other worries. He wasn't a killer by nature, but he excelled at anything he put his shoulder to. Ask Stubbs.

The newscast at noon lightened his mood. Another county supervisor got frog-marched across the back parking lot and into jail. Jonce hated politicians and public officials in every form, not for their greed and corruption but for their authority. Give a man of unimpressive intellect a little power and suddenly he's swinging his sword like Mel Gibson in Braveheart. Like a hall monitor with a whistle. Like Bull Conner with a firehose. The trouble with laws is they don't allow for revenge, and revenge is the only tool a poor man has. *Let the law handle it* is another way of saying shut up and mind your place.

Jonce grinned at his use of logic. In a fair world he would be at the top looking down instead of on the bottom looking up. He wasn't alone on the bottom though. Some newcomers had joined him and more were shaking in their boots. The local station played the frog-march on a loop, over and over the slump-shouldered supervisor walked from the black SUV toward the back door of the jail house through which suspects are booked. The female anchor blathered on about the mayor and how his efforts had sent shockwaves throughout the community. Mayor Pigg was some kind of hero now, which was laughable because it had been Jonce who freed the damning evidence from Tipton Palo's wall safe and got the shit storm howling. Palo was still out on bond, which was a problem because he owed Jonce money and he was the kind of weasel who would throw Jonce to the wolves if he could figure out how to do it without incriminating himself. Jonce went back and forth on the threat Palo did or didn't pose. It's hard to guess a man who has no moral code.

A pounding erupted against Jonce's apartment door. Cop pounding, not Bobbie Booth come home for a lunchtime quickie pounding. Not female cop pounding either, but the kind of pounding that if not answered quickly results in a battering ram taking the door off its hinges.

Jonce rushed to save his door and threw it open a split second before he realized no one had yelled POLICE. By the time he saw four eyes staring at him through ski masks it was too late. They advanced on him and pushed the door open with him trying with all his might to close it. His bare feet slipped on the floor as he tried to hold on.

Once inside, they slammed the door and seized him. Jonce folded around a fist to his gut, then went to his knees as a double-fisted blow struck him between the shoulder blades. Instinct told him to protect his vulnerables and ride it out. It wasn't his first beating. A boot struck him in the head and knocked him dopey, then another one found his left kidney. Within seconds the room was a blur. Everything hurt. He heard a rib crack and felt a sharp pain in his side that overpowered all the other blows. The room bounced in and out of focus as they kicked him with unbridled fury. He struggled to remain conscious. Giving up wasn't an option. He closed his eyes and imagined himself alone in a dark room, no longer feeling the blows, plotting his revenge. They would tire soon and he would make his move. Everybody tires eventually.

When he came to the men were gone. Jonce lay in a pool of vomit and blood and piss. When he tried to move he realized he had shit himself. Every fluid his body contained was represented in the slick, sickening soup in which he lay. Every orifice had emptied itself.

His brain spun up and began to work again. Were the men gone or were they hiding? Were they ransacking the bedroom looking for the documents Prichard had sent them for or were they sitting at the kitchen table drinking his beer, waiting for him to wake up so they could begin round two?

He closed his eyes and pretended to be unconscious, giving his body time to recover enough that he might make a move if they came back. His ears rang with the intensity of a buzz saw, making it impossible to listen for their sounds. Survival meant not dying at that instant. One second into the future was the extent of his planning.

An undetermined amount of time passed. He had lost his ability to measure its passage as he went in and out of clarity. His brain began to assemble a list of suspects: Prichard, Palo, Wazenski. Prichard stood the most to gain. Palo's motive could only be revenge. The Polack wasn't high enough up on the food chain to have goons working for him and he was too poor to hire that kind of muscle. Another possibility struck him as he remembered the female cop glancing up at him from behind the steering wheel of her SUV. The ski masks could have been hiding cop faces.

The buzzing in his ears slowly degraded into a hum. If the goons were ransacking the place they were wasting their time. He wasn't dumb enough to make that mistake twice.

Jackie pulled her white Hyundai into the employee parking lot where Bobbie Booth sewed cushions for cheap sofas and loveseats. The place had a guard shack but no guard. The look of security without the expense. She recognized the green Nissan Sentra from seeing Bobbie leave her apartment earlier that morning. It had an unmistakable dent in the right front fender.

She parked two spaces up and waited. At half past three the employees began spilling out from every door and scattered in all directions. Jackie had worked factory jobs in Detroit before enrolling in the police academy. Union jobs with decent pay and benefits with union bosses who took their share off the top before it trickled down. Unions didn't fare so well in the South, she had heard, and she wondered if the people she saw trailing off to their cars were better off or worse. Politics was not her thing. She voted democrat because she was supposed to, though lately she had been having second thoughts.

She spotted Bobbie with a young man tagging alongside, chatting her up and making her laugh, the back of his right hand almost bumping against her left as they walked toward her car. Jackie wore her civilian clothes for the same reason she had driven her personal car, but she hadn't planned on him. She needed information, and the worst thing she could do was cause trouble for the potential informant.

Bobbie and her friend stopped at a jacked up four-wheel-drive two spots in front of Jackie's car. For a moment she thought they might kiss, then Bobbie poked him in the ribs and hurried away laughing. He watched after her for a moment then climbed up into his truck. The brake lights flashed before his dual exhausts thundered and he pulled away with more noise than go.

Bobbie reached Jackie's window without noticing her.

"Can we talk a minute?"

Bobbie stopped and looked at Jackie with a moment of confusion followed by recognition. "No," she said and continued walking.

Jackie opened her door and got out. "Either I talk to you or I talk to your husband."

Bobbie spun with a menacing look. "Stop harassing me." She wasn't the scared little sparrow Jackie had imagined her to be.

"You'll know when I start harassing," Jackie said.

Bobbie stopped again, then she looked around to see if anyone was watching. "I don't know anything about that man," she said.

"I'm not here to judge you."

"Judge me for what? Living next door to a pervert?"

"I never said Nash was a pervert," Jackie said. "Has he bothered you that way?"

Bobbie's face flushed. Jackie instantly knew the next thing that came out of her mouth would be a lie. "I've never talked to the man. Now please leave me alone."

"Are you afraid of your husband?"

"No, and I'm not afraid of you so leave me alone."

"What *are* you afraid of?"

Bobbie looked at her without answering.

"I know you've been in his apartment."

Bobbie opened her mouth to deny it then didn't.

"More than once," Jackie said, "but like I said, I'm not here to judge you. And I'm not here to cause trouble for you."

"Then why *are* you here?"

"I told you. Information."

Bobbie steeled herself with a heavy breath. "I told you I don't know anything. That old bitch in twenty-three's crazy."

"He's trouble, Bobbie. Real trouble. You don't know what you're getting yourself into."

"I'm not getting myself into anything, and you better stay away from me or I'll call a real cop."

"I am a real cop," Jackie said. "If you want to make this bigger than it is and get your husband involved that's your business. I'm trying to keep you from getting hurt."

Bobbie laughed. "Fat chance of a cop worrying about me getting hurt."

"Have you ever heard of a man named Perry Stubbs?"

"I read the papers," Bobbie said.

"I believe Jonce Nash knows something about that murder," Jackie said. "It's very possible he was involved."

"I don't know anything about that either."

"The crime scene reminded me of a gang killing."

Bobbie held out her arms. "No gang tats on me."

"Hayes doesn't have that type of gang yet."

Bobbie shrugged.

"It's the kind of thing a man might learn about in prison," Jackie said. "The way Stubbs was killed. It was extraordinarily gruesome. His throat was cut from —."

"Spare me the gore," Bobbie said. "It won't change my answer."

"Did you know him before?"

"Before what?"

"Before he got out of prison, or before he went in?"

"I never laid eyes on him before he moved in next door. Can I go now?"

It was time for the backup plan. Jackie pulled a 5x7 glossy of Stubbs from her purse and shoved it into Bobbie's face. Bobbie recoiled and slapped the photo away. "That's disgusting!" Her chest heaved and she cupped her hand over her mouth and gagged.

"That's what the man you're sleeping with is capable of, Bobbie. If you don't care about yourself, think about your husband."

"You're sick!" Bobbie said. "Stay away from me or I'll sue." She spun and ran back to her car. There was nothing Jackie could do to stop her short of physical restraint so she let her go. It wasn't the outcome she had hoped for but it would have to do. She had delivered her message. The rest was up to Bobbie.

Nothing in the apartment had been touched. Prichard was out as a suspect and Wazenski and the female cop were front and center. Palo would have made sure Jonce knew, the way he had instructed him to make sure Stubbs knew. Since Jonce wasn't dumb enough to wage war on the entire Hayes police force, the little Polack was about to learn himself a lesson. He drew the short straw.

Bobbie knocked on the wall and told Jonce to come over. What an upside down day it was, her summoning him. He hadn't moved from his prone position on the sofa since his long soak in the tub to get the stink off. He was completely naked.

She knocked again. "It's important. The cops are asking about you."

His ears perked but the rest of his body was too sore to move. "You come over here," he said, but the words barely carried beyond his lips. Minutes passed with his curiosity getting the better of him. Finally, he lifted himself up off the sofa and staggered to the wall and repeated his invitation. She didn't answer so he rapped the wall with his knuckles. They were the only part of his body that didn't hurt. "I'm hurt," he said. "You'll have to come over here."

"Okay," she said. "Is your door locked?"

He didn't know. "No. Come on."

Seconds later his door swung open and in she popped, closing the door behind her as though she were being chased. When she saw him she gasped. "You're hurt!"

"I told you I was hurt," he said, still leaning against the wall for support.

She rushed to him and grabbed him by the shoulders. "What happened?"

"Let go of me!"

She stepped back.

"Don't touch me," he said. "I'm all busted up."

She crinkled her nose. "What's that horrible smell?" She looked at the floor behind him. "Gross!"

"Never mind that," he said. "Help me back to the couch."

"You told me not to touch you."

"Gentle me," he said.

She took his arm and waited for him to push himself off the wall, then together they made the short trip back to the sofa where he lay down with grunts and groans of agony until the soft hug of the cushions supported his full length.

"Who did this to you?"

"Maybe your cops," he said. "Or maybe it was somebody else. I don't know yet. Get me a beer. I'm parched."

She rushed to the refrigerator and returned with a beer and opened it for him. He couldn't drink it without spilling it down the side of his cheek but he didn't care. The moment the cold liquid hit his throat his entire body relaxed.

"That hit the spot," he said, allowing her to pull it back from his lips. "Now what about them cops?"

"She was waiting by my car when I got off work," she said. "She knows about us."

"Knows about us what?"

"You know what," she said. "About us ... being together. In here."

"What did she want?"

"Information on you."

"What kind of information?"

"She never said, but she showed me a picture of that man who got murdered."

His brain spun into overdrive. So she suspected him now. She couldn't have any proof or he would be in jail, but she suspected and that was enough to cause concern. Cops have a way of squeezing suspicion into evidence.

"What'd you tell her?"

"Nothing."

"Don't make me beat it out of you."

"I told you I didn't say nothing." She looked hurt at the accusation, which meant maybe she was telling the truth. Besides, what *could* she tell?

"You didn't say nothing about my arm?"

"No. She didn't ask about that."

"Good. You sure you didn't say nothing?"

"I swear. I told her to leave me alone or I'd sue."

He groped for her arm and found it, then he slid his hand down her wrist to her hand. "Good girl. Just keep your mouth shut and I'll be fine."

Bobbie pulled away. "You'll be fine? What about me? What about how I'll be?"

"She ain't after you."

"She threatened to tell Don."

"Don ain't no prize," Jonce said. "Don't worry about him."

She sat down on the coffee table. Tears clouded her eyes. "I knew it wouldn't last."

"Ain't nothing gotta change," Jonce said. "They got nothing on me." He put his hand on her knee and slipped it between her thighs.

"I'm talking about my marriage, you idiot. Don married me because I got pregnant." She sniffed. "He's noble. Imagine that." She turned away either to be dramatic or because remembering was hard. Jonce didn't know which and he didn't care. "I lost the baby so don't ask."

It hadn't occurred to him to ask. He was as unconcerned with the yarn she was about to spin as he was with whether or not the moon landing had been faked, or who really killed John Kennedy. She wiped her eyes with the back of her hand and turned to face him again. "I've never been pretty and Don was always so handsome."

"The way you two go at it I'm surprised you ain't got a house full."

"I told you already he's sterile," she said.

"Then how was you pregnant?"

"The baby wasn't his, genius. I wasn't sure at the time, but later after he got tested I knew. I thought he would dump me but he didn't."

"Yeah, he's a real Samaritan," Jonce said.

"Most men would've called it quits," she said, wiping her eyes dry again. "But not Don. He said it didn't matter because it happened before we met."

"Don sounds like a real mathematician."

"We dated for nine months. It could've been his if he wasn't sterile."

"Ain't no shame in being a whore," Jonce said.

"I ain't no whore."

He hadn't meant the offense she took. The world needed whores the same way it needed every other profession. People have different talents. "Of course you're not," he said, not wanting her to leave. All of a sudden he felt hungry and he didn't have the strength to go to the kitchen. "I used the wrong word."

"If a man likes sex he's normal," she said. "If a woman likes it she's a whore."

"It ain't fair," Jonce said, pushing his hand farther up her thigh without her seeming to notice. "People is people and wants is wants."

She moved his hand away without any anger behind it. "You're not gonna kill me are you?"

It was a question he hadn't entirely pursued yet. If the cops were snooping around she might be a liability. On the other hand he liked having her around, and what she knew didn't amount to more than a bullet in his arm that could have come from anywhere. As long as Palo kept his mouth shut about the shooting he was good. If Palo talked, the scar on his left bicep would damn him with or without her. "I'm harmless as a kitten," he said, putting his hand on her leg again.

"Is the Stubbs guy the one who shot you?"

"That was something else."

"Tell me."

"It ain't none of your business."

"You would've died if it hadn't been for me."

"You can't tell what you don't know," he said, then he remembered the lie he had meant to tell her. "Fine, I was somewhere I shouldn't have been."

"That's obvious."

"Me and this woman who I won't name because she's married was occupying ourselves while her husband was supposed to be working late."

Bobbie rolled her eyes.

"You can't trust nobody no more," he said.

"Poor you."

"I was out the window quicker'n a cat can lick its ass but he licked his quicker." He eyed her to gauge her reaction. She didn't believe him but it didn't matter because she couldn't prove different. "Ever since I was fifteen they've clawed at me."

"Cats?"

"Women. Married women especially. It got to where I couldn't leave the house with being mauled."

"Liar."

"My friends started calling me Elvis."

"Like you had friends," she said.

He adjusted his position with a groan. "I need you to wrap my ribs. I think one got cracked."

"I ain't your nurse."

He put his hand on her leg again. "And don't get lustful because I'm too stove up."

"Don't confuse boredom with lust."

"You're lucky I can't swing my arm," he said. "You can rip up one of my sheets for a bandage."

"I'm not wrapping your ribs."

"Rip up the one with the stain," he said. "Not the good one."

She stood with a sigh and stared down at him, then she disappeared into the bedroom. He heard the unmistakable rip of a sheet. After she wrapped his ribs she mopped the floor, then she went home.

Seeing Bobbie Booth leave Jonce Nash's apartment had been a stroke of luck for Jackie. Timing, good and bad, plays a role in police work as it does in life. She had worked late at the station and Jordan had already texted her three times asking when she would be home.

"Where's the pizza?" Jordan asked as soon as she stepped through the door. His appetite for unhealthy food knew no bounds.

"We've got leftovers from last night in the refrigerator."

"Gross."

She dropped her purse onto the coffee table and sat down on the sofa. "Did you do your homework?"

"I'm homeschooled, remember? It's all homework."

"Did you do it?"

"Yes."

"Yes what?"

"Yes ma'am."

She kicked off her shoes and squeezed her feet through her pantyhose. "Order your pizza," she said. "We'll look at your schoolwork after dinner."

She lay back and stretched out on the sofa and closed her eyes. Soon she was in a dark room with no doors or windows. Her husband called out to her. His voice was hard with anger, the way he sounded when he was mean. Her blood ran cold as she tried to conceal herself in the darkness but she knew he could hear her heart pounding. Suddenly Jordan called out to her. It wasn't right for him to see. He was too young to understand so she refused to answer, thinking if she ignored him he would go back to his room where it was safe.

Jordan kept calling. "It was him! Wake up! It was him!" She groped the blackness but couldn't find him, then she felt his hands clamp her shoulders and shake her. "Wake up!" She opened her eyes and saw her son standing over her, terrified at something or someone. She sprang from the sofa and grabbed her purse from the coffee table and drew her weapon, not sure if she had actually moved or if it was still part of the dream. Jordan backed away and threw his hands up. "Don't shoot me!"

The shrillness of his voice cleared the fog of sleep from her brain and her hands began to shake. She had almost shot her own son. She lowered the gun and scanned the room. The door was locked and the deadbolt was horizontal. "What happened?"

"The deliveryman," Jordan said. "It was him! The one who tried to come in the other day!"

She pushed past him and threw open the door with her weapon leading. No one was at the door so she stepped across the threshold and swung her weapon in both directions in rapid succession. The fog of sleep was completely gone and she was in full cop mode. A light popped on in a car three rows back and five spots down. Both doors on the car swung open and a Mexican couple she recognized climbed out. The man saw her and froze. Jackie lowered her weapon but kept her elbows locked. No other sign of life existed. She stepped out between two cars and looked up toward Nash's door. It was closed and he was nowhere in sight.

"Is he gone?"

"Yes," she said. "Are you sure it was him?"

"It was him all right. He looked like somebody had worked him over."

"What do you mean?"

"His face was bruised and swollen, like he'd been in a fight and lost."

"Did he hurt you?"

"No, he just stood there holding our pizza. I slammed the door."

"Describe him."

"Mom, it was him. He stole our pizza. I saw the delivery car turning out of the parking lot."

She took a deep breath to calm herself, then she threw her arms around her son and pulled him into her chest.

He struggled to free himself. "You're breaking me."

She released him. What she was about to do required her to be absolutely certain Jonce Nash was the man Jordan saw at their door. "Now I want you to think very carefully before you answer," she said, "and try to remember every detail. Describe the man you saw at the door."

"It was the same man who came here the other day," he said. "The same man in the picture you showed me."

She closed the door and ordered him to go sit on the sofa, then she followed and put her weapon back in her purse. When he was younger she had been careful to keep it in a lockbox but he was old enough now not to touch it. Her heart still raced as she sat on the opposite end of the sofa and looked him in the eyes. "I don't want you to *tell* me who you saw," she said firmly. "I want you to *describe* who you saw. Every detail."

Jordan sighed his frustration. "Well, he was about this much taller than me," he said, holding his hands about two inches apart. "He was thin. He had light brown hair with a mustache and a goatee."

"How long was his hair?"

"Normal."

"And his mustache — was it thick and bushy or —."

"No," he said. "It was scraggly."

"What was he wearing?"

"I don't know. I was looking at his face. Oh, and he had mean eyes. The way he looked at me I thought he was going to kill me."

"Jordan, now I need you to be completely honest with me. Are you describing the man you saw just now, or the man you saw the other day?"

"Both," he said. "He's the same man."

The anger inside her began to bubble up into her chest. She grabbed the phone from her purse and called the pizza place and demanded to speak to the driver who had delivered the pizza to her address. When the woman on the other end told her he hadn't returned yet, Jackie identified herself as a police officer and told the woman to tell the delivery man to call her.

"I'll tell him when he comes back," the woman said. "We're pretty busy for a Monday night."

"I'm speaking to him in five minutes or your place is closed down in ten," Jackie said. "And after I get through with my investigation, I'll call the city inspector just to make sure you're building's up to code. Then I'll call the health —."

"I get it," the woman said. "He'll call. What's this about anyway?"

"My pizza was cold," Jackie said, then she hung up. Forty-five seconds later her phone rang with an unknown number. She answered. "Detective Deen."

"Uh, I was, uh, I delivered your pizza," the nervous young male voice said.

"We never got our pizza," Jackie said. "Apparently you gave it to someone else."

"He said he lived there."

"Are you in the habit of giving people's pizzas to total strangers?"

"Uh, yes ma'am," he said.

Jackie realized how silly the question was. Of course he gave pizzas to strangers. He was a delivery boy. Jordan watched her with curiosity. "Describe the man."

"He was an old guy," the kid said. "He looked like somebody had beat him up. I was scared so I got out of there as soon as he paid me."

"When you say he was an old guy, how old do you mean?"

"At least thirty."

"Do you remember what color hair he had?"

"No ma'am. Am I in trouble?"

"No," Jackie said. "You're not in trouble. Do you remember what he said to you?"

"Nothing really," the kid said. "He had a twenty in his hand and he was standing by the door to number fifteen and that's what was on the ticket so I naturally assumed —."

"You didn't ask?"

"No ma'am. Well, uh, maybe I said something like *you waiting on me* or something, just to make conversation you know. Sometimes I get a better tip if I make conversation."

"You didn't think it strange for him to be standing outside with the door closed?"

"No ma'am. I get that a lot. Especially in that part of town."

"What part of town is that?"

"Uh, well, uh, I guess just that part of town."

"You mean where black people live?"

"No ma'am, I, uh, I'm sorry for saying it that way. The man I gave the pizza to was white."

"He was white so you naturally trusted him," Jackie said. "How old are you?"

"Seventeen."

Two years older than Jordan. In two years it might be him delivering pizzas. "I'm sorry," she said. "You didn't do anything wrong and I appreciate you calling me back."

"Should I bring you another pizza?"

"No. We're fine. Thank you. Just be more careful next time."

"Can I tell you something?"

"Yes," she said, hoping he had remembered something important.

"Just so you know, I'm black too."

"Okay,' she said, feeling embarrassed for assuming he was white because of the way he spoke. She hung up and looked at Jordan, who had not stopped looking at her.

"That was brutal," he said.

"I wasn't brutal."

Jordan rolled his eyes. "He'll probably spit on it next time."

Jackie grabbed her purse and shot to her feet. "Deadbolt the door when I leave and don't open it for anybody," she said. "And I mean nobody. Got it?"

"Where are you going?"

"Do you understand what I just said to you?"

"Yes."

"If anyone but me knocks on the door call the police."

Jordan looked suddenly worried. "You're going after him aren't you?"

"I'm going to have a talk with him," she said. "He needs to learn where the boundaries are." She turned and marched toward the door with long angry strides.

"Shouldn't you call for backup?"

She hesitated with her hand on the knob. What she was about to do wasn't a police action. It was a mother action. "Don't worry," she said, sensing the concern in her son's voice. "I'll be back in five minutes."

"How long should I wait before I call someone?"

She realized her hands were shaking. Anger dulls the senses in much the same way alcohol does. Jordan had every right to ask the question. "Fifteen minutes," she said, then she opened the door and stepped out into the cold night air. She waited until she heard the deadbolt engage, then she followed the sidewalk past fourteen doors and fourteen windows to the base of the stairs. What if Nash was hiding in the parking lot watching her? Waiting for her to leave so he could go after her son? She mounted the stairs and continued up, unable to reason herself out of doing what she had arrested people for doing more times than she could remember. Wasn't she reacting exactly the way Nash wanted her to react? Wasn't she walking straight into his trap?

Halfway up the stairs she saw the light around the curtains of his window. She hesitated long enough to scan the parking lot again. From her vantage point she could see the door to her apartment. Jordan was still safe. If Nash wasn't home, or if he refused to answer, she would hurry back down and wait for another day. The logical side of her brain knew it would be better to catch him when he wasn't expecting it, but the angry side of her brain refused to concede, so she climbed.

At the top of the landing she hesitated again to shift her purse from her right hand to her left, gripping it from the bottom with her wrist bent in and up so that it sat cradled between the inside of her arm and her torso. She made a mental note of her weapon's exact position in case Nash forced her to use it. A tinge of fear soured her stomach as she pounded on the door with the side of her fist. She often felt fear when going toe to toe with evil. There's no shame in fear. Fear sharpens the senses.

Jonce Nash gave no response.

"Police! Open up!"

It wasn't an official police matter. There would be no report. No call to dispatch to show her out at Nash's location. No safety net if things went south. She thought of the fifteen minute window she gave Jordan. A lot can happen if fifteen minutes.

She pounded on the door again. Nash could be at her apartment at that very moment kicking in her door. She stopped pounding and listened. A dog barked somewhere in the distance. She heard muffled laughter from an apartment down the row, then she heard a rattle at the door in front of her.

It opened and she stood face to face with Nash. He was barefoot wearing a white tee and dirty jeans with a hole in the left knee. His face was bruised and swollen. Dry blood matted both eyebrows. His hair was a mess. Jackie planted the ball of her right hand into his chest and pushed him back as she entered, keeping an arm's length between them in case he decided to pounce. Her left hand cradled her purse.

Jonce stumbled backward but didn't fall. "Easy, bitch. I'm hurt."

He couldn't know how accurate his description of her was about to be. She left the door open at her back. "Where were you five minutes ago?"

"Right here licking my wounds."

"Liar."

He grinned. She glanced at the pizza box on the coffee table. It was open and there were four slices left. The blood on his bottom lip was probably sauce, but someone had definitely worked him over. She could feel his heart beating against her hand with a slow steady rhythm. Her own heart rate outpaced his two to one.

She became aware of how easy it would be for him to grab her arm and take the advantage. She stepped back. Instinct told her to rest her hand on her purse but she didn't want to present fear. "Go near my son again and I'll put a bullet in your brain."

"You got the wrong man, lady."

"Don't make the mistake of thinking I'm a lady," she said, struggling not to finish what someone else had started. She could tell by the way he favored his right side that he was in pain. Her first strike would be to his ribs if he forced her hand. She glanced at the pizza again. He had paid the delivery boy so she couldn't charge him with misdemeanor theft. They both knew she had nothing.

"Help yourself," he said. "I ain't greedy. Take a slice to your boy."

Her hand moved to her purse. His eyes followed, then bounced back up to make contact with hers. He wore the look of a puppy intrigued by a bouncing ball. She understood at that moment how easy it could be for one human to kill another in anger. How a person with no criminal history whatsoever could cross the line that separates innocence from guilt. Good from bad. The line between living a life and waiting to die a death.

He glanced at her purse again. He wanted her to know he was reading her mind. Smelling her fear. Tasting her hatred of him. He *wanted* her to hate him. She exhaled half a second before realizing she had been holding her breath. Her anger vanished and in its place rose an overwhelming sense of foreboding. She backed out the door and left him, knowing she had walked into his trap. Wondering what his next move would be.

Chapter Twelve

The desk sergeant looked up when Jackie walked into the station Tuesday morning. He was a burly man with a dour disposition on his good days. On his bad days he could be downright insufferable.

"I don't know what you did but he's pissed," he said, nodding toward the chief's office. Jackie's brain ran a quick inventory of possible infractions and came up dry. Her only thought as she reached the chief's door was that her counterpart with the MBI had complained. Maybe she had stepped on his toes by going to see Gain Prichard. Then Bobbie Booth sprang to mind. Had she complained? Surely Bobbie didn't carry the kind of weight that would piss off a chief. Maybe she was related to an alderman.

The chief's door stood open and Gant took his time noticing her. Every ear in the place was bent toward her back. All conversation had stopped. She was only a week on the job and hadn't earned the trust of her fellow officers yet. Camaraderie needs time to form. Rumors don't.

"Close the door," the chief said. Then after she had completed the first task, "Sit."

She knew enough about protocol not to defend herself before she heard the charge.

Gant watched and waited as she completed the second task. The sergeant hadn't exaggerated the chief's mood.

"Tell me about last night?"

"Last night?"

"Yes, last night. And don't leave anything out. You've got one chance not to lie to me."

Suddenly she knew. "I overreacted," she said. "It was a mistake and it won't happen again."

He looked at her with no change in facial expression.

"It wasn't about the pizza," she said. "It really wasn't the delivery boy's fault. I'll call him and apologize."

Gant's looked confused. So it wasn't the boy who complained, it was the manager.

"I may have exaggerated my ability to shut the place down," she said, trying to remember exactly the threat she had made. "I was angry because she gave me the runaround when I asked to speak to the delivery boy."

Gant stopped her. "Tell me about Jonce Nash," he said. "And let me remind you that you're still on probation. I can fire you for tracking mud on the floor."

"Jonce Nash stole my pizza."

"You assaulted a man over a pizza?"

"Assaulted? Is that what he's saying? I talked to him." She remembered telling him she would put a bullet in his brain but it was his word against hers. Unless he recorded the conversation. Of course he recorded it. He knew she was coming up because he had set the trap. Gant had already heard the conversation and was testing her honesty. Maybe he had seen a video.

"When he opened the door I used my hand to keep him at arm's length while I stepped inside," she said. "I pushed him but I didn't shove him. I didn't assault him. I may have told him I would put a bullet in his brain if he went near my son again."

She realized her mistake the moment Gant's mouth dropped open.

"You have a son?"

If Gant had heard a recording or seen a video he would have known she had a son. He would have heard the threat. She had just made the mistake of admitting something he didn't know.

"Okay, yes, I have a son. His name is Jordan and he's fifteen. Two times Nash has been to my apartment and frightened my son and it wasn't an accident."

Gant looked less angry by a fraction. "I see," he said.

"Do you have children?"

"No."

"Then you don't see," she said. "He threatened my son to get to me. I don't know why but he did. Twice. I've thought about it all night and the only answer I came up with is that my investigation is getting too close. He didn't like me going to see Prichard so he's trying to make me back off by coming after my son."

"You should've reported it to me," Gant said. "I can't protect you if you go rogue."

"Rogue? All I did was talk to the man. Maybe I threatened him, but I'm guessing you didn't know that so it's my word against his."

"I saw the man," he said. "You did more than talk."

Jackie remembered the bruises on Nash's face and suddenly she knew what she was up against. The trap she had walked into was much bigger than she had imagined.

"Oh hell no," she said. "That wasn't me. He looked that way when I got there. Ask the delivery boy if you don't believe me. Ask my son." She thought of Bobbie Booth. "He's sleeping with his neighbor," she said, "so don't be surprised if she backs up his story. Her name's Bobbie Booth and she's married on weekends."

"On weekends?"

She gave him the rundown on her interactions with the Booths and with the elderly woman who lived on the other side of Nash.

"I doubt she'll involve herself," Gant said. "It might be hard to explain to her husband."

Gant tapped the pen against the desk. "You're confined to your desk until further notice."

She opened her mouth to protest but his demeanor stopped her. Desk duty was better than no duty. It wasn't the first time in her career she had been sidelined. Any cop who hasn't had a charge leveled against them probably isn't doing their job. It wasn't something she would post on social media, but the cold hard truth was that police work is sometimes ugly. A cop is expected to throw a touchdown pass every time the ball is snapped. One fumble and the knives come out.

"Do you have anything else you'd like to say?"

"No," she said. "Just that I hope this doesn't cause you to lose confidence in me."

"We're all under the spotlight right now," he said. "That badge makes you a target."

"Can I continue my investigation of Nash? From my desk I mean."

"As long as you're careful. Don't give the DA anything to use against you."

"Jonce Nash is a psychopath."

"Is that your medical opinion?"

"It's my cop opinion," she said. "I've been around a few. I

recognize the behavior. I've checked into his past and he fits the profile. Did you know he abused his son?"

"I didn't know he had a son," he said. "That seems to be a thing with me lately — not knowing people have sons."

Technically she had lied on her paperwork, which was enough to get her fired if the chief wanted her gone. She wanted to tell him her story. She desperately needed a friend and he seemed like a man who took friendship seriously, but she couldn't take the chance. "I found newspaper articles and police reports," she said. "The boy ran away. It was horrible what that kid went through. His wife overdosed while Nash was in prison.

The way he looked at her gave her chills. It felt as though he was looking directly into her soul. Some small part of her expected him to recite her situation verbatim, but instead he nodded and told her that his door was always open. There was a lot packed into that statement — *my door is always open.*

"So how long am I confined to my desk?"

"Until I say otherwise."

"Strictly enforced?"

"Leave this building without my permission and I'll fire you on the spot. No questions asked. No second chances. If you can't obey my orders I have no place for you."

She stood to leave. "Just so we're clear," she said. "If Jonce Nash comes near my son again I'll kill him."

Gant looked at her with no expression she could put a name to, then he turned his attention to some paperwork on his desk. His lack of a reaction confounded her. She sat back down, thinking as she did that she was about to make a huge mistake. "Do you really want to know why I left Detroit?"

He looked up. "If you want to tell me."

She spent the next half hour baring her soul to a man she hardly knew.

It didn't take long for the movers and shakers to start circling the wagons across Jonce's toes. Gain Prichard was the first dog to yelp. He called Jonce two minutes before noon and lectured him on the complications of being stupid. "You'd better withdraw that complaint," he said.

Jonce laughed.

"Or get the hell out of town."

"Run ain't in my vocabulary," Jonce said. "I think the doctor cut it out when I was born."

"I think the doctor cut out your brain," Prichard said. "Yours ain't the only nuts in a vice you know."

"My nuts is hanging gentle."

Prichard groaned. Jonce savored his discomfort. He had long ago ceased to wonder how men of low intellect rise to powerful positions. It was a mystery best left to the ages.

"Leave town and I'll slow-walk the paperwork," Prichard said. He sounded desperate to get Jonce out of his hair.

"I wouldn't miss this show for all the noodles in China," Jonce said. Authority had pushed him around all his life and now he was going to push back. Hayes was teeming with state and federal investigators peeking up the skirts of everybody who was anybody. It was all over the news. Perry Stubbs was the boogeyman and everyone who had ever passed him on the street was a suspect. They had already netted themselves two county supervisors, a constable, a justice court judge, a jailer, and, of course, a high-priced attorney by the name of Tipton Palo. All were out on bond except for the jailer, who the judge deemed a flight risk.

Instead of continuing the conversation, Jonce hung up and pulled another beer from his fridge, wishing it was closer to four so Bobbie could come over and help him celebrate. He was still sore from his beating but the important parts were ready for action.

He reclined on the sofa and flipped on the TV with the beer in his hand. His eyelids grew heavier with each passing minute. Next thing he knew it was two hours later and someone was pounding on his door. No way was he falling for the same joke twice.

"Go away!"

"Police! Open up!"

He limped to the door and checked the peephole. "Show me your badge."

A gold shield appeared at the hole. Jonce cracked the door and peered out, recognizing the police chief immediately. He grinned. "Second chief in two weeks. I feel important." He threw the door open and stepped back. "Welcome to my castle."

The chief stepped inside but didn't close the door. Jonce offered him a beer.

"You filed a false report on my detective," the chief said. "I want you to retract it."

"And if I don't?"

Gant stepped close, nose tip to nose tip. "She has a son. Go near him again and I'll personally beat your brains out."

Jonce laughed. "You was a lot nicer this morning."

"I've got two witnesses who say you had your injuries before my detective came to your apartment. You also provoked her. Filing a false police report is a crime."

"That kid of hers'll say anything," Jonce said. "And that pizza boy couldn't see me clear because it was dark."

"I'll take the word of three people over the word of one convicted felon any day of the week."

Just as well. Jonce hadn't really expected the charge to stick. All he wanted to do was rattle her and the presence of a police chief at his door satisfied him that he had accomplished his mission. "I'll study on it," he said.

"Remember what I said about the kid or I'll be back."

Patrolman Roy Birch leaned head and shoulders through Jackie's door with a concentrated look on his face. It was Tuesday afternoon, her first day of desk confinement. All day she had been attracting stares the way a magnet attracts steel filings.

Birch patted the wall with his large hand. "Just wanted to say if you need anything you can count on me," he said.

"Ok."

"Well, that's it," he said, then he retracted himself and disappeared down the hall. Odd, she thought, since he had said nothing at all to her since she joined the force. It was also the first time she had seen him without a mischievous grin on his face.

She stared at the empty doorway long after he had gone. Was he hitting on her now? And why now? She had heard some of the other officers kidding him about being a heartbreaker. He certainly had the looks for it but he was too young for her. She had ten years on him easy, not that she would have been interested otherwise. Romance was the furthest thing from her mind at the moment.

Desk confinement rankled her. To be punished for something she didn't do, by someone as loathsome as Jonce Nash, had her in a foul mood. Otherwise she would have thanked Birch for his encouragement instead of suspecting him of ulterior motives. Some men want the new girl simply because she's new. Maybe Birch wanted to put his brand on her before the others did, or maybe he was simply trying to be supportive of her plight. The only way to find out was to ask him. Since he was known to frequent the break room, she decided to go grab a bottle of water from the fridge. As she neared the door she heard the nasally voice of Ray Cline. Cline was another officer who had barely said three words to her since she joined the force. She stepped through the doorway and saw Cline and Kale Ramey sitting at the table nearest the microwave splitting the last slice of pound cake the jailer had brought from home. Officer Birch stood propped against the counter with his legs crossed at the ankles. He raised his eyes from the conversation when she entered.

"She wouldn't have to worry about any of that if I —."

Birch cleared his throat and interrupted Cline. Both officers at the table looked at her. Ramey dumped cake crumbs from his palm into his mouth. "Old man Tilman shot another one of Jorge Alverez's dogs last night," he said to the quiet room. "Of course Alverez can't prove it."

Cline focused on Jackie as she brushed past them and pulled open the refrigerator door. She felt two sets of eyes burning hot against her back. Birch was close enough that she could smell his cologne. There was a lot to find attractive about the man had she been interested.

"Don't let me interrupt," she said as she backed out of the refrigerator with a bottle labeled spring water that had probably come from a corporate well. No one spoke. She glanced up at Birch and noticed the smile he was trying hard to suppress. She turned her back to Birch and looked down at Cline and Ramey. "I believe you were talking about someone shooting a dog."

"You don't know old man Tilman I guess," Cline said. "He's been pissing people off for as long as any of us can remember. Hell I'd have shot that dog myself if I'd known he'd get so riled up about it."

"We were talking about you," Birch said. "We all think you got a raw deal."

She wanted to look back at Birch but she felt suddenly embarrassed by her miscalculation.

Cline rubbed his chin. "Yeah, I guess that's about right."

"Chief told us to keep our eyes and ears open," Ramey said.

"What else did the chief tell you?"

"Just to watch your six," Cline said.

Jonce sat outside his apartment in a chair from his kitchen and watched Bobbie Booth exit her car and climb the stairs like a windup toy with a busted spring. He alternated the cigarette in his left hand with the beer in his right, pulling from each without a thought in the world other than how long it would take Bobbie to top the stairs and crawl into his bed, or her bed. Location mattered not. As soon as her head bobbed above the top stair she caught sight of him and frowned.

"That's not the hello I expected," he said, grinning because the beer in his veins had lifted his spirits.

"I'm tired, Jonce."

"Fine. Let's hop in the sack."

She reached her door and stabbed the lock with her key. "You're drunk."

Jonce took a final sip and tossed the can over the rail and heard it hit the hood of a car parked below. Bobbie looked at him and rolled her eyes. "That's classy," she said as she defeated the lock and tried to slip through a small crack in the door without Jonce following. He sprang from his chair and pushed his way in behind her and closed the door.

"You're not invited," she said. "Go home."

"Take your hair down," he said, looking her over and deciding he didn't like the way she had it pinned in every direction. "Your head looks like a pin cushion."

"I didn't wear it this way for you."

"You look butch."

"Good, maybe you'll leave me alone."

Her mood befuddled him, then he remembered his visit from the female cop. "Last night wasn't what you think," he said. "She came up here uninvited. Tried to scare me."

Bobbie dropped her purse onto the counter and turned with both hands planted on her hips. "Who? I don't have a clue what you're blabbering about."

"That she-cop," he said. "Weren't nothing to it on my end, though I think maybe she had her heart set on something if you know what I mean." He winked.

"Go home, Jonce. I've had a really hard day and all I want to do is kick off my shoes and smoke a joint."

He stepped close and traced her naked shoulder with his finger where the strap of her halter top lay. "Shuck them britches and I'll show you what helps me relax."

She swatted his hand away. "Go home and shuck yourself, drunk."

"It's true I'm lubricated," he said. "But not so well-oiled that I can't cause a little friction." He winked again and calculated how many seconds it would take to strip her jeans off if they worked in tandem — her unfastening and him pulling from the other end.

She blew upward at her bangs. "It's hard to believe you were married."

He reached for her shoulder again. "Ellie weren't a talker like you."

She slapped his hand away. "Oh, so now I talk too much?"

"No ma'am. Not today. Today I'm all ears, like that baldheaded doctor on television — the shrink. What's his name?"

"Some shrink you are," she said. "You probably pull the heads off kittens."

"I'll shrink your head so little they won't recognize you at work tomorrow."

"Before or after you get my pants off?"

He flashed his best grin. "During, I reckon."

She unpinned her hair and shook it out the way he liked. "The store's closed," she said. "If Don finds out you've been coming over here he'll kill us both."

They moved into the living room as they negotiated. She pried off her shoes with one foot then the other. Jonce liked the way she asserted herself. "You let me worry about Don," he said.

"Ha! You couldn't whip his shadow."

Jonce backhanded her across the face. She wiped her nose with the back of her hand and looked at the blood without flinching. "Get out!"

"You asked for that," he said, reaching for her again. "Weren't nothing personal."

"You've got five seconds before I call the cops!"

He laughed. "They won't come. I got myself immunity in that regard." It wasn't as true as it had been before the police chief paid his visit but she had no way of knowing. He reached for her face and grabbed her chin and held her as she tried to twist away. She kicked at his groin and missed but managed to pull free.

"I hope whoever beat you up comes back and finishes the job!"

"Me too," he said. "Next time I'll be ready."

She dabbed at her nose and came away with more blood. "You could've broke my nose you know."

"Still could," he said, grinning. "Momma used to tell me nosebleeds is from thinking too hard."

"Good for her. She taught you not to think." She pushed past him and went to the kitchen and tended her nose with cold water from the sink and a paper towel.

Jonce tilted his head back and made a show of inhaling. "Smells better'n my place."

"A garbage dump smells better than your place."

"The woman who lived there before me had kids," he said. "Ain't nothing leaves a stink like kids."

"When's the last time you took a bath?"

He sniffed at his armpits. "I been studying about you and Donnie and me. Why you came after me so hard."

"Ha! I think you've got that backwards." She was pouty now instead of mad. Women get at a thing in predicable stages, like a movie where everybody sees the end coming halfway through. Jonce didn't mind the drama because it came with the date, like a dance before sex, or sometimes just a meal.

"My dead wife would've hated you," he said. "In a jealous sort of way."

Bobbie let go of her nose and sniffed, then she refolded the paper towel to find a spot that wasn't red and dabbed again. It came away clean. "She's probably glad she's dead so she doesn't have to put up with you."

"You're everything she wasn't," he said, ignoring the jab. Women need a certain latitude when it comes to popping off. Every mouthy thing doesn't deserve a slap. It's one of those things a man gets a feel for after spending time with a woman. "And I'm everything Donnie ain't."

"Is that what you think?"

He joined her in the kitchen and put his hand on the side of her neck and squeezed. "That's what I know."

She tried to pull away but he held her fast. "You're hurting me."

"That's why you come at me so hard," he said. "Because you know I'll hurt you."

She pulled harder. "I'll scream."

He closed his fist around a clump of hair and jerked her face toward his. "Women like to be hurt."

132

She put her hands against his chest and struggled. "You're breath stinks!"

"You don't smell like no bed of roses yourself," he said.

"Because I worked all day! Now let me go!"

He pulled her into the bedroom with her slapping and clawing. The bedroom was a mess with clothes strewn everywhere and the bed unmade. He threw her onto the bed and fell on top of her before she had time to slither away. She tried to scream but he clamped his hand over her mouth. She bit his finger so he slapped her again.

"We can do this easy or hard," he said. "Personally I enjoy the struggle."

She stopped struggling. "Just get it over with," she said. He worked open the snap on her jeans and kissed her hard, tasting the fresh blood on her bottom lip. She stared up at the ceiling until he was finished, then she disappeared into the bathroom and slammed the door.

Chapter Thirteen

J ackie sat at her desk and worked her case Wednesday morning in exactly the same manner she would have had she not been chained to it by Chief Gant's reprimand. So much of her job could be done from her computer. She even had a brief video chat with her MBI counterpart. Timms, as expected, had nothing new to offer. If he knew about her desk restriction he didn't mention it. Still, she chafed at being punished for something she didn't do.

Twenty-six hours and counting. Gant hadn't given her sentence an end date so she had no way to pace herself. Even prisoners are given a release date.

She picked up the phone to call Gain Prichard when she saw her boss standing in her doorway. She waved him in and aborted the call. He stepped inside without closing the door. He had bad news written all over his face.

"You have a meeting with Tipton Palo," he said matter-of-factly. It was not at all what she had expected him to say.

"When?"

"In half an hour."

"Where?"

"His office.

"What about my —."

"Temporarily suspended," he said. "After you talk to Palo you come back here."

"I thought he was off limits."

"He asked for you," Gant said. "In fact he insisted on it."

"Why?"

"I was hoping you could tell me," he said. He looked at her with an accusatory stare, or was she misreading him? He defied almost everything she knew to be true about men.

"What's this meeting about?"

"I was hoping you could tell me that, too," Gant said. "When you return you *will* tell me. Exactly. Word for word."

The chief's vagueness confused her. Did he really not know? Did he suspect her of something? "Will you at least tell me how this meeting came about?"

"All I know is he claims to have information about who killed Stubbs and he refuses to talk to anyone but you."

Her brain scrambled into defense mode. Was Palo setting her up? Was he in cahoots with Nash? Did she need to wear a wire to protect herself?

"And if I refuse?" The instant the question cleared her lips she wished she could un-speak it, but with it said she stood her ground and watched his face contort into a mix of surprise, amusement, and discontent. He wasn't just a man, after all, he was the chief of police.

"It's not a request, detective."

She tried hard not to squirm. "Point taken," she said. "Will I be interviewing him alone?"

"That's how he wants it."

"And you have no idea why he asked for me?"

"Insisted on you," Gant said. "And no, I have no idea."

She had read everything she could find about Palo and didn't like the assignment. Palo was a powerful man. Ruthless. In many ways he reminded her of her husband.

Gant stood.

Jackie stopped him with a question. "Can I ask you something unrelated?"

His look gave her permission.

"Did you tell anyone about my problem?"

"No."

His answer displayed no more indignation than if she had asked him if it was raining outside. For the second time during their conversation she asked herself what kind of man he was.

"One of the men said something yesterday," she said. "I probably misinterpreted it."

"Anything you tell me in confidence stays that way," he said. "I expect the same treatment from you."

She nodded her agreement. It was a good arrangement, if they could keep it.

Twenty-five minutes later she stood outside the door to Tipton Palo's law office certain she was about to see the other side of humanity. She disliked lawyers in general and considered them all dishonest at the most basic level. During her numerous times on the witness stand testifying against criminals she knew to be guilty, she had seen every dirty trick in the book trotted out from both sides of the aisle. Winning mattered more than guilt or innocence. Verdicts were the scorecard.

She straightened herself then opened the door and stepped into a very swanky lobby with an attractive secretary who made her wait almost half an hour for no apparent reason other than to show that she could.

"You can go in now," she finally said with no detectable communication from her boss. Waiting is a penalty important people impose on the less important. The longer one waits the less important they have been deemed to be. She had no way of knowing how far up or down the scale half an hour was to Tipton Palo. Probably he disliked cops as much as Jackie disliked lawyers. More so, perhaps, given his current predicament.

Jackie freed herself from the deep hug of the leather sofa and pinched out a smile to the woman behind the desk as she breezed past her toward the door with Tipton Palo's name affixed in gold letters. A bit gaudy, she thought as she twisted the handle and stepped into an office large enough to host a dinner party. The floor was the same hardwood as the outer room, and the walls were painted the same color of beige, but the paintings on the walls were gallery quality instead of so-so reproductions. He had a unique collection of *things* scattered about the room, the most notable of which was a globe that appeared to be suspended by a hand attached to the wall. Whatever his failings, the man had taste, or at least he had enough money to hire a decorator who did.

He saw her looking at the globe. "That one gets the most attention," he said without rising. "Feel free to look around. Take your time."

"No thank you," she said, purposefully looking at her watch. "I have other appointments and you've already used up half an hour of our time having me wait in the lobby."

He smiled cheerfully. For a man about to spend a very long time in prison he seemed in good spirits. "I hope Candice made sure you didn't want for anything." He remembered his manners and stood. "Please, sit," he said, gesturing toward two padded chairs sitting half a foot apart on her side of a desk almost large enough to serve dinner on.

"Is Candice your wife?"

"Unfortunately no, but thank you for thinking it possible," he said as they both sat.

"You know what they say about money and power," Jackie said. She already disliked him more than she had before she walked in. They were off to a great start.

His smile dwindled. She made a mental note in case she needed to tweak his attitude later.

"I'll get right to the point, Miss Deen."

"It's Detective Deen," she said. She had learned the hard way never to let anyone disrespect her on purpose or through oversight.

"*Detective*," he said, his smile returning. "You didn't introduce yourself so I wasn't sure."

"Let's not jerk each other around here, Mister Palo," she said. "You asked for me specifically so you obviously know who I am. How about you stop wasting my time and tell me what this is all about?"

His smile vanished. "Maybe I won't," he said. "Maybe I'll keep the information I have to myself."

Jackie stood as though she were going to leave, hoping he didn't call her bluff because she wasn't about to return to her boss empty-handed. He folded his hands and peered up at her as though unsure how far he could or should push her. Like most men he would get away with everything he could for no other reason than because he was a man and she was a woman.

"Do I go or stay?"

"Stay," he said. "Sit down and let's talk."

She hesitated so he wouldn't think her too eager, then she sat because she didn't want to overplay her hand.

It was his move.

"The short version of why I asked you to come here today is that I know who killed Perry Stubbs," he said matter-of-factly. "But before I give you his name you have to listen to the long version."

"I'm listening."

"The state will never solve this case," he said. "You know that, right?"

"I'm wondering why you aren't offering this information to the state in exchange for some sort of deal."

He laughed. "Trust me, the state couldn't care less about a local murder."

"They're leading the investigation."

"Only because they thought they might catch a cop or a mayor," he said. "You're new here but you've seen the papers."

"The local newspaper seems to be in your corner," she said.

"You've done your homework."

"You were telling me about the man who killed Stubbs," she said, trying to steer him back on target. Her gut told her he was lying.

"He tried to blackmail me," he said.

"Stubbs?"

"No, the man who killed him. Unfortunately I'm a meticulous note-taker. It's a hazard of my profession, I'm afraid. He broke into my home and cut open my wall safe. When I refused to meet his demands he handed the documents over to Stubbs."

"And Stubbs gave them to the mayor," Jackie said. "I'm afraid I'm not seeing a motive here."

"Don't rush me, detective. This may not be dinner theater but I've seen your office so sit back and enjoy the change of scenery. I have it on good authority you have nothing better to do, which will make what I'm about to tell you well worth your time. Trust me."

"I make it a point never to trust lawyers who say trust me," she said. "But go ahead, I'm listening."

"He — the killer — attempted to extort a quarter million dollars from me in exchange for destroying the documents he had stolen from my safe. He also raped my wife, but that's no longer important."

His callous attitude toward women reminded her of her husband. "It might be important to your wife."

"She's moved past it," he said. "As have I."

"If you knew what he had, why didn't you pay him?"

"Hindsight, detective. At the time I thought he was bluffing. I didn't know Stubbs was involved and even if I suspected it I didn't think Stubbs would double-cross me."

"Because you were partners?"

"Business associates," he said. "I found out later that it was Stubbs who sent him to my house."

"What's in this for you? Revenge?"

Palo laughed. His cocksure manner pushed her buttons. "You know how this stuff works, detective. First I want a deal."

"Ah," she said, "but just a moment ago you said the state doesn't care about our local murder."

"I'm not talking to the state," he said. "I'm talking to you."

"About a case the state's leading. I'm a lowly detective."

"It's a chance for you to secure a place for yourself here."

"I feel reasonably secure."

"Since you're not going to ask the terms of my offer I'll spell it out for you," he said, speaking as though he still held all the cards. "In return for the man who killed Stubbs I walk."

Now it was Jackie's turn to laugh. He had to know his demands were ridiculous. "You say you know how this works and that's your first pitch? Be serious, Mister Palo. Perry Stubbs was a low life bookie with dirt on half the important people in this town. I've been here less than three weeks and even I know no one is sad to see him dead. If the case goes unsolved, who cares?"

"So you don't want the name?"

"Yes, I'd like to solve my first case in my new job," she said, "but I don't have a magic wand. Besides, the charges against you aren't misdemeanors."

"I think this is where you make a counter offer," he said.

"Give me the name and I promise to do what I can for you. Maybe they'll put you in one of those satellite prisons instead of Parchman. You might even get to come home on weekends after a few years."

"That's your offer?"

"Even that's a stretch," she said. "A lot of people can't wait to see you behind bars."

"Does that include you?"

"I'm new here, remember?"

"You're tough," Palo said. "A lot of cops would've promised me anything to get the name."

"I don't make promises I can't keep," she said. "Or threats I can't back up."

Palo reclined back in his expensive chair. "I know all the tricks in the world, detective. I'll never serve a day in jail. It'll be years before my case comes to trial and by then everyone will be sick of all this public corruption nonsense and I'll get a slap on the wrist and maybe lose my law license." He smiled. "I practice law to make money and gain power. I've got money and, well, unfortunately my thirst for power will have to go unquenched. Not all dreams are realized."

"Which brings us full circle," she said. "Why am I here?"

Palo leaned forward with a hard look. "Because this lowlife is threatening me again. In addition to the documents, he stole ten-thousand in cash I kept put back for special emergencies."

"What's ten grand to a high roller like you?"

"It's not me losing the money," he said, "it's him having it. He threatened to tell the cops that I paid him to kill Stubbs."

"Did you?"

"When I told him to go to hell he came after me. He said he'd kill me the way he killed Stubbs." Palo touched his throat. "He showed me pictures. He's an ex-con with money he shouldn't have. The state wants me behind bars so of course they'll believe his story."

"Sounds nice," Jackie said, wanting the name but trying to seem disinterested. "But without corroboration it won't stand up in court. Surely you —."

"Do you think I'm stupid?"

"On the contrary, I think you must be very smart to have gotten away with so much for so long," she said. "But you did get caught, so there's that. And the state already has enough on you to put you behind bars for a very long time."

"Wrong again, Detective. Like I said, I can fight this corruption stuff for years, but murder is something else entirely. If they can pin a murder on me they'll have me where they want me."

He opened a desk drawer and pulled out a handgun. Jackie's hand instinctively went to her purse. Palo placed the weapon on the desk and slid it toward her.

"When he couldn't scare me he threatened to kill my wife," he said. "I agreed to his terms and met him in an abandoned warehouse in the industrial park. When he came to collect I shot him, but I'm a much better attorney than I am a marksman. I hit him though. I know because he left a blood trail." He pushed the weapon closer. "On the off chance he still has the bullet in him you'll find that it matches this gun."

"How do I know he's not dead?"

"Because you've met him."

Her brain spun up half a dozen names.

"In fact, he's the reason you're restricted to your desk."

"Nash?"

"Jonce Nash." Palo smiled as he consumed her shock. "Be careful with him. He's a real hard bastard."

Jonce washed a turkey and cheese sandwich down with the last beer from his fridge. It was the last of almost everything edible in his apartment. He raised the empty can and sighted the trash pail like a basketball goal, pumped twice then released. The can ricocheted off the plastic rim and struck the wall and rolled to a stop practically at his feet. He had never been any good at sports, especially basketball. His parents had made him play baseball for half a season until he threw his arm out of its socket and the coach had to yank it back in. At recess he was always the last one picked for whatever game the other kids were playing. It never bothered him, at least not that he could remember. People had always come second with him over anything that wasn't people.

He liked Bobbie, though, and she was people. He didn't want to like her, but he seemed not to have any say in the matter. It was a hard twist for him to figure out. She wasn't the sort of woman a man would stop on the street and look at when she passed, and he wasn't the sort of man to get his feet tangled over a woman.

It was half past noon and he needed groceries so he put on his boots and headed out. Halfway down the stairs he saw a black SUV parked two spots from his truck. He hesitated mid-step. The dark windows made it impossible to see inside. He turned and beat it back upstairs toward his apartment. At the top of the stairs he glanced back and saw the door swing open. He made it into his apartment and stuck his eye to the peephole, seeing the man half a minute later when he stepped into view outside his door.

Jonce opened the door when he knocked.

"Jonce Nash?"

"Depends on who you are," Jonce said.

The man flashed a badge. "Sergeant Timms, Mississippi Bureau of Investigation. Can I come inside?"

"Do I have a choice?"

"No."

"Then by all means," Jonce said, stepping aside with a broad sweep of his arm. "Enter my humble castle and trample my rights like they trained you to do in the academy."

Timms wore a charcoal suit with a white shirt and navy blue tie. His hair was white except for a bad dye job on top. Jonce guessed him to be pushing retirement. A real man's man from the way he carried himself. Probably used to getting his way back when he was young enough to back up the swagger.

"You first," Timms said, apparently not wanting Jonce at his back. A good move under most circumstances. He closed the door and followed Jonce into the living room.

"I don't have no beer to offer."

"I've got a warrant to search your person," Timms said, opening his coat so Jonce could see the paper sticking out of his inside pocket.

"If this is about that female cop beating me up I've dropped them charges," he said. "Weren't worth the attention I was suddenly getting."

Timms wasn't amused. "Strip down to your underwear."

"Whoa, cowboy. My chute's exit only."

"Would you rather I call a couple of uniforms up here to do it for you?"

Jonce grinned. "Would that female detective be one of 'em?"

Timms pulled his phone from his coat pocket.

"Hold on," Jonce said, throwing up his hands. "No need making it a foursome." He dropped his pants to his ankles. "I don't mind losing the drawers if you're into that kinda thing, just no touching."

The sergeant's face turned fire hydrant red. "Now the shirt."

Jonce wondered who talked as he pulled the shirt over his head and dropped it on the floor. The only two people who knew were Bobbie and Tipton Palo. "I don't have much chest hair," he said. "Momma said my great-great grandpa was two-thirds Navajo."

The scar on his left bicep drew the investigator's eyes like a magnet. "That looks like a gunshot wound to me."

"She weren't even all that pretty, either," Jonce said, "but I'd been locked up so long it didn't matter. It mattered to her husband, though. It mattered a lot to him."

"Because you raped his wife?"

"Rape? I barely hung on. Didn't know she was married until the third time."

"Enough with the dumbass routine," Timms said. "I know who shot you and I know why. And I know you killed Perry Stubbs, so turn around and put your hands behind your back and come along peaceably so I don't have to spend the afternoon doing paperwork for beating your ass."

❖

Jackie watched Timms through the two-way mirror as he prodded Jonce Nash with gotcha questions that didn't get him. He was too professional. Too predictable for the street smart felon who sat slouched in the straight-backed wooden chair with his hands cuffed to a chain threaded through the vertical slats that formed the back. Timms had dragged the table over against the wall as a psychological ploy meant to make Nash feel vulnerable. He had probably used the same setup hundreds of times with success. Instead of sitting, he stood, and he moved about the tiny room showing too much frustration at having fired and missed again.

"You've been arrested twenty-seven times," Timms said, reading from an inch-thick folder, his back to Nash because he had turned and stepped toward the opposite wall again.

Nash stared at his back half grinning. It was probably the grin that threw Timms off balance. Men in Nash's position weren't supposed to grin.

The interrogator continued with a raised voice. "Grand theft. Larceny."

"Ain't them two words for the same thing?"

Jackie saw the interrogator's back stiffen. No doubt Nash noticed too. Timms closed the folder and turned, piercing Nash with his eyes. "Child abuse!"

Jonce frowned. "It says that? I never laid a hand on that boy. Ask anybody."

Timms flipped the folder open again and found his place with his finger. "Petty theft. Petty theft. Petty theft." He raised his eyes. "Need I continue?"

"It's your party," Jonce said. "You ain't gonna find no murder in there."

"I'll pencil it in," Timms said. He closed the folder and dropped it to his side.

Jackie felt the chief's presence behind her before she saw his reflection in the glass.

"How's he doing?"

"Knocking it out of the park," she said. "If you're asking about Nash."

"That bad?"

"The man's a psychopath."

"And I suppose you'd like a crack at him."

143

"Not on this evidence," she said, not taking her eyes off the unfortunate scene playing out behind the glass. "Timms jumped the gun. Nash is not the backwards hick he plays himself up to be. It's a game he plays."

Inside the little room Timms propped his foot on the chair between Nash's legs in an effort to reclaim his alpha status. Jackie released an audible sigh. It was painful to watch. "He's playing right into Nash's hands," she said. "See the way Nash is grinning?"

"He's acting tough," Gant said.

"I don't think so. Pay attention to his eyes. I think he's really enjoying this." Nash's eyes smiled in sync with his mouth. A man can control his facial muscles but his eyes take their cue from subconscious thought.

Timms asked Nash if he enjoyed prison.

"I never was one for joining clubs," Nash said.

"Stubbs probably has a lot of friends there," Timms said.

"You didn't know Stubbs."

"Tell me about him," Timms said. "What sort of man was he?"

Jonce laughed. "Depends on what sort of man you was."

"Explain that to me."

"Okay, well, let's suppose you was a judge ... or a police chief ... or just about any other public official who might be of some use to him. To them Stubbs weren't such a bad fella. Except now of course. They ain't liking him too much now."

"What sort of man was he to you?"

Jonce grew somber. He lowered his eyes to the floor and lost himself in thought.

"Here it comes," Jackie said.

"I loved that man like he was my own daddy," Jonce said. "It was him who got me out of prison early. He gave me a job. Treated me good. Gave me a truck to drive." He looked up at Timms again. "It weren't no loan, neither. You can check the title."

"And yet you killed him."

Jonce shook his head slowly. "No sir, weren't me."

"This is too hard to watch," Jackie said. Gant mumbled his agreement. Beyond the glass, Timms dropped his foot to the floor and asked Nash how he *really* got the bullet in his arm as though the question still mattered.

"I already told you how," Nash said.

"Tell me again."

"I was sneaking out of a certain bedroom window and —."

"We've got the gun," Timms said.

Jackie saw a flicker of hesitation in Nash's face. "Did you see that?"

"See what?"

"That look in Nash's face when Timms said we have the gun."

"Looks the same to me," Gant said. "Hook him up to a polygraph and I bet he'd pass. He'd be lying his ass off but he'd pass."

"He hesitated," she said. "It surprised him. Timms didn't see it."

"Neither did I," the chief said.

Beyond the glass the back and forth continued. Jonce shrugged off being shot as though it meant nothing.

"Wouldn't you like to see the man who shot you punished?"

"Punished for what?"

"For shooting you," Timms said with incredulity.

"I was in his henhouse," Nash said. "With his hen."

"Is that why you didn't go to the hospital?"

Nash shrugged. "Weren't much of a wound."

"It went in the front and came out the back," Timms said. He reached down and grabbed Nash's arm. Nash flinched. "Still hurts, doesn't it? I bet it really hurt when it happened. I bet it took a lot of willpower not to rush to the ER."

Nash recovered his composure. If his arm still hurt he bore it well. Timms let go and stepped away, turning his back again. Even with his back turned Nash remained defiant.

"He knows we're watching," Jackie said.

Slowly Timms began to speak again. "Who helped you?"

"Who helped me what?"

Timms spun back toward Nash and raised his voice. "Who took that bullet from your arm?"

"Weren't no bullet in my arm," Nash said. "It went clean through."

"Suppose I told you it wasn't a jealous husband who shot you? Suppose I told you it was Tipton Palo?"

"Is that what he's claiming?"

"Was it his wife you were with?"

"Did she say that?"

"I'm asking you," Timms said.

"She ain't hard to look at."

"So you admit it was Tipton Palo who shot you?"

"Weren't him," Nash said. "I wish it was though."

Timms was beginning to let his aggravation show. "Why?"

"Because then it wouldn't've been that other guy."

"Where's the bullet?"

"I threw it in the trash."

"Why? Because you know we can run ballistics on it and prove it came from Tipton Palo's gun? With your DNA on it?"

"No, because it weren't no use to me," Jonce said.

"I don't believe you threw it away. We can get a warrant and search your apartment."

"If you could do that you'd be searching it instead of in here talking to me," Jonce said. His smile evaporated. "Tipton Palo's lying to you because he wants a deal and I'm a con and he thinks I'm an easy mark, but I ain't. You tell him that for me."

"Why you and not some other con?"

"Ask his wife," Nash said, grinning again. "She's got a dark mole inside her right thigh right up close. I told her she oughta have it looked at but she said it's been looked at plenty."

Jonce strode out of the front door of the police station with his shoulders back and his chin up. Palo may have thrown him to the wolves but the alpha male was toothless. It crossed his mind to pay Palo a visit in an hour or so when it got dark enough that he could move around without being seen. By the time he reached the broken down Impala with City Taxi on the door he had dismissed the idea as something an amateur would do.

As he slid into the back seat he glanced over his shoulder at the unmarked SUV already queued up to follow. "The least they could do after arresting a man for no good reason is pay for his taxi ride home," he said to the driver. The old man raised his eyes to the rear view and asked where to.

"Just do me five dollars in a zig zag pattern," Jonce said. "The more alleys the better."

The car rolled away from the curb with the two brown-gray eyes sizing him up. "I'm packing if you got any squirrelly ideas," the man said.

Jonce laughed. What a world to live in. Even the taxi drivers were against him.

They turned into the street and coasted through a stop sign two blocks later, then a left onto Fourth Street followed by a hard right onto Sycamore. Why did every town have to have a street named Sycamore?

"Still back there," the driver said, with his eyes in the mirror. "For twenty bucks I can lose him permanent."

"I don't want you to lose him," Jonce said. "Just piss him of a little."

The old man did a fair job of weaving his cab down one street then up another. Enjoying himself a bit too much, it seemed.

"I've always wanted to do some cop show shit," the driver said as he wheeled a hard left that sent Jonce scrambling to stay upright. The SUV was no longer in the back glass when Jonce looked around. "Damned Uber punks 'bout took all my business."

Jonce gave him the address to his apartment and told him to take it easy the rest of the way. He didn't want to die in the back seat of a cab that smelled like foot fungus and throw up. At the corner store he told the driver to stop and wait while he went inside and bought a carton of cigarettes. Then the driver dropped him at the stairs. Jonce climbed them two at a time and banged on Bobbie's door until she answered.

"I thought maybe —"

The look on her face stopped him mid-sentence. She mouthed the word *Don* two seconds before the door flew open and there the big guy stood behind her glaring down at him. "What the hell do you want?"

Jonce tore a pack of smokes from the box he was holding and offered it up. "Returning a pack I borrowed yesterday," he said as though it were the perfect truth. Bobbie's eyes bounced wildly in their sockets as her dim brain probably tried to cipher how to keep up. "I ran out and asked to bum one and she gave me a pack. Like sugar, you know, without the cup."

Bobbie took the cigarettes. "He's right," she said. "I forgot."

"You shut up," Don said. "I'll handle this."

"Ain't nothing to handle," Jonce said. "Unless of course you're thinking I should pay her back with interest, in which case, you being big and me being such a little feller —."

"You shut up too."

Jonce winked at Bobbie.

"Stop winking at my wife."

"He wasn't winking," Bobbie said.

"I told you to shut up! Since when do you smoke regular

cigarettes?"

"I gave him a pack of yours," she said. "He promised to replace them before you got home."

"Well I'm home," Don said, looking at the carton in Jonce's hand. "And that ain't my brand."

"I didn't figure you'd mind the upgrade," Jonce said. "And if you think about it you'll see that we weren't trying to slide one past you or I would've bought your brand and she would've told me you were coming home early."

"She didn't know," Don said.

"She done me a solid, see, because I was drunker'n Otis and these cops around here would love to catch me driving down to the corner store with my load on, and I really needed a smoke — you know how it is when you drink beer and run out of cigarettes."

Don looked undecided so Jonce shook out a second pack from the carton and offered it up. "A token of my appreciation," he said. "For your wife's neighborly generosity which probably saved some little kid's life because I didn't drive drunk."

Don snatched the pack from Jonce's hand. "Stay the hell away from my wife."

"Wouldn't touch her with a ten-foot pole," Jonce said as Don slammed the door in his face. He tore open a pack and smoked one at the railing before going inside just so Don would know he wasn't scared.

Chapter Fourteen

J ackie's police-issue cell phone rang Saturday morning at exactly a quarter past seven. She answered with sleep still in her eyes. The caller was not in her contact list but she paid no attention to the number beyond that. She had given the number to a handful of people she had interviewed in the Stubbs case in the unlikely event their memories suddenly improved. The voice she expected — hoped — to hear was that of Bobbie Booth. She had a strong feeling about Bobbie.

"Deen," she said sleepily into the phone, suddenly realizing how close she had come to saying Mulvaney. The caller didn't respond. She tried a second time. "Hello?"

She hung up. Robo calls have that lag before the recorded pitch begins. "My car's new," she said to the ceiling. "I don't need your extended warranty." Almost forgetting to use her new name had her fully awake now. Instead of going back to sleep she began thinking about her case. It was a reflex action. Learned behavior from working too many unforgettable cases. Being a small town detective wasn't the cakewalk she had thought it would be. Murder was routine in Detroit. If you couldn't solve one case there was always another waiting. No one expected them all to be solved, except occasionally when the violence strayed into the wrong neighborhood.

Her brain switched to autopilot. The victim was a known criminal who had been allowed to operate unfettered for years in a community that from the outside looked pristine. He had possessed a book of names and figures that rendered him untouchable. His murder had been deliberate. There was no robbery component. His killer —.

Her phone rang again. "Detective Deen," she said clearly. Practice makes perfect. Instead of speaking, the caller exhaled. It sounded exactly the way they make it sound in the movies when a stalker is terrorizing some young wife or mother. Her chest tightened but she refused to panic. "Who is this?" She knew it was a mistake to play into his hands by attempting conversation. The caller was definitely male. The husky expulsion of air had not come from a woman. "I can trace this call you know," she said, knowing she couldn't. The phone was most likely a burner. There was silence, then another husky breath, then nothing.

Just like that her morning was shot. The caller had achieved his objective. She ran into the bathroom and vomited into the toilet, then she checked the call log and saw the Detroit area code. How did he find her? She had been so careful.

The phone was her work phone. Her cop phone. The phone her boss had given her. The only person she had told was Gant. He had double-crossed her. With all the corruption dropping around him he had exposed her. Why? It had to be money. She shouldn't have told him Kelton was rich. She shouldn't have told him anything at all. Now she would have to move again. Start over.

She splashed water on her face then moved back to the bed and sat, running her fingers through her hair hard enough to scratch. She found Gant's name in her quick-dial list. Her finger hovered. Her heart pounded against her chest. It was anger now instead of fear.

"You bastard!" she said when he answered. He wasn't her boss anymore, he was her enemy.

"What? Who is this? Jackie?"

"You couldn't help yourself could you!"

"What are you talking about? What's wrong?"

"Nothing's wrong! I hope you choke on your thirty pieces of silver!"

She hung up. It felt good to vent.

"Momma?"

She glanced over her shoulder and saw Jordan. "Go back to bed," she said.

"Who were you yelling at?"

"Nobody," she said, slipping the phone underneath the blanket. "It was just a bad dream. I'm fine."

Her phone rang. Jordan stared at her. He was too old not to understand. He looked more sick than afraid. It was the same way she felt. Sick.

"Who's calling?"

"Go back to bed," she said. "We'll talk about it later."

Jordan came and sat beside her. "No," he said. "Tell me who it was."

She pulled the phone from underneath the blanket and showed him the screen. Chief Gant. It was still ringing.

"Aren't you going to answer?"

"No," she said. It rang once more then stopped.

"Why were you yelling at your boss?"

The phone rang again. She looked at her son, who looked all grown up sitting there ready to protect her. She owed it to him to be honest. She answered the phone and put it on speaker.

"Jackie? Detective?"

"Who did you tell?"

"Who did I tell what?"

"You know what," she said, no longer yelling because she needed to teach her son to keep his head.

"What's going on with you? Are you in danger?"

Tears filled her eyes and spilled over onto her cheeks. "I trusted you," she said, then she hung up again. Gant called right back.

"Stop hanging up on me!" he said. He sounded mad now. *He* was mad.

"What did you do to my mother?" Jordan said.

"Who's that? Is that your son? Talk to me Jackie or I'll send a car over."

"It's too late to send a car," she said. "He knows where I am."

Jordan grabbed her hand. The terror in his eyes reminded her that she was supposed to be the strong one. She was the protector, not Jordan.

"Who knows? Your husband? Did he contact you?"

"What did you expect him to do?"

"I don't know what you're talking about," Gant said. "If you think I told him you're wrong. I haven't told a soul. I swear it."

"No one else knew," she said. "No one." A possibility occurred to her. She looked at Jordan. He understood immediately and shook his head. "It wasn't me," he said.

"If you were just trying to talk to your father I —."

"No! I'm never talking to him again!"

"I'll be there in ten minutes," Gant said.

"No. I don't need your protection," she said.

"Then meet me at the station. Drive your personal car. I'll have Ray check it for a tracking device."

She hadn't considered a tracking device. Kelton hadn't known she was leaving. He had never seen the car. She bought it right before leaving Detroit. She made sure to use a dealership they had never used before. Unless …, the thought made her feel sick again. What if Kelton was having her watched before she left? He was a control freak. It made sense, but why did he wait so long, and how did he get her work number?

"I can check my own car," she said, but she heard the helplessness in her own voice.

"Not the way Ray can," Gant said. "He's an ace. And if you have a laptop bring that too."

"I didn't bring a computer," she said.

"My video game," Jordan said. "What if he's tracking that?"

She didn't know. Could a video game be tracked? It was a computer, she supposed, but Kelton had never touched a video game as far as she knew. He hated to see Jordan playing it. Said it made him lazy.

"Give me time to think," she said. She felt confused. Dazed. She needed to throw up again.

"I didn't tell anyone, Jackie," Gant said again. He sounded sincere. Jordan squeezed her arm and nodded. He believed him.

"I don't know."

"Break your phone," Gant said. "Back over it with your car, or drop it in the toilet. I'll replace it with a different number."

"He knows where I am," she said. "It's too late for that. You can send someone to pick up my car at my apartment. I'll leave the keys under the floor mat."

"You're quitting?"

"I'm leaving," she said. "What choice do I have?"

"And go where?"

She hung up. Her gut told her he was telling the truth, which meant her husband had found her by some other means. No knowing meant she couldn't stop it. It would happen again. There was nowhere to hide. Nowhere to be safe.

"Go pack," she told Jordon. "We're getting out of here."

❖

Three nights of hearing the neighbors' overly dramatic lovemaking had Jonce in a foul mood as he rolled out of bed and went to the kitchen without bothering to brush his teeth. Instead of coffee and eggs he gorged himself on beer and potato chips, contemplating the problem of Bobbie having or not having the bullet she dug from his arm. If she threw it away as she claimed, fine, but if she kept it, problem. Big problem. The female cop was poking around with a curiosity that made him nervous, especially now that she had a score to settle. Mistakes and blunders can end careers, even lives. Nixon should have burned the tapes, and Lincoln should have posted a more reliable guard at the door of his box at Ford Theater. Kennedy should have put the top up. Jonce had no intention of adding his name to the list of blunderers.

The trouble was that he *needed* Bobbie. Needed her in an unfamiliar way. Every moment he spent with her broke new ground. The problem, if he got to the nut of it, was Don. How long before she accidentally or on purpose said too much? Don was a hothead. One slip to him and he might go to the cops without thinking it through. And maybe if he thought it through he might go anyway. Maybe Bobbie getting into trouble didn't matter to Don, or maybe he thought it might teach her a lesson. Make her more obedient.

He was the strong, dumb type, Don. More muscle than brain. Prison was full of his kind. Their solution to every problem is brute force. He suited Bobbie because she liked it rough. She liked a little pain with her pleasure, like that rock song Jonce remembered from prison but couldn't name. Pleasure spiked with pain. Mostly he liked country, but a con don't always get to control the radio.

Bobbie liked getting slapped around. That was the attraction. Ellie hadn't cared much for it but she tolerated it well enough. She stayed.

He opened the refrigerator and found a package of ham slices and a jar of mayonnaise. It wasn't a hard find because the shelves were mostly empty. In roughly thirty hours Don would hit the road again. Not a bad setup for Bobbie. She had the security of a man with a solid job without the full time responsibility of being a wife. Jonce didn't mind sharing. His longing for her lived in his loins, not his chest. Hearing her and Don through the wall going at it like Grant shelling Vicksburg didn't make him jealous, it made him impatient.

Thirty hours, give or take. Don wasn't punctual. He wasn't one to set your watch by.

Jonce poured room temperature Coke into a glass without ice and

153

opened a fresh bag of chips and sat down to breakfast. For some reason he always thought of prison when he ate breakfast. Waking up and eating breakfast was the hardest part for him. Starting another day in confinement was like getting sentenced all over again. There's a hopelessness in being locked up like an animal. Fed slop like an animal. Yelled at and ordered around and kept dirty like an animal. Next time it would be permanent. Next time the judge would put him up for life. No parole. No time off for good behavior. No hope. He renewed his vow not to go back. Not ever. They might kill him but they would never send him back. The joint was full of men who had sworn that same oath. A man has a natural reflex against dying, like jerking back from a hot stove.

Bobbie's shrill voice blew through the wall like a cannonball. "If you think you're tromping off to meet some whore you've got another thing coming!"

Jonce jumped from the suddenness of it. Until that moment he had thought them still asleep. They didn't do anything without noise.

"Don't start on me with that crazy shit this morning!"

Something crashed and broke. Don's heavy boots hit the floor and stomped a line to the door.

"If you go out that door —."

SLAM!

End of conversation. It was like shooting off a Chinese bottle rocket. There's quiet, then an explosion, then quiet again.

Jonce left the table and put his ear to the wall. "You sure told him," he said with mock admiration, holding his half eaten sandwich because he hadn't thought to put it down.

"Shut up!"

"Get your ass over here," he said. "We got something to talk about."

"Go to hell!"

"And take a shower first just in case."

"Screw you," she said.

Jonce laughed. "He slammed that door too hard to be back before dark. Late afternoon at the earliest."

"You don't know anything."

"He's probably on the phone with some floozy right this minute, telling her what a terrible bitch you are."

Something broke against the wall at his ear. He jumped away then laughed. She was a wild one for sure. Untamed in every respect. She had the personality of a pulled-back rubber band, but it suited her somehow. That was the nut of it — it suited her.

Jonce stepped out to the rail and searched the parking lot for Don's truck. It was gone. He was probably slapping the steering wheel, cursing with every breath. Women do that to the Dons of the world. Men who don't know how to confront something they can't shoot or kick.

He jiggled her doorknob. "Let me in."

"Go away."

"I'll break it down."

"Try."

"One word from me and they'll hang you for being my accomplice," he said. "One little word."

"Accomplice to what?"

"Sooner or later they'll pin something on me and all I have to do is say your name," he said. "That female cop already suspects you."

"They won't believe you. I ain't done nothing." She was worried all right.

"Cops like believing stuff," Jonce said. "They show up at your door and find that pot you got growing in the spare bedroom and all of a sudden you're public enemy number one. All they need is a grain of truth and they'll manufacture the biggest lie you ever heard. The jury'll believe it too. Pothead like you, screwing around on your husband the way you do. They'll hang you up crooked like a dollar store picture frame."

"You got no reason to get me in trouble," she said. "I helped you." She had moved close to the door.

"Like a rabbit helping a wolf," he said. "I had my leg in a trap and you was stupid. Now open this door, little bunny. Let me stroke your fur."

A crack appeared in the door and her eye appeared in the crack. Jonce burst through the door like a goose sucked through a jet engine. Bobbie stumbled backward and barely caught herself.

"What the hell! I thought you was supposed to be hurt!"

Jonce stopped short and closed the door with his foot. She had noticeable swelling in her right cheek and the red marks of Don's fingers on her throat. The fingerprints were probably from rough sex, but the cheek was more recent.

"I heal quick," he said.

Bobbie straightened herself with defiance. One step forward and she would be within easy reach. Neither of them moved.

"Looks like Donnie gave you a shiner."

"It's nothing compared to what he'll give you if he catches you here."

"Or what he'll give you," he said. "Husbands and cops think alike."

"He said he was coming right back," she said. "You'd better go."

"Where's that slug you took out of my arm?"

"What slug?"

He stepped forward, eying the puffy cheek, thinking one more smack might help her remember. "Hand it over," he said.

"I threw it away. How many times I gotta tell you that?" She balled her right hand into a fist.

"Where?"

"In the trash."

"My trash or your trash?"

"Your trash," she said. "In the bathroom. I ain't dumb enough to bring it here."

"You sure you didn't keep it?"

She laughed. "Sure, I kept it as a souvenir. Bastard. You men are all alike."

Maybe he believed her. It was impossible to be sure.

"If the cops get their hands on it we're both in the shit," he said. "Me and you. Bonnie and Clyde. I'll swear you're the brains behind everything I've ever done."

"I threw it away," she said. "So I wouldn't catch no prison disease."

"I was in prison but prison weren't in me," he said. His eyes stroked her. The flimsy shirt she was wearing clung in the right places and struck her mid-thigh. It was blue with a pink flower. Ideas popped into his head but she hadn't had time to shower since Don.

"If you ever touch me again I'll kill you in your sleep," she said, reading his mind.

He touched her cheek with the tip of his finger. "You don't mean that," he said, tracing her injury.

She brushed his hand away but she wasn't violent about it. "He saw where you burned me," she said. "I told him I did it with my curling iron."

Jonce looked at her shoulder. The cigarette burn was hidden beneath the shirt. "Good thing for you he ain't too bright."

"I could've told him you raped me."

"Rape's a strong word."

"It's the right word."

Jonce shrugged. He somewhat believed her about the bullet. More accurately he didn't *not* believe her. When he left her apartment he saw an unmarked car with dark windows roll into the parking lot and park in the third row. A man got out and disappeared toward one of the downstairs apartment. He couldn't be sure which, but he guessed.

Jackie jumped when she heard the knock at her door. She grabbed her purse and pulled her weapon. Training took over and her brain ticked off the possibilities as she slowly approached the door, weapon leading, and stuck her eye to the peephole. Instead of the scarred face of a thug, she saw the clean-cut face of her boss.

She opened the door with a mix of embarrassment and anger. Embarrassment that he had scared her; anger that he had the gall to show up. It hardly mattered that she had already convinced herself that he was telling the truth.

"Can I come in?" His eyes dropped to the gun then back up again.

"We were just leaving," she said. It was almost true. She still had to pack what she could carry from the kitchen. Their money was almost gone and there was no way of knowing how long it would be before she landed on her feet again. She couldn't afford to leave anything behind.

"Where will you go?"

Did he seriously think she would tell him her plans? "Somewhere safe," is all she said. The cold hard truth was there was no place where she would feel safe. If her husband could find her in the backwoods of Mississippi, he could find her anywhere.

"He'll expect you to run," Gant said. "Hayes may be the safest place for you right now."

She stepped aside and let him in. He was right about Kelton expecting her to run. Maybe she should stay in Hayes. A person in trouble wants to believe the easiest solution. Wherever she went she would be looking over her shoulder. At least in Hayes she had a job, and a legal reason to carry a firearm. In fact her job required it. The question was whether or not she could trust Andrew Gant.

She closed the door and locked it. It seemed a bit overdone as she engaged the deadbolt. Two cops, both armed, against a phone call.

"You shouldn't have come," she said. "I'm okay." She felt a tinge of embarrassment at not having done more with the place since moving in. The tiny apartment was a hard fall from the home she had fled in Detroit. Gant would have been astounded had he walked into *that* home instead of where he now found her. In her former life she had a chandelier in the main dining room that cost more than the entire furnishings of the two-bedroom apartment. After thinking those things she thought how trivial it was of her to care what he thought about her lifestyle.

"A threat against one of my cops is a threat against me," he said. It was the kind of automatic thing a cop would say.

She offered him a cup coffee. It was already made and she had to empty the pot anyway. He accepted and followed her into the kitchen. She wondered what her fellow officers would think if they saw the chief leaving her apartment mid-morning. Her brain was already conditioning her to stay. "You'll have to excuse the mess," she said as they settled into chairs on opposite sides of the small kitchen table. Inviting him into the living room seemed a bit too intimate. "We were just getting settled in and now this."

"Have there been any more calls?"

She looked at him with incredulity. "Isn't one enough?"

"One is too many," he said. He sounded legitimately concerned but she had seen plenty of good actors.

"Do you have kids, Chief?"

"Bachelor," he said. "Maybe if I find the right woman."

"It's no picnic. Don't get me wrong, I love being a mother, and I wouldn't trade my son for all the world, but once you have a kid your priorities change. You have to think about someone other than yourself."

He nodded. "I've heard that." He sipped the coffee and told her it was good. He was being nice. Trying to be pleasant. What was his angle? They hadn't known each other long enough to form a bond.

"Even if I wanted to stay I have to think about my son. If something happens to me —."

"I'm not trying to talk you into anything."

"Aren't you? Isn't that why you're here?"

"I'm here to help," he said. "In any way I can. Even if that means helping you load your car."

She smiled accidentally. Either he was honest or he was the worst kind of liar. The kind with no conscience. No, she couldn't believe it of him. Maybe it was the mayor who outed her. Maybe he hadn't meant to. What a stupid thing to think. You don't accidentally let something slip in Mississippi and get overheard in Michigan.

"Tell me about the call."

She shrugged. What could she tell him? "He was male. Husky breathing. Didn't speak."

"Was it your husband?"

"No, more animalistic than my husband."

"Animalistic?"

"More tank top than white shirt and necktie," she said. "One of his goons."

"Your husband has goons?"

"When you're wealthy there's always people willing to do things for you," she said. "I don't mean to make him sound like a mafia kingpin or anything. He's not. Mostly he's an honest businessman, but there's no such thing as a completely honest businessman."

"I know a few who would argue the point," Gant said.

"Are they rich?"

"No."

Jordan popped out of his bedroom carrying his duffle bag on his shoulder. He stopped short when he saw them sitting at the table drinking coffee. He didn't look frightened but he did look surprised.

"This is my boss," Jackie said. "Chief Gant, this is Jordan."

Gant nodded toward the boy but didn't speak to him directly.

"Should I wait in my room?"

She waved him in. He dropped his bag on the sofa and joined them in the kitchen. Instead of sitting he propped his elbow on the bar.

"This concerns you too," she said.

"I was telling your mother that I think you should stay," Gant said. "The best way to keep you both safe is to catch this guy."

"It's not just *this guy*," Jackie said.

"We catch this guy — assuming he shows up — and we make him talk. Is your husband such a big man in Detroit that he can't be arrested?"

"The mayor was a regular at our dinner parties," she said. "But no, I don't think he would stick his neck out if we have a good case. Kelton donates to his campaign. They're not friends."

"Then we flip this guy and go after the source." He looked quickly at Jordan. "I'm sorry for putting it so bluntly. I know he's your father."

"Jordan knows what we're up against," Jackie said. She was thinking Detroit thugs are hard, then she remembered she was working a case where the victim had his throat sliced open.

"The important thing is that we deal with it now," Gant said. "Don't kick the can down the road."

"We?"

"If you stay, yes," he said. "I'm responsible for everyone under my command." He glanced at Jordan. "Being a police chief is the closest thing I know to being a father."

She wanted to believe him. It would have been easy because of the drop dead exactness of his phrasing, but men lie and she had been burned.

"At least do the paperwork," he said. "It's important to make it official just in case."

"In case he kills me?"

"In case you kill him."

"Just do the paperwork, mom," Jordan said. She looked up at her son and saw the fatigue in his eyes. He was tired of running. They both were.

"I suppose it won't hurt to file a report before we go." She cast a hard look at the chief. "But that doesn't mean we're staying."

Gant absorbed her defiance with no hint of victory or defeat. If he was running a game on her he was very good at it. What was his secret? He stood almost alone in the rubble of fallen men who had once been the backbone of the town. Could any man be as honest as Chief Gant and Mayor Pigg seemed to be? Neither of them claimed honesty for themselves, but you felt it. Two minutes with either man and you felt yourself believing them. Wanting to believe them.

"If you're playing me —."

"I'm not," the chief said. He asked Jordan to give them a minute, then he waited until the boy had gone to his room before continuing. "You came here with a giant chip on your shoulder. I get it, but —."

"Do you? Do you really get it? Do you know what it's like to be a woman in a man's world? A black woman?"

"No."

"Do you know what it's like to live in fear and shame every day of your life?"

"You didn't corner the market on emotional trauma," he said. "Your husband is one man. He's not all men."

"And how about the man who told him I'm here?"

"You're making assumptions. As a detective you —."

"I'm following the evidence," she said.

"Meaning you still think I betrayed you."

"It could've been the mayor."

"Did you tell the mayor?"

"No."

"Then he doesn't know so it wasn't him."

"Then I guess that leaves you," she said, "because I haven't told anyone else."

"But it wasn't me, so you'd better start looking at the evidence from a different angle. Surely someone other than me knows. Someone in Detroit maybe. Have you talked to anyone there since you left?"

She felt sick in the pit of her stomach. "Two people," she said. "I trust them with my life." Did she really? At that exact moment she didn't know.

"Then your husband found out some other way. Until you figure out how, he'll keep finding you and you'll keep running. Wouldn't it be better to stand and face whoever's coming for you knowing they're coming?"

"Why do you care so much? What difference does it make to you if I run?"

He looked into his coffee mug before answering, searching the dark liquid for the right words. It was hard not to believe him because he bore none of the traits of a liar.

"What reason would I have for telling your husband where you are?"

"Money."

He frowned. "Here I am neck deep in what the papers are calling the worst corruption to hit the state of Mississippi since Reconstruction and somehow I waited until you came along to want my cut."

She smiled without meaning to. Though she couldn't explain it, his presence made her feel safer.

He pushed his coffee mug aside and folded his hands on the table, leaning in on his forearms, elbows pointed in opposite directions. "Every minute you spend focused on me is one more minute you waste."

"I wondered when you'd get around to saying that."

"I don't expect you to believe me," he said. "If I were in your shoes I wouldn't believe me either, but that's exactly *why* you need me. I *know* I didn't do it, so I'm not distracted by the possibility that it might be me."

"You're asking me to believe you over the two people who have proven their loyalty to me."

"No, I'm asking you to let me help you. Suspect me. Investigate me. But let me help you."

She couldn't look him in the eye. She was thinking like a victim, wanting to believe there really were knights in shining armor searching the world for damsels in distress.

"Stop blaming yourself," he said.

"Blaming myself for what?"

"For what your husband did to you. For the way he treated you."

How could he possibly know that? Those nights afterward, lying in bed beside the sleeping animal, staring up at the dark ceiling as her face swelled and her eyes turned from red to blue-green to black, reliving the moments before it happened, searching for a reason why. Searching for the impossible. Feeling the weight of guilt settling on her chest like a slab of granite crushing her.

He reached across the table and took her hand. She wanted to pull back but didn't. "It wasn't your fault," he said.

She felt the tears creeping into her eyes but she was powerless to stop them. She stared at his hand on hers, then she pulled away.

"I'm sorry," he said. "I wasn't trying to —."

"I know."

"We all have skeletons in our closets," he said.

"What's that supposed to mean?"

"It means sometimes when we get close to someone they try to use our mistakes against us. They convince us that we deserve to be punished."

"And they are the punisher," she said. Was he reading her mind?

"Exactly."

"How many skeletons do you have?"

He smiled. "We're talking about you."

It felt good to have a conversation. He made it easy to forget he was her boss.

"You almost smiled," he said. "It came and went but it was there."

"I want to believe you," she said.

"But?"

"But I have my son to think about. It's not just my life I'm putting on the line by staying here."

"Staying here is the best way to protect him."

"I don't know."

162

"Sooner or later he'll catch up with you, or the law will. If he's as powerful as you say he may already have lawyers working to get him custody. They may issue a warrant."

"All the more reason not to be where he can find us," she said. "If a judge issues a warrant for my arrest I don't want you being the one to enforce it."

"Better me than a stranger."

"You're forgetting that you *are* a stranger."

"Am I?"

She looked away. "No. But you *would* enforce it. You're too by-the-book not to."

"I'd have to," he said. "But I'd be so sloppy about it you'd probably slip away."

She looked into his eyes for a long time. "I appreciate what you're trying to do," she said. She did, really.

"But?"

"That's all I was going to say."

He surprised her with a question completely off target. "Do you know why Timms hauled Nash in knowing he couldn't hold him?"

"Are we changing the topic now?"

"He did it because he had your back," Gant said. "He did it to send him a message that if he messes with one of us he messes with all of us."

His response startled her. "He said that?"

"He didn't have to. Every cop in this department is itching for a chance to teach Jonce Nash a lesson. If he spits on the sidewalk he'll get hauled in."

"Your orders?"

"No."

"I don't want that," she said. "If we harass him on the small stuff it'll be harder to make the big stuff stick."

Gant smiled. "That's exactly what I told them."

The truth was she *did* want it that way. She wanted Jonce Nash to suffer every moment of every day, but being a cop isn't about getting what you want.

"I've seen cops go through this department and never get that kind of respect," Gant said. "All I'm asking is that you think twice before you give that up."

"Is it because I'm female? They think I need protecting?"

He shrugged. "Beats me. Could be, I guess. Part of it anyway. Men are predisposed to protect women."

"Tell that to my husband."

"I said men," Gant said. "From what you've told me about your husband, he doesn't qualify."

"Do they really feel that way?"

"To a man."

She felt an overwhelming need to confide in Gant. He had a quality about him that was becoming impossible to resist. He already knew her big secret — the one that put her in danger. The one he may not have kept. Still. "I met Kelton at a church social. He was tall and handsome, … and rich." She watched for a reaction and saw no detectable change in his face. "Don't get me wrong, I didn't marry him for his money, but when it's part of the package it certainly doesn't hurt."

"There's nothing wrong with being attracted to success," Gant said.

"He was so confident, so strong. I was too mesmerized by him to see what he was hiding. I should've known better."

"Love is blind."

"It was too early for love."

"We see something shiny on the ground and we hope it's a silver dollar," he said.

She laughed. "Are you sure you're a cop and not a psychologist?"

"Police work requires a lot of psychology."

"We were married almost a year before he hit me the first time. It was a Tuesday morning and he was late for an early meeting. I burned his toast." It surprised her how embarrassing it was to say those words aloud. "Burnt toast," she said, still feeling the sting of the memory. Gant was right about the self-guilt. She remembered thinking at the time that if only she were more attentive.

"Why didn't you leave?"

"He said all the right things. *I'm sorry. It won't happen again.* That sort of thing." She took a breath and made eye contact again. Gant wore the proper expression. "You've probably heard a hundred women tell the same story."

"More than a few."

"Six months later, almost to the day, I forgot to pick up his suit from the cleaners. He had plenty of other suits. I didn't leave that time either."

"But you *did* leave eventually," he said. "That's all that's important now."

She nodded. As strange as it felt to think it, she was one of the lucky ones. "It's more than black eyes and swollen lips," she said. "Everything became my fault. The insults were barely noticeable at first. During normal conversation he would say things — little things that meant nothing except inside his own warped mind. I remember one time I said it was going to rain and he said *you'd like that wouldn't you*, and I didn't know why he said it until later when I found out he had a deadline on a construction job and if he was late he had to pay a penalty. That was his thought process. Everything was my fault. Everything I did became an affront to him." She made eye contact and broke it again. She wanted to stop talking but at the same time it felt good to unburden herself to an actual person instead of to the imaginary friends she conversed with inside her head when she was alone. A person's heart can only hold so much pain before it spills out, like water topping a dam. Restrain it too long and something important might break — something that can never be fixed.

"Well it rained, and he missed his deadline." She felt the tears welling in her eyes and tried to shut them off but it was too late. They spilled over onto her cheeks. "I shouldn't be telling you this."

"That's what friends are for."

"Is that what this is? You trying to be my friend?"

"Everybody needs at least one."

She forced a smile. "I bet you have a lot of friends."

"You'd be surprised how many parties I don't get invited to because I'm a cop," he said, then he laughed. "Sometimes that works to my advantage."

"Have you ever been in love?"

"I thought we were talking about you."

She laughed through her tears. "Friendship has to go both ways. I spill my guts then you spill yours."

"Okay, if that's how we're playing this. No. I've never been in love."

"I don't believe you."

"It's true. I guess I'm not cut out for it."

"Everybody's been in love at least once."

"I almost got married once," he said.

"What happened?"

"She dumped me."

"I'm sorry."

"Don't be. After I wallowed in self-pity for a few days I realized I hadn't really been in love with her."

"A few days?"

"Okay, weeks, but it's the same outcome. I only thought I loved her because she was beautiful. She did me a favor."

"Let me guess," Jackie said. "Now she weighs three-hundred pounds and has moles on her face with hair growing out of them."

"No, she's still beautiful," he said. "And on her third marriage and from what I hear he's already drinking." He laughed. "Beauty's hard to hold onto."

"Are you speaking from personal experience?"

"Are you saying I'm beautiful?"

"You're handsome," she said, then she felt her face grow hot as she watched his turn red. "Don't tell me that's the first time you've heard that."

"My mother told me once," he said. She couldn't tell if he was being serious. Lots of people have a hard time seeing themselves the way others see them.

"Men don't understand why women like me stay with men like my husband," she said.

"Maybe it's not about gender," he said. "I've seen a few men reach their breaking point. Something had to push them to it. Maybe suffering is universal."

Was he unburdening? "Have you ever suffered? Besides the near-miss marriage?"

"Not that I can think of."

"And you're what? Forty?"

He overplayed being offended. "Not for three more years thank you very much."

She smiled easily, then it vanished. A burst of sunlight in a terrific storm. "Two years older than me," she said, "and you've never suffered? You should give lessons."

"I've also never been in love," he said. "Don't forget that part."

"I've heard of unicorns but can't say I've ever met one until now," she said.

"Unicorns?"

"Fictitious creatures. Beings that exist only in the imagination."

"Meaning you don't believe me?"

"Don't take it personal. I don't trust easily. If you knew me you'd understand how uncommon this is for me. Opening up this way."

"Anything you tell me stays between us," he said. "You've got my word on that."

"Don't forget I pack a gun."

"So you'll stay?"

"Let's just say I'm not leaving right now," she said. "We'll see how it goes."

"Fair enough." He wore the look of someone with a difficult question on his mind.

"Go ahead and ask."

"Ask what?"

"Whatever it is you're wanting to ask me."

"You're really good at this," he said. "Maybe you're the psychologist instead of me."

"Like you said, it's part of being a cop."

"Okay," he said, "so why didn't you fight back? You're trained. You look like you can handle yourself."

"It wasn't a physical war," she said. "He knew all the tricks."

"Like what?"

She realized she was talking to a man. A real man. A man who couldn't understand hitting a woman because he wasn't an animal. "Hitting me was a symptom of a bigger problem. The real abuse was the way he controlled me. Everything I did became calculated. I overthought everything. It got to where I didn't turn my head without wondering if he might read something into it. He did, sometimes. More often than you might believe. It's crazy."

"What made you finally leave?"

The answer formed on her lips but she couldn't speak it because she knew the dam would burst and she would fall apart in front of a man she barely knew. Instead she turned her face toward Jordan's bedroom door and felt Gant's eyes following her, then she felt his hand envelop hers and close around it. This time she didn't pull away.

"Get your wormy ass down here PRONTO."

Jonce recognized Gain Prichard's voice two syllables into the order. It was Monday afternoon, not Thursday, but schedules meant nothing unless Prichard said they meant something.

"I'm busy," Jonce said, refusing to submit without some semblance of resistance. He didn't care Monday from Thursday but he didn't like being jerked around.

"Un-busy yourself." The line went dead. Jonce dropped his phone into his pocket and waited half an hour before driving downtown. Through the big plate glass window he saw Prichard perched behind his desk like an overgrown frog who had learned to sit like a man.

"You should think about dropping a few pounds," Jonce said once inside. Prichard didn't look up. "And by a few I mean fifty."

"Shut up and sit."

Jonce let the door pull itself closed behind him. "A treadmill might be something to think about."

Prichard looked up for the first time. His face had the sag of a man walking the last two yards of a fifty yard dash. He was played out. "Sit down, Nash."

Jonce stepped fast to the chair and slid into it with terrible posture. "If not a treadmill then at least a window shade. Some blinds or something."

"Shut UP."

"A curtain."

Prichard wagged his finger. "One more word and I'll come over this desk and stomp you into mush. You got that?"

Jonce bit his lips together and nodded.

Prichard glared at him for an eternity, then he looked at a paper on his desk as though refreshing his memory on some key point. When he raised his eyes again he asked Jonce what took so him long to get there.

"You ever had a shit pain hit you just as you're walking out the door?"

"Never mind," Prichard said.

"I would've tried to hold it but I got me a relaxed anal muscle."

"I said never mind!"

"And you ain't got no bathroom. How come they don't give you a bathroom?"

"Your anal muscle is why I called you here," Prichard said. "You've got to leave town."

"What's leaving town got to do with my rectum?"

"Because if you don't leave town you'll be back in the joint getting your anal muscle relaxed again."

Jonce shot straight up in his chair. "No sir, Mister Prichard, that ain't why. I was born with it. Call my momma and ask her. She said when I was a baby I —."

"Shut the hell UP!" He took another deep breath. "What I'm trying to tell you, Jonce, is that —." He suddenly stopped himself and glared at Jonce. "How do I know you're not wearing a wire?"

"Why would I wear a wire?"

"Maybe that's why it took you so long to get here."

"I told you I had a call of nature." He shot to his feet and peeled his shirt over his head.

"Stop that!"

Jonce unbuttoned his jeans.

"I said STOP!" He blew through his nose like a mad bull and told Jonce through clenched teeth to put his shirt back on and sit down.

Prichard glanced toward the big window so Jonce looked too. A woman advanced in years stood with her mouth agape looking in.

"She'll be awful disappointed if these pants don't fall," Jonce said.

"If they do fall I'll have you arrested for indecent exposure."

"She's old," Jonce said. "Might be her last chance to see one like mine."

Prichard shooed the woman away by flicking his hand. She gathered herself and hurried off down the sidewalk.

"You better hope she doesn't report this," Prichard said. "I'll have your hide." Gain Prichard was an idiot doing idiot work. Squeeze an unimportant man into an unimportant space doing unimportant work and he'll soon think he's the most important cog in the wheel. He'll convince himself the world can't spin without him — that without him everything that *is* will stop itself and look around and say where's Gain Prichard?

Jonce pulled his shirt back over his head and sat.

Prichard leaned back in his chair and folded his hands behind his head. The chair protested, but it held. "What I was trying to explain to you, Jonce, is that a certain somebody is squeezing me to violate your parole."

"Squeezing?"

"Pressuring me, Jonce. Pressuring me real hard."

"And who might this certain somebody be?"

Prichard leaned forward again, causing more groans from the helpless chair. "Don't matter who it is. You let me worry about that. All you got to do is skip town. Scram. Vamoose. Got it?"

"Ain't that illegal? I mean, ain't that what you're supposed to keep me from doing?"

"Ordinarily, yes, but these ain't ordinary times, Jonce. These are

169

extraordinary times."

"And you want me to just pick up and go?"

"The sooner the better."

"Just leave town and don't look back?"

"The farther away you go the more I'll like it."

"No more Thursdays?"

"I never want to hear from you again."

Jonce mulled over the proposition. As much as he wanted to be free of Gain Prichard and the terms of his parole, he didn't trust the man. "No," he said. "I won't do 'er."

"The hell you won't."

"I leave and next thing I know they'll be scooping me up and sending me back to prison. No thanks. Ain't happening."

"It ain't like that, Jonce. You can trust me."

Jonce laughed. "I ain't trusted nobody since third grade."

Prichard planted his face in his hands and rubbed all the way up his forehead and over the top, then he crossed his arms on the desk and leaned in. "Okay, so I'll be straight with you, Jonce. Either you get the hell outta Dodge or you'll go back to prison for killing Stubbs. That's the rest of your miserable life, which'll probably be around twenty years because that's about how long it'll takes 'em to stick a needle in your arm. They'll strap you to a gurney and have all those people sitting on the other side of the glass watching you and placing bets on how long it'll take you to die, or on whether or not you'll cry and beg for mercy. There won't be no mercy, Jonce. Just that needle in your arm and several minutes of that juice burning through your veins like liquid fire. You'll scream your brains out but no one will hear you because you'll be paralyzed. You'll feel every second of it because they want you to feel it, otherwise they'd put you to sleep first. Paralyzed don't mean numb. It means helpless."

He stopped and looked hard at Jonce with his arms still crossed. "Or, you can pack your little bag and take your happy little ass on down the road and disappear."

"I didn't kill Stubbs," Jonce said. It seemed the thing to say. Maybe Prichard was wired, or maybe the state had his office bugged.

"Save the denial for the cops," Prichard said. "It'll be your word against Tipton Palo."

So Palo was going to talk after all, huh? It was just the sort of thing a man like him would do. Jonce had feared it but he had hoped Palo had better sense.

"I've still got all that evidence on you," he told Prichard. "Don't forget about that."

"It ain't me doing this, Jonce. It's me giving you the heads up. I'm giving you a chance to save yourself."

"So I don't use what I got on you?"

"Exactly."

"And you won't turn me in as soon as I'm gone?"

"No."

"Won't they miss the paperwork?"

"I'll keep turning it in like always."

"And when they find out I'm gone?"

Suddenly Prichard fell mute. Jonce grinned. "That's what I thought. As soon as they find out I'm gone they'll come asking you where I am and you'll say that boy must've gone on the lam. You'll say catch him boys, I think he went to see his momma in Florida."

"Then don't go to Florida. Go someplace else. Don't tell me where you go."

"But that's how it'll go," Jonce said. "And I'll be a fugitive."

Prichard leaned back again. "Well, of course if they find out … I'll have to tell them something."

"Uh huh."

"But you'll have a big head start."

"They'll send federal marshals after me."

"I doubt they'll go to that extreme. You're not that important."

"For the man who killed Perry Stubbs?"

"Nobody much cares who killed Stubbs," Prichard said.

"They'll care all right," Jonce said. "They'll care because it'll be their chance to snatch up ole Jonce Nash and throw him in the clink for good."

"That new female detective called here asking about you."

"I fixed her," Jonce said.

"Yeah, well, maybe she don't know you fixed her. Ever think about that?" He pulled his keyboard to the edge of his desk and pecked on a few keys. "I'll set a long check-in date and drag out the paperwork," he said. "You can be in Mexico before anybody knows you're gone."

"I don't speak the language."

"Mexico's got lots of beautiful women."

"Who all get real ugly by the time they're my age."

"You've got a boy down there don't you?"

Jonce bristled at the mention of his kid. Jayrod was a man now but he wasn't in Mexico anymore. He was in Texas. First Brownsville, then Dallas, then Jonce lost track but he was still in Texas. People who get a taste for Texas don't leave without a good reason, and the way he heard it Jayrod had a blond blue-eyed reason to stay.

"I'll see you Thursday, Mister Prichard."

Prichard sighed. "Then you better start thinking about what you're going to do about Palo."

Jonce stood. "You're trying too hard, Mister Prichard. I'll see you Thursday."

Chapter Fifteen

Over the next two weeks Jackie received fourteen phone calls from fourteen different numbers, all having Detroit area codes. Each call lasted exactly thirty seconds. The caller never spoke, but Jackie always heard breathing. In the beginning she called the numbers back, but it soon became clear the numbers were fake so she stopped.

No one at the department knew she and Jordan had spent two nights at Chief Gant's house, using two spare bedrooms in his three-bedroom house. It began as a one-night invitation after the third anonymous call, then another call came and Gant insisted they stay one more night.

Ten days had passed since she and Jordan returned to their tiny apartment. Ten days and ten more mysterious phone calls to keep her nerves on edge. She had felt safe at Gant's house. He lived in one of the old neighborhoods that wasn't gated. An old dog-eared fence enforced privacy along both sides and the back, and his front lawn comprised half an acre with three rows of mature pecan trees that gave him a plantation view from his front porch. She had felt guilty for imposing because he was a decent man and their secret might have cost him his job, or at least some respect. No one would believe it was nothing more than one friend helping another. Sometimes she wanted not to believe it herself, but Gant had not displayed the first hint of romantic interest in her, and the last thing she needed was to further complicate her life. Two weeks ago having a friend seemed an impossibility. Now, on occasion, when she lay in bed with nothing but her thoughts to keep her company, friendship seemed not enough.

Kelton was trying to scare her and it was working. She was scared for Jordan more than for herself. Scared of the legal system that might take him away and force him to stay with his father. Scared of what she might do if it actually happened.

Jordan spoke and jerked her out of her private world. "I like Mister Gant," he said, bringing her another plate to rinse. She had cooked pasta for dinner and her son had spent the entire meal talking about a new video game he had downloaded. For the life of her she couldn't remember much of what he had said.

"So do I," she said, taking the plate and holding it under the faucet. "He's been a good friend."

"I wish we could go stay with him again."

"We can't," she said.

"How much does he know?"

Their situation was forcing him to grow up too fast. "Some of it," she said, then she busied herself scrubbing the plate so he wouldn't see the tears creeping into her eyes. "I had to tell him because it was affecting my job. You go finish your schoolwork and I'll finish the dishes."

He went to his room without the usual resistance, as though he understood her need to be alone. It broke her heart to think what he must be feeling, but there was nothing to do but to keep moving forward. Turning back would be a death sentence for her. For Jordan too, in the grand scheme of things. Sometimes the thing that doesn't kill you turns you into a hollow shell. She wanted more for her son. It was too late to give him a normal childhood, but maybe she still had time to give him a future.

The phone rang. Not again, she thought. Not now. She pulled the phone from her pocket and breathed a sigh of relief at seeing Gant's name.

"It's warm out tonight," he said. "Feels like spring."

She dabbed away her tears. Gant had an easy way about him. Strong and decent, the way Kelton was in the beginning. Aren't all men strong and decent until they're not? "Do you believe in synchronicity?"

"Synchro-what?"

"Synchronicity," she said as though it were the most common word in the English language. "Google it."

"No, you use it in a sentence," he said. "My high school English teacher always told us if you can't use a word in a sentence you shouldn't be saying it, so let me hear that big word in a sentence."

"I did use it in a sentence."

"No, you used it in a question," he said. "You asked me if I believed in it."

"Well, do you?"

"No, because I don't know what it means."

"Jordan was just telling me how much he likes you," she said, changing the subject. She turned off the water and dried her hands on a towel.

"I like him too," Gant said. "You've done a fine job with him. Now back to that word you used on me."

"Synchronicity means when unrelated events seem to be related," she said.

"Oh."

"Like Nash showing up at my apartment then I start getting these phone calls, and then Tipton Palo takes a special interest in me. And —." She almost included Gant in the mix but stopped.

"And me?"

"You have to admit it's strange."

"I hope you don't still think I'm part of what's happening to you."

"No, I don't,' she said. "These phone calls are making me paranoid. You've been a terrific friend."

"How could Nash or Palo know about you?"

"They couldn't," she said, tossing the towel onto the counter. "That's what has me so worried."

"You're welcome to come stay with me for as long as you like."

The offer was tempting but she had leaned on him too much already. She needed to stand on her own two feet so she declined. Being a gentleman, he didn't press the issue.

For two weeks Jonce had stalked Tipton Palo, learning his patterns until he could accurately guess where he would be at any time of day or night. At precisely eight sharp every morning the security gate at the end of his driveway swung open and out he rolled in his cherry red Porsche. Every morning he stopped at the diner down the street from his law office for breakfast, usually sitting alone but Jonce suspected it hadn't always been that way. Palo wasn't the loner type. Men like him need to be the center of something, and what Palo was the center of now was not to his liking.

After breakfast he would make the short drive to his office and park behind the building in a lot that was visible from a side street that was always busy that time of morning. Throughout the day he came and went between his office and the courthouse at irregular intervals, but he rarely took lunch outside his office. Most days his secretary — a long-legged brunette Jonce wouldn't mind getting to know — went down to the diner and brought something back. Some days a delivery boy brought pizza.

At five on the nose, day in and day out, he left his office but he didn't always go straight home. On Tuesdays and Thursdays he went to a local gym with large windows that allowed Jonce to see inside from the parking lot. Palo spent half an hour on a treadmill next to a brunette who was not his wife. It was not always the same treadmill but it was always the same woman. Their workout routines were either coordinated or unbelievably coincidental. After half an hour of jogging they disappeared into the back. Some time later Palo would reappear and leave alone, wearing a fresh shower and carrying his gym bag. Jonce never hung around long enough to see the woman come out. Palo was his target, not her.

Weekends were the wildcard. The first weekend the Palos didn't leave home except for church on Sunday morning. The second weekend they skipped church.

It was Monday night again and Jonce had just returned home from tailing Palo to his mansion fortress. He tapped on Bobbie's apartment door and waited the polite amount of time, then he knocked harder.

"Go away," she said through the door.

"Open this door."

"Why? Did she throw you out?"

"She who?"

"Whoever you've been screwing these past two weeks."

Jonce laughed, which was a mistake because it set her off and she yelled something obscenely impossible at him through the door, then he heard her stomp away. Women.

He sank into his own apartment and put his ear to the wall in an attempt to determine her whereabouts. Her television was playing a Lifetime movie. Lifetime had been Ellie's favorite channel until he put his foot down.

He pounded on the wall with the side of his fist. "You'll come over here if you know what's good for you."

Silence.

He struck the wall again. "I only got an hour," he said. His meet-up with Emil Wazenski was too important to postpone. Getting at Palo was going to take more than one man and the Polack was going to pitch in and help whether he liked it or not.

"That's fifty minutes more than you need," she said with her acid tongue. She was at the wall though. It crossed his mind to punch through and teach her a lesson but explaining the damage to Donnie Boy would be a bitch come Friday. Jonce was already pushing his luck in that regard. He wasn't afraid of the big man but he wasn't yet healed from his previous beating.

"Suit yourself," he said. "It's your loss. I only offered because I felt sorry for you." He retreated to his couch and stretched out for a quick nap before striking out for Tupelo to meet Wazenski.

They met in a seedy little bar on the outskirts of town. It was the kind of place where bikers sold dope in the parking lot and three Mexican girls sold something more addictive in a room off the back. Waz had picked the place and quickly pointed out a cute little Mexican sitting on a biker's lap at a corner booth. "That's my future wife," he said proudly. "Her name is Juanita."

"You can't marry a whore, Waz," Jonce said with a cigarette dancing between his lips.

"Why not?"

Jonce shrugged. "People just don't marry whores, that's why not. I didn't make up the rule."

"After she marries me she won't be a whore anymore."

Jonce offered Waz a cigarette but he declined. "Whores is always whores. Look at her over there with his hands all over her."

"She's only doing her job, Jonce Nash. She's got bills to pay."

"And little papooses running around all over the place I bet."

"No papooses. She's Mexican, not Indian."

"Pardon my ignorance," Jonce said. "Little wetbacks."

Wazenski frowned. "You shouldn't say that."

"She didn't hear me."

"But I heard you," Wazenski said. "And she's going to be my wife." He cut his eyes at her again. "Why do all you white people have to be racists?"

"You're white."

"I'm Polish."

"You look white to me," Jonce said, studying him. "Maybe if you trimmed your eyebrows a little you wouldn't look so much like a muppet."

Wazenski sighed. "I'm Caucasian but I'm Polish, meaning I understand what it's like to be discriminated against." He waved his hands in the air as if erasing the conversation. "Never mind. Juanita is a nice girl and she has no children and she is going to be my wife."

"Well if she keeps rubbing herself against that biker like she's doing she'll have children soon enough," Jonce said. "But like you said, never mind all that. Ain't my business if you marry a whore or a nun."

"You can't marry a nun without going to hell, Jonce Nash, and I don't want to go to hell so I'll marry Juanita."

Jonce looked in her direction again and gave a slow nod. "In that case you'll need money. Lots of money." He returned his attention to Wazenski. "And quick because Romeo just slid his hand up her skirt and she didn't flinch."

"I told you she's working. She has bills to pay. I fry chicken and she does what she does."

Jonce cut his eyes again. She wasn't bad to look at. "How much exactly does she get for *working*?"

"Fifty dollars for one hour. As much as the other two girls combined."

Jonce looked around for the other two but only saw one. She wore more makeup than Juanita and was a little heavier up top. "Two for the price of one," he said. He pointed his finger across the table at Wazenski. "You should rethink your future."

"A man can't marry two women."

"Maybe not, but with the kind of money I'm fixing to send your way you can sign 'em up on a lease." He flashed his best grin. "How does a quarter million United States greenbacks strike you?"

Waz's eyes lit up as he did the math in his head, using his fingers in some undecipherable pattern. A smile spread across his face. "For that amount of money I could have her younger sister."

"Good," Jonce said, looking around to make sure they weren't being listened to. "Now all you have to do is help me take care of a little problem."

The phone call Tuesday morning proved different in a terrifying way. Jackie had been in her office for all of twenty minutes when her cell phone rang with the familiar Detroit area code. She resisted the urge to answer for three rings, then answered on the fourth. Through the slow rhythmic in and out of the caller's heavy breathing, she heard the muffled chatter of a male voice in the background. Her cop senses kicked in and she managed to pick out a few words. *Unseasonably warm with a thirty percent chance of rain.* The line went dead.

"You okay?"

She looked up and saw her boss standing in the doorway. "Unseasonably warm with a thirty percent chance of rain," she said, repeating the phrase. "I thought I was onto something but it was just a weather forecast."

"Am I supposed to guess?"

"He called again," she said. "Same area code. Same heavy breathing, but this time he had the television on. Or a radio. Maybe he was driving in a car. He's getting careless."

Gant stepped in and closed the door, then he pulled the chair close to her desk and sat. "If you need a few days off —."

"No," she said. "That's the opposite of what I need. Work is the only thing keeping me sane." A thought occurred to her and she rapidly typed a Google search into her desktop computer. "The forecast for Detroit today is forty-two and clear." A chill went up her spine. She typed again. Her heart almost stopped. "Sixty-five with a thirty percent chance of rain for Hayes," she said. "He's here."

"Go home and get Jordan," Gant said, peeling a key from the ring he pulled from his pocket. "Take him straight to my place. That's not a suggestion, it's an order."

"You can't order me to move in with you."

"Stop wasting time."

She gathered her purse and stood. "We'll be fine at my apartment," she said. "I'm a cop. I'm not supposed to be scared."

"You're human. We all get scared."

"I've never seen you scared," she said.

"I'm scared right now," he said. "Now get moving. I can send a car with you if you want."

"No, I'll be fine."

"And you'll take Jordan and stay at my place until I get there?"

She took the key. "Yes." She was more scared than she was willing to admit. In fact she was terrified in a way that only a mother can understand.

Just then Gant's phone dinged in his pocket. He looked at the display and raised his eyebrows. "Gain Prichard says he's got something important for us on the Stubbs murder."

"Why did he text you instead of me?"

"Don't worry about that right now," he said. "He'll keep. Go be with your son."

She started for the door then stopped. "Jordan trusts you," she said. "He'll open the door for you if I call him."

"What's that supposed to mean?"

"If you go get him and take him to your house I'll know he's safe and I can go talk to Prichard."

"You're restricted to your desk, remember?"

"Only until you say otherwise." She offered him back his key. "Please don't make me explain why this is so important to me."

His eyes dropped to the key then up again as he weighed the consequences of her request. "Keep it," he said. "I've got a spare."

"Thank you. I'll call Jordan on the way and tell him you're coming."

"Okay, but then you call Timms and have him meet you here."

"I'd rather —."

"Call Timms. It's his case too, remember. Let's not burn any bridges unless we have to."

"He never answers when I call," she said.

"Leave a message."

"How long should I wait?"

"However long it takes," he said. "That's an order."

She waited almost an hour. When Timms arrived he offered no apologies and no excuses, he just stuck his head into her office and told her he was ready to go. They took his car and barely spoke during the ride over beyond him telling her to let him take the lead. Maybe it was because he was state and she was local, or because he was a he and she was a she, or because he was white and she was black. His reasons were his own. Her suspicions were hers.

She found Prichard to be an unlikable sort. A bastard. Big and loud and obnoxious. She had known plenty of men like him. Too many to count. Timms shook his hand and the two of them chit-chatted about the job as though putting bad guys in prison and helping them stay out amounted to the same thing.

He only had the one chair so Jackie stood. So much for chivalry. The boys exchanged man talk for what seemed forever. Eventually they fell silent and Timms took some initiative.

"About our murder."

Prichard's frat boy smile vanished. "Yes, about that," he said. "I've had my suspicions about Jonce Nash for quite some time now." He leaned back in his chair and made it scream. "When a man runs afoul of the law and gets caught, he either submits himself to the demands of society or he digs in his heels and bares his teeth and snaps at anything that moves." He clasped his hands behind his head and tilted his face toward the ceiling. "I get both kinds, and let me tell you there's no middle ground. Not a single man who comes through this office takes the center lane. I can read 'em like first grade primers. See Dick run. See Dick chase Jane."

"I don't dispute your expertise," Timms said. "But what does this have to do with Stubbs?"

Prichard feigned annoyance. "If you'll let me finish I was getting to that."

"By all means," Timms said. He glanced at his watch. "I've got a dentist appointment Friday so get to the point."

Jackie suppressed a smile. Prichard frowned. "I was simply trying to frame what I'm about to tell you with my years of experience dealing with degenerates. The information I'm about to give you is not what you detectives might call … concrete."

"So in other words you're hypothesizing," Timms said. "It means —."

Prichard collapsed forward and landed with his arms folded on his desk. Jackie almost mistook the move as an attack but Timms didn't flinch. "I know what the hell hypothesizing means!" He glared at the detective while he reset himself. Tension has a way of squeezing every nanosecond out of a pause. Eventually he cut his eyes to Jackie, seeming to notice her presence for the first time. "What I was trying to tell your partner, was that at the very outset I thought Jonce Nash was capable of murder."

"Why so?"

Prichard looked suddenly sad and shook his head. He was a terrible actor. Overly dramatic at all the wrong moments, like a soundtrack out of sync with the picture. "I sit at this desk and look across at every sort of scum imaginable. Murderers, thieves, child molesters … you name it and I've seen it."

"We see quite a bit of that ourselves," Timms said, trying to re-insert himself into the conversation.

"When *you* see it they're still claiming to be innocent," Prichard said. "By the time they get to me they don't give so much of a damn about appearances anymore. Sure, they may *say* their innocent but they know that I know better. And I *always* know better." He raised his eyes toward Jackie again and apologized for his language, then said he had no real evidence linking Nash to the murder, just a hunch based on Nash's strange behavior during their last meeting.

Jackie asked him to explain.

"He kept asking me if I thought Tipton Palo would ever go to prison for all the crimes he's committed. I told him I didn't know, then after a while I asked him why he cared, and he said that he didn't want Palo to go to prison. I think Nash may be gunning for him." He cut his eyes away from Jackie and focused on Timms, as if waiting for him to ask the question that would make the meeting understandable. Instead, Timms asked if he thought Palo paid Nash to kill Stubbs. Prichard's eyes widened. "Is that what happened?"

"We don't know," Jackie said quickly. "We're just trying to cover all the bases."

The three of them looked at each other in a sort of scrambled awkwardness. Prichard leaned back in his chair and made it groan again, stroking his chin between his thumb and forefinger until it turned red. "So that's why he was so nervous," Prichard said. "Nash said Palo was threatening him and he asked a lot of questions about self-defense and whether or not his being on parole meant he couldn't defend himself."

"Did you believe him?"

Prichard looked at Timms, who had asked the question, then back at Jackie. "Do you think maybe Nash did kill Stubbs and Palo found out about it somehow and now Nash is scared?"

"Anything at this point is possible," Jackie said. Prichard was trying too hard to steer them toward his Nash theory. Experience had taught her that when someone tries too hard they usually have a motive. What Prichard's motive might be she couldn't guess. Maybe he was just trying to get another ex-con off the streets and out of his hair. He struck her as the type.

Prichard stood abruptly and offered his hand to Timms. "I'd keep a close eye on Nash if I were you," he said as they shook, then he dismissed them with the clumsy excuse that he had lost track of time and had a newbie coming in for his first interview. "I have to come down hard on 'em at first," he said. "Scare the hell out of 'em and sometimes they stay in line for a while." He laughed from the belly and shook head to toe. "I think some of 'em break the rules just so they can go back and get away from me."

"Is that what you think Nash is doing?" Jackie asked. "Trying to get away from you?"

He shook his head slowly, side to side. "No, not him. That boy's too dumb to be scared. Too dumb to be stopped, too."

"Stopped from what?"

"Killing Palo, if that's what his angle is."

"Is that what you think his angle is?"

"That's exactly what I think," Prichard said. Jackie didn't believe him, but she was willing to let it play out.

"This ain't Detroit," Timms grumbled as he slammed his car door. "Down here the lead detective runs the interview." He twisted his head and looked at her with more annoyance than anger. "And in case your boss didn't tell you, I'm the lead detective in this case."

"No disrespect intended," Jackie said. "I had questions and I asked them. That's how I work."

"Not when you're working with me you don't."

"Prichard called my boss, not yours," Jackie said. "And I've worked cases with the FBI so you can lose the superior attitude. They don't work on me."

Through the windshield she saw Prichard dial the phone at his desk, then mouth what appeared to be an angry exchange. "Twenty bucks says he's talking to Palo," she said as Timms twisted the ignition and started the car.

"He could be talking to his mother for all we know," Timms said. He backed into the street without looking and almost hit a PT Cruiser in the passenger door. The driver swerved and blasted the horn without stopping. Timms sat immobile with his foot hard on the brake, glaring angrily at the steering wheel with his hands at ten and two. "See what you made me do?"

"Like it was my foot on the gas," she said, straining to choose her words wisely lest she find herself restricted to her desk again.

Timms eased the car back into the street then started forward. Neither of them spoke again until they reached the station and he switched the car off. "I apologize," he said without taking his eyes off the windshield. "It was me that almost hit the car, not you."

Jackie laughed. "Don't take this the wrong way," she said, "but you reminded me a little bit of my father back there. Every time he messed up driving he always blamed my mother."

Timms grunted and got out of the car. Jackie followed suit, hoping he wouldn't follow her inside the station. He did.

"We may as well brief your boss together," he said as they reached the door and she pulled it open.

"To make sure our versions match?"

"Something like that."

"What about your boss?"

"I'll handle that part alone," he said.

"Meaning he's not interested in my version?"

"Don't take it personal," Timms said. "To tell you then truth he's not much interested in mine either."

They both laughed and the tension between them vanished. Jackie wasn't ready to invite him over for dinner but she no longer felt the urge to punch him in the throat. She remembered that the chief was not in — he was out taking care of her son — so she suggested they call him from her office.

She called Gant and was quick to tell him he was on speaker with Timms in the room lest he blurt out something about Jordan. She already knew from a text he sent that her son was safe.

Timms gave his version of the interview first. It was a long, rambling, exaggerated account of an interview she only slightly recognized. He oversold Prichard at every level, even saying at one point that if the case got solved it might very well be because of the information gleaned from their interview.

When Jackie's turn to speak came she hesitated. Either she backed up what amounted to a lie, or she torched a bridge her boss had warned her not to burn. "I don't find Prichard very credible," she said. "He lacks candor if you ask me."

Timms gasped. "The man's practically one of us!"

She tried to choose her words carefully. "From my perspective he just wasn't believable. It has nothing to do with who he is or what position he holds. At times I felt like I was watching a B movie."

"That's absolutely ridiculous," Timms said, sitting on the edge of his seat now, leaning toward the phone between them as though being closer to it meant being more right. "You should put a detail on Palo."

"I don't have the manpower," Gant said. "You're welcome to bring in some of your boys."

Timms frowned but gave no audible reply.

"The evidence isn't there," Jackie said. "Or Prichard knows more than he's telling us, which I think's a no-brainer. He seemed nervous to me."

"He wasn't nervous," Timms said. "He was reluctant to give evidence against a man in his charge."

"Oh please."

"Let's not turn on each other," Gant said. "We're all on the same team here."

Jackie wondered if that were true, though she kept those sentiments to herself. She didn't believe Timms to be a bad man, though he did seem to have a chip on his shoulder. Not that long ago Gant had said the same thing about her. Prichard, on the other hand, reeked of corruption.

"The quickest way to close this case is to wire Prichard's office and have him bring Nash in again," Timms said. "Let the cocky bastard hang himself."

"Which cocky bastard?" Jackie asked. "Nash or Prichard?"

Timms gave her the eye. "Of course Prichard would have to cooperate," he said.

"And if Prichard and Palo are setting Nash up?"

"It's dog eat dog," Timms said. "Nash chose the life he's living."

"And if Palo paid for the murder we'll be helping him get off scott free."

"What a conclusion to jump to," Timms said. "No one said Palo paid Nash to do anything."

"Just connecting the dots," Jackie said.

"I like the idea of a wire," Gant said. "If Nash is innocent he has nothing to worry about."

Innocent seemed a strange word to use on Jonce Nash.

"Make sure Prichard understands the ground rules," Gant continued. "He's to bring Nash in and get him to incriminate himself."

Timms beamed with satisfaction.

But Gant wasn't finished. "After which we squeeze Nash to give up Palo."

"And Prichard," Jackie added. "We may as well kick over all the dominos."

Chapter Sixteen

Thursday at noon Jonce took delivery of a pizza he had not ordered. The boy double-checked the name and address on the ticket and confirmed that it had been paid for in advance, so Jonce gave him a dollar and sent him on his way, then he plopped down at his kitchen table with a beer from the fridge and fell into it before the delivery boy realized his mistake.

When he opened the box and saw pepperoni and cheese he felt jilted, but free was free and any pizza without pineapple was edible, so he downed the first piece without breaking for beer, then he took a quick swallow from the can and grabbed a second slice. As he lifted the triangle to his mouth he noticed something in the box that didn't belong. Sticking out from underneath the next slice was a small piece of clear plastic that looked to be the corner of a sandwich bag. Thinking he was about to call and complain and get a replacement with every meat they had in the kitchen, he flipped the slice and uncovered the baggie. Inside he saw what looked to be a receipt folded in half. He tossed the uneaten slice onto the table and retrieved the grease-slick sandwich bag and turned it over to examine the other side. Through the clear plastic and the thin white paper he saw something written with a pen but couldn't make out the letters. With great caution he fingered open the bag as though diffusing a bomb and fished out the note, expecting when he unfolded it to see a threatening message from Palo, or a warning from the female cop. Instead he saw a warning of a different nature. MEETING IS A STING. At first he didn't connect the dots, then he remembered that Prichard had called yesterday and rescheduled his Thursday afternoon to Friday morning, which was tomorrow. His first thought was to warn Prichard that the

186

cops were onto him lest he say something stupid and give them both away, then it occurred to him that Prichard might still be in cahoots with Palo, so he decided to let him sink or swim on his own. The art of trusting people is not to. Ever.

It didn't occur to him until several minutes later, after he had finished most of the pizza, to wonder who had warned him. He studied the problem over another beer and concluded that it had to be Palo. Who else would go to so much trouble? But why? Unless the meeting wasn't a sting at all and he simply wanted to shut Jonce up.

He closed the box and belched. Warning or no warning, Palo had to be dealt with and it would have to be done right. No half-baked operation was going to work against a man who had his hooks into so many people. The problem wasn't so much how, but when and where. Dead men don't talk, but killers leave clues no matter how careful they are. Timing and location are critical. Every advantage has to be seized. Cameras hide in the most ridiculous places.

Palo's law office was off limits. Too easy to be seen. Without a doubt he had cameras, and even if he didn't there would be one around somewhere to pick up his coming or going. It only takes one. Palo lived a short distance from his office so catching him on the street was out of the question. Even if he found a secluded spot there was the problem of stopping him and getting at him before he could call the cops. The devil of every plan is in the details. Surprise was his only option, and he had an idea that just might work. One that didn't involve the Polack, meaning there would be no messy tracks to cover. He had grown somewhat fond of the little man and didn't want to have to kill him. He especially didn't want to have to pay him.

Bobbie's door slammed. At first he thought she was home early, then he checked the stove clock and realized he had been sitting at the table for over an hour. He slipped from his chair and slinked to the wall. She made soft noises as she moved about her apartment. Female noises, like a cat trying to avoid the dog in the yard. He wrapped lightly with his knuckles and invited her over using his softest tone.

"Why should I?"

"I need a favor."

"I've got a headache."

"It's not that kind of favor."

"The answer's still no."

"I'll give you fifty dollars."

He knew he had her hooked when she hesitated. "You better not stiff me," she said, then half a minute later she knocked on his door. He opened it and invited her in but she stood her ground and demanded to see the money first. Jonce pulled two twenties and a ten from his pocket and waved the bills under her nose. She grabbed for them but he jerked the money away.

"Not so fast, sugar foot," he said. "Get in here before somebody sees you."

"You ashamed of me now?"

She wore jeans and a flimsy shirt with three buttons at the neck, all of them undone, and enough makeup to paint a hog. He offered cold pizza. She declined.

"You'd be halfway pretty if you'd smile every now and again."

"You've got two seconds to tell me the favor or I'm leaving."

"There might be two favors if you play your cards right."

She turned to go.

"Okay," he said. "The favor is you say I was home all evening if anybody asks."

She turned back. "Which evening?"

"Tonight, dummy," he said.

"Don't call me a dummy."

"Anybody asks, you tell 'em I was here when you got home from work and you heard me moving around until you went to bed at ten."

She looked confused. Being bright wasn't her superpower.

"That's the favor," he said. "And you have to be convincing."

"Let me guess," she said. "By *anybody* you mean the cops."

"By anybody I mean anybody," Jonce said. "Cops, firemen, the mailman, even that old deaf woman on the other side of me. Anybody means anybody."

"Why would the *anybody* believe I keep track of you coming and going?"

"Say you heard me singing or something. Tell 'em you kept banging on the wall telling me to shut up but I wouldn't. Not until ten o'clock."

She rolled her eyes. "And if they ask what song you were singing?"

"Songs," he said. "Lots of songs. From six until ten. Rolling Stones. I do a pretty good Mick Jagger."

"I could go to jail for lying to the cops," she said. "Fifty dollars ain't worth going to jail."

"That's just something cops say to scare people," Jonce said. "It only counts if you're under oath, and they can't put you under oath unless you swear on a Bible. Just don't swear on no Bibles and you're in the clear."

"Suppose they make me swear on the Bible?"

"Tell 'em you're an atheist."

She stuck out her hand for the money. He counted the bills into her palm.

"Especially mention that you heard me singing somewhere between six and seven. Got that? Six and seven. That's the most important part. And don't change your story because cops are tricky bastards."

"Care to tell me what I'm making myself an accessory to this time?"

"Never you mind that," he said. "Just say what I told you and don't say nothing else no matter how hard they prod."

Instead of going home after leaving his office, Tipton Palo drove in the opposite direction for three blocks then took a left. Jackie tailed him at a safe distance though the traffic was too sparse to conceal herself if Palo had the wherewithal to be careful. He struck her as a man so used to getting away with his illegal activities that he hadn't yet learned to think like a suspect, or perhaps he wasn't doing anything illegal at the moment. His destination might very well be the grocery store, or Walmart. Or, as it turned out, a local gym.

Midtown Gym anchored one end of a row of businesses and empty storefronts. There was a shoe store where all shoes were fifty percent off according to a sign in the window, a beauty salon with a full-time manicurist, and a tax preparation service with a bilingual sign above a yellow and red canopy. Palo parked two spots from the front door and entered the gym carrying a small gray gym bag. Had he looked back he might have seen Jackie's blacked-out Mustang parked in front of the flower shop across the street. She watched through a pair of miniature binoculars as he entered the building and disappeared toward the back. The heavy tint on her windows made her invisible but made the car conspicuous. The flower shop was closed and it was almost dark enough for the streetlights to start popping on so she backed into a narrow space between the flower shop and a large metal dumpster. Satisfied that she was sufficiently hidden, she shut off the engine and waited. Within a matter of minutes he reappeared wearing dark sweats and a ball cap that changed his appearance dramatically. If not for her binoculars he might have mounted the treadmill unnoticed.

He skipped the warmup and began his run. She stared at him and he stared at her, except that in all likelihood he saw only his reflection in the plate glass window. Fitting, she thought, for a man such as him, though she wondered if what he saw satisfied him as much as it probably had only a few short months ago. She had seen pictures. He was beginning to let himself go despite the treadmill.

Five minutes into his run a brunette mounted the treadmill next to him and quickly matched his speed. He turned and spoke to her. She smiled and spoke back. Jackie wished she could read lips. They both increased their speed. They never stopped talking. Even from a distance it was clear they were flirting. Was it more? The woman certainly wasn't his wife. Palo had a brother but no sister. Perhaps the woman was a friend. Men and women can be friends without sex being involved. Perhaps she was a client. His wife's sister. Jackie hadn't checked his wife's background. Whoever she was, they definitely knew each other. Were they brazen enough to meet so openly if they were lovers? Maybe their relationship hadn't reached that stage yet.

They ran awfully fast. The human body can accomplish great feats when the mind is focused on the task. It can endure enormous strain when the mind is distracted.

Jordan texted and asked when she was coming home. He was alone at the apartment again after spending Tuesday night and all day Wednesday at Gant's house. Stalker or no stalker, she couldn't relinquish control of her life by turning their safety over to a man she barely knew. Jordan, she told herself, was probably safer being alone in the apartment with neighbors close by than at her chief's secluded house with both of them working. She had wanted to bring him to the station but he balked at the idea. Stop treating me like a baby, he had told her. Is that possible for a mother to do? Ever?

She texted back and told him she would be home soon, then she reminded him not to open the door for anyone, no matter what, to which he replied with an emoji she didn't understand. It began to settle on her that no one knew where she was. She was off the clock. Tailing Palo was an unofficial act. Her stalker could be lurking in the shadows behind her at that very moment, sneaking closer with every passing second because she had provided him with the perfect opportunity. She checked her mirrors with increasing frequency as the chill of fear threatened to push the man on the treadmill into oblivion. A few minutes more, she told herself. The doors were locked. She had her weapon. Her radio. Her training.

She pulled her weapon from her purse and held it ready in her lap, allowing its heft to calm her. Fear became the enemy. Not the man who had tracked her from Detroit. Not her husband. Not Jonce Nash. Fear — the most patient of emotions.

Palo switched off his treadmill and dismounted, reclaiming Jackie's attention. The brunette slowed but didn't stop as Palo shrank from view and disappeared behind her. Exactly two minutes later she abandoned her machine and followed in the same direction. Only a handful of people were in the building. Five, exactly, if counting cars in the parking lot could fix the number. Jackie had seen four in total, but never more than three at any given time. It would be a simple thing for the brunette to join Palo for a quick shower, or perhaps a long one.

A single streetlight remained dark in the parking lot. Nightfall had coaxed the other three to life. There were none where she was parked, giving her fears a fertile playground. She checked her mirrors again but saw only darkness. A second text from Jordan startled her with its noise. He was hungry, but safe. Nothing short of a distress call from him was going to move her from that spot until she had completed her mission. Or was it simple curiosity now? Was there any value in knowing whether Palo left alone or with the brunette? She began to second-guess her motives. A cop who doesn't second-guess herself is too complacent. Her former captain had told her that, though at the moment she couldn't recall the context of the conversation. All manner of trivial thoughts pass through a person's mind when they are alone and idle.

Palo reappeared alone, dressed exactly as he had been when he arrived. Freshly showered, she assumed. It was too dark to tell if his hair was wet. He walked with the confidence of a man who has the world at his feet, then he folded himself into his small expensive car and sped away, leaving the brunette to do whatever women in her position do after the deed is done.

It was all conjecture, of course. She could have been a cousin. Deal with facts, Jackie reminded herself as she watched the taillights of his red Porsche fade into the darkness, wanting to follow but knowing she had duties more important. It was only a short drive to Palo's mansion. No sense following. The brunette had not left the gym. Jackie had not witnessed anything illegal.

❖

The plan was simple. Twenty feet up Palo's driveway from the street was a large steel gate anchored on each side by twin stone columns. The gate split in the middle and swung inward when activated. There was a pipe painted black anchored in a concrete pad at the edge of the driveway that rose to the height of a car window then protruded forward at an arc with a call box attached. A camera atop one of the stone columns pointed downward at the call box. The gate could be operated by remote control from within the house or either of the Palos' cars. Half an hour earlier the wife had returned home from wherever wives of rich men go when their husbands are away. She was a schoolteacher, but school had long since dismissed. It was full dark and the light that splashed against the gate was artificial. Soon, if he stuck to his routine, Palo would turn his flashy red car into the driveway and roll through the moving gate with the precision of a seamstress threading a needle, except this time the gate wouldn't open because Jonce had secured the two halves together with his leather belt at the bottom where it would be impossible for Palo to see without leaving his car to investigate. Naturally he would, being a man who wanted to get home, and his attention would be on the malfunctioning gate instead of the black-clad man darting from the ditch behind him with a tire iron bearing down on the back of his skull.

That was the plan.

Jonce had stolen the tire iron from the back of a pickup truck in the parking lot of his apartment complex and had not handled it without the gloves he now wore. His face was fully covered with a black ski mask, and he wore coveralls that he would douse with gasoline and burn in a dumpster behind a carpet store on the outskirts of town after the deed was done. The dumpster was full of cardboard and scraps of carpet and foam backing and its burning would attract every cop on duty the way a lamp attracts moths. Everything would burn. Boots, socks, gloves, coveralls, and ski mask. Even the belt had to be sacrificed. Anything that might connect him to the crime scene had to be completely destroyed, and what better place to do it than right under their noses?

Jonce prided himself on his ability to plan a job to perfection. Palo would get out of the car. Jonce would spring from the ditch as soon as his back was turned. He would reach Palo just as Palo reached the gate and saw the belt. He would strike Palo in the back of the head with the tire iron hard enough to bring him down but not hard enough to kill him. Blunt force trauma was too easy. Jonce wanted Palo to know he was dying. As soon as Palo's knees hit the concrete, Jonce would pull the plastic bag from his back pocket and force it over Palo's head, then he would secure it with duct tape from the roll he wore on his left wrist. For good measure he would tape Palo's wrists together behind his back, and if need be he would strike him in the head a second time.

He checked his watch. It was a Seiko that he stole from an insurance salesman back in his heyday. He considered it a good luck charm and only wore it when he pulled a job. It wasn't always lucky but it was incredibly accurate.

Palo was two minutes behind schedule. Jonce didn't worry because he had no place else to be.

A short time later, headlights slashed the darkness toward town. Jonce heard the sexy purr of the Porsche engine. He checked the other direction for traffic. Traffic was the one element of the job that Jonce couldn't control. Every job requires a certain degree of luck. Without risk there can be no reward.

The car slowed as it approached the driveway. The big gate trembled but didn't budge. Jonce's leather belt held.

Jackie had just put chicken in the oven when her phone rang and Chief Gant told her Tipton Palo had been brutally attacked in his driveway. She arrived on the scene just in time to see the helicopter lifting off with Palo aboard, en route to the hospital in Tupelo. The street was lined on both sides with emergency vehicles of every description. Local and state, as well as an ambulance, a fire truck, and at least a dozen volunteer first-responders. Red and blue lights exploded against the darkness like a light show run amuck.

She picked Gant out of the throng of people crowded around Palo's Porsche. The driver's door of the Porsche was open. Gant saw her walking up and stepped away to meet her. "Are you okay with going to the hospital and getting a statement from his wife?"

Jackie nodded that she was. It was her job to go, and she had never been one to shirk her duty.

"You can drop Jordan off at my place on your way," he said. "I'll get home as soon as I can."

"I'll take him with me," she said. "He can sit in the waiting room while I talk to her. He'll be safe there."

Gant gave her the rundown. Someone had split the back of Palo's head like a melon then sealed it with a clear plastic bag and two wraps of duct tape around his neck. No doubt about the intended outcome. Luckily his wife noticed something odd on the security monitor and investigated.

Jackie wondered aloud if the wife noticing had been accidental or planned.

"She seemed pretty upset about it," Gant said.

"Suppose she was watching on the monitor and got cold feet?"

Gant clearly hadn't considered the possibility. "Suppose for now we don't hit her with that question," he said. "Unless you know something you're not telling me."

She decided against telling her boss about her unofficial surveillance just yet. "I'll be gentle," she said. Interviewing the spouse is always tricky. "Do I get to do this one alone or do I have to take my shadow?"

"Alone," Gant said. "As far as we know this has nothing to do with the other murder."

"Other murder? Is he dead?"

"Not yet," he said. "All the more reason for you to get moving. If they tell her he's dead I wouldn't mind you being there to see her reaction."

"Any witnesses besides the wife?"

"Just the camera," Gant said, pointing toward the stone column that anchored one side of the gate. "I've got Ramey up there retrieving the DVR now. Mrs. Palo said she saw his car sitting here with the door open and thought it looked strange so she came to investigate."

"Instead of calling it in?"

"It always looks different in hindsight," Gant said.

Jackie looked toward the house, trying to guess how long it might take a wife to walk from there to the gate. It was a chilly night so she would have probably put on a jacket first. It doesn't take long to suffocate. It seemed a terrific coincidence.

"See that," she said, suddenly noticing the speaker on the call box. "Why didn't she call down to him instead of walking all this way in the dark?"

"Go ask her."

She left in a hurry, telephoning Jordan on her way back to the apartment with instructions to be ready. His first question had been were they moving again. Running was what he meant. No. Be ready.

He was full of questions when she picked him up. He begged her to take him by the crime scene so he could see the action. At the hospital he balked at the idea of sitting in the waiting room while she interviewed Mrs. Palo.

"If you move out of that chair I'll tan your hide," she said as she left him.

"How am I supposed to learn how to be a cop if you won't let me go with you?"

She stopped short and turned. "Why would you want to be a cop?"

He shrugged. "What else would I be?"

An elderly woman sitting nearby smiled at her. Jackie returned to her son and sat in the chair beside him. "You get this being a cop business out of your head," she said at a forced whisper. "You're going to college so you can be something important like a doctor or a dentist."

"Being a cop's important," he said.

"It's also dangerous and the pay is low. Be a scientist, or an engineer. Be a journalist. That's important. Tell people the truth they can't get anywhere else. Be something that makes a difference, like those doctors and nurses who are back there trying to save this man's life."

"Like you finding out who did it might save someone else's life?"

Jackie looked into his eyes, struggling for a way to get through to him that she wanted more for him than she had for herself.

"Sounds like someone is proud of his mother."

Jackie turned and saw the elderly woman still smiling at her. She smiled back. It hadn't occurred to her that her son might be proud of her. The idea seemed foreign somehow. She resisted the urge to tell the woman to mind her own business.

"We'll talk about this later," she said to Jordan.

Autumn Palo was sitting alone in a small room down the hallway from a set of doors that opened from the other side by a button pressed at the nurses' station. At first glance she showed all the signs of a grieving wife — red puffy eyes, tear-streaked mascara, a tissue wadded in her hand ready to tidy the nose when needed.

Jackie flashed her badge and introduced herself in the kindest manner she could summon, armed with knowledge about Mrs. Palo's husband that may or may not have factored into the attack. Jealousy is a powerful motivator. Revenge even more so. It wasn't her job to break up marriages.

Mrs. Palo dabbed at her nose with the tissue. "Can we do this some other time?"

"It's important that we do it now," Jackie said, then she rattled off the standard line about memories being the most accurate when they're fresh, and how in a crime such as this the first few hours are the most critical. Mrs. Palo glanced at her watch twice during the exchange. Did she have somewhere more important to be? Was she waiting for someone to arrive? Timing how long it took her husband to die?

Jackie dispensed with the most basic questions first — questions Mrs. Palo had already answered at the crime scene. The important thing was to see if the answers changed.

Jackie: "When did you first suspect something was wrong?"

Mrs. Palo: "I happened to look out the window and I saw headlights at the gate. The gate was closed so I went to the monitor in the den. That's when I saw Tipton's car sitting there with the door open and I thought it was strange."

Jackie: "Is that when you went outside?"

Mrs. Palo: "No, not at first. I called out to him over the speaker but he didn't answer. I thought something was wrong with the gate so I opened it from inside. When he didn't return to his car I went to see what was keeping him."

"Why didn't you call nine-one-one?"

"It didn't occur to me."

"Weren't you afraid going out alone in the dark with your husband missing?"

"He wasn't missing. His car was there so I knew he had to be ... I thought he ... may have been talking to someone."

"Did you have reason to believe he may have been talking to anyone in particular?"

Mrs. Palo averted her eyes.

"Was your husband having an affair?"

Mrs. Palo twisted her hands in her lap before making eye contact again. "You would think with all that's happened ... with all he's been accused of ... that a silly thing like that wouldn't bother me."

"Do you know her name?"

"No. I don't even know if it's true. I suspected him. That's why I walked down to the gate." She wrung her hands again. "To be honest, I told you a little white lie. I didn't call out to him over the speaker. I didn't even open the gate until I got down there. There's a box on

196

both sides."

"So you tried to sneak up on him … to catch him in the act."

Mrs. Palo nodded.

"This is very important, Mrs. Palo. At any time did you see anyone at the gate with your husband?"

Tears flooded the grieving woman's eyes. Whatever role she played or didn't play in the scene that unfolded at the gate, she was racked with pain. "I saw someone. Just a glimpse on the monitor. I thought it was my husband but now I realize it wasn't. The way he moved — it was too fast to be Tipton." She looked at Jackie with pleading eyes. "Did I see the man who murdered my husband?"

Jackie had inquired at the nurses' station about his condition. "Your husband's still alive, Mrs. Palo. They have very good doctors here."

Mrs. Palo blew her nose into the tissue then wiped her eyes with the back of her hand, smearing mascara like kindergarten paint. "They won't tell me anything but I see it in their faces. For the life of me I don't know why I care after all he's done." She sniffed again. "I ripped the bag with my fingers so he could breathe."

"Was he conscious?"

"No. I thought he was dead until I heard him gasp. He never opened his eyes. There was blood everywhere. I thought he'd been shot."

"You saved your husband's life, Mrs. Palo."

Mrs. Palo dabbed at her eyes with a fresh tissue from the box beside her. "I don't know why I should care very much." She stiffened herself. "Tell me, detective, am I a suspect? We're getting a divorce you know. I don't know why I cared who he was with at the gate. It's over between us."

"It's never easy," Jackie said. She had not yet filed her own divorce papers.

Mrs. Palo looked at her very directly. "You haven't answered my question."

"Until we rule you out, yes. It's routine."

"I understand. I should've called the police instead of going down to the gate myself. I realize how that must look to you."

"Your husband has a lot of enemies," Jackie said. "Had you not gone out to check on him he would be dead right now."

"He didn't do some of the things they're accusing him of." She dabbed her nose again. "Sure, he did plenty, but not everything. He's a good man."

Jackie understood the statement. Admitting failure doesn't come easy. She recalled all the times she had made excuses for Kelton. "Do you have any idea who may have wanted to harm your husband?"

A hard change gripped her face. "Can I list the ones who don't instead?"

"I know it's difficult right now but it's important that you try," Jackie said.

"Did you know they invited us *not* to attend church anymore? *Our* church. My husband practically built the recreation hall out of his own pocket."

"Have you heard your husband mention the name Jonce Nash?"

Mrs. Palo's face grew hard. "I've heard the name."

"Do you remember in what context? Was he ever at your house?"

"No."

She was lying. Jackie felt certain of it. Her reaction to the name had emotion behind it. Either pain or anger, she could not yet tell, but it was harsh. Too harsh not to be personal. Jackie decided to keep her suspicion in her pocket for now.

On the way home Jackie called Gant and gave him the rundown, including her hunch that they should take a hard look at Nash. Mentioning him as a suspect almost seemed redundant.

"He's certainly on the list," Gant said. "Whoever it was did a good job covering his tracks. So far we've got nothing."

She asked about the surveillance video.

"Palo falls into view after the blow to his head," Gant said. "Then a man dressed like a ninja pulls the bag over his head and secures it with duct tape. Maybe we'll find some DNA on the bag or the tape but it's a long shot. This guy was careful. After taping the bag over Palo's head the suspect goes toward the gate and out of the frame for a few seconds. Next time we see him he's carrying something — a strap of some kind — in his right hand. He probably used it to tie the gate so it wouldn't open. Good thing for our victim he didn't leave it behind or the wife might not have gotten the gate open in time."

"I tailed him this afternoon," Jackie said. "He went to the gym and appeared to be friendly with a woman."

"Nash?"

"Palo. I would've followed him home but Jordan called and said he was hungry. I could've caught this guy."

"I don't remember authorizing overtime."

"I was off the clock."

"I see," he said. "Turn in your time and put what you saw in your report. And no more freelancing. It's too dangerous."

"Would you say that if I were a man? Never mind. That was out of line."

"Borderline insubordination," he said. "Knock it off. You're better than that."

"Am I?"

"You'd better be. I put my neck on the line with the mayor."

"I thought it was the other way around."

"Whichever way it was, we both took a chance on you and I'm the one who'll have to answer for it if you screw up, so knock it off and work the case."

"This woman Palo was with could be a lead," she said. "Maybe she's got a jealous husband."

"See if the gym requires its members to use access badges," he said. "If we're lucky we'll get a name without having to jump through the hoops of getting a court order."

Getting the name would be easy. Jackie excelled at prying information out of business owners who hid behind privacy rights. Business owners fear code enforcement the way everyone else fears the IRS. No one likes having their shorts checked.

"What's your take on the wife?" Gant asked.

"Possible suspect," Jackie said. "She certainly had motive. He practically ruined her life, plus he's cheating on her."

"Do I sense a *but* coming?"

"But I didn't really get that vibe from her. She's hiding something — I'm sure of that — but I don't think she hired someone to kill her husband. And she did save his life."

"Her behavior in the video looked legitimate." Gant said. "Either she's a good actor or she had no idea what she was walking up on."

"She could easily have stayed in the house," Jackie said.

"Or walked slower. Another thirty seconds and he would have been dead."

"Him dead saves her from a very messy divorce," Jackie said. It was the cop in her talking, not the woman. She didn't believe Autumn Palo tried to kill her husband.

Chapter Seventeen

J once walked into Prichard's office loaded with the knowledge that every word he was about to utter would be listened to by the cops and recorded for posterity. He had studied on it all night, trying to concoct something to keep them chasing their tails instead of chasing him.

It struck him as strange that the morning news hadn't mentioned Palo. Surely they had found the body by now. School had started so the missus would have left for work and she couldn't very well have driven over him. Or could she? Not the car, but him. She probably wanted to. Maybe they would pin her as a suspect and take the easy way out.

"You're late," Prichard said.

"It's my feminine side showing."

"Sit down and shut up until I tell you to talk," Prichard said. He was nervous. Laden with guilt because of what he was about to do. Jonce could smell the deception on him. He had the look of a dirty rat about to make off with all the cheese.

Jonce sat. "If this is about me getting a job I already told you --."

"Did I tell you to talk yet? Did I?"

Jonce zipped his lip and threw away the key the way he had done when he was a boy. Prichard adjusted himself straight in his chair and rubbed at his nose with a knuckle. "Tipton Palo's saying you killed Perry Stubbs, Jonce. Claims he can prove it."

"Okay."

"Doesn't that make you nervous?"

"Why should I be nervous? I ain't done nothing."

"Says he can prove it."

Jonce threw his leg up on the arm of the chair. "If he could prove it I'd be in jail instead of here jawing with you. He's a liar. He ain't got nothing on me because they ain't nothing on me to get."

"Look Nash," Prichard said in a suddenly father-like manner. "If you did do something then it'll go easier on you if you get out in front of it. I can help you."

"Why would you help me?"

"It's my job."

"Helping me's your job?"

"Well, sure it is."

Jonce sat up straight and summoned all the seriousness he could muster. "Well, if that's how it is Mister Prichard then I guess I'd better come clean with you." He watched Prichard's face grow stiff with worry at what he might say. "I ain't done nothing. N-O-T-H-I-N-G. Nothing." He slouched back to his former posture. "Now let Tipton Palo bring his evidence."

Prichard sighed. "You need to think about your future, Jonce. If Palo's telling the truth it could be a one-way ticket back to Parchman for you. They might give you the needle."

Jonce pulled a cigarette from his shirt pocket and stuck it between his lips.

"You can't smoke that in here."

Jonce struck a match and stared into the flame. "You know they used to make matches you could strike anywhere? On the side of your boot, a fence post, even on a fingernail."

"Don't light that cigarette."

Jonce moved the flame close to the tip. "John Wayne could strike a match on a horse's ass. Didn't matter if they'd just swum a crick. Hell, Clint Eastwood could look at a match and it'd strike itself." He lit his cigarette and waved out the match just as the flame reached his thumb. "No, sir, they don't make matches like they used to." He tossed the charred stick to the floor, took a deep drag, then blew smoke straight up toward the ceiling. "There is some evidence Palo's got," he said. "But it ain't agin *me*."

A primal noise escaped Prichard's throat. "We're done here!" he bellowed. "Get out!"

Jonce winked. "Want me to tell you exactly who oughta be afraid of Palo talking?"

Prichard slapped his desk with the flat of his hand. "Dammit Nash, did you kill Perry Stubbs or didn't you? Tell me straight out and stop jerking me around!"

"What I was about to say was —."

Prichard shot up like he had been kicked in the seat of his pants. "Get out before I throw you out with my bare hands!"

Jonce smelled fear on Prichard like a three day sweat. The man was in over his head but he was too dumb to know it yet. Jonce collected himself up out of his chair and stubbed his cigarette out on the corner of Prichard's desk, eyeing him with a grin as he turned for the door. If the cops weren't interested in Prichard before, they sure would be now. It was a dangerous game for Jonce to play, but Gain Prichard had to be brought to heel.

Jackie stared at the monitor on her chief's desk in disbelief as Jonce Nash stood up and left Prichard's office in real time. She sat on Gant's right. Timms sat to his left. The live stream was effectively over, though their technician had not yet cut the feed. Prichard appeared completely disheveled.

"What the hell was that?" Jackie asked the room, leaning back, palms up as though she were about to be handed a package.

"That," Timms said with an apathetic sigh that Jackie thought overdone, "was a great big waste of our time." He was the first to stand. "No need to watch the credits roll on this movie."

"Are you serious?" She couldn't believe his reaction. "You don't think Prichard's hiding something?"

"Based on what? Bad acting?" He stepped around the desk then turned. "Nash was suspicious from the moment he came through the door." He took another step and turned again. "Not that he knows anything worth telling. The man's a two-bit hustler and petty thief."

"And quite possibly the man who murdered Perry Stubbs," Jackie said.

Timms laughed. "Jonce Nash doesn't have the brains to kill a gnat. Corey Pickle murdered Stubbs. We should be looking for him instead of wasting our time settling personal scores." He resumed his exit with Jackie seething.

"Get back here," Gant said as Timms reached for the door. "And be careful how you talk to my detective."

Timms turned and glared at the chief. "Or what?"

"Or I'll call your boss and have you removed from my town," Gant said.

"Ha! I'd like to see you try it." Timms opened his jacket to reveal the badge attached to his belt. "In case you've forgotten, this is a state badge and Stubbs is *my* case."

Gant picked up his phone.

"Okay," Timms said. "No need getting anybody else involved." He looked at Jackie. "I was out of line and I apologize."

Gant dropped the phone back into the cradle. "Jonce Nash knew this meeting was a sting before he walked in. He played Prichard like a cheap fiddle."

Timms stepped back to the desk but didn't sit. "Okay, let's assume you're right. So how did he know? Who tipped him off?"

"Had to be Prichard," Jackie said. "Or one of us three. No one else knew."

Timms frowned. "It certainly wasn't me. What about that kid who set up the equipment?"

"Not a chance," Gant said. "Ray left a good job installing car stereos to become a cop. I can promise you he took a pay cut."

"There's more than one way to make money as a cop," Timms said.

"He lives in the same single-wide trailer he's lived in for years," Gant said. "If he's taking payoffs he's awful slow about spending it."

"Nash has something on Prichard," Jackie said. "I can smell it."

"Seemed that way to me too," Gant said.

"And I think you're seeing something that's not there," Timms said. "The way Prichard behaved is more common than you think. People get nervous when they're wired. I've seen it a thousand times."

"That wasn't nerves because he was wired," Jackie said. "He's scared of something."

"So we do a deep dive into Prichard," Gant said. "Scour his financials. Find out who he associates with. Who he owes money to."

"You can't be serious," Timms said. "He's one of us. My father was a parole officer. It's a thankless job. The cons hate you for making them follow the rules and the cops treat you like a security guard."

"Prichard's not your father," Gant said. "Jackie can take the lead if you're not comfortable with it."

"I've never let my personal feelings prevent me from doing my job," Timms said. He looked at Jackie. "Unless you don't trust me, in which case I'll make myself scarce and let you lead."

"Trust is a two way street," Gant said. "We need all hands on deck. Whoever murdered Stubbs is still on my streets and I want him off."

"In that case I'll check Prichard's undershorts for stains," Timms said, reaching for the door. This time Gant didn't stop him. After he left, Gant asked Jackie if she thought Timms was dirty.

"I think he's staring at retirement and getting lazy," she said. "Probably thinks he should've made captain by now." Her cell phone rang in her purse. It was Jordan. He was breathless when she answered, talking in incoherent bursts. Her blood turned to ice. "Calm down," she said, trying to remain calm herself. Panic makes every situation worse. "Take a breath." Gant touched her arm. She glanced at him and saw the concern in his eyes. She heard the word apartment and shot to her feet with Gant suddenly at her side. She was out the door and running toward the exit before she realized she had moved. "Is he still there? How long has he been gone? What did he look like?"

Gant was on her heels every step of the way. Roy Birch had appeared from nowhere and was running too. She heard Gant ordering all units to her apartment over the radio he had grabbed from his desk. When she threw open the door the sunlight hit her in the eyes and temporarily blinded her. Gant grabbed her arm and steered her toward his car. She didn't resist because she knew she was in no condition to drive.

Jonce sat on his couch with his bare feet propped on the coffee table and a soap opera playing out on his television. An empty plate with the crumbs of a bologna sandwich lay on the cushion next to him as he clanked the ice in his glass and wished he had just one more sip of Coke to wash the last remnants of bread from his teeth. The kitchen seemed a mile away, relaxed as he was. Proud of the way he had handled Prichard. Knowing — feeling — it had been Prichard who sent the pizza with the note.

A funny idea struck him. He called up the pizza joint and ordered a large with everything to be sent to Prichard's office. The part that made it funny was the note he had asked the kid on the phone to put underneath the pie. "Say thanks for the warning and write it sloppy so he can't read it then put it underneath so the grease can get to it."

"Huh?"

Jonce laughed. "It's an inside joke between friends," he told the kid. "Add a ten-dollar tip for yourself."

He gave the location of Prichard's office, then rattled off the long series of numbers from the preloaded credit card he had purchased at the corner store the day before. Jonce had never had a real credit card before, preferring to keep his business transactions unrecorded, but the preloaded cards allowed him to function in an ever changing world.

Just then the wail of a siren pierced the walls of his apartment and pulled him from the couch to the tiny kitchen window where he looked out and saw two cop cars wheel into the parking and race toward the building. When they stopped he could see the tail of one and nothing of the other through his window. Within seconds another car arrived with the same urgency, then another. They were making a show of it. He let the curtain fall back into place and unbolted his door so maybe they wouldn't knock it down. Getting the landlord to fix anything was like getting the prison cook to salt the potatoes.

He stripped naked and stretched out on the couch with his hands behind his head and his feet propped and crossed on the arm. If they were going to haul him out he may as well have some fun with it, especially if that pretty little sip of coffee from downstairs was with them. Of course she would be. They'd probably pin him down with half a dozen knees in his back while she clamped the cuffs tight enough to make his wrists bleed, mad as hell because their ruse hadn't worked, knowing they couldn't hold him because all they had was a body and a video of a man perfectly concealed. It wouldn't matter that the man he had killed topped their most-wanted list. Cops are funny that way.

He laughed continuously as he waited. He wanted to be laughing when they burst in so he kept it up. Laughing, then breathing, then laughing again, refusing to stop until he saw their pitiful faces. Minutes passed. Where were they? Why hadn't they come? He laughed harder. Louder. They were probably massed outside his door afraid to come in. Afraid of Jonce Nash. Killer extraordinaire.

Jackie burst through the door of her apartment and found her son standing in the middle of the living room trembling, the way he had stood outside her bedroom door and trembled the first time he saw his father hit her almost three years ago. He had seen it many times since, but that first time had robbed him of his innocence. Kelton had lost a lot of money on a bad investment and had come home in a foul mood, slamming doors and complaining about everything that crossed his path. They had dinner reservations and Jackie was just getting out of the shower when he came into the bedroom and threw his coat and tie on the bed instead of hanging them up the way he always did. Kelton was meticulous with his clothes. Wrinkles were the bane of his existence. The little man with the hat who ran the dry cleaning store around the corner from Kelton's office probably cringed every time he came in to pick up his suits because her husband always complained. She had asked him once why he gave his dry cleaner such a hard time. Their marriage was young and she wasn't afraid back then. If you don't complain they'll get complacent and stop paying attention to detail was his answer. It should have been a warning of things to come.

Chief Gant and half of Hayes PD followed her into the apartment and flooded every room. Any one of them would have given his life to protect her son. It was an empowering feeling to be surrounded by the blue wall of which she was a part, yet she wondered whether or not that wall could protect her son from the only man in the world she feared. As she held her trembling son, she thought about the mothers who weren't cops. Mothers who stood alone against their Keltons, at the mercy of a legal system designed to react to crime instead of prevent it. The entire ordeal had been a blur.

She felt a firm hand on her shoulder.

"We need a description," Gant said in his easy manner. She wondered how calm he would be if it had been his son who had been attacked. He couldn't know how she felt because he didn't have children. He couldn't possibly know, but he was right. Every second counted. Every second the would-be abductor remained free increased his chances of escape. She forced herself to release her son and step back. Her training took over and she nodded permission for Gant to do his job. Gant was precise and thorough, but Jordan's answers were mostly head shakes and shoulder shrugs. The only question he answered with any certainty was that he had never seen the man before, then more specifically that it was not Jonce Nash. As if reading her mind, Gant told the men to start knocking on doors. It was early afternoon so most of the apartments were empty but she had a few neighbors who would be home.

"Stay away from Nash," he said as the men began to filter out. Jackie understood why. Jordan was certain it wasn't him, and Nash wouldn't tell them anything even if he knew, or he might feed them false information and send them on a wild goose chase. Better to let him wonder. Make him think they were asking the neighbors about him.

Jordan began to calm down after the room cleared and it was just the three of them. Gant moved to the doorway and stood looking out into the parking lot.

"I'm sorry," Jordan said, unable to look his mother in the eye. "I know I wasn't supposed to go outside."

She grabbed him by the shoulders and shook him without meaning to. He raised his eyes to meet hers. "I'm not mad at you for going outside," she said. "What happened isn't your fault."

He dropped his eyes again.

"I need you to think," she said. "Picture him in your head and tell me what he looked like. What was he wearing? What color was his hair? His eyes? Did he have a big nose or a small one? Did you see any tattoos or scars? Anything at all that might help us catch him?"

"His nose looked kinda funny," he said.

"Funny how?"

He shrugged. "Just funny. Like it was bent or something. And his shirt was dark. Black maybe, or gray."

"Did you see what he was driving?"

"The car was blue."

"Light or dark?"

"Medium." His eyes suddenly brightened. "It was a Chevrolet."

"Are you certain?"

"I remember seeing the bowtie in the grill." He looked over at Gant, who had turned to watch them, and smiled.

"Did you see the license plate?"

He shook his head. "I only saw the front of the car."

"We should check all the car rental places in Tupelo and Oxford," Jackie said to her boss, knowing that Hayes didn't have any.

"He would have flown into Memphis," Gant said. "The shuttle to Tupelo is more trouble than it's worth and Oxford doesn't have one at all."

She knew it would be an uphill battle to get information from the Memphis rental companies without a court order, and no judge was likely to grant one based on a hunch.

"There's probably a lot of blue Chevrolets between here and Memphis," Gant said.

Jackie knew the odds of catching him were low. "We'll have to move. We're not safe here."

"If he found you here he'll find you in the next town," Gant said. "We've been over this already."

"Thanks for the reassurance."

"Sooner or later you're going to have to make a stand."

"And you think I should make it here. I get it, but you don't know everything."

"Here's as good a place as any. You've got people here who've got your back. You saw how the men reacted. They're working their tails off right now trying to catch this guy. He'll expect you to run. Do the opposite. You can stay at my place until it's over."

"I can't."

"Why not?"

Her brain swirled with a thousand reasons why not. He was her boss and people would talk. He might even get the wrong impression himself. Some men get caught up in playing the role of protector and mistake gratitude for romantic desire. She had never had a male friend because men don't know how to be friends with women. Men don't know how to be anything but conquerors.

"I just can't," she said.

"I'm tired of running," Jordan said. "Why can't we stay with him?"

Gant smiled. "See? I'm not so bad."

"It won't look right," she said. "People will talk."

"Let them talk," Gant said.

"You say that now, but wait until they start calling the mayor."

Gant laughed. "I wish they would."

"Please," Jordan said. "I like it at his house."

"Consider it protective custody," Gant said.

"We'll go to Birmingham."

"That's the first place he'll look."

She knew he was right. Kelton had found her in Hayes. He would find her anywhere. Her best option was to stand her ground and fight. "Okay," she said. If Kelton forced her to fight she would rather not have to fight alone.

Chapter Eighteen

J once kept the television on for noise. Back in the day, the Saturday morning fare would have been cartoons — Bugs Bunny and the Road Runner, or Tom and Jerry. Something funny. By noon there would be wrestling out of Memphis, or basketball. These days he had fifty cable channels and nothing to watch except twenty-four-hour news and infomercials. There were movies if you could stand the endless commercials. He couldn't.

It was too early to drink. When he was in prison he used to lie on his bunk and dream of a cold bottle of beer. In prison he would have drank it for breakfast, but now that he was out, and could, he didn't want to. That's the way life is. The things out of reach are the most attractive. A man dreams of something he can't have, then he gets it and suddenly finds he doesn't want it anymore. At least not for breakfast.

He had no particular plans now that Tipton Palo was dead. They couldn't link him to Stubbs now. Not to his murder anyway. From here on out it would be smooth sailing. Prichard couldn't touch him. Nobody could.

A commercial came on, then a teaser for the midday news. The old man with the walrus mustache said the words *attempted murder* with a headshot of Tipton Palo hovering over his left shoulder. Jonce sprang from the sofa without knowing where he was going, then he sat down again. It had to be a trick. Cops are tricky bastards when it comes to dispersing information. They were trying to trick him into doing something stupid. It was a tactic they used in all the cop shows. Make a man think someone he killed didn't die, then hide and wait for him to come finish the job. No sir, he wasn't falling for it. Not Jonce Nash.

Palo was dead all right. No two ways about it.

In the minutes after the teaser, he grew worried. The cops in Hayes weren't smart enough to invent a story like that. Somehow Palo had worked himself free. Maybe he had come to and ground his face against the concrete and ripped the bag so he could breathe. He should have hit him harder, or used a better-quality bag.

He spent the remainder of the morning racking his brain trying to reconstruct the attack in minute detail. Had he made a mistake? Another mistake, that is, other than the obvious one. One mistake leads to another, and the one he had made was a humdinger. Mistakes accumulate. They breed. Had he shown himself to the camera? Every inch of flesh was covered, but had he shown his eyes? Had he looked up into the camera and given them enough to do a retinal scan? The things cops can do with technology these days are incredible. They have too much power. More power than the Founding Fathers intended. Freedom died with the high definition camera.

Jonce looked around for his cigarettes and fired one up. Not being dead didn't mean Palo was up and walking around. There's a lot of possibilities between alive and dead. He replayed the downward swing of the tire iron, remembering the sound of Palo's skull cracking, like dropping an emu egg on pavement. In the dark it was hard to tell how severe it was, but the blow had dropped Palo like a sack of flour, and there was blood. Alive could mean vegetable. A man can't go more than a few minutes without air before his brain begins to die. He might be alive with just enough brain activity to know he's not dead. Suffering. Conscious but unable to speak or move or, most importantly, give a statement to the cops.

A lot of people had reason to want Tipton Palo dead. A lot of people. It was an indisputable fact.

Jonce was nervous and smoked the cigarette all the way to the filter, then he stubbed the butt out on the coffee table and left it there to smolder. The wooden table was peppered with old burns and scratches. Every piece of furniture in the place was either scratched, torn, or broken. What did he care about another burn on a table he didn't own?

For some unexplained reason he thought of his mother. Maybe it was the table. His mother would have gone ballistic if his old man had snuffed a cigarette on her coffee table. She would have yelled until she was blue in the face, then she would have broken down into tears and cried like a baby. Afterwards she might have recited a verse or two from the Bible, slinging God at the old man like a club. Life had slapped her back and forth like a ping pong ball. It was all peaks and valleys with her, never flat ground where she could take her feet off the pedals and coast. She was good, though. All mothers are good. Maybe when things settled down he might call her and let her know he was out of prison. His parents had moved to Florida when he was eighteen and he wasn't big on keeping in touch. They didn't seem to mind. He had visited them a few times when Ellie was still alive. Ellie liked the beach and was always nagging him to go, using his parents as an excuse when they both knew his mother had never approved of her. It didn't seem to bother Ellie — not being approved of. It was probably old hat to her.

He fished another cigarette from the pack and smoked it. Prichard crossed his mind. Thanks to certain documents from Palo's safe sticking to Jonce's fingers, Prichard was still a free man. Palo could change that with a simple statement to the prosecutors in exchange for consideration, then Prichard might deal Jonce into the pile. Every little bit helps when the boot of justice is on your neck. Every little easing up helps you breathe better. Maybe Prichard didn't know that yet. He didn't strike Jonce as an especially bright man. Most big men aren't. Very few get to have it all. Jonce wasn't a mountain but he had brains, and with brains a man can move a mountain.

A Mississippi state trooper stopped a blue Chevrolet Malibu barreling toward Memphis on I22 between Holly Springs and Potts Camp just before daylight Saturday morning. It was doing eighty-five in a seventy, and the man behind the wheel had a Michigan license. The car was registered to Hertz.

Jackie didn't recognize the name David Regal Sansing. A quick background check turned up a slew of low-level street crimes in Detroit. Drug possessions, petty theft, and more than a dozen simple assaults. An old contact she had with anti-crime knew him as a street hustler with more ambition than brains. There was no need for her to hide from her Detroit friends now. Her husband knew exactly where she was. How, she didn't know, but the immediate threat was that he knew.

It was a little past two in the afternoon when Sansing arrived in Hayes. Gant had sent Ray Cline to Holly Springs to fetch him, then he had taken charge of the interrogation personally, not allowing Jackie in the room for obvious reasons. Less obvious were his reasons for not using the room with the two-way mirror. Jordan had positively identified the suspect as the man who tried to abduct him.

She fumed as she waited outside the closed door behind which her boss questioned the man who had almost taken her son. Was he asking the right questions? Did he understand the makeup of a big-city street thug? Was Gant being played?

Forty-five minutes slogged past with them locked away and her standing in the hallway. Sansing should have lawyered up by now. Surely he knew the drill.

At the fifty minute mark the door opened and Gant stepped out into the hallway. His face was impossible to read.

"Well?"

He shook his head.

"Nothing?"

"Nothing we didn't already know," he said.

"You spent an hour with him and he didn't say anything?"

Gant looked at his watch. "Fifty-two minutes and thirteen seconds, and no, he didn't say much."

"What *did* he say?"

"Take Jordan and go home," Gant said. "There's nothing for you to do here."

"You should've let me sit in."

"Go home."

"Maybe there's something you missed," she said. "I've interviewed hundreds of men like him. I know how they think."

Gant took her by the elbow and stepped away from the door. "We've got criminals down here, too," he said. "I'm not letting you blow this case." She didn't object to his grip on her elbow. It wasn't menacing in any sort of way. He wasn't trying to overpower her. Physical contact between the sexes isn't always one extreme or the other, sex or assault. Gant was simply leading her away from a place she had no business being, but she wasn't concerned about a conviction. She didn't care if David Regal Sansing went to jail or not. He was nothing more than an actor in a play. Jackie wanted the director. She wanted Kelton.

They reached her office where Jordan had been waiting since morning. Gant released her arm. "Take him to my house. I'll be home after I've finished the paperwork."

"You're awfully determined for us to stay with you."

"Your apartment's not safe," he said. "It's time you stop being tough and start being smart."

"What happens to him?"

"He'll be charged with attempted kidnapping and assault on a minor," he said. "And anything else I can think up when I get back to my office."

"Did you offer him a deal?"

"Go," he said. "This ain't my first rodeo."

"I didn't mean to imply —."

"Yes you did," he said. "And I don't blame you. Now take Jordan and go back to my place." He fished his keys from his pocket and peeled the house key off the ring.

"Why are you doing this?"

"Which part?"

"Being overprotective. Is it because I'm a woman?"

"Yes."

She had expected a different answer. "Are you always so honest?"

"No."

Jordan looked up from his portable game console and said he was hungry. "Officer Birch brought you Burger King two hours ago," she said.

"He brought me a kiddie meal."

"Well a kiddie meal is better than no meal," she said. "Gather your things. We're going —." She glanced back at Gant. "We're going back to Chief Gant's house."

Jordan smiled.

"But only for tonight," Jackie said. She didn't want either of them thinking the arrangement was permanent. While Jordan gathered his things, she and Gant stepped back out into the hall. "Sansing won't give up my husband."

"Then he'll learn how hot a Mississippi summer can be in jail," Gant said. "Maybe that'll change his mind."

Jackie figured they had a decent chance of getting a judge to deny bail since he had no connection to Hayes. If he made it back to Detroit he would disappear and never be heard from again. Kelton would see to that. Summer was three months away.

"He'll keep sending people until they get me," she said.

"All the more reason for you to stay with me."

"Kelton has important friends. The mayor is a regular at his parties."

"You keep telling me that as though it matters. Detroit should have our mayor. He doesn't go to anybody's party. Drives the Joneses crazy."

"Do you go to their parties?"

"Detectives don't get invited to those parties," he said. "No offense. And I haven't been chief long enough to make the list."

Gant stayed behind while she took her son home. Home being Gant's house, which was cozy but not elaborate. He lived the way one might expect an honest cop to live. His street had no painted lines and his driveway was gravel. A privacy fence separated him from his neighbors in the rear and both sides. The front was open to the street. No sidewalk. Logistically it would be harder to defend against the next David Regal Sansing than her apartment. Jordan could scream his head off and no one would hear.

When Gant came home she had dinner waiting. Supper, he called it. Chicken spaghetti with green beans and diced potatoes. He ate without complaint or compliment, though Jordan turned up his nose at the vegetables. Afterwards Gant helped her clean the kitchen without discussing the case. The avoidance of it was both obvious and welcomed to her. The fatigue of worry had begun to take its toll and she supposed it showed. It seemed like a week since she'd slept.

"I asked you once before why you never married," she said. "I think you gave me some lame answer about not meeting the right woman."

He was rinsing a plate at the sink while she finished clearing the table. "It was a perfectly good answer."

"It's too boilerplate."

"Even if it happens to be true?"

She delivered the last of the dirty dishes to the counter beside the sink. "Is your dishwasher broken?"

"Is that your follow-up question?"

"Well it's none of my business," she said, transferring a plate into the soapy water. "It's just that you strike me as the kind of man who should be married."

"I thought we were talking about the dishwasher now," he said, taking the plate and scrubbing it with a rag.

"Dishwashers are boring," she said. "Tell me about Hayes. What was it like here before all this corruption business started?"

He shrugged. "Same as any small town I guess. The same people always running things. Same people always complaining about how things are run. Now the names that used to mean something are tarnished."

"All of them?"

"A lot. More than I would've believed if someone had told me a year ago."

"Detroit could use your mayor," she said. "The same people have been running things there too. A thing like this could never happen there."

"The corruption?"

"No, the comeuppance. They're too powerful. It's one big circle jerk."

He flashed surprise.

"Sorry," she said. "I mean one big mess."

He laughed. "No, I think you had it right the first time. I'm just not used to hearing ladies talk that way."

"Who said I'm a lady?"

"I do."

Their conversation moved into the living room and to the town's mayor and how he had blown the lid off the good ole boy political system singlehandedly. Gant told her how Mayor Pigg had refused to do interviews on the cable news channels and rarely even showed his face on local stations. No one could have blamed him had he rode the story to fame and fortune, but that wasn't Walter Pigg's way. Gant admitted to not being able to figure him out, and he lamented the fact that he still refused police protection even though his life had been threatened numerous times.

"He walks around town like he's invisible," he said. "Abraham Lincoln without the hat. If he knew I had men watching out for him he'd probably fire me." He laughed. "And let me tell you he could if he wanted to because the town council learned its lesson on bucking him."

Jackie remembered the first time she met Mayor Pigg. She had just come to town and needed a job. "I thought he was the saddest little man I had ever seen," she said. "Then he said something funny and I didn't know what to make of him after that."

"Then I'd say that puts you in the same boat with everybody else in this town," Gant said. "I like the man, and I admire the hell out of what he's done, but I'd hate to be a shrink and have him on my couch."

❖

Jonce paid Emil Wazenski fifty dollars to go to the hospital in Tupelo and get the lowdown on Palo's condition. He didn't trust anything he saw on the news or read in the paper about his so-called miracle recovery. So far Jonce hadn't been mentioned publicly as a suspect, though he knew his name had to be on the short list. The upside was that the short list probably wasn't so short.

Waz's report proved thorough. The two men sat back-to-back in a burger joint two traffic lights down from the hospital exchanging conversation like two spies in a James Bond flick. The lunch rush had come and gone so they had the place to themselves except for a Mexican man and woman with three small children who sat at a table against the back wall. The teenager working the counter was too absorbed in her phone to eavesdrop.

Jonce ate his cheeseburger while Waz detailed his reconnaissance. Palo occupied a private room on the third floor and had no visitors during the three hours Waz surveilled the place. Two different nurses entered his room at various times, one of them more frequently than the other. Each room had different colored lights above the door and Palo's light came on more frequently than any of the others. The delay between the light coming on and the nurse going into his room increased with each occasion, as did the look of annoyance on the nurse's face. He managed to work himself close enough at one point to hear her tell another nurse at the station that they couldn't discharge 324 soon enough.

"And?" Jonce spoke because Waz stopped. Talking as he chewed, Waz picked up where he left off and explained how he entered Palo's room pretending to have gotten the numbers mixed up. Palo was alone and the room was clean and tidy. There were no flowers or balloons, and no clutter around the chairs where visitors would sit.

"Was he conscious?"

"Very much so," Waz said. "He asked me what the hell I wanted so I told him I was looking for my cousin and apologized for bothering him."

"How many tubes and hoses was he hooked to?"

"One empty IV bag that didn't look connected."

Jonce turned to see the back of Wazenski's head. "No tubes up his nose or down his throat?"

"None."

"And he was talking?"

216

"Yes."

Jonce turned back to his own table and pondered the possibility that Wazenski might be mistaken. "You sure you had the right room? I hit him pretty damned hard."

"Killing a person is harder than it looks in the movies."

Jonce smiled inwardly. "You'll have to tell me about it sometime."

Wazenski's voice was sad when he spoke again. "Killing my wife was the biggest mistake of my life. I should've hired it done. Maybe it's best you leave Palo alone now. I don't think you're cut out to be a killer."

Jonce pushed the last bite of cheeseburger into his mouth and contemplated his next move. "His wife not being with him might mean something."

"It means she's rich," Wazenski said. "Rich people don't grieve like normal people."

"He'll probably get out soon," Jonce said. "If you're telling the truth."

"What reason do I have to lie?"

Jonce couldn't say if he believed him or not, but fifty dollars had been spent and he figured that made them partners in the deal. "I've got something else for you to do," he said.

"I don't think I want any more of your money."

"I ain't asking," Jonce said. "I'm telling. I wouldn't be in this fix if it weren't for you." He waited for Wazenski to protest. He didn't. "Now the way I figure it, if she didn't sit with him in the hospital she won't let him back in the house. She's wiped her hands of him. He's orphaned." He turned and looked at the back of Wazenski's head again. "We're gonna steal ourselves an orphan."

Chapter Nineteen

J once paid Wazenski another fifty dollars to return to the hospital and find out when Palo was going to be discharged, then he drove out to Palo's street and made a few passes looking for activity at his house. School was out for spring break so the missus had the week off. Eventually he parked his truck on a parallel street and slipped through the woods to watch the place. Sooner or later she would come or go, unless she had gone already and didn't plan on coming back. Rich women don't sit on the front porch all day sipping tea.

Noon came and went. Jonce ignored the growling in his stomach as he watched the house from a safe distance. In the old days he could have hopped the fence and skirted the yard until he found a safe approach to the house then looked through the windows, but these new security systems alert people through their phones so they could sit from anywhere in the world and see everything, and it wasn't just for the rich, either. Anybody could have a system like that and lots of people did. Palo certainly would, being rich and crooked the way he was. Maybe he was watching the place from his hospital bed, wondering where his wife was.

At two-fourteen Waz called and told him Palo was being discharged in the morning, which was Tuesday. Still no visitors. If Mrs. Palo didn't show herself soon he would have to assume she had flown the coop.

At three o'clock on the dot the gate jerked and swung open, then a white Land Rover rolled down the driveway and turned toward town without stopping at the end of the driveway. He recognized Palo's wife through the windshield. He immediately called Waz and told him to keep a close watch on the room in case she showed, then he hoofed it back across the woods to his truck and went home.

When the factories let out Monday afternoon, Jackie went to Bobbie's apartment and knocked on her door. Nash's truck wasn't in the parking lot so she didn't have to be careful.

"I ain't talking to you," Bobbie said through the crack in the door

Jackie pushed her way inside.

"What the hell!"

Jackie flashed her badge just to make it official. Bobbie was wearing jeans with horizontal cuts across both thighs, and an olive pullover with a marijuana leaf between her breasts. Her hair was down and her highlights needed touching up.

"I can smell the marijuana from the sidewalk," Jackie said. "You're two seconds away from handcuffs unless you cooperate."

Bobbie couldn't help but glance back toward a closed door that was meant to be a bedroom. Jackie knew the floor plan because she lived in its downstairs twin.

"I don't know anything."

"I haven't asked anything."

"Well whatever you're gonna ask I don't know so you may as well leave."

Jackie scanned the place from where she stood. It looked clean enough. No dirty dishes in the sink. "I know your husband's the jealous type so I'd rather not get him involved. I'm not here to cause you trouble."

"Get him involved in what?" Her defiance was weakening. She didn't strike Jackie as an addict. The pot was probably recreational. She had checked her record and Bobbie was clean. No arrests and she had been at the same job for over a year. "I need to sit down," she said. "I've been on my feet all day."

"I thought you sewed cushions."

"Yeah, well, today I filled in for the utility and they ran my ass off and my feet hurt."

"Does marijuana help take the edge off? Is that why you smoke it?"

"It's legal everywhere but here."

"Not exactly," Jackie said, "but I'm not here about the pot unless you force me to play that card."

"If this is about what happened last week I don't know anything about that. I was working. Is your kid okay?"

"Yes, thank you," Jackie said. "I'm not here about that either."

"Did you catch the guy? I mean, having somebody like that loose around here's scary."

"We caught him." She noticed a stack of hunting magazines in the floor underneath the coffee table. "Is Don a hunter?"

Bobbie shrugged. "He mostly reads about it. Sometimes he goes with his buddies."

"It must get lonely," Jackie said. "Him being gone so much."

"I manage."

Jackie looked toward the wall Bobbie shared with Jonce Nash. "Does he help you manage?"

"Hell no. I wouldn't let him touch me with a ten foot pole."

Jackie forgave the lie. A young woman should defend herself even when she's wrong. "Do you know if he was home last Thursday around six?"

Bobbie rolled her eyes toward the ceiling, thinking. "Last Thursday? I think so. Yeah, sure, he was home."

"Are you sure?"

"I'm positive."

"Would you swear to it in court?"

"Yeah."

"Under oath?"

"What's this about anyway? I told you he was home."

"Are you sure it was Thursday and not Wednesday? Or Friday?"

"It was Thursday," she said. "I was watching that show I always watch. The one about the little smart kid. Sheldon."

"Doesn't that come on at seven?"

Bobbie squirmed a little. "He was making noise. Singing. I pounded on the wall and told him to knock it off because my show was coming on."

She was lying, but why? Was she in love with him? "How much do you know about him?"

"I know he was in prison for robbing a pawn shop or something."

"Besides that," Jackie said.

"I don't keep up with him."

"What do you know about him being shot?"

Bobbie broke eye contact. "I don't know anything about that. He always wears a shirt."

"I didn't say where he was shot."

She squirmed again. "Okay, so he wears pants too. I don't know nothing about him being shot. You don't think I shot him do you?"

Jackie had her off balance now. "No, I don't think you shot him. I also don't think you heard him singing last Thursday evening. Why are you covering for him?"

Bobbie stood. "I want you to leave now."

"Your feet hurt, remember? Sit down."

Bobbie sank back into her chair. She couldn't keep her hands still, or her eyes. She was scared of something. Life or death scared.

"You're a young attractive woman living alone while her husband's out of town. Jonce Nash is a dangerous man who may also be a murderer."

"I can take care of myself."

"He used to beat his wife and son before he went to prison. The boy ran away from home because of it."

"That's a heartbreaker," Bobbie said. "But what's it got to do with me? The only reason I know the man's name is because when he moved in he looked like a convict so I looked him up. If he's as bad as you say why'd they let him out?"

"Because the system doesn't always get it right, Bobbie. Sometimes it screws up and lets a Jonce Nash go free."

"And what happens to me if he catches me talking to you?"

"You don't have to talk," Jackie said. "I've got a different idea. I'd like to plant a listening device." She pointed at a small table with a lamp that sat against the wall Bobbie shared with Nash. "We could put it there. In the lampshade, or underneath where it can't be seen."

"Don wouldn't like that."

"Don't tell him."

"What if he finds it?"

"It's tiny," Jackie said. "Virtually impossible to see unless you're looking for it."

"And what happens when *he* finds out," Bobbie said, glancing toward the wall.

"There's no reason for him to find out." It was a lie. If they picked up something useful and charged him his lawyer would find out in discovery. Hopefully by that point his parole would be revoked and he would be on his way back to prison.

Bobbie shook her head slowly. Thinking. "No. It's too risky. You can't make me do it can you? I mean if I refuse you can't make me?"

"No, Bobbie, I can't make you."

"Good, then I won't do it," Bobbie said.

"Does the name Tipton Palo mean anything to you?"

"I've seen his name in the papers."

"He shot Nash in the arm when Nash tried to shake him down for money. Last Thursday between six and seven, Palo was attacked and left for dead. It's a miracle he's still alive."

Bobbie had stopped paying attention.

"I live downstairs. I know how thin these walls are. I believe you know something. Perhaps you heard something, or saw something. If it's something you're involved in I can help you. We're not out to hurt you."

"I don't know anything."

Jackie recognized defeat when she saw it. She stood. "Be careful, Bobbie. You're playing with fire."

Bobbie stopped her at the door. "If you know he was shot why can't you arrest him?"

"Getting shot isn't a crime," Jackie said.

"Then why does it matter? Why ask me if I know about it?"

"We have the gun," Jackie said. "What we don't have is the bullet. The bullet would have Nash's DNA on it. If it matched the gun we'd have a case."

"Could you lock him up? Forever I mean?"

"I don't know, Bobbie, but I'd sure as hell try."

Waz hid in a janitorial closet for three hours waiting for the nurse to wheel Tipton Palo out of his room, into the elevator, then out to the front curb where a taxi awaited to take him to a nearby hotel. They followed in Jonce's pickup truck and watched from the parking lot as the cabbie lugged Palo's suitcase into the hotel lobby.

"I don't like it," Waz said as the glass doors slid closed behind the slow-moving lawyer. "Hotels have cameras."

"And we have disguises," Jonce said, pulling two black wigs from a plastic shopping bag. "One for you and one for me." He put his on and pulled it down so that the artificial hair covered his ears.

"You look ridiculous."

"No more ridiculous than you will," Jonce said, tossing the other wig into Waz's chest. "Put it on and let me see how pretty you are."

Waz sighed as he donned the fake hair.

"You look like one of them high-priced movie stars ," Jonce said.

"If I didn't know you was a man I'd kiss you on the mouth. He pulled another bag from behind the seat and tossed his sidekick a white blouse with lace around the collar and a pair of dark slacks. "I figure you for hairy legs so I forwent the dress."

"If you think I'm wearing that you're crazy!"

Jonce winked. "Be careful he don't pinch you on the squeeze box."

Waz looked at the female clothes then back at Jonce with defeat written all over his face. Jonce slipped out of his jeans with ease, being thin and not having a gut to get in his way. The steering wheel tilted up so that it was no hindrance at all. He slipped his feet into a short blue skirt.

"I always had nice legs," Jonce said. He had spent half an hour in the bathtub shaving. The clothes came from Goodwill and he picked up the wigs at a consignment shop. Bobbie Booth loaned him the pantyhose with a warning not to bring them back with runs. "Don't you think I got nice legs?"

"I think you're going to get us arrested," Waz said. "Or killed. What if Palo has a gun?"

"They don't let patients have guns," Jonce said. "We followed him here from the hospital. Don't be stupid."

They finished dressing then entered the hotel through the automatic front door. Jonce asked for Palo's room number in a female voice he had practiced while shaving his legs.

"He bought that girlfriend nonsense," Waz said with a laugh as they mounted the elevator. "What a putz."

"Men are dogs," Jonce said. "He thought we were hookers." He laughed and the elevator stopped on the third floor. Waz complained again about the likelihood of getting caught. Jonce stepped out and followed the sign toward room 310. The hallway was empty but the ceiling had black bubbles that concealed cameras. "Swing your hips," Jonce said, thinking the guy at the front desk might be the perverted type. Waz overdid it. Jonce almost popped him but remembered the guy at the front desk. When they reached room 310 Jonce put his thumb over the peephole and knocked. Palo opened the door without asking who it was.

Jonce pushed his way in, knocking Palo back against the dresser at the foot of the bed. He teetered, then sat down hard on the floor.

"Expecting somebody?"

Palo looked up at him with confused terror. "Who the hell are you?"

Jonce slipped a knife from his purse and pressed the tip into the soft flesh of Palo's cheek. "You so much as fart sideways and I'll slit your goozle."

They took the elevator down and left through a side door.

An unidentified female called 911 in a panic and reported Tipton Palo missing from his hotel in Tupelo. By the time Jackie was notified, Tupelo P.D. had learned from the hotel clerk that Palo left with two transvestites. His cell phone and all his personal effects were found in the room. It took less than three hours for a Tupelo detective named Greg Abacore to email Jackie a link to the hotel surveillance video.

"The hotel has forty-eight registered guests today," Abacore told her over the phone. "Thirty-three of those guests were not at the hotel at the time Mr. Palo left with his two companions. Only two of those who were at the hotel had rooms on the same floor. Bottom line is we got jack when it comes to eyewitnesses."

Jackie had just reached her desk and was in the process of logging onto the hotel server using the link Abacore had shared. "I appreciate you getting this to me so soon," she said.

"It's a good setup the hotel has," Abacore said. "Everything's in the cloud. They gave us a login and our guys identified all the pertinent camera feeds and downloaded to our server. What I sent you is the spliced-together version with all the angles so it might be a little choppy. It'll take a while to download everything but we'll go back a few days just in case this turns out to be more than your boy getting his pole greased. If you ask me we're wasting our time but your boss called my boss so here we are."

"Thank you again for your cooperation," Jackie said. "Tipton Palo's pretty high on our radar over here."

"Yeah, I know who he is. A first rate scumbag who deserves what he gets, but who am I to pass judgment? Serve and protect, right?"

Jackie thanked him again. She was eager to view the footage and reach her own conclusions.

"Oh, and that tall one in the video," he said before letting her go. "He told the desk clerk he was Palo's girlfriend." He laughed. "But who am I to judge, right?"

The video began at exactly 11:53:18 AM with an inside view of the lobby door. Two seconds into it the door slides open and an unidentified white male enters pulling a black rolling duffel. Eight seconds later Tipton Palo steps into view. It takes him thirteen seconds to walk from the sliding door to the desk. He tips the unidentified male, who then leaves.

Jackie jotted a note reminding her to ask Detective Abacore if he interviewed the man, presumably a cabbie or a ride-share driver. People sometimes mistake the back seat of a taxi for a psychiatrist's couch. Palo struck her as more careful, but he had suffered a head trauma and may have been off his game.

After checking in, Palo appeared to have a brief disagreement with the clerk, then he pulled his suitcase around the corner and disappeared. The video flickered — a splice — and Palo reappeared stepping into the elevator. Another flicker and Palo stepped out of the elevator and pulled his suitcase down the hall to his room and entered. The next splice was almost unnoticeable. The lobby doors opened and two women — one tall, one short, — entered. They stopped briefly at the front desk, had an exchange with the clerk, then took the same elevator to Palo's floor.

The timestamp when the tall *female* knocked on Palo's door was *3/19/2019 12:04:21 PM.*

The door opened and the two subjects entered the room with moderate force. At 12:08:03 PM, the door opened again and Palo exited the room followed by the two subjects. They flanked him in the hallway down to the elevator and disappeared. At 12:08:42 PM the elevator doors opened and the trio stepped out and left through a side entrance.

Jackie jotted another note to ask Abacore if the hotel had a camera in their parking lot.

Gant stuck his head in and asked her how it was going. His timing was perfect, assuming he wanted the information without having to watch the video.

"How many transvestites do you know?" she asked her boss.

"None," he said. "Call me old fashioned but I'm an original recipe guy."

She invited him to her side of the desk and showed him a still of the three subjects stepping off the elevator. It was the best angle for possible identification.

"Know either one of these two?"

Gant leaned in close. "The tall one looks familiar."

"I thought the same thing," Jackie said. "They're definitely not trannies."

"How can you tell?"

"Transvestites put more effort into their appearance."

An email from Abacore hit her inbox. It was a still shot of a brunette from an overhead angle. The message identified her as the probable 911 caller.

"Says she went to Palo's room less than half an hour after he left," she told Gant. She zoomed in until the photo became grainy. "I'm not certain, but she looks an awful lot like the woman I saw with Palo at the gym." Jackie had gone to the gym last Friday but the manager was out of town for the weekend and the employee claimed not to have access to the records but did confirm that members were required to swipe their membership card to gain entry.

"I think we've got ourselves a mistress," Gant said. "Maybe you need to have another talk with Mrs. Palo."

"That explains why he opened the door," Jackie said. "He was expecting her."

She backed the video up to where the two subjects escorted Palo from the room and watched it again with Gant. As they turned to face the elevator doors she stopped it. "There," she said, pointing to the tall subject's hand against Palo's back. "Does that look like a knife to you?"

Gant asked her to zoom in. "Could be," he said. "It's definitely something."

They had themselves an abduction.

Chapter Twenty

Tipton Palo sat tied to a tattered office chair with a ripped cushion and squeaky wheels. Jonce had found the chair in a pile of junk in the back corner of the mostly-empty warehouse where less than two months prior the crooked lawyer had shot him in the arm in a sloppy attempt to tie up a loose end.

"I had you dead," Jonce said to the face illuminated by a flashlight small enough to fit into his pocket. The warehouse was dark and the air was heavy with the stench of disuse. The noise of Waz digging through the pile of junk in the far corner echoed throughout the confines of steel and concrete with the volume of a wrecking ball.

"Found one," Wazenski yelled in triumph, meaning another chair. "No wheels but it'll sit."

"See if you can drag it over here without waking the dead," Jonce yelled, then in a normal voice to his captive, "He's not bright but he works hard."

Jonce heard him getting closer in the darkness, chair legs banging against the concrete as he walked. He swung the flashlight toward the noise and saw Waz with a metal folding chair underneath each arm.

"I found two," he said, unfolding one then the other. "Maybe we should tie him in one of these then we can take turns with the soft one."

"He stays where he is," Jonce said. He swung the light back into Palo's eyes. "I want him comfy while he wonders how bad I'm gonna hurt him."

Palo's eyes danced wildly against the light. "You'll never get away with this. Hotels have cameras. They're probably looking for me already."

Jonce flipped off the light. Except for a few shafts of daylight that seeped in around the big dock door and through the closed louvers of the half dozen fans mounted high in the walls, the place was completely dark. "Forty-seven days ago in right about this spot, you put a bullet in my arm," Jonce said. "Shot me like a coward when I was here on honest business."

"I made a mistake," Palo said. "I'm sorry."

"Life's a hard biscuit to eat," Jonce said. "I got me a knife in my pocket that'll shave the fuzz off a peach."

"Don't. I'll give you anything you want. You want money? Just name your price and I'll get it."

Jonce flicked the light on again and lit up Palo's face. "See how trembly he is, Waz?" He snickered. "And you thought he was a bear. Boo!"

Palo jerked back against the chair. "It was a misunderstanding between us, Jonce. That's all it was. Let me go and I'll give you anything you want ... and I won't say a word about this to anyone."

Jonce turned off the light. "Promise?"

"I'll swear it on the Bible."

"Cross your heart and hope to die?"

"Yes, I'll cross my heart and hope to die."

Jonce flipped the light on again and illuminated Palo's pasty white face. "Maybe after I've cut off your ears," he said.

"Cut out his tongue so he can't talk," Wazenski said.

"Shut up stupid," Jonce said. "See what I mean," he said to Palo. "P-O-L-A-C-K. Dumb."

"Cut that out," Wazenski said.

Palo began to squirm. He pulled at the nylon zip ties that bound his wrists to the spine of the chair. Identical ties secured his ankles to opposite shafts of the pedestal base. "You'll get the needle for this!"

"Needle smeedle," Jonce said. "Hickory dickery dock."

Palo fought harder. The chair squeaked and groaned but the nylon ties held. "Please," he said. "I'm already ruined. Isn't that enough? I'll probably spend the rest of my life in prison."

Jonce sniffed the air. "You smell that, Waz?"

Wazenski said he didn't smell anything.

Jonce sniffed again. "Mister high and mighty done shit his pants." He laughed hard enough to rattle the metal louvers of the inoperable fans. The echo bounced off the walls like rolling thunder.

Palo began to cry.

Jonce stopped laughing. "Oh, I've hurt him wittle feelings." He laughed again though without the effort.

"Let's get this over with," Wazenski said. "I don't like this place."

"Shut up."

Jonce flipped on the flashlight and swept the floor in all directions. "Right about here," he said, drawing an X on the floor with the light. "Is where you was standing. Your car was parked right about there. I came in through that bay door blind as a hamster in a bull's ass, but you saw *me* all right. You stood here with your gun pointed at me like dilly whack." He flipped off the light.

"Please. I made a terrible mistake."

"Oh, you made a terrible mistake all right. You made one humdinger of a mistake. Rule number one in the book of modern warfare is if you shoot Jonce Nash you'd better kill Jonce Nash. You better kill him good and dead and put bricks on him so his ghost can't get up and kick your ass."

Jonce crept silently toward the sound of Palo sobbing and groped the darkness for the back of his chair, then he swung the chair around with all his might and ran as hard as he could toward the wall with Palo screaming for all he was worth. He guessed the distance in his head, then released the chair and heard it crash into the steel wall with thunderous result. Palo shrieked in pain, cursing and swearing threats he couldn't execute even if he wasn't tied. Jonce threw back his head and buried the threats with laughter that bounced off the steel walls like steel shot.

Jonce stopped laughing and the place fell silent except for Palo's whimpering. "I don't know how that happened," Jonce said. "You just took off." He turned toward Waz's last known position in the darkness. "He just took off, Waz. Right into the wall. Damnedest thing I ever seen."

"Come on, Jonce Nash," Waz said. "Let's get this over with and leave this place. I think it's haunted."

"Getting this thing over with is a mountain we all three have to climb," Jonce said. "It'll take patience and cooperation from all parties involved."

"I don't like this place," his sidekick said again.

"Your reluctance is duly noted," Jonce said. "The vote is two to one. This place ain't liked." He flipped on the light and found Wazenski. "Go fetch him back." He swung the light toward the blubbering heap against the wall. Wazenski sulked over and rolled the lawyer back. "Now you stay put this time," Jonce said to Palo. "Don't go rolling off or I might have to cut your hamstring."

"Just tell him what we want," Waz said.

"Yes, please," Palo whimpered. "Tell me. Anything. I'll give you anything you want."

"Here I find myself saddled with a sissified lawyer and a yellow Polack," Jonce said. "Since I'm outnumbered I'll get on with it. Let's get this show on the road." He swung the light into Palo's eyes again. "First and foremost you owe me for killing Stubbs. With compounded interest and past due penalties I'd fix that amount at half a million dollars. Then you shot me in the arm and that, I believe, is what you lawyer types call pain and suffering, so, rounding it out in my head, I'd say you owe me an even million."

"A million dollars! You're out of your mind! I can't raise that kind of cash!"

"See how quick *anything* becomes too much, Waz? I told you I'd have to cut his ears off to prove I mean business. Grab his head."

"Wait! I'll pay but it'll take time. I'll have to liquidate some assets."

"Then you'd better start liquidating," Jonce said, "or I'll have to start amputating."

"It's not that easy," Palo said. "You don't know what you're asking."

"I ain't asking."

"Okay." Palo's heavy breathing stabilized. "I can't do it here. I'll have to go to my office."

"No office," Jonce said.

"But I need my laptop. And an internet connection. It's all online."

Jonce hadn't considered that complication. His involvement with the internet had been mostly limited to porn sites at the library. "What about it, Waz? You think he's telling the truth?"

"Yes," Wazenski said. "I think he's telling the truth."

"Okay," Jonce said. "Tell you what. You give me your keys and I'll send the Polack after your laptop."

"I'll need internet," Palo said.

"One thing at a time," Jonce said. "I ain't as dumb as you think I am."

Tuesday afternoon, three days after his arrest, David Regal Sansing sent word to Chief Gant that he was ready to talk. Gant buzzed Jackie at her desk and asked if she wanted to observe the interview through the two-way mirror. She did.

Sansing sat slumped forward at the small table in the center of the room with his hands cuffed to a chain that ran through a loop in a heavy leather belt around his waist. He wore an orange jumpsuit and looked terribly disheveled.

He raised his head when Gant entered the room. "I want a deal in writing. I tell you who sent me in exchange for full immunity."

Gant chuckled. "And I want a supermodel wife and a Porsche. I guess we're both out of luck."

Jackie watched Sansing straighten himself and lean back in his chair. Three days ago he had spent his one phone call on a two-minute exchange to a Detroit area code. Since then nothing. No high-priced lawyer swooping down to rescue him. No visitors. No one calling to inquire. Nothing. Kelton had left the sick calf to the wolves.

"I know my rights," the prisoner said.

Gant lowered himself into the chair directly across the table. "Do you?"

"My lawyer should've been here by now. Somebody's pulling some shit on me."

Gant glanced at the mirror. "Sounds like somebody decided you're not worth the trouble. In legal terms that means you're screwed."

Sansing quickly grew agitated. "I know things," he said. "You want the information because that lady's a cop."

"This is the last conversation you and me have," Gant said. "After I leave this room it'll be you and the district attorney. He flies a Confederate battle flag in his front yard and there's nothing he likes better than putting yankees in prison.

Sansing twisted his hands and scoffed. "Yeah? Well this is still the United States of America ain't it? You rednecks know about the Constitution don't you?"

"Sure, we've heard of it. We even teach it in school. Personally I'm against all that Stars and Bars flag business, but my wife didn't run off to Boston with a beer salesman."

Sansing adjusted himself. Jackie watched both men in profile. One was clean cut and confident, the other looked as though he had spent the night underneath the porch with dogs. "I wasn't gonna hurt the kid," Sansing said. "My orders were to bring him home."

"To Detroit?"

"Yes."

"To his father?"

"First I need something in return."

"You've just admitted to kidnapping a minor for the purpose of transporting him across state lines," Gant said. "That's federal time. Day for day. No time off for good behavior."

Sansing smirked. "That's easy time. I might learn to play golf."

"They save the golf courses for the rich business types," Gant said. "You'll be soaking your teeth in a jar by the time you get out. *If* you get out." He leaned in again. "But that's after you serve time in our prison for felony assault and attempted rape of a minor."

"Attempted rape! What the hell? I didn't touch that kid!"

"That's your word against his," Gant said.

"Is that what he's saying?"

"He'll say whatever his mother tells him to say."

Sansing jerked at his shackles and tried to stand but Gant shoved him back into his chair. "I want a lawyer! A public defender because I ain't got no money!"

Gant sighed, then he stood. "Okay. Have it your way." He stooped and rested both hands on the table, looking down at him. "When word gets out that you tried to rape a fifteen-year-old boy you won't last the afternoon back there. We don't tolerate that kind of activity down here in Mississippi." He straightened himself. "The only good lawyer we got came up missing this morning, but I'll put your name on the wheel. They'll send somebody over in a few days." He turned and started for the door.

"Wait!"

"Too late," Gant said, still walking. "Once you ask for a lawyer it's over. My hands are tied."

"I take it back!"

The chief stopped and turned. "You have to put it in writing."

"Okay, bring me the paper to sign. I don't want a lawyer. I'll tell you what I know but you knock off that rape stuff. I ain't no fag and I damned sure ain't no child molester."

"You're making a wise decision," Gant said. He returned to the table and sat. "Now tell me who sent you and why."

Sansing hesitated. "Kelton Mulvaney sent me."

"For what purpose?"

"To bring his kid home."

"Did he pay you?"

"Half up front and half when I deliver."

"How much?"

"Two grand."

"Two-thousand dollars for felony kidnapping? You work cheap."

"He said I couldn't get in trouble because I wasn't doing anything wrong."

"Are you that dumb?"

"Yeah, I mean ... well, I didn't plan on getting caught."

"But you did get caught."

"He said I was like a bounty hunter."

"Do you have a license for that?"

"No."

"So you're not a bounty hunter. You're a kidnapper."

"Wait a minute, I thought we had a deal."

"The deal is that you tell me everything I want to know and in return I'll drop the attempted rape charge."

"That charge is bogus and you know it! I oughta get something for spilling my guts."

"Okay, I'll drop the felony assault charge too."

"No deal," Sansing said. "You gotta drop the attempted kidnapping charge."

"Fat chance," Gant said. "The DA wouldn't go for it."

"Then I'm back to wanting a lawyer."

Gant stood. "Okay, then I'm back to charging you with attempted rape."

"Wait a minute," Sansing said, twisting his hands and squirming. "I'll take the deal."

"Too late," Gant said. "I've already got all I need."

Sansing jerked at his restraints. "I'll deny everything," he said. "You ain't got nothing until I sign a statement. This ain't my first time you know!"

Gant smiled and pointed at the video camera in the ceiling. "I got it all right there."

Sansing's face collapsed. "I've got something else," he said.

"I'm listening."

"Do I get the original deal?"

"Depends on what you've got."

"How do you think I got here?"

Gant studied him. "A plane to Memphis and a rental car?"

"Yeah, but how do you think I knew where to come?"

Jackie's pulse quickened. Gant played it cool. "That no longer matters," he said.

Jackie almost pounded the glass and screamed at her boss to make the deal.

"She'll wanna know," the prisoner said, turning to the glass. "I know she's watching. I can tell you who ratted her out."

Gant appeared to mull it over. Jackie realized what he was doing and began to breathe again. "Okay," he said. "You've got your original deal."

Sansing hesitated again. He looked up at the camera then back at the chief. "And I want the attempted kidnapping charge knocked down to simple assault."

"Don't get greedy," Gant said. "You've got five seconds before I walk out that door and I won't be coming back."

"It was some Mexican lawyer," Sansing said. "I heard Mulvaney talking about it on the phone."

"Does the Mexican lawyer have a name?"

"Pablo," he said. "That's all I know."

Jackie left immediately and drove to the gym where she had seen Palo talking to the unidentified female. Armed with a still shot of the woman from the hotel surveillance video, she managed to get a name from the manager without having to threaten her with a warrant.

"Her name is Jerri Barlow and she's a real bitch," the short muscular woman said from behind her modest desk. The office was little more than a storage closet with a desk, a chair, and a lamp amid the clutter of stacked boxes and propped brooms. The manager looked to be in her forties and had probably once been attractive. "They were here together that night, you know — before he left and got his head caved in. If you ask me he had it coming." She frowned. "Does that make me a suspect?"

"In this town I'd say it makes you normal," Jackie said.

"Good. And too bad Jerri wasn't with him. She's got some stuff coming too."

"I'm listening."

"It ain't the first time she's gone after somebody's husband."

"Yours?"

"Ha! She wouldn't want mine. He's a bum."

"How many people knew about their affair?"

"Everybody. They tried to keep it quiet for a while, then I don't think they cared."

"Did his wife know?"

The woman shrugged. "If she didn't she should have. Do you think she did it? The wife I mean."

"Does Jerri have a husband?"

"Not last time I checked."

"Boyfriend?"

"Lots of those."

"Anyone in particular who might be the jealous type?"

"You ever seen a man who wasn't the jealous type?"

"Can you give me any names?"

"I don't wanna get anybody in trouble," the manager said. "Guys like that get mad then they find another tart to chase. I don't think any of them did it. You might check into that new car she's driving though."

"Why?"

"She didn't pay for it herself. I know that much."

"Do you know who did?"

"No, but I know who can afford it and who can't, and there ain't but one who comes here with that kind of dough."

"Palo?"

She nodded.

Jackie left the gym and drove to Canal Street and found Jerri Barlow at home. Their conversation was short and sweet. Jackie's gut told her it was a dead end.

Jonce donned his female attire one last time and used Tipton Palo's key to let himself in through the front door of Palo's law office, then he punched the four-digit code into the alarm system keypad while a tiny speaker beeped a warning that he had better hurry and that he had better get it right. Waz had strict instructions to slit Palo's throat if Jonce wasn't back in one hour, but he doubted the Polack's resolve. Palo was probably plying him with slick words at that very minute, trying to talk himself free. All the more reason for Jonce to hurry.

The tiny red light turned green and the beeping stopped. Silence persisted. The code had worked. Jonce pointed his flashlight in the direction Palo had told him, then flicked it on for a split second to get his bearings. It was darker inside than out, and he couldn't risk someone seeing the flashlight through the window. He felt his way toward Palo's office until he bumped into the wall. His heart beat steady. His senses were keen. He kept his head down in case the cameras had night vision. He wore gloves. Jonce Nash was in his element.

He groped for the doorknob, opened the door, then flashed the light again and saw a desk big as a twin bed. He inched his way forward until he found the desk with his hands. Everything to that point had gone according to plan. Palo had not deceived him. The laptop was exactly where he had said it would be.

The same code that disarmed the alarm armed it back. He locked the door with the key, leaving everything as he had found it minus the laptop. Jonce had never been one to destroy a person's property for sport the way some people in his profession did. The longer it takes the victim to realize they've been burgled, the colder the trail gets. In this particular instance, Jonce hoped the secretary wouldn't notice the laptop missing for the time it would take Palo to liquidate and transfer his assets without the cops getting wise and freezing everything.

He walked the two blocks back to his truck with the laptop tucked underneath his arm, swishing his hips in case the headlights approaching from behind belonged to a cop. The town was dead except for that one car. Half a block from his truck he heard the car slowing as it overtook him.

"Hey there sweet thang," a voice rang out in the darkness. The car was a pickup truck occupied by two old drunks. The truck veered to the sidewalk and slowed to match Jonce's gate. "What you walking so fast for honey? How about we give you a ride?" The passenger was hanging arm and shoulder out the window, laughing the way a drunk does when he doesn't know he's making a fool of himself. It occurred to Jonce to lift his dress and flash his cargo just to see the looks on their faces, but drunks sober up and one or the other might talk and blow his cover. Or they might pile out and beat the shit out of him.

He reached the corner of the block and made a hard right toward his truck. The drunks would have to either give up the chase or get out and follow him on foot because the small parking lot had no entrance from Main Street. Jonce had chosen it because it was isolated and his daytime reconnaissance turned up no cameras. If the men followed, he would wait until they were hidden from the street and teach them a thing or two about how to treat a lady. He snickered as he played the scene out in his head. Of course there was the safety of the laptop to consider.

The two drunks gave up the chase and rumbled away with their dual exhausts thundering, offering themselves up as an unwitting diversion should a cop happen to be lurking nearby. Sometimes luck is on your side and sometimes it's against you. Jonce sucked in the night air and savored it as he reached his truck unmolested by drunks or cops. The high of a job well done filled him with nostalgia. Prison had almost broken his spirit. He renewed his vow never to go back, no matter what. Jonce Nash belonged in the wild.

He stripped off the dress and wiggled back into his regular clothes before leaving the parking lot, then on a whim he stopped by the apartment complex and offered himself up to Bobbie for a quickie. May as well make Palo sweat out the remaining half hour.

"Quickie yourself," Bobbie said through the door. "I'm good."

"You ain't the only game in town," Jonce shot back.

Her door swung open and there stood Bobbie wearing a long white t-shirt that struck her mid-thigh. Her eyes were red and puffy.

"You been crying?"

"You've put me in a helluva mess," she said, then she told him not to stand in the door like an idiot where the neighbors could see. He followed her into the living room.

"You better not be talking to the cops."

She sniffled. "No I ain't talking to the cops. Not that they ain't trying."

Jonce halved the distance between them. "Trying how?"

"Never mind that," she said. "You've put me in a real fix."

The sight of her standing in front of him practically naked caused his heart to beat fast. Pressure built up in his face and head and chest until he thought he would burst. "Maybe if things work out the way I plan, you and me'll go away someplace fancy."

She turned on him with a suddenness that caught him off guard. "I wouldn't go away with you if you were the last man on earth! I hate you and I hope you die!" Her red swollen eyes were tight and fierce. Her jaw was set. She looked determined.

Jonce balled his fist ready to knock her down if she charged him. "What the hell's wrong with you?"

"I'm pregnant you son of a bitch!"

Jonce took a minute to soak it in. "Well," he said, thinking hard.

"Pregnant ain't no hill to climb."

He took a step toward her but she recoiled. "Don't touch me!"

"The way you and him go at it I'm surprised you ain't got a houseful of kids."

"It's yours, stupid."

He laughed. "Well maybe you want it to be mine but I don't see how you can know."

She started crying again. Sobbing. Wiping snot and tears with one hand then the other. "How am I supposed to tell Don? He'll kill me."

Jonce stepped toward her again but she balled her hand into a fist and cocked it at his head. "If you come near me Jonce Nash I swear I'll kill you."

He believed she would try. He wasn't scared of her but the noise of him having to correct her attitude might attract the cops and he definitely didn't need that tonight of all nights. "Okay," he said. "Calm down."

"Don't tell me to calm down!"

"Fine, work yourself into a knot then. I'm just trying to help." He took a step back. "See, I ain't on you. I just don't understand the situation, that's all."

"Do you understand pregnant?"

"You're married, and what's more you and that overgrown husband of yours go at it like rabbits on acid from Friday night to Sunday afternoon."

"Remember me telling you he's got a low sperm count?"

Jonce remembered.

"It can't be his and he'll know it can't be his. He'll leave me and I'll be stuck here by myself raising your kid."

"Well, maybe one of Donnie's little sperms made its way through. Low don't mean no does it?"

She shrugged one shoulder and sniffed.

"I bet if you act excited when you tell him he'll be overcome with joy."

"Fat chance of that," she said. "He'll probably backhand me across the room."

"Then you scream at him for not being happy about it. My Ellie screamed at me for two months because I didn't dance a jig when she broke the same news to me."

She smiled underneath her sadness. It came and went in less than a heartbeat but Jonce saw it and he knew she was coming around.

Women have their moods.

"Even if he believes me, I'll know," she said.

"You think you know," Jonce said. "Women are always thinking they know."

Her face grew tight again. "I know a lot of things, you bastard. A lot of things you may end up wishing I didn't know." Tears filled her eyes again. "I could make a lot of trouble for you."

"You don't mean that."

"That woman detective says you killed a man."

"She's lying."

"She wants to bug my apartment so she can listen to you through the wall."

Jonce struggled to control himself. A few kicks to the abdomen would solve two problems at once. "Be careful," he said. It occurred to him that the place might already be bugged. Bobbie might have walked him into a trap.

"I told her no," Bobbie said.

Jonce scanned the room. There was a table against the wall with a lamp. Bobbie saw him looking and told him that was the place, but not to worry because she had refused permission. He checked it anyway. Trust had never been one of his failings.

"Never trust anything a cop tells you," he said. "And you better get rid of that stuff you've got growing in the bedroom."

"She said she wasn't concerned about that."

"That's what she says now," he said. "When the time comes she'll use it against you to get what she wants." He stepped into her face and grabbed her wrist and applied just the right amount of twist. "Just remember what I told you about accessary after the fact. If I go down you go too. Don't matter what deal they offer because all that stuff is tricks."

She tried to pull away but he was too strong. "Let go of me. I said I didn't tell her nothing."

"Just make sure it stays nothing," he said. He released her arm. "I'd hate for your kid to be an orphan before it's born." He stepped back to access her mental condition. Wazenski expected him back soon. "I've got business someplace. Important business."

"More important than this," she said, pointing at her stomach.

"To a certain somebody it is."

"I could get rid of it if I had some money," she said. Don wouldn't have to know.

"Drink some Drano."

She lurched forward and slapped him. He slapped her back twice as hard. She stared at him in stunned silence.

"I'll give you the money," he said. "I was just having a little fun."

She rubbed her cheek. "I don't believe you."

"Find out how much, and I want it on paper. Now I gotta run take care of something important. If anybody asks, I was home all night."

Chapter Twenty-One

Detroit police arrested Kelton Mulvaney early Wednesday morning. His attorney sprung him by noon, less than half an hour before Jackie's former captain called her with the news. He never saw the inside of a cell and the DA said the case was Swiss cheese.

The district attorney was a sometimes guest at Kelton's dinner parties, though Jackie herself knew the evidence against her husband was weak. He paid a man to bring his son home. On the surface it seemed harmless. She had worked hundreds of cases just like hers and she knew the outcome was hopeless.

She thanked him for pushing the arrest through as a favor to her. The risk was that it would annoy her husband more than it intimidated him. Kelton Mulvaney was a man accustomed to getting what he wanted, and no one wants to be handcuffed and marched out of their office in front of their employees.

Less than an hour after the first call, her captain called back with bad news. Her husband had filed charges against her for abducting their son. Tit for tat. Push Kelton and he punches.

"The mayor's backing him," her captain said. "The DA promised to drag his feet on the paperwork but expect to be extradited."

The first place she went was Gant's office. "I'm in deep trouble," she said. "I made a big mistake having Kelton arrested."

"He sent a goon to kidnap your son."

"Now he's charging *me* with kidnapping. My captain told me they'll extradite me."

She saw a flash of defiance in Gant's face, then the crash of defeat. They both knew the extradition order would be honored.

"We'll squeeze Sansing again," Gant said. "Maybe he knows more than he's telling us."

"I doubt it," she said. "My husband's too careful. I should've known better than to think I could get away from him."

"I know a shelter where you can hide for a while. They'll take Jordan too."

"You think I don't know how those places are?"

"It's better than losing your son ain't it?"

Being a cop's the only thing I know how to do," she said. "If I don't stand and fight this thing I'm finished. I'll never wear a badge again. Besides, Jordan deserves better than hiding out in a shelter."

Gant nodded. "Okay, so we fight it."

"We?"

"You think I'm gonna let you fight this alone?"

"It's not your fight."

"When somebody threatens one of my men it damned sure is my fight."

"I don't want you losing your job over me," she said. He had already put himself out. "Jordan and I will move back into the apartment tonight."

"That's a bad idea."

"It's a good idea," she said. "I don't want you caught up in this."

"Give it a few days," he said. "Sansing may not be working alone."

"Kelton's fighting me in court now. He won't send anyone else."

"At least wait until Saturday," Gant said. "No sense moving all that stuff back in the dark."

She laughed. "It's two suitcases." It felt good to laugh. "Okay," she said. "Saturday. But don't try to talk me out of it."

Everything Jonce Nash knew about computers could be written on a postage stamp folded three ways. Waz knew even less. All morning they had prodded Palo to transfer the money but he kept saying he couldn't do anything without an internet connection. Hayes didn't have public Wi-Fi and Palo had left his phone at the hotel. Jonce's phone didn't have hotspot capability and Waz's phone was the old flip type.

"They got internet at the Wing Empire," Waz said, meaning the chicken place where he worked. Jonce shot the idea down for obvious reasons.

"You can take me to my house," Palo said. He was still tied to his chair. The glow of his laptop screen illuminated his face.

"Fat chance."

"Or my office."

"Wrong again."

"Well, there's the motel," Palo said. "You don't have any other options if you want the money."

Jonce flipped on his flashlight and found Wazenski sitting in his folding chair with his legs crossed at the ankles. "Go to the motel and rent us a room."

"Why me?"

"Because I said so that's why. Now scat before I put my foot up your ass."

Wazenski scrambled out of his chair and mumbled something incoherent as he walked toward the door with Jonce's flashlight against his back.

"And get one around back so nobody can see us," Jonce called after him. "And use a fake name."

"He'll have to pay with cash," Palo said.

"Shut up. He ain't stupid." Jonce found Wazenski with his flashlight again. "And pay with cash."

After the door opened and closed and they were alone, Jonce pulled a chair up close and propped his feet in Palo's lap and smoked a cigarette. A beer would have been nice but he had to keep his head and not let his captive outsmart him. Prison is full of men who might still be free if they had stayed sober that one time that mattered. "I like what alcohol does to my brain," Jonce said to Palo. "It makes me forget about people like you. High and mighty with all your money and laws. Thinking you're better'n the rest of us."

"I worked hard for what I have," Palo said.

Jonce put his boot against Palo's chest and applied just enough pressure to make him squirm. "The hardest work you ever did was ripping off insurance companies."

"Well it pays a hell of a lot better than breaking into people's houses and stealing guns."

Jonce shoved with his boot and sent Palo rolling backward into the darkness.

"Shut up when I'm talking." Jonce planted both feet on the floor and adjusted himself in his chair. "Know what that wife of yours was out doing while you was laid up in the hospital?"

"I don't care."

"She weren't home crying for you, that's for sure. I watched her come and go, all dolled up with her tits pushed up to her chin." He laughed. "Of course that took some pushing."

"Shut up about my wife."

Jonce laughed. "She ain't no looker, that's for sure, but she's got a good feel to her."

"I told you to shut up about her."

"She was eager," Jonce said. "Did you find her eager? I mean at first, when you got married. I guess all wives get tired of their husbands. We're all dogs. Was you a dog? Be truthful now. I bet you was." It disappointed him that Palo gave up so easily. "That little gal at the gym sure is a fireball. Looks it, I mean. I ain't got around to seeing for myself yet. Is she better'n your wife?"

Palo remained silent.

"I bet she is … at first I mean. They all start nagging after a while. What's the matter with you? Cat got your tongue?" He flipped on his flashlight just to make sure Palo hadn't pulled some magic trick and escaped. He hadn't. Jonce's light caught him with his head hung in defeat. He wasn't even trying to get away. Jonce extinguished the light. The laptop had gone dark too.

"It's eerie in here," Jonce said after several minutes of boredom. "Like one of them horror movies right before the guy wearing the hockey mask jumps out. I bet you scream like a teenage girl, don't you? Huh? Is that how you'd scream if Jacob jumped out at you?"

"Jason," Palo said. "The man in the hockey mask's name was Jason."

Jonce chortled. "Well listen to you."

"If you insist on babbling, at least get the names right."

"Don't mind me," Jonce said. "I'm just nervous coming into all this money. Do you remember when you made your first million? Well? Do you?"

"Yes, I remember."

"Well?"

"Well what?"

"How'd you make it?"

"Unlike you I earned it," Palo said.

"Earned it how? Who'd you sue?"

"An insurance company."

"You stole it from them now I'm stealing it from you," Jonce said. "It's not good for the economy to hoard money. Money's supposed to be circulated."

"Spare me the economics lecture," Palo said.

"Jonce Nash, millionaire. It's got a nice ring to it don't you think?"

"You're forgetting about your partner. You'll only be half a millionaire."

Palo hadn't taken in the whole picture the way Jonce had. Partners were for when a man was needing, and after Palo transferred the money Jonce wouldn't be needing anymore. He left those thoughts unsaid because he knew Palo was trying to bait him.

"Half a millionaire sounds fine," he said. "I ain't one for greed."

"Why not let me keep my money then?"

Jonce laughed. "I'm doing you a favor. Helping you get through the eye of that needle the Bible talks about. Besides, your wife would get it all anyway."

Palo scoffed. "She'll be lucky to get out with the clothes on her back by the time I'm through with her."

"I weren't talking about divorce," Jonce said. "I was talking about after you're dead."

Palo flooded the place with silence. Jonce lit a cigarette and smoked it to the filter then thumped the butt toward his captive. It missed and fell harmlessly to the floor where it glowed orange then faded out over the next several seconds. Smoking was more luxury than habit with Jonce. He had always had an unnatural ability to deny his cravings.

"I was casing this house one time," he said to the darkness. "Bertie Portman promised me a thousand dollars for a rifle he said the owner kept locked in a safe. The only catch was I had to deliver before opening day of deer season which was less than a week away. The house was supposed to be empty one particular morning but the wife didn't go to work that day so I sat out in them woods for three days and nights waiting for that house to be empty. Three days and nights without food or water. Three days and nights with mosquitos tormenting every inch of exposed skin. I rubbed myself down with mud and I waited. On the fourth morning she finally left the house and I got me that gun, then I sold it to Bertie Portman for a thousand dollars and I got blind drunk."

"Is there a moral somewhere in all that?"

Jonce thought for a minute. "No, I was just passing time. Ordinarily I don't mention the names of my clients but Bertie bragged so much about that rifle that the man who owned it tracked him down and beat him half to death. Everybody in Chutahachie knew about it."

"What happens to me after I wire the money?"

"We go our separate ways and call it square," Jonce said.

"You're lying."

"Okay."

"Why should I give you anything if you're going to kill me?"

"There's different ways of dying," Jonce said. "There's easy, then there's the other way."

"What if there's not any money?"

Jonce flicked the flashlight on and aimed it at Palo's eyes. He was scared all right. Terrified.

"My wife's divorcing me. All the accounts may be frozen."

"Except the ones she don't know about."

"It may take a couple of days to liquidate that much money."

"You've got until the banks close tomorrow," Jonce said. "After that I cut off your ears. Day after tomorrow I'll cut off your nose. See how it works?"

They waited until dark to move Palo from the warehouse to the motel. Jonce tied his hands and feet and stuffed him into the trunk of Wazenski's car with a warning to keep quiet, then he pulled him back out and stripped off one of his socks and stuffed it into Palo's mouth until he gagged.

The parking lot behind the motel was empty and all the windows but one were dark. Waz had paid cash for two nights. They pulled Palo out of the trunk and carried him into the room like a rolled up carpet, then they tossed him onto one of the beds and Jonce glared down at him. "Before I take my sock out I'll warn you," he said, meaning every word he was about to say. "One peep and I'll cut out your tongue." He plucked the sock from Palo's mouth. Palo coughed and gagged and spat into the carpet.

"Keep it down," Jonce said. "Remember what I told you about peeping."

Palo looked up at Jonce with wild eyes. "You ever do that again I'll kill you." He spat again. "When's the last time you washed your feet!"

Jonce jerked him up by the hair of his head and cut his hands and feet free, then he pulled him to his feet and marched him to the little desk against the wall and shoved him into the chair. Wazenski put the laptop in front of him. "Start liquidating," Jonce said.

Waz made a food run and brought back hamburgers and Cokes all around. Palo persisted in his argument that the stock market was closed and wouldn't reopen until nine the next morning.

"He's right," Waz said with his mouth full.

"How the hell would you know?"

"Everybody knows the stock market closes at night." He sounded sure of himself.

There was nothing to do until nine the next morning but sleep. It had been a tiresome day and Jonce was beat. "We ain't got but two beds so you can either sleep on the floor or with the Polack."

"He's not sleeping with me," Waz said.

"Then floor it is," Jonce said. He told Wazenski to tie him good and tight, then he checked his work to make sure it was done right.

At nine sharp the next morning they untied their victim's hands and set him to work at his computer. Jonce watched his fingers dance across the keyboard without a clue what he was doing. He changed screens so many times that Jonce got sick of watching. Shortly after ten, Palo closed the lid on his laptop and said the deed was done.

"It won't show up in the account until tomorrow," Palo said. "I can't help that. It's the best I can do."

Jonce felt the cleansing wash of wealth come over him. If he could spend three days and nights in the woods for a thousand dollars, one more night in a motel room for a million was a piece of cake.

Candice Bey telephoned at fifteen minutes before ten Thursday morning and told the 911 dispatcher that her boss, Tipton Palo, was being held hostage in room 112 of the local motel by Jonce Nash and a man he called Waz. The dispatcher kicked it directly to the chief, who summoned Jackie to his office where he had been discussing the department's budget with the mayor.

Her first thought when she saw Mayor Pigg was that she was about to be fired, or worse, handcuffed and transported to Detroit to answer her husband's charges against her. Gant wouldn't do it on his own, so the mayor was forcing him. That was her thought process.

"Should I close the door?"

"No," Gant said. "We just got a call that Nash and an accomplice are holding Tipton Palo hostage over at the motel."

Her relief was immediate. Instead of being fired, she was about to close a case and nail Nash's hide to the wall as a bonus. She had a score to settle with him and it was going to be a pleasure.

She glanced at the mayor, wondering what role he played in the case. Curiosity, probably. He seemed the sort.

"You've had more direct contact with Nash than I have," Gant said. "What's your gut tell you?"

"He's unpredictable," she said, glancing at the mayor again. "I wouldn't want to be Palo when SWAT shows up." She remembered where she was. Hayes didn't have a rapid response team. "Or us," she said. "Unless you want me to take it alone."

"Birch and Ramey are on their way there now," Gant said. "We'll take your car."

She glanced at the mayor a third time. This time he noticed. He shrugged. "I was already here," he said. "Discussing the budget. If you want my opinion, bomb the room."

Gant stood and grabbed his radio. "We'll talk budget later."

They left the mayor sitting.

"His secretary called it in," Gant said as they left the parking lot with Jackie driving. "Apparently he sent her an email and told her he was being held captive."

She blasted her siren and blew through a red light.

"I've worked one hostage situation in my life," he said. "It was a domestic dispute that got out of hand. The husband was drunk and thought his wife was cheating on him so he pulled a gun on her. He held us off for half an hour before I talked him out of the house."

"Sounds like a perfect track record."

"The gun didn't have a firing pin," he said. "My only hostage situation has an asterisk."

"You had no way of knowing."

"What about you?"

"I've observed my share," she said. "But I've never taken the lead."

"Great," he said. "I'll call Tupelo and request SWAT. It'll take half an hour at least. We'll have to handle it until then."

They were three blocks out. Jackie passed a car without the siren just in case Nash didn't yet know he was trapped. Birch and Ramey were on the scene but had not made contact.

"We establish a line of communication and keep him talking," she said. "Nash likes to talk so that part should be easy."

"We could always go with the mayor's suggestion," he said. "Except we don't have a bomb."

Jackie wheeled the car into the parking lot and rolled past the front entrance. Two cars and a pickup truck were parked in front of three street-facing rooms.

"So was he squeezing you on the budget?"

"Would you believe he said I didn't ask for enough money?"

They rolled around the side and saw two patrol cars parked nose to tail behind Jonce Nash's pickup and a green Pontiac.

She parked behind the second car. "Does this mean I get a bigger office?"

"No," he said, "but we get the new vests we've been needing. I wish we had them now. The tourism committee is going to hate us."

Jackie opened her door. "Hayes has a tourism committee?"

"Not anymore."

Officer Birch trotted over and pointed at the room directly in front of Nash's truck. "Quiet as a mouse, Chief," he said.

"Good," Gant said. "Go help the manager clear out the other rooms." He looked at Jackie. "Now let's see how unstable our guy is."

Chapter Twenty-Two

J once jumped at the chattering ring of the old beige phone on the nightstand. Waz stuck his head out of the bathroom where he had been busy stinking the place up for the better part of half an hour. How a man could smell that bad from what little they had eaten stymied Jonce, but cracking a window was not an option because motel windows don't open.

"Get that," Jonce barked. The hair on the back of his neck stood at attention.

"Who is it?"

"Answer it and find out, stupid."

Waz got in no hurry reaching the phone. The little hammer striking the tin bell made a harsh sound that can't be duplicated by electronic gadgets. Jonce held his finger to his lips as a warning to Palo to keep quiet. They had tied him to the chair again as soon as he finished transferring the money. Electronic wire transfers were foreign to Jonce but he had heard about them in prison and had the slip of paper in his pocket on which Palo had jotted the numbers and codes he would need to turn computer keystrokes into cash. Palo had resisted being tied to the chair, thus the swelling around his left eye. The chair had sturdy arms and legs, and seemed well suited for tying a man. The seat and back were padded, though apparently not to Palo's liking. He complained incessantly.

"Sometime today, Waz," Jonce barked over the noise of the phone's bell. Since childhood he had hated hearing telephones ring.

Waz reached the phone and raised the handset to his ear. "Hello," he said in his lazy accent. His eyes flashed wide and he jerked the phone away and covered the mouthpiece with his hand. "It's the cops!"

Jonce looked at Palo and watched a smile creep into his face. "If this is your doing I'll gut you like a hog." Wazenski hadn't moved since pulling the phone from his ear. "Well ask him what he wants, dummy."

Wazenski returned the phone to his ear. "Jonce said what do you want?"

Jonce rushed toward him and snatched the phone away and slammed it back into the cradle. "Don't say my name you dumb Polack!"

"He said look outside," Wazenski said.

Jonce glared down at his captive, slapping him every way but Sunday in his head. Beating him now would only make matters worse.

Palo laughed.

"You ain't out of the woods by a long shot," Jonce said. He looked toward the heavy curtains that covered the window. Light seeped in around the edges and through a razor-thin gap where the two halves met in the center. The door was the only way in or out. "Check that window," he said to Wazenski.

"Why do I have to check it?"

Jonce grabbed him by the collar and jerked him to his tiptoes. "Do what I say or you'll get it worse than him!" He released him with a shove that sent him stumbling back against the nightstand, toppling the ugly lamp and scattering some change Jonce had removed from his pockets before going to bed the night before.

"Looks like you've been outsmarted," Palo said.

Jonce turned and kicked the lawyer in the shin. Palo yelped with pain. Jonce pulled the knife from his pocket and exposed the blade with a flick of his thumb. Palo's eyes grew wide with terror as Jonce pressed the tip to his throat. "You don't learn good," Jonce said, pushing the tip into the soft flesh of Palo's throat until a trickle of blood ran down his Adam's apple. "One more word. I promise you, just one more word."

"Don't kill him," Wazenski said. "We'll need him to get out of here."

Jonce withdrew the knife. "We ain't leaving this room alive," he said to Wazenski. He swung his attention back to Palo. "None of us. We're like the Three Musketeers. One for all, all for one." He pushed his fingers through his hair front to back, thinking. "Help me scoot him up against the window. If they shoot their way in they'll have to shoot through him."

The phone rang again. "Let it ring," Jonce said. Together they wrestled Palo's chair in front of the window and positioned him so that the shaft of light spilling through the gap between the curtains cut a vertical line between his eyes. Jonce ordered Wazenski to grab one curtain and he grabbed the other. On his signal, they jerked the curtains back and filled the room with light. Palo twisted his head and fought to no avail. The chair was stout and the nylon ties were strong.

"That's right," Jonce said. "Show 'em how scared you are." He laughed. There's a certain humor in death. The phone continued to ring. "Answer that damned phone!"

Jonce peeked around the curtain and saw two patrol cars and the female detective's Mustang. Her head and the chief's head stuck up above the front passenger fender of the second patrol car. The chief had a phone to his ear.

"He wants to talk to you," Wazenski said. "He said you may as well talk because we're not going anywhere."

Jonce walked backward, making sure to keep out of a direct line of fire, then he crawled across the bed and dropped to the floor. He snatched the phone and stuck it to his ear. "See what I got me in that window?"

"You need to release your hostage and give yourselves up before somebody gets hurt," the chief said. "No need turning this into a murder."

"This is a private matter that don't concern you," Jonce said.

"In fifteen minutes there'll be a SWAT team here," the chief said. "The only way you're leaving that room is in handcuffs or on a gurney with the sheet pulled all the way up."

"If we die, Palo dies," Jonce said.

"You should've picked a better hostage," the chief said. "Don't expect us to give you a plane to Brazil and a million dollars in cash for Tipton Palo."

Jonce tried to laugh but it came out wrong because his stomach was twisting itself into knots. "I already got a million dollars," he said. "And airplanes give me the shits. I want your cop to unblock my truck and you give me a five minute head start. I'll drop the lawyer off at the county line."

He hung up the phone so he could think. All they had him on so far was kidnapping. He studied the back of Palo's head. The light from the window lit him up like an angel. "How much time can they give me if I let you go?"

"Not enough," Palo said.

"You say we was pulling a joke and I'll give you the money back."

"Half that money belongs to me," Wazenski said

"Shut up you dumb Polack. Half a million dollars don't mean nothing if you're dead."

"But half a million dollars means a lot in prison," Wazenski said.

"He's thinking like a real loser," Palo said.

"You shut your yap," Jonce said. "I'm trying to think."

"You've got no right to give back my half of the money," Wazenski said. "I won't consent to it."

"They won't let us keep the money you idiot. All we got is a piece of paper with a bunch of numbers on it," he said, pulling the paper from his pocket and holding it up for Wazenski to see. "They take this paper and we got nothing."

Palo began to laugh. Jonce watched his entire body shaking from the effort. It infuriated him but now was not the time to lose his cool.

"Make him stop laughing," Wazenski said.

Jonce kicked at the Polack but he was out of reach. "What am I? His daddy? You make him stop if it bothers you so much."

Wazenski went to Palo and punched him in the back of the head with his fist. "Shut up!"

"That a boy, Waz, you dumb Polack. Make yourself a target."

Palo fought hard against his restraints. "The joke's on you," he said. "Morons! You didn't really think I was going to give you a million dollars did you?" He laughed hysterically. "That paper's worthless! The numbers are gibberish! I outsmarted you! Instead of transferring money into your fake offshore account I sent an email to my secretary and told her where I am!"

Wazenski's jaw dropped. "You're lying," he said. He turned to Jonce. "Tell him he's lying."

"He ain't lying," Jonce said. He pulled the paper from his pocket and wadded it into a tiny ball between his fingers then flicked it against the wall.

"We watched him transfer the money," Wazenski said.

"You watched me liquidate my stocks and mutual funds and transfer the money into an offshore account. Did you pay attention to the numbers I wrote down?" He laughed again. "Now my wife can't touch a dime of it and you bozos helped me pull it off."

Jonce crawled on his hands and knees and grabbed Palo by the hair and toppled him backward to the dingy carpet. "Shut them curtains," he said to Wazenski. "Now!"

Wazenski jerked the curtains closed with great danger to himself. The sudden change from light to dark temporary blinded Jonce as he twisted Palo's hair into his left fist while his right hand retrieved the knife from his pocket.

"Kill him," Wazenski said. "Cut his damned throat!"

Palo's hysterical laughter turned to begging. The phone rang again. Jonce lay on his stomach between the beds and rested his cheek against Palo's head so that his lips brushed against the captive's ear when he spoke. "I knowed not to trust you," he said as he pressed the flat of the blade against Palo's throat. "Feel that American steel against your goozle?"

"Please," Palo said. "I was lying. The money's yours. I was just —"

"Shut up," Jonce said, still whispering. The phone continued to ring.

"I'll tell them it was a joke! I'll swear I came here of my own free will!"

"Ssshhhh," Jonce said. He eased his grip on Palo's hair. "Be quiet, little butterfly, and let me think."

Jackie had seen her share of hostage negotiations in Detroit. Some ended well, some didn't, but they always ended with the perp either dead or wearing handcuffs. Cops don't hand out airplanes and satchels full of cash the way they do in movies.

Communication with Nash had been in short bursts.

"Did you mean what you said about Palo?"

Gant broke his concentration on the motel door. "What did I say?" She grinned.

"If you're asking me if I'm going to try everything in my power to get him out in one piece, yes. If you're asking me if I'll be sorry if it doesn't turn out that way, yes again."

"Good."

"But Nash doesn't have to know that." He looked at her with resolve. "Neither does Palo."

"I wish his email had told us if they're armed," she said. "And if so, with what."

"That email business strikes me funny," Gant said. "Either he's awfully clever or those two are awfully dumb."

Officer Birch approached and told them the plate on the Pontiac came back to an ex-con named Emil Wazenski. The front desk clerk recognized him from his mugshot and said he paid cash for the room.

SWAT was two minutes out. Gant tried the phone again.

Jonce heard the clatter of a diesel engine and peeked between the curtains again. The SWAT truck rolled to a stop and men fanned out in all directions. He let the curtain fall closed and turned to Waz. "Shit just got real."

"Why don't you answer the phone and get this over with," Palo said. His bravery surged in direct disproportion to the closeness of the knife to his throat. His demeanor rode Jonce like a fat cowboy.

Jonce barked at Wazenski. "Tell the chief we want food."

"He wants to talk to you," Wazenski said. "It's a different man this time."

"Two large pizzas with everything," Jonce said. "And three big Cokes."

Wazenski spoke into the phone then lowered it again. "He said he won't do anything until he talks to you."

Jonce peered through the curtain again. The gig was up. They had less chance than a rabbit in a bear cage. He crossed the room and took the phone. "You heard the man," he said. "We want pizza and Coke. Not Pepsi. Coke. And none of that diet stuff."

"First I need some assurances from you."

"Okay, I assure you that unless you get us two large pizzas and three big Cokes I'll cut off this lawyer's ear and throw it out the door to you."

"I'm sending for the food now. In the meantime —."

"And breadsticks," Jonce said. "I don't think good on an empty stomach."

"In the meantime we need to agree to some ground rules."

"I said I don't think good when I'm hungry." He hung up the phone in a calm manner then cocked his gaze toward Waz. "My grandma would say our goose is cooked. Grandpa would say we're up shit creek without a paddle. How do they say it in Poland?"

"I've never been to Poland," Waz said.

"How can you be a Polack when you never been to Poland?"

"How can you be an asshole when you've never been to Assland?"

"You're both in deep trouble," Palo said. "Let me go and I'll represent you in court. You don't have to die in prison."

Jonce hadn't yet decided how they would leave the room. Murder would put him on death row for the next twenty years, then the needle, or whatever new way they might come up with by then to kill a man and call it humane. Twenty years was a long time. Death row scared him not so much because of what lay at the end of it, but because of the isolation. At least in general population he could live. A man can get used to almost anything except being alone. A few hours ago he would have sworn to leave the room in a bag, but staring death in the face made it more real. The closer a man gets to dying, the more he concerns himself with the accommodations. "Do you believe in hell, Waz?"

"I prefer heaven."

"I think that ship has sailed, my little Polish friend. It's hell or a dark tomb of nothingness for me and you."

A deep sadness gripped Wazenski's face. "The Bible is the Bible," he said.

"Well that's profound," Palo said. He was lying on his back still tied to the chair. Jonce told Wazenski to kick him in the head but Wazenski ignored him.

The phone rang again. Jonce picked it up and immediately dropped it back into the cradle. They hadn't had time to get the food so he had no interest in talking.

"If you stop talking to them they'll storm the room," Palo said.

"Shut up."

"First they'll fire a teargas canister through the window then they'll break through the door with a battering ram and shoot everything with a pulse. Except me, because I'm down here on the floor with my blood rushing to my head."

Wazenski kicked him in the head but not hard enough to make him stop talking.

"Give up now and we'll all live."

The phone rang again. Jonce picked it up and dropped it. "Ambitious cat, ain't he?" He looked at Wazenski and saw tears. "You crying, Waz?"

"I killed my wife," Waz said as though her dead body lay at his feet. "I'm going to hell to burn in a pit of fire forever and ever."

Palo spat an audible sigh toward the ceiling. "Please kick in the door and shoot me now," he said.

Jonce stepped toward him and put his foot on Palo's forehead. Palo howled in pain. Jonce pressed harder and twisted, grinding the leather sole of his boot into Palo's flesh. "Say one more word and I stomp." Palo bit his lip and groaned. Jonce lifted his foot and parted the curtains with a finger. The parking lot looked like a Christmas parade stuck in traffic, except Santa and his elves were wearing bulletproof vests and pointing rifles.

The phone rang again. Jonce turned to Wazenski. "Don't it say in the Bible that a man can be forgiven for anything if he asks?"

Wazenski nodded. "Something like that."

"Then what's the problem?"

"I haven't asked," Wazenski said.

"Well ask."

"The Jesus I know wouldn't spit on either one of you," Palo said.

"Then you know the wrong Jesus," Waz said. He sat on the edge of the bed and stared down at his feet. "I was a good Catholic. I went to Mass. Every Saturday morning I went to the church and confessed my sins to the priest so I could start the new week clean. It was a good way to live."

The phone continued to ring.

"Just like that? You confessed and that was it?"

Waz nodded. "Confession cleanses the soul."

"So if I pick up that phone and tell them to put a priest on the line I can confess and I won't go to hell?"

"Are you Catholic?"

"What's that got to do with it?"

"I think you have to be Catholic to confess to a priest," Wazenski said.

Jonce looked down at Palo. "What are you?"

"Leave me out of this."

"You're guilty too you know. It weren't just me."

"You cut his throat," Palo said. "Not me."

"You hired me."

"But I didn't pay you," Palo said. "I shot you instead. The contract wasn't completed so legally I —."

Jonce kicked him in the head. Palo's eyes rolled back but he didn't pass out.

The phone kept ringing. The confession angle intrigued Jonce and he wanted to know more about it. "How does somebody get to be

Catholic?"

Wazenski shrugged. "I think you have to be born into it."

"Like being a Jew?"

"I guess so."

"So why'd you quit confessing?"

He lifted his head and locked eyes with Jonce. "Because I killed my wife."

"Come home early one day from confessing and catch her with her feet in the air?"

"No."

"Riding the priest?"

"She was a faithful wife."

"So why kill her?"

"Too much salt," he said with all the seriousness of a condemned man. "Everything she cooked. Salt, salt salt."

"You killed her over salt?"

"Too much salt dries your blood. I begged her to stop. I threatened her. She ignored me. She even put salt in her apple pies."

"Did you slap her? Knock her around a little? One good slap cures a thousand ills," Jonce said, cocking his hand back to demonstrate. "Of course they need the occasional booster."

"I would never strike a woman," Wazenski said. "It's unmanly."

Jonce ignored the slight. Every culture has its quirks. "So how'd you do it? Poison?"

"No."

"Push her out a window?"

"No."

"You doctored the brakes on her car and sent her over a cliff?"

"I smothered her." He glanced up then back down. "With a pillow. My pillow. The pillow I slept on in the bed beside her for six years."

"Well I'll be damned."

"It takes a long time to smother a woman. At first she scratches and claws, then she twists and shakes and whimpers."

"I never would've figured you for the smothering type," Jonce said. He dipped his head toward Palo. "Maybe I'll let you show me how it's done. Sounds clean."

"Smothering your wife takes a lot of commitment," Waz said. "First you decide to do it, then you have to keep deciding and keep deciding until it's done."

"But you wouldn't hit her?"

"Never." When he looked up again his eyes were dry. "Sometimes at night I wake up and I'm still on top of her, holding my pillow over her face wishing she would hurry up and let me stop." He looked at Palo, who had regained his senses and was looking at them. "I think we should let him go."

"For our souls?"

"No, Jonce Nash. For his."

Jonce weighed the opposing outcomes. Prison for Palo would be a thousand times worse than a few minutes chewing on a pillow. "After we eat," he said. "Might be the last time we get pizza."

The standoff ended without injury exactly one hour and thirteen minutes after Gant delivered two large pizzas, three Cokes, and breadsticks to their room. He had insisted on handing the food off himself, refusing to put one of his officers at risk and declining the commander of the SWAT team's offer to fire a teargas canister through the window and take the room by force.

Jackie admired the way he handled himself during the crisis. He had been firm but calm. A true leader. Some people rise to an occasion and some shrink from it. His strength surprised her.

"You take the lawyer and I'll take Nash," he said to her when they arrived back at the station and the two perps had been booked. They had Palo in the interrogation room with the two-way mirror, reminding everyone within shouting distance who he was, demanding to be released. Nash waited in the private interrogation room. Wazenski was cooling his heels alone in a holding cell, minus his belt and shoelaces because he looked the type.

Jackie entered the room with Palo, wondering why her boss had allowed it. She was about to face the man responsible for destroying her life. He wasn't cuffed because he wasn't under arrest. The first thing out of his mouth was a demand to be released immediately. Jackie disliked him immensely. "You might try thanking us for saving your life," she said as she settled into the chair opposite him and placed a blank white legal pad on the table in front of her.

"You're holding me against my will," he said. "I'll sue."

She scribbled the date and time across the top of the legal pad, then she wrote both their names and a brief description of the interview about to take place. She had excellent penmanship. "Now, Mister Palo, tell me in your own words what happened."

"Those two lunatics abducted me and tried to extort a million dollars from me." He spat an off-balance laugh. "Told me to wire the money into an offshore account."

"Did you?"

"What offshore account? The idiot doesn't have an offshore account."

"So what did you do?"

"I bought twenty shares of Amazon stock and emailed my secretary," he said. "Then I checked a few other stock accounts and transferred fifty thousand from my joint checking account into an account my wife doesn't know about." His demeanor improved dramatically so that when he spoke again his voice was calm. "Those two idiots thought I was setting up an offshore account for them. I scribbled some gibberish on a piece of paper and gave it to Nash."

"So he thinks he's rich?"

"You think I'd let him leave that room thinking he outsmarted me?"

Jackie took notes as he talked, jotting down the highlights since the interview was being recorded by a microphone on the table between them and a camera mounted in the ceiling.

"You went from the hospital to a hotel. Why?"

"That's none of your business."

"You opened the door as though you were expecting someone."

"Room service," he said. She knew he was lying. She had seen the surveillance video and she knew about the girlfriend.

"A short time after you left with the two suspects, a woman came to your room."

"I didn't leave with the suspects, Miss Mulvaney, I was kidnapped." He smirked at his use of her real last name.

"It's detective," she corrected him.

"My mistake."

The microphone didn't need to hear what she *wanted* to say, so she continued with the task at hand. "We found your cell phone in the room and the hotel surveillance video doesn't show either of you carrying a laptop. Where did the laptop in the motel come from? Is it yours?"

"If you were a real detective you'd know the laptop from my office is missing. You would have checked my surveillance video and seen Nash let himself in with my key and take it off my desk."

"I'm sure your secretary would have denied us access to your surveillance video without a warrant," Jackie said. "We'll need a copy."

"Absolutely," he said. "As soon as you show me a warrant."

"Proving my point," she said.

"Forgive me if the lawyer in me refuses to allow you to trample my civil rights."

"Is there something on the video you don't want us to see?"

"I don't know. I haven't seen it yet."

Someone knocked on the door so she excused herself and stepped out into the hall and found her boss waiting. He asked for the rundown. She gave him the ten-second version.

"Nash is asking for a Bible," he said. "Says he feels a rebirth coming on."

"This one in here probably put the idea in his head."

"Palo? Why?"

"He's throwing up roadblocks."

Gant pondered the information. "So are we looking at an abduction or a scam?"

"Ask me when it's over and I'll give you the benefit of hindsight," Jackie said. In a normal world Palo would be screaming to the top of his lungs for Nash and Wazenski to be burned at the stake. She asked for a crack at Nash but Gant refused. His complaint against her was too new. As much as it rankled her, she ultimately agreed with his decision. They couldn't afford to blow the case against Nash on a technicality.

She looked around to make sure they were alone. "He called me Mulvaney," she said, kicking her head toward the room Palo was in. "It was all I could do not to punch him in the face."

"You got it on video?"

"For what good it'll do."

"Every little bit helps," Gant said. "You know it wouldn't surprise me if Palo shows up later as Nash's attorney."

"It's hard to believe Nash is dumb enough not to know the difference between an email and a wire transfer."

"He works at being dumb."

"How long do we keep Palo?"

"As much as I'd like to make him miserable for as long as possible, we need the room for Wazenski." He looked at his watch. "You know what? It's almost two and I don't know about you but I'm starved. Let's you and me go to the diner for a nice long lunch and kick Palo

261

when we get back."

Chapter Twenty-Three

T wo days had passed since the arrest of Jonce Nash and Emil Wazenski. Nash had persisted in his request for a Bible until Gant relented and told the jailer to accommodate him. It seemed a strange thing to Jackie to deny an inmate a Bible, but she understood Gant's concern. Juries are suckers for jail house conversions. Good people have a hard time fathoming evil, and Jackie believed with all her heart and soul that Jonce Nash was evil.

She also believed in the power of redemption.

It was Saturday, and unless something major happened she and the chief were both off for the weekend. If felt strange to wake up and start her day in a house with a man who was not her husband. She had cooked eggs and pancakes for breakfast, then sandwiches and soup for lunch. Gant seemed to enjoy having someone cook for him, and if she were honest with herself, she enjoyed cooking for someone who showed appreciation.

After lunch she went out to the back patio and immersed herself in a novel. It had been months since she had picked up a book. Her love of books had irritated Kelton, though she never figured out why. It was as though he felt jealous of anything that occupied her time. He denied it of course. Accused her of trying to make him look silly, but it was there every time she settled into her favorite chair with a book. Eventually she avoided reading in his presence, sneaking around as though the book were a lover, or a pornographic magazine. It had become that way with a lot of things near the end. Small things. Ordinary everyday things normal people do without thinking about unless they live with a Kelton.

Gant stepped out from the kitchen. "Where's Jordan?"

She looked up from her book and saw him standing with his back to the door. It was a beautiful spring afternoon. The back yard was heavily shaded and the breeze was fresh with the scent of spring. Each season has its own smell and she loved spring above all others. Spring is a new beginning. A promise that life will always out pace death.

"Parked in front of his video game," she said. "Where else would a fifteen-year-old boy be on a beautiful afternoon?"

"Mind if I join you?"

"It's your patio."

He sat in a matching wicker chair. A small wicker table separated them.

"My reading doesn't bother you does it?"

"Why would it?"

To most people it would seem ridiculous. Soon, hopefully, it would seem ridiculous to her again.

"What I meant was," she said, trying to wiggle out from underneath an embarrassing peek at what she had allowed herself to become, "I borrowed it from your bookshelf without asking." She held the book up for him to see. "Ivanhoe. You don't mind do you?"

"Of course I don't mind," he said. "Borrow anything you like. I've resigned myself to using my Kindle. Convenience over tradition. Does that make me a sellout?"

"Yes."

"One of these days Jordan will go into your attic and find all your paperbacks and learn what kind of person you were. My son will find my Kindle and the battery will be dead and I'll remain a mystery to him."

"I never thought of it that way," she said. "That explains why I couldn't find anything new in your bookcase."

"I was speaking hypothetically about my son of course," he said. "My window of opportunity is closing fast."

"Do you want kids?"

He contemplated the question, as though he had never been asked. He had a way of putting thought into questions he had probably answered a thousand times. "Two," he said. "A boy and a girl. I want the boy to be the oldest so he can take care of his little sister, but I don't want too much difference in their ages so they'll be friends." He frowned. "And I'd like to still be young enough that people don't mistake me for their grandfather."

They laughed. She found it easy to laugh with him. Men are

supposed to be strong and gentle with unyielding integrity yet malleable under the right woman's influence. Andrew Gant seemed to be all those things while Kelton Mulvaney was the exact opposite. Instead of strength her husband effused brutality. Instead of unyielding integrity he practiced base dishonesty. Her influence had broken against him like waves against a rocky shore.

"Life really isn't fair, is it?"

He looked at her with the curiosity of a boy. "Did I trigger something?"

Instead of answering, she simply smiled and turned back to her book. If life were fair people would grow complacent, and when complacency became the norm mankind would die from lack of trying to live. It's the struggle that makes people strong. She had read somewhere that God doesn't put anything on a person they can't handle if they try hard enough. That simple concept had carried her through the rough patches, and she had repeated it so many times to her son that it had become a joke between them.

"Do you think he'll get away with killing Stubbs?"

"It's Saturday," he said. "You're supposed to be thinking how much you enjoy my company."

She looked at him again. "I do," she said. "Very much. Thank you for letting us stay here."

He blushed. Had he wanted to he could have reached over and took her hand and she would have let him, but he didn't. Instead he said he should let her get back to reading her book and he went back inside. Thirty seconds later she realized she had just read the same sentence three times.

Jonce sat on the ground in the center of a circle of inmates preaching the gospel as he envisioned it, borrowing from the Bible tucked underneath the mattress in his cell and making up the rest out of whole cloth. The assembled group varied in age from young to old — three whites, four blacks, and two who probably didn't understand a word he was saying. Gathering an audience was easy. The men were so bored they would have listened to him read a phonebook.

There were no guards in the compound because technology had eliminated the need. Instead the guards lounged in a room with a lot of monitors attached to cameras that covered every inch of outside space, and they were eager to pounce at a moment's notice should the need arise. They also were watching Jonce. He knew because his cellmate had told him they offered to knock three months off his sentence if he got Jonce to admit he killed Perry Stubbs.

"Ain't no better friend than Jesus," he said after misquoting a scripture about walking through the shadow of death. Wazenski approached the circle and wedged himself in directly across from Jonce. "Take this poor dumb Polack here. He murdered his wife with a pillow. Smothered her. Rode her into the ground like a Fat Albert on a two-year-old gelded mare and all he has to do to walk them pearly streets of gold is ask for the forgiveness that can't be denied him because the Book says it's so."

"Mares can't be gelded," a little whip of a man sitting at Jonce's left elbow said with authority.

"Anything can be anything if you believe hard enough," Jonce said. "If Jesus will save a Polack he'll save you," he said, casting his eyes toward the two Mexicans. "Even you boys. It's true. Look it up. Last night I read about when they nailed him to that cross and he saved them two thieves."

"He only saved one of them thieves," the black man who sat nearest him said. "That other one didn't ask."

"Which proves my point," Jonce said. "All you gotta do is ask. That's it. Just ask and it's yorn. Don't matter if He saved one or both. Don't matter if He looked out over that crowd of gawkers and saved every single one of them or just the ones with blue eyes. What I'm telling you is He'll save you if you ask. Don't hurt to ask. Both them thieves died that day and one went to heaven because he asked. The other one, well, I guess he's probably still down there dancing around on them hot coals with his two broke legs playing grab ass with the devil."

Jonce closed his eyes and rested his Bible on his crossed ankles. "Now, fellow sinners, if you'll join me in a closing prayer we'll make this meeting official. He opened one eye to confirm they were complying. Wazenski was the only holdout. He closed his eyes when he saw Jonce looking at him. "Dear Heavenly Father I ask you to lay hold on this pitiful group of sinners and squeeze the wickedness out of us so we can follow Your ways and spend our eternities enjoying the wondrous kingdom of heaven. Amen."

One by one the assembled men opened their eyes and left the group until only Jonce and Wazenski remained.

Wazenski glanced over both shoulders then leaned in with a whisper. "Is this real or are you pulling some kind of scam?"

Jonce raised the Bible and kissed it. "I've seen me the light, Waz."

"Well, okay, I guess. If you say so."

"Ain't me who says so," Jonce said, tilting his face toward the sky. "It's Him."

❖

First thing Monday morning Gant put into action a plan he and Jackie had hatched on Sunday. It involved Tipton Palo. Hinged on him, in fact, though he had not yet been told.

He walked into Palo's office without an appointment and had no difficulty getting past his pretty secretary.

"There was a time when you would've had to wait," she said with a hint of sarcasm. "Now he just sits in there and pretends he's still important."

Gant went in and closed the door. Palo looked up with disinterest. "Come to arrest me again?"

Gant sat where countless men and women with legal troubles had sat. "Tell me what you know about David Sansing."

"Who?"

"Wrong answer," Gant said. "This'll go better for both of us if we skip over the part where you pretend you didn't contact a man in Detroit by the name of Kelton Mulvaney."

Palo rubbed his chin and repeated the name as though he were trying to remember. "Doesn't ring a bell," he said. "I can have Candice check my case files."

"I can get a warrant for your phone records if that's how you want to play this."

"Do you really think you can?"

Gant laughed. "Against you?"

Palo frowned. "All I did was tell the man where he could find his wife. What he did with that information is his business."

"What he did was hire a man to kidnap her minor son for the purpose of transporting him across state lines."

"You're wasting your time if you think you can pin that on me. My secretary could get that charge thrown out."

"Maybe so, maybe not. These aren't ordinary times. An awful lot of people want you put away for good. Powerful people."

"No deal, Chief. Kelton Mulvaney sent a friend to bring his son home. If anybody's facing jail time here it's your girlfriend."

"She's not my girlfriend."

"Everybody knows but you, huh?"

"She's a battered wife in fear for her son," Gant said. "For once in your life do something decent. I know charging you as an accessory may be a long shot, but she's a good person and a damned good cop, and I swear if you don't help undo what you did to her I'll do everything in my power to make your life miserable."

Palo sighed. "You haven't even told me what you want."

"I want you to contact Mulvaney again and tell him Sansing's talking. Tell him his wife is filing for divorce and she's going to clean him out. You've handled enough divorces to make it sound good."

"Won't work," Palo said. "In the first place, why would I call him with this information? What's in it for me?"

"I was getting to that," Gant said. "Tell him you know a guy who can make her go away. Make sure you're clear that it's a hit. Be specific. You know the legal requirements better than I do so make it airtight."

"He won't buy it."

"I've heard you in the courtroom," Gant said. "He'll buy it if you sell it hard enough."

"I don't even know the man," Palo said. "Why would I commit a felony for him?"

"For the same reason you told him where to find her in the first place. Money."

Palo smiled. "I didn't do it for money."

"Why then? Because she was getting too close to Nash and you're afraid he'll talk?"

Palo's smile faded. He studied the chief. "Suppose I agree to this hair-brained scheme. What's in it for me?"

"The satisfaction of knowing you helped right a wrong."

Palo laughed. "You should write Hallmark cards."

"For what it's worth, I'll talk to the DA afterwards and tell him what you did. I'll talk to Judge Bishop, too."

"That's worth exactly nothing," Palo said. "No good deed goes unpunished." He picked up a pen and clicked it with his thumb. "There is something I want from you."

"I'm listening."

"I want the mayor to stop writing lies about me on that infernal Facebook page of his."

"I don't control what the mayor writes," Gant said.

"No, but you have his ear. He likes you."

"I'll see what I can do."

"It won't be easy to sell this to Mulvaney," Palo said. "He's a shrewd businessman."

"I thought you didn't know him."

Palo smiled again. "I do my research."

"As would a shrewd businessman," the chief said. "I googled you before I came over and it's not pretty. Tell him you've spent everything on legal bills."

Palo clicked the pen again. "Now for the ten-thousand-dollar question, Chief. What's in it for you?"

"I stand up for my cops."

"Especially the attractive females?"

"It's not like that," Gant said.

Palo tossed the pen onto the open file he had been perusing when Gant barged in. "Okay, I'll play along. You buy her with a favor and I buy you."

"Nobody's buying anybody," Gant said. "This is you fixing what you did to her. Nothing more."

Palo winked. "We'll do it here."

"I'll send my tech over to set up the equipment," Gant said.

"Not necessary," Palo said. "I have the best recording equipment money can buy. Besides, I don't trust your man not to accidentally leave something behind when it's over."

Gant rose to leave. "Okay, but don't forget Mulvaney has to say what the money's for. He has to be specific."

"We'll trod this slippery slope together, you and I," Palo said. "How does it feel to have so much power over a man's life?"

Gant didn't answer. Instead he asked the million dollar question: "How'd you find out about her anyway?"

Palo smiled. "Nash told me."

"Nash? How did he find out?"

"He didn't say."

All morning Wazenski stuck to Jonce like a tick. Lurking, always underfoot. Something was up and Jonce had a notion what it was. The Polack had been turned.

He had just finished church service with a group of blacks when Wazenski motioned for him to step over to a private spot. He went expecting to get served a baited question about Perry Stubbs. Wazenski stood with his right shoulder against the fence looking nervous, avoiding eye contact. "I'm going to finger Prichard and I need your help."

The statement surprised Jonce. "Finger him how?"

"Those papers," Wazenski said.

"Them's my papers."

"I want them back. I figure I can give them Prichard in exchange for my freedom."

"What about my freedom?"

Wazenski raised his eyes. "They'll never let you go, Jonce, you know that. Me they don't care about so much."

Jonce grabbed Wazenski by the collar and jerked him close. "How much have you told?"

"Nothing! I swear! I haven't told them anything."

Jonce released him with a shove. "Good," he said, looking around to see if they had attracted unwanted attention. Everyone seemed to be going about their business of being bored. "Don't you say a word about Prichard. Not one word. Got it? He's my property."

Wazenski looked ready to cry. He was weak. The chief and his detective could break him easy. "I should've killed you when I had the chance," Jonce said. "And I still might so don't go braining up no ideas about selling me out."

"I wouldn't sell you out," Wazenski said. "We're friends."

"Not one word to anybody about what we got on Prichard."

"Okay, I won't."

Jonce poked him in the chest with his finger. "I got me a plan for us."

Chapter Twenty-Four

Tuesday morning for Jackie began with a summons to the chief's office. She stepped into his office carrying a fresh cup of coffee from the break room.

"Sit down," he said. "And close the door."

She pushed the door closed. "That bad?"

Gant waited for her to sit. "Jonce Nash cut a deal with the DA."

Until that moment Everett Mosby had been a name attached to an office, nothing more. She had met him but had not formed an opinion of him as the county's chief prosecutor. "What kind of deal?"

"The kind of deal where he walks," Gant said.

Jackie almost crushed the Styrofoam cup in her hand. They had Jonce Nash dead to rights. The case was airtight. "That's impossible," she said, knowing by the look on Gant's face that it wasn't. "What's he offering?"

"Gain Prichard," Gant said. "On a silver platter with all the trimmings."

"That explains a lot," she said, remembering how Prichard had steered Nash during the sting operation. "So we trade a murderer for a crooked parole officer?"

"Technically we're trading a kidnapper for a crooked parole officer," he said. "Contingent on the documents Nash claims to have in his possession being legitimate."

"Documents?"

"Nash claims to have a trove of documents he now admits he stole from Tipton Palo's safe. Stubbs sent Nash to Palo's house to find the safe and burn it open. Nash combed through the documents and found Prichard's name."

"So he removed a little something for himself," she said. "He's not as dumb as he pretends to be."

"Something like that," Gant said. "Birch and Ramey are at that burned-out gas station down the street from Nash's apartment retrieving them as we speak."

"Should I go?"

"No. They can handle it. I don't want Nash saying you tossed anything if it turns out he's lying."

"I hope he's lying," she said. "He's too dangerous to be back out on the streets."

"All the more reason for you to solve this homicide and put him away for good."

"So you believe he did it?"

"He admitted to blowing open the safe and stealing the documents that got Stubbs killed. We know he went through them before turning some over to Stubbs. Maybe he tried to play both ends against the middle and it got too hot for him."

"I've been thinking about how he found out about me," Jackie said. "I know he was outside my door at least twice, but I don't remember saying anything about Detroit."

"Maybe he was outside your door more than twice," he said.

"I'm too careful. He had to find out some other way."

"Maybe Palo was lying," Gant said. "Maybe Nash had nothing to do with it."

"Why would he lie about it?"

"To spook you."

"I guess it makes no difference now," she said, thinking she might sleep better knowing exactly what she had done to trip herself up. "I hope Nash killed Stubbs."

"I hope you can prove it."

"I hope Palo paid him and they turn on each other," she said, but she knew that was asking a lot. Things don't always wrap up nice and clean in real life. Sometimes the bad guy wins. "Aren't you concerned about a conflict of interest letting me go after Palo now?"

"No, but go slow. We don't want to jeopardize our other deal. Focus on Nash for now. Let Palo think he's smarter than we are. After he makes the call to your husband he's all yours."

Gant's phone rang. He had a very short conversation and hung up. "That was Ramey," he said. "They found the box of documents right where Nash said they would be. They're on their way back here with it now. If Prichard's guilty, we might be taking dozens of Jonce Nashes off the street."

Jackie shuddered at the thought of a dozen Jonce Nashes, but she knew that Prichard didn't create him. Nash's kind of evil wasn't taught. It couldn't be passed from person to person like a bottle of whiskey. "What about Wazenski? Did Mosby kick him too?"

"No."

"There may be an opportunity there," Jackie said. "The man who masterminded a kidnapping goes free while his accomplice takes the full ride."

"Explore it."

"Any chance Prichard knows something on Nash?"

"Explore that too," Gant said. "Explore everything."

"How long do I have before he's out?"

"I asked Everett to drag his feet on the release. I'll certainly drag mine." He glanced at his watch. "We need to get this business with Palo and your husband over with as soon as possible."

"Does he know about Nash's deal?"

"Not as far as I know," he said. "Mosby promised to keep it under wraps until after Palo makes the call to your husband but you know how this sort of thing gets around. I've got it set up for one o'clock at Palo's office."

"I'd like to be there."

"I wouldn't have it any other way," he said. "But only as a spectator. I'll handle Palo."

Everett Mosby was a short round man with a bad comb over and tiny round spectacles that reminded Jonce of a picture he had seen once of Ben Franklin. Their one and only meeting had taken place in a private room at the jail. The next meeting, Jonce hoped, would take place in an office someplace with no bars on the windows and no guards hovering. The scent of freedom fit well in Jonce's nostrils.

Wazenski had been asking questions and making a general nuisance of himself. Sooner or later he would learn the truth and go ballistic, but that was his hill to climb. When it gets down to the nut cutting, a man has to look out for himself.

"You heard from Prichard yet?"

"No, Waz, I told you five minutes ago I ain't heard from Prichard yet. Now go the hell away and let me think."

A lanky billboard for jail house tats approached Jonce from nine o'clock and asked him what time he was holding church.

"I quit all that," Jonce said. "Go suck on somebody else's tit." He waited the patient amount of time. "Well, go on. Get outta here!" The man sauntered off in an aimless direction. Jonce asked Wazenski if he had ever seen such a pitiful bunch of losers. When he got no answer, he looked around. Wazenski had walked away in the opposite direction, aimless in his own regard. Jonce felt almost sorry for him. Almost. Sympathy was an ailment Jonce rarely suffered.

After a while he noticed Wazenski propped against the fence in the shade talking to a large black man named Daryl. Wazenski glanced his way, then Daryl glanced. He was a big man in both physical stature and in the sway he held over the jail's black population. Jonce flipped them both the bird.

The sting took place in Palo's office at one o'clock on the dot. The disgraced attorney sat behind his enormous desk with the smugness of a banker who had just landed the Apple account. Gant and Jackie sat on the client side in leather chairs that were more comfortable than most people's living room furniture. Oversized paintings hung on the walls in frames that were almost gaudy.

Palo placed the call with his phone on speaker. It was an expensive model with superb sound quality. Kelton Mulvaney's voice sent a chill up Jackie's spine when she heard it for the first time in weeks. It was hard for her not to picture herself in the room with him.

The call was being recorded by Palo's personal equipment. He often recorded his calls, he had told Gant. Some of those recordings would be used against him and his associates in court at various future dates.

"That wife of yours has got our police chief wrapped around her little finger," Palo said after announcing himself. He looked at Jackie and smiled, ignoring Gant completely. She resisted the urge to look at Gant. If any finger-wrapping had taken place, Palo had the roles reversed.

"You have five seconds to convince me not to hang up," Kelton said. "Five … four …"

"You're in a lot of trouble," Palo said with the delivery of a disinterested party. "You sent an idiot to do what should have been an easy job. He botched it, and now he's talking to the cops."

"I don't know what you're talking about."

"Ordinarily I wouldn't care, but since I'm the one who told you where to find the boy, well, you can understand my predicament."

"I should think you have more important things to worry about, Mister Palo. Why concern yourself with my problems?"

Palo laughed an easy laugh. "Let's not kid each other. I could give a rat's ass what happens to you one way or another and I'm sure the feeling's mutual, so let's get down to business. I need money."

"Are you blackmailing me?"

"That's one way to look at it, of course I'd prefer to think of it as me offering you a service."

"And why should I pay you for a service I don't need?"

"Oh, but you do need it, Mister Mulvaney. You need it very badly. You're about to be indicted on attempted kidnapping charges and a few other technical offenses."

"I'm not afraid of your small town southern sheriffs," Kelton said.

"Well this small town southern sheriff happens to know a federal prosecutor," Palo said. "We have those down here, you know, and they don't all have fat bellies and tobacco stained teeth. "The prisons down here are extremely uncomfortable. Especially during the summer, and our summers run April through November."

"Are you speaking from future experience?"

"I'm too good an attorney to go to prison," Palo said. "You on the other hand —."

"I have good attorneys too, Mister Palo. Don't concern yourself with my comfort."

"Detroit attorneys in front of a southern jury equals conviction, but if you're okay with that I'm sorry I wasted your time."

Jackie tensed at what she perceived to be a white flag by Palo. Gant touched her knee, then jerked his hand away as though he had touched a hot stove. She glanced at him and saw his embarrassment.

"I'm not comfortable discussing legal matters over the telephone," Kelton said. Jackie's hopes renewed. His tone told her Palo had his attention but his paranoia was an impenetrable firewall.

"If you don't trust your phones," Palo said, "then perhaps I've said too much already."

"It's not my phones I don't trust."

Palo laughed. "Have you ever heard of a firm called Hermetics?"

"No."

"You should look into it," Palo said. "It's a security firm based in Brussels and they specialize in communications. They use the same technology our government uses to secure the President's phones on Air Force One. Their service is very expensive. Between the time I dialed your number and when your phone rang, their technology had already swept your line for bugs."

Kelton hesitated, then he told Palo to make his pitch.

"The idiot you sent to grab up your son is ready to testify under oath that you paid him to kill your wife."

"That's absurd!"

"Absurd it may be, Mister Mulvaney, but that's what's about to happen if you don't do something to shut him up."

"My lawyers will rip him to shreds."

"Maybe so, maybe not. Like I said before, southern juries can be peculiar, but you've got bigger problems. Your wife is planning to divorce you and take everything but your shorts. She'll allege spousal abuse, and she's got a damned good case thanks to Sansing and his big mouth."

"How do you know all this?"

"Because your wife came into my office this morning and put down a ten-thousand-dollar retainer for my services."

"Why you dirty bastard!"

"Dirty bastard indeed," Palo said. "And more. I'm also a very good lawyer. Fortunately for you I'm for sale to the highest bidder."

There was a long silence. Jackie and Gant had begun passing notes to each other. Palo was going off script. Gant signaled him to end the call but Palo waved him off.

"Exactly what are you suggesting, Mister Palo?"

"Hayes is a crooked town," Palo said. "I know because I had a hand in corrupting it. I may be in trouble but I've still got people on my payroll. People who know how to make certain problems go away … for a price."

"Meaning what exactly?"

"For half a million dollars, David Sansing will hang himself in his cell."

"And my wife?"

"I'll handle her divorce and she'll walk away with the clothes on her back." He looked at Jackie and winked. "And you'll have your son back home with you."

"Suppose I want her dead too?"

"We don't kill our women down here," Palo said.

"I'll need time to think about it."

"You've got thirty seconds."

The seconds ticked off before Kelton Mulvaney spoke again. "Hang the son of a bitch."

Palo hung up the phone and reared back in his chair looking very proud of himself. "How's that for a sales job?"

Jackie understood now what Gant had meant when he said Palo was a master in front of a jury.

"I've never heard of this security company," Gant said. "What was the name? Hermetics?"

Palo laughed. "Doesn't exist. I made it up on the fly. The feds are probably analyzing the call as we speak."

"Suppose he googles it?"

"Does it really matter at this point?"

"We don't have a case until money changes hands," Gant said. "You shouldn't have given him a name to search."

"Giving him the name is what sold the lie," Palo said. "Besides, if he googles it and comes up empty, so what? Would a firm that secures the President's phones allow itself to be googled?"

Jonce sat in the small windowless room down the hall from the cellblock shuffling his feet against the discolored tile floor. They had him shackled hand and foot like an animal while the DA teetered about someplace totally oblivious to the fact that he had an afternoon appointment. He was probably taking a long lunch with all the defense attorneys letting them slap his back and congratulate him on the smart way he had sent their clients upriver with the paddle jammed up their backsides.

The door opened and Jonce looked up. "You're late."

Everett Mosby had a twitchy look about him as he entered the room with his briefcase swinging at his side and his hard-soled shoes pecking at the floor, pretending not to notice that he had been spoken to until he reached the table and pulled out the wooden chair so that its feet scrubbed against the floor like fingernails on a chalkboard.

"My apologies, Mister Nash, did you have someplace to be?" He flashed a toothy grin. "Perhaps some more pleasurable engagement than trying to convince me that the story you told me this morning is anything but horse shit?"

Jonce hit the table with his fist. "We made a deal damn you!"

Mosby looked ready to bolt. "Calm down," he said, looking about himself as though someone might rush to his aid. "We made a deal and I'm sticking to it … against my better judgment I'll have you know. I saw your … documents. I read them in fine detail."

"And?"

"And … they seem sufficient … meaning they paint Gain Prichard in a bad light. A very bad light. I don't enjoy these kinds of deals very much." He had regained his composure from the scare. "He and I are on the same team, so to speak."

"Well I do enjoy it very much," Jonce said. "I enjoy the hell out of it. You be sure to tell him I sent you." He eyed the DA's comb over. "How come you don't cut that?"

Mosby didn't comprehend, then he did. His cheeks flushed and his hand flew to his head and patted his pink scalp. "I'll thank you to keep your snide remarks to yourself. It's not too late to put your documents in the shredder and send you back to a cell."

Jonce grinned. "I was just funning."

Mosby opened his briefcase and produced a small stack of papers Jonce recognized, then he closed it again and placed it on the floor beside his feet. "Now you told me in our first meeting that you stole these documents from a safe in Tipton Palo's home. Is that still your story?"

"Took," Jonce said. "Not stole."

The DA frowned. "From a safe in his home?"

"Yes."

"Describe the safe, including its location."

Jonce framed the width and height of the safe with his shackled hands as he described it, then added that it was flat enough to hide behind a picture hanging on the wall in Palo's study. He then told Mosby how he cut it open using a blowtorch he had borrowed from the pawn shop.

The DA interrupted. "The pawn shop belonging to Perry Stubbs?"

"That be the one," Jonce said. "I think I told you all this last time."

"I'm seeing if you can tell the same story twice."

Jonce grinned. "How'd I do? Did I get it right?"

Mosby had a perfect scowl. "Fine. We'll skip the rest for now. You'll have to repeat it all in front of a jury, though, and you'd better tell it the same way or I'll lock you back up so fast it'll make your head spin."

"And if that wife of his says she helped me find that safe she's lying. She weren't nowhere to be seen."

Mosby raised his eyes and looked across the table at Jonce without lifting his head. "I'm not amused by your hick persona, Mister Nash. If you'd like to get out of those handcuffs so you can go home and take a much needed bath, I suggest you cooperate."

Jonce assumed his most serious expression. "I sincerely apologize for my behavior. You're a busy man and I've been wasting your time and —."

"Knock it off." Mosby pulled a paper from the folder and examined it. "Who else knows about this?"

"Prichard knows," Jonce said. "And Tipton Palo. Stubbs would've known but he died."

"Anyone else?"

"The little Polack who helped me grab Palo knows because he —."

"Refrain yourself from xenophobic remarks, Mister Nash, or this meeting will be over before it starts."

"I've very sorry, sir," Jonce said. "The size-unmentioned Polack who —."

Mosby slapped the table with the flat of his hand and turned red in the face. "My grandmother was Polish you miserable little bastard and she almost died in one of Hitler's death camps!" He sucked a deep breath and held it until he regained the color in his cheeks.

"My apologies again, sir. I meant no disrespect to your dearly departed grandmother who I'm sure was a fine woman of unquestionable virtue. Hitler was a depraved bastard who I hear had a very tiny —."

"DOES ANYONE other than your accomplice, Emil Wazenski, know about these documents? Yes or no?"

"Prichard."

"Except Prichard."

"No."

"And how did he — Wazenski — come to know about them?"

"Prichard told him."

The DA looked surprised. "Prichard told him?"

"See, the — uh, Wazenski, worked for Prichard, doing illegal stuff, so when I tried to blackmail Prichard with the documents he sent the little — Wazenski — to my apartment to steal 'em, which he did until I beat his ass and stole 'em back."

"Prichard?"

"The aforementioned Polish gentleman."

"So Wazenski can corroborate your story?"

"If that means what I think it does, yes."

"It means if I ask him, he'll tell me the same thing you just told me."

"If he don't he'll be lying."

"Okay," Mosby said, flipping through the first three pages then back to the start. "Let's go over the finer points of what we have here." For the next hour he read line after line, page after page in his monotone voice, pausing only to ask Jonce if he knew this thing or that thing.

Finally able to take no more, Jonce interrupted. "Do you believe in God, Mister Mosby?"

Mosby stopped reading and looked Jonce in the eye. "Most certainly."

"Well for the love of Him would you please stop asking me about stuff I don't know?"

Mosby sighed, closed the folder, and jotted another notation on his pad. "Are you prepared to testify in court?"

"Can't wait."

"You'll have to behave yourself and not act a fool the way you have today."

"I'll make you proud to know me."

"I doubt that very much," Mosby said. "Something tells me I'll regret this, but you're free to go."

"Right now?"

"As soon as you're processed out."

"Can you tell 'em to shake a leg? They work harder getting a man in than they do getting him out."

"I'm sure they're as eager to get rid of you as you are to be gotten rid of." He stood. "Stay away from Tipton Palo or I'll rip up our agreement and throw the book at you."

"Tipton who?"

"And stay away from Detective Deen and her son. Especially her son. If she shoots you I very well may look the other way."

Jonce jiggled the handcuffs. "Can I get these off? They're starting to chafe."

Mosby collected his papers and left the room. A short time later a guard entered and began the process of making Jonce Nash a free man again.

Chapter Twenty-Five

T wo days elapsed between Palo's phone call to Kelton Mulvaney and David Sansing's jail house execution. He had agreed to cooperate in exchange for the charges against him being dropped. Gant ordered a utility shed behind City Hall to be cleared out for the photo shoot. Only one tight shot was needed but it had to be believable, which meant the use of real blood they had obtained from a local veterinarian. They had decided against a hanging because it was difficult to stage.

"Stop being so nervous," Jackie said to their model. "We're not really going to kill you." She had applied and wiped off and reapplied makeup on the same spot on his forehead five times without getting it right. "Maybe stabbing him in the back would be easier," she said to Gant. "Tape a handle to the back of his shirt and pour some blood on him and be done with it."

"Yeah, do that," Sansing said. "You're rubbing the skin off my head."

Gant said he wanted one shot and it had to include the face with enough clarity to remove all doubt it was Sansing. They kicked around ideas and discussed angles and lighting like two stage managers behind the scenes of a play.

"Get on the floor," Jackie said. "Lie on your right side and stick your right arm out a little." She waited until he was on the floor. "Now draw your legs up a little. Bend your knees. Let your other arm hang loose." She stepped back and peered at him through a finger camera. "I think if we shoot from the front … somewhere about here … we can get a clean shot of his face and the handle of a knife sticking out between his shoulder blades. We can break the blade out of the handle

282

and mount it to the floor somehow instead of trying to glue it to his skin."

"I like it," Sansing said. "Do it quick because this concrete's hard as a rock."

"Shut up," Jackie said. "After what you tried to do to my son I've got a good mind to use a real knife."

Gant rolled his eyes and smiled. Earlier he had grilled her to be sure she was okay with trapping her husband this way. Kelton was evil, and she was tired of being afraid, so yes. She was tired of not fighting back. She wanted Jordan to know that it was okay to fight back, even against people you are supposed to love. The plan was for Palo to send the photo, then wait for her husband to make the payoff.

"I'll sleep fine," she said, answering a question Gant hadn't asked. She knew by the way he watched her that he was expecting her to back out.

"So will I," he said.

"You won't hold it against me for dragging you into something that goes against your conscience?"

"Honest men don't hire hitmen," Gant said.

"It's no different than setting up a drug buy."

"No different at all," he said.

She began to second-guess herself. If she was willing to entrap her husband to save herself, would she be willing later to entrap someone else she thought was guilty to save his victim? The difference was that she knew her husband was guilty. There was no doubt. Did that make it right? Did wearing a badge give her special protections?

Sansing groaned. "Can we please get this over with?"

"Shut up," Gant said.

They spent the next half hour taking pictures that all looked too clean. Finally it occurred to Jackie that a man who had just knifed another inmate would get away as fast as he could. If he had to have proof he would snap the picture quickly and run. She went outside, then ran in and took a picture without aiming, then looked at it. It was too blurred. She repeated the process five more times, each time either blurring the photo or missing the details. On the sixth attempt she got the shot she wanted. A blurred image that was a little off center but captured the face and the handle of the knife. The pool of blood was the icing on the cake.

❖

Sansing raised hell at not being set free as soon as his death photos were taken, but Gant wasn't about to release the bait before the trap they had set for Kelton Mulvaney had sprung. Instead of sending him back to a cell, they stuck him in one of the interrogation rooms and posted a guard at the door with strict instructions that the prisoner was to have no contact with anyone. No exceptions.

Jackie was having second thoughts now that the photos were ready to be sent. What had seemed like a no-brainer a few hours ago now felt like a millstone around her neck. She was about to send Jordan's father to prison for a very long time. Sure, he was an abusive husband and a terrible father, but he wasn't a killer. Palo had sold him on the hit like a used car salesman. A good lawyer might get it thrown out, or a sympathetic jury might not punish it. Then where would she be? What would he do to her then?

Gant knocked and entered without being invited. Being the boss, he could come and go as he pleased, but being a good boss he didn't. He placed a thumb drive on the edge of her desk and sat. "All ready to go," he said. "Palo's waiting." The plan was for them to deliver the pictures to Palo and be present to witness him emailing a private link to Kelton. Once the money changed hands it would no longer be her decision. Mosby had seemed eager to bag himself a Detroit businessman, thinking perhaps it would make good copy for whatever campaign ads he decided to run in the near future.

"It seems more real than it did a few hours ago," she said.

"We can't hold Sansing much longer," Gant said. "The first call he'll make will be to your husband."

Her head swirled with guilt and indecision. Kelton Mulvaney was a bad man but she didn't hate him. There had been a time when she loved him with a ferocity that rivaled anything she had ever felt. There were times when she thought she hated him. Times when she wanted him dead. But he was the father of her son. Their son. She couldn't send her husband to prison without sending her son's father to prison. "You know, I haven't even mentioned this to Jordan. He should have a say in what happens to his father." She raised her eyes, expecting Gant to say something he didn't say. She envied his strength. "Well, shouldn't he have a say?"

"No."

"It's his father."

"You asked me a question and I answered it." His eyes dropped to the thumb drive on her desk. "I could take that over myself," he said. "You don't have to be involved at this point. As a matter of fact, you probably shouldn't be."

"I'm a cop."

"A cop who also happens to be the victim. Let me take care of this for you."

"He wasn't always like this," she said.

"Sure he was. Maybe not with you — not at first — but men don't change what they are."

"I can't stop thinking about Jordan. If both his parents end up in jail who'll take care of him?"

"You're not going to jail."

"Once they extradite me I'll be on his turf. I've seen how justice works when the system is rigged."

A movement in the doorway caught her eye. The mayor stood with his cane hooked across his left forearm and his hat in his hand. "What's this about extradition and jail?"

Gant seemed suddenly aware that he should have closed the door when he came in. "Nothing, Mister Mayor," he said, turning to see the man standing behind him. "We were just having a hypothetical conversation."

"Hypothetical," the mayor said, stepping forward and closing the door behind him so that the three of them now occupied her small space. "I consider myself something of an authority on the hypothetical. Fill me in."

Gant rose and offered the mayor his chair.

"Keep your chair, son. The effort it takes to plant and un-plant myself is hardly worth being off my feet for a few minutes." He looked at them both with no small degree of curiosity. "Or is this hypothetical a personal matter that's none of my business?"

Gant stepped back from the chair. "I really don't think —."

"I was eavesdropping," the mayor said. "And you left the door open. We share the blame. Now what is this about my detective being extradited?"

"I'm married," Jackie said. "My real name is Mulvaney. My husband is an important businessman in Detroit."

"I dislike him already. I bet he has terrific connections."

"Her husband was violent," Gant said.

"Please, let her tell her story if you don't mind," the mayor said. He looked at Gant, then at her, then back at the chief. "Unless this is some kind of love triangle."

"No, absolutely not," Gant said with an abruptness that made Jackie wonder if he found the idea repulsive. "Our relationship is completely professional."

"But the detective and her son *are* staying at your house."

"How did you —."

The mayor laughed. "I've fielded five calls this week from concerned citizens asking me if I knew what my police chief is up to."

Jackie felt the need to jump in. "My husband sent one of his thugs down to kidnap my son and Chief Gant offered us a safe place to stay. Nothing improper happened."

Mayor Pigg tossed his hat onto her desk and eased himself down into the chair Gant had vacated. The discomfort in his face aged him beyond his years. He sat for a moment in absolute silence.

"So you're a battered wife?"

"Was."

"And your son? How old is he?"

"Fifteen."

"And did your husband also —?"

"Once. That's when we left and came here."

"Why here?"

"Hayes needed a detective and I needed a job."

"You had no previous connections to here?"

"No sir."

"And that story you told me about your father in Birmingham?"

"Partly true."

The mayor seemed to ponder the situation. She and Gant exchanged a series of furtive glances. She had lied on her application and was probably about to be fired.

"I've never quite understood our judicial system when it comes to battered women and children," the mayor said. "If a man punches a stranger in the nose he gets arrested and charged with assault, but if he punches his wife, nothing happens. Can either of you tell me why that is?"

"Battered wives too often refuse to press charges against their husbands," Gant said.

"Because they're afraid? Of course they're afraid. Why shouldn't they be? Why doesn't our courts protect them? Why don't fathers and brothers and uncles protect the women in their family from these ... these monsters?"

"Sometimes they don't know," Jackie said. The mayor's passion touched her. "We go to great lengths to keep it hidden."

"Why? Because you're afraid?"

"Because we're ashamed," she said.

"Ashamed? Of what? You haven't done anything wrong."

"Failure."

The mayor looked puzzled. "Failure? Help me understand. Please."

"Failure in our marriage. In our lives. Failure that we allow someone to have so much control over us."

Tears clouded the mayor's eyes. "Do you blame your father for not protecting you?"

"Sir?"

"Your father," he said. "Do you ever ask yourself why he didn't protect you?"

"Of course not. He didn't know."

"Why didn't he know?"

"Because I never told him."

"Why didn't you tell him? Didn't you trust him? Was he weak and you were afraid he wouldn't protect you?"

Jackie searched Gant's face for help. "I, uh, ——."

Gant came to her rescue. "Perhaps if you tell her why you're asking."

Jackie's eyes shifted back to the mayor.

"Yes, the dreaded backstory all readers hate," the mayor continued. "My daughter Amy. She's serving a sentence in a California prison because she killed the monster she was married to." A tear rolled down his cheek and he didn't bother to wipe it. He seemed utterly lost in his thoughts.

"I'm sorry."

He looked at her as though he had forgotten she was in the room. "We sent her to Ole Miss, thinking we were doing the right thing. Every parent wants their child to get an education. She ran off to California with a football player who was supposed to end up in the NFL. I have a grandson by him that I didn't know existed until a short time ago. He lives with my wife and me now. No one knows where his father is."

Jackie felt suddenly confused.

"No, he wasn't the man my daughter killed. She never married the boy's father. His NFL career didn't pan out and he abandoned her. She married a rich man in California without telling us. We didn't hear from her for years other than the few calls she made to tell us she was all right." He hesitated, then continued. "She was afraid of how I would react to her having a child by a black man." He hesitated again, perhaps waiting for her to respond. She didn't. "Well, to be honest with you she was probably right. I would have reacted badly." He sniffed and tried to regain his composure. "Long story short, her husband beat her and she ran away. She came home but he found her. He sent someone to kidnap her and drag her back. Apparently he didn't want the boy. My wife and I, along with our grandson, were abducted and on our way to California to be killed when I ... well, that's why I'm in this broken physical state."

"The mayor was a hero," Gant interjected. "CNN and Fox News sent crews down to cover his story."

Mayor Pigg waved him off. "All that hero stuff is hogwash. The truth of the matter is that my daughter killed her husband because she didn't trust me to protect her. You see, I've always been something of a coward."

"I don't believe that," she said.

"No, it's true. I'm ashamed of it but I no longer deny it. I was a coward when I grabbed that demon and rode him out the door of that RV. I lived and he died. There was nothing heroic about it. It was pure desperation and abject fear on my part."

"It sounds pretty brave to me," she said.

"You are in the presence of one of the sorriest specimens of the male gender that God ever produced, but I'm no longer afraid. Fear is the worst of human emotions. Worse than hate because fear gives birth to hate. Fear will eat at your soul until there's nothing left but shame and self-loathing." His eyes were dry now. "Don't let your husband destroy you." He turned his attention to the chief. "Don't you let her destroy herself. Whatever you have on that thumb drive ... use it. Employ it to whatever lengths necessary. Don't hide behind the law or some misguided sense of morality and let them drag her back to Detroit. That's an order."

"Chief Gant can't stop an extradition," she said.

"Nonsense! If he won't hide you out at his house then you come to mine. We'll hide you — Mildred and I."

"Extradition is a legal process," Gant said. "The only way to fight it is through the courts."

"The only way to fight it is tooth and nail. Don't confuse right and wrong with justice. Justice admits its blindness. It brags about it." He shook his finger at the chief. "If you let them take this young woman back to Detroit I'll take your badge. You won't get a job as dogcatcher in this town as long as I'm running it, and make no mistake about it, young man, I'm running it."

"I'll do my best, sir," Gant said.

Mayor Pigg nodded. "I know you will." He looked at Jackie, calm again. "I picked him, you know. Did he tell you that? We're cleaning this town up, him and me. The crooks around here don't know what hit 'em." He winked. "God not only gave us the right to protect ourselves and the ones we love, he demands it. He charged us with that duty, not Thomas Jefferson and George Washington, and if we carry out that duty He'll protect us. Either down here or up there," he said, pointing toward the ceiling.

"Thank you, sir," Jackie said.

Mayor Pigg struggled himself free of the chair and took his hat from the desk. "May I make one more suggestion?"

"Of course," Jackie said.

"The next time the two of you have a private conversation, close the door."

Jonce couldn't resist the temptation of telling Gain Prichard in person what he had done to him. He waltzed into his office Thursday afternoon and sat down and looked across the desk at him with a contrived hangdog look on his face.

Prichard eyed him with agitated confusion then checked his calendar. "You're not due in until next week. Scram."

"Won't be no next week for you, Mister Prichard."

"What's that supposed to mean?"

Jonce fished a cigarette from his pocket and pushed it between his lips, challenging Prichard to enforce the no-smoking rule.

"You know you can't smoke that in here. Now get lost. I'm busy." Suddenly his face snapped to life. "Say, how'd you get out of jail?"

"They turned me loose."

"Turned you loose? Nobody told me they were turning you loose." He snatched up his phone and stabbed at the keypad.

"I wouldn't poke that bear if I was you, Mister Prichard"

Prichard's finger hovered over the last digit. Jonce dipped his eyes toward the cradle. Prichard lowered the phone. "What's going on here?"

"They threatened to send me back until the hairs on my nut sack turn gray. I did the only thing I knowed to do."

The muscles in Prichard's face danced and twitched as the understanding of what Jonce had done settled on him. "You fingered me?"

"So deep I had to wash my elbow," Jonce said.

Prichard shot to his feet and glared down at Jonce like a wild animal. "I'll break you in two!"

"Sit down, Mister Prichard. Let's be men about this." He watched Prichard's emotions twist and turn. "Come on. Sit down. Big men like you don't need to be jumping around and putting all that strain on your heart."

Prichard maintained rigid eye contact as he lowered himself back into his chair. "If this is some kind of joke I don't think —."

"You know it ain't."

Prichard's face twisted and contorted itself into panicked confusion. "Why? We had a deal."

"They had my nuts in a wringer. It was either squeal or be a eunuch."

The blood drained from Prichard's face and left his cheeks white as milk. Jonce lit his cigarette and took a drag. "The district attorney is a mousy little fella but he riles easy. Don't ask him about his comb over. He's touchy about it."

Prichard stared off into space and moved his lips but no sound came out.

"Are you having a stroke?"

"Get out."

"You'll have a bad time of it in prison, Mister Prichard. You know that don't you? Better ask for isolation or you won't be able to hold a quart fruit jar in your ass by week two. I seen this one guy who'd been a security guard at a tire plant and they —."

"Shut up!"

Jonce stubbed his cigarette out on the arm of his chair and thumped it toward the trash can. Prichard's color began to come back as his anger rose. "You'll probably recognize plenty of old clients. Long as you gave 'em a fair shake they'll treat you all right I reckon. Of course your idea of a fair shake might be their idea of a raw deal."

Prichard dropped his forehead into his hands. "I've got a gun in my desk drawer," he said. "If you're still here in five seconds I'm going to shoot you." He pulled open the drawer. Jonce stood and saw the revolver. "Five. Four."

"I'm going."

"Three."

Jonce quickstepped it to the door. "If I was you I think I'd go ahead and use that."

"Two."

"A man your age … with what they've got on you."

"One!"

Prichard's hand went for the gun at the same time Jonce turned and threw the door open. As he bolted out the door a shot hit the glass and shattered it. People on the sidewalk began to scatter and scream. Jonce ran as hard as he could for half a block then ducked behind his truck for cover in case Prichard came out after him. When he peeked up over the right front fender he saw the shattered glass on the sidewalk but not Prichard. A siren wailed in the distance. He stood. He hadn't broken any laws and there were witnesses so he decided to stay put and watch the fun. A second shot sealed it.

Gant walked the thumb drive containing Sansing's death photo down the street to Palo's law office and made it past his secretary without her looking up from her phone.

"You know you could've emailed it," Palo said. "Saved me the trouble of offloading it to my laptop then sending it to my phone."

"I don't want it getting out except to Mulvaney," Gant said.

"I'll Snapchat it," Palo said. "He gets to see it then it disappears."

"I'll wait," Gant said.

"Don't trust me?"

"No."

Palo smiled but didn't laugh. He inserted the stick into a USB port on his laptop and brought the picture up on his screen. "Looks real enough. I like what you did with the eyes."

"I've seen my share of dead bodies," Gant said.

Palo worked his mouse then picked up his cell phone and opened his email. "You can come around and watch if you want to," he said. "It's a really simple process. I email it to myself then copy it from the email on my phone and paste it into Snapchat." In a matter of seconds it was done. "There. As soon as he opens it and sends me the money we're all set." He looked around as if realizing for the first time that Jackie wasn't there. "She get cold feet?"

"Just send the picture," Gant said. "And you'd better not pull any shenanigans like you did with Nash."

"Speaking of Nash, I hear he's out."

"I had nothing to do with that deal," Gant said. "He went straight to Mosby with it."

"He's a problem you know."

"Leave him to me. He'll screw up again."

Just then Gant's cell phone rang. It was Jackie calling to tell him Gain Prichard had just been shot. She was on the scene and it was bloody. Prichard's office was just up the street. Close enough that he would have heard the shot had he been outside. He ran out and saw the large crowd already gathered around Prichard's storefront office. An ambulance roared past him as he jogged the short distance and took command of the scene.

"Looks like a self-inflicted gunshot wound through the mouth," she said as he reached her elbow. Prichard was slumped down in his chair with a spray of blood and brains on the wall directly behind him. "He's not wearing a wedding ring so I don't know if he's married."

"He's not," Gant said.

"Kids?"

"Not that I know of. I didn't know him all that well. Hardly at all, actually. Why is Nash outside talking to Roy?"

They could both see Jonce Nash through the window standing on the street beside officer Birch. "The woman in the blue dress said she heard a gunshot and saw Nash running out, then a few seconds later she heard the second shot."

"That explains the shattered glass," Gant said. "It wasn't enough to destroy the man, Nash had to make sure he finished the job. He probably goaded him into it."

Jackie studied Nash's face through the glass. He was smiling. The deal he made with Mosby set him free. His interaction with Prichard secured that freedom. "Look at him. He's proud of himself."

"I want him off the streets for good," Gant said. "Do whatever it takes."

Chapter Twenty-Six

At nine o'clock Friday morning Kelton Mulvaney wired seventy-five thousand dollars into a newly-created account bearing Tipton Palo's name. He had flatly rejected Palo's initial demand of half a million. His counter offer had been fifty thousand, but Palo talked him up to seventy-five. The amount made no legal difference.

The account was officially owned by the Hayes police department and would subsequently be handed over to the FBI as evidence. Gant called the agent from his office the moment the bank manager notified him that the transfer had gone through.

"This is really happening," Jackie said after her boss got off the phone. She had been in his office most of the morning going over evidence from the Prichard suicide with her MBI counterpart. Timms had departed two minutes before the call from the bank came in. He knew nothing about the sting operation and Jackie hoped to keep it that way. The fewer people who knew, the better. She still had mixed feeling about going to such an extreme despite the mayor's emotional endorsement.

"It's happening," Gant said. "And it's the right thing to do."

"Because of what the mayor said?"

"No, because you and Jordan deserve to have a life. No one forced him to do this so stop beating yourself up."

She wanted to believe him. "When do you think the FBI will pick him up?"

"Maybe today," Gant said. "Maybe next month. You know how they work."

"But they *will* pick him up," she said. "I mean he can't beat this can he?"

Gant reached across the desk and squeezed her hand. "Relax," he said. "You know how all this works better than I do. We've handed them an airtight case. All we can do now is wait."

"Waiting is the hard part," she said. "I'm sitting here thinking about all the times I've told victims not to worry, knowing they *should* worry. Now I'm the victim."

"I'll wait it out with you," he said, then he released her hand and shuffled some papers on his desk. "Now get busy and put Jonce Nash back in jail where he belongs."

It was Friday afternoon when Jonce got the idea to pick Bobbie up at work and take her someplace to celebrate his freedom before her husband blew back into town and occupied her time. He knew where she worked because he had followed her one morning. Knowing details came second nature to him.

At half past three he heard the blaring of a distant horn that lasted exactly two seconds, then a throng of people poured out of the factory like mice from a sinking ship. Cars and pickup trucks came to life and sped away. Friday was payday and there was money to be spent and beer to be drank. Jonce had worked in a factory for a short stretch so he understood the urgency of getting clear of a place as quickly as possible. Soon he saw Bobbie, then she saw him and her face sank. She slowed her pace, unable to avoid him because he was parked beside her car. The fat woman walking behind her swung out and passed without so much as a well wish for the weekend. Everyone had someplace to be.

"Come along now," he said to the windshield, not at all dissuaded by her hesitation. He wore a white t-shirt and sat with his arm hanging out the window as though he were carrying the truck door under his arm. His truck was so close to her car that he could have patted her roof on the passenger side.

Eventually she came up. "You're supposed to be in jail."

"Well howdy do yourself, Mrs. Bobbie *my husband won't be home till late* Booth."

She jerked open her door. "Go away." She looked around to see if anyone was watching. "Did you escape or something?"

"Something," he said. "How about me and you go someplace cozy and celebrate?"

Bobbie spat a laugh at him. More *ha* than *ha ha*. "How about you crawl off someplace and die?" Before he could answer she had ducked below the roofline of her car and slammed the door.

"That's fine," he said loud enough for half the world to hear. "You lead the way and I'll follow." He giggled as she tore away and headed for home. When she reached the apartment complex, she hurried up the stairs with him on her heels. He overtook at the top of the stairs and pinched her on the left ass cheek. She jumped the top step and made a dash for her door but she didn't have her keys ready so he caught her again and pulled her into his apartment with her elbowing and slapping and threatening to scream.

But she didn't scream.

Jonce bolted the door and flung her toward the living room sofa. She regained control of herself and turned on him. "What the hell's wrong with you? I don't want this anymore."

"Just like that," he said, grinning ear to ear. "That's how I knowed you'd be." He moved forward and grabbed a fistful of hair and tilted her mouth toward his. "You been missing me."

"I ain't been —."

He kissed her hard as she struggled to twist her face away. She tried to knee him in the groin but he had turned his bottom half rightward with his left leg blocking. He caught her leg in the bend of the knee and scooped her up into his arms, then he carried her kicking and screaming to the bedroom and dumped her on the bed. She stopped fighting and stared up at him with her hair half covering her face. "If Don catches us he'll kill us both," she said, then she stripped her shirt off over her head.

Jonce grinned down at her naked upper half. Life was swinging his way again.

Gant received the call at home that Friday evening just as the three of them sat down to dinner. She knew it was *the* call by the way he picked at the words he used, and because he kept glancing her way as he listened and spoke. Jordan didn't seem to notice. Calls at the dinner table had become a new normal for them since moving in with Gant. A police chief doesn't have the luxury of not answering his phone.

Her curiosity spilled over after the call ended and Gant went back to eating as though nothing had happened. "Is everything all right at the station?"

"Yes," he said, cutting his eyes toward Jordan. "That case we were working on broke our way."

She felt a tremendous gush of relief, then an almost equal wave of guilt. Jordan would have to be told, but she hoped he never learned the entire truth. A boy shouldn't know that his mother sent his father to prison by framing him, even if the father deserved it. Then, as she picked at her food, she began to second-guess even that again. *Did Kelton deserve it?* The logical answer was yes, but the emotional answer took more effort. Kelton Mulvaney had worked very hard to carve out a spot for himself in a culture he believed to be rigged against the common man. He donated to all the right causes because he believed in giving back, and he greased the right palms because he had learned the hard way how the system works. It was his violent temper that he couldn't control. He was a good father ninety percent of the time, but he had crossed the line and struck his son — her son — and in her mind that stripped him of the right to call himself a dad. He would always be Jordan's father, but he would never again be his dad.

Dinner seemed to last for all eternity, then Jordan asked to be excused and left the table, leaving her sitting with an almost untouched plate and a man who had no reason to care but did.

"So it's done?"

"He'll get bail of course," Gant said. The call had not lessened his appetite. His plate was almost clean. "You did the right thing."

She raised her eyes from her plate and saw more compassion in his eyes than she had seen during her entire marriage to Kelton. Across the table sat a man with no family to care for, yet he found a way to care for someone else's family. Someone else's wife and son. It wasn't just her — she couldn't write it off to lust, or romantic feelings — he cared for her son, too. Perhaps he cared for everyone. He seemed the type. Big, strong, handsome man with a heart the size of Texas, the way men used to be portrayed in Hollywood movies before society changed and began the process of tearing them down.

"Thank you," she said, barely able to push the words past the lump in her throat. She wanted to cry but didn't because she was afraid he might hold her, and she was afraid of what might happen if he did. It was too soon for that. Too soon to mix those emotions into the pot with all the others.

"A battered woman can't change her abuser's behavior," he said in a soft, quiet voice. "But she can change her own. That's what you did when you put your son in the car and left Detroit."

"I can't help thinking it was selfish of me." She looked at him again and tried to laugh but it came out pitiful. "I know it sounds silly."

"It sounds perfectly human."

She smiled. "Why couldn't he be like you?" He didn't answer. She felt embarrassed. "What I mean is why did he have to be so mean? He's not a bad man if you take away the meanness."

"The same could be said of a lot of men," Gant said. "Charles Manson, Adolph Hitler, maybe even Jonce Nash."

She laughed. "I wouldn't go that far."

Gant reached across and took her hand. "Life is full of *what ifs* and *whys*. All we can do is take things as they come."

She straightened her shoulders and tried to lighten the mood. "How come you're not married?"

"You've asked me that already. Next question."

"You're kind and gentle. Strong. Handsome."

He laughed. "I was hoping for that last part." He released her hand and dropped his napkin into his plate. "But apparently southern women don't share your estimation of their police chief. Or maybe they know how much money I make."

"Well I think your southern women are crazy. One of them should have snatched you up by now and put her brand on you."

He got up and carried his plate to the sink and rinsed it. When he turned back toward her, he asked her if she thought Timms was phoning it in.

"So we're talking shop now?"

"I think we'd better."

"Was I getting too personal?"

"Every time I ask Timms how it's going with the Stubbs case he tries to change the subject."

"Like you're doing now?"

"Well I thought I'd better before you start putting my picture up on dating sites."

So there it was. She thought they were flirting and he thought she was auditioning him for Tinder. Maybe he didn't go for the interracial dating thing. People like what they like. It's not always a conscious choice. It doesn't have to be good or bad. "Okay, well, it's a frustrating case. Nash is slippery as an eel."

"He's all over the Prichard suicide."

"Maybe he sees the other investigators getting all the press and the Prichard case is his chance to grab some of the spotlight." She watched him pondering her explanation and wondered if he had passed the same judgment on her performance. Technically it was her case too. "If you're wondering if he's hiding anything from us I don't think so. There's no gain in it for him so why would he? No one cares much if it gets solved or not."

"Maybe that's the problem."

"If you're insinuating that I don't care, I do."

"I'm not questioning your motives," he said. "There's just something about Timms that sticks in my craw. Speaking of sticking, I hope you don't plan on leaving us after this thing with your husband blows over."

"Divorces don't just blow over," she said. "Though I wish it were that easy. Kelton will always be Jordan's father, even if he's in prison."

"Does that mean you're moving back?"

"No. I'll never live in Detroit again."

"What about the house? And your friends?"

"You're assuming I'll get the house," she said. "And that I have friends."

"The friend part I would put money on. The house depends on how good your lawyer is."

"My friends were his friends. He didn't like me going outside the circle."

"Jealous *and* abusive," Gant said. "You picked a real winner." He winced. "Sorry. That was out of line."

"Yes it was, but I forgive you."

"It's settled then," Gant said. "Hayes needs you and you have no place better to be."

She couldn't see herself making Hayes her permanent home but she kept those thoughts to herself. One doesn't tell her boss she considers her job temporary. She wanted Jordan to have opportunities not available in a small southern town. Maybe they would go to California, or New York. Chicago was too close to Detroit both politically and geographically, as was Philadelphia, but she was getting ahead of herself. First she had to ride out the storm of divorcing Kelton.

❖

Jonce prepared himself for Donnie's arrival by transferring two D-cell batteries from a flashlight he kept in the kitchen drawer to a sock he found in the floor beside his bed. Any man can be brought down with the proper technique, and Jonce could swing a loaded sock as good as any man. Donnie, being bigger and dumber, would probably come empty-handed. His size advantage would be his undoing. That and the batteries in Jonce's sock.

Eight o'clock came and went with no explosion next door. Jonce began to think the big boy had abandoned her, then he heard voices. Low voices in conversation. He sprang from the couch and put his ear to the wall but couldn't make out the words. She talked then Donnie talked, then she talked for several minutes without stopping. Bobbie had an annoying amount of words inside her and she was always trying to get them out.

Nine o'clock came with Jonce having stashed the sock in his pocket. Nothing annoyed him like people not behaving the way he expected them to. He supposed she could call the cops and claim rape but it would be her word against his, and he would tell the world about the bun he put in her oven. He knew for a fact she had not yet spent the abortion money he gave her. She would be showing through her clothes soon. The clock was ticking. Maybe Donnie would get her naked and notice the roundness of her belly the way he had when she stripped off her shirt. That could take some explaining on both their parts, which brought him full circle back to the loaded sock in his pocket.

At eleven o'clock Jonce startled awake on the couch and wiped the drool from the corner of his mouth. The sock was still in his pocket and the door still on the hinges. It was quiet next door. Too quiet. He went to bed.

Chapter Twenty-Seven

Monday was April Fools' Day and Jackie was ready. No one had fooled her on the first day of April in three years. The last time almost didn't count because of its cruelty. Her husband had called her early in the morning and told her their son had fallen down the stairs and was at the ER with severe head trauma. She had rushed to the hospital with her lights and siren only to be told they didn't have a Jordan Mulvaney.

Kelton thought it was terribly funny and loved telling the story at their parties to friends and acquaintances and hangers-on who laughed politely or not at all. It was the first time she fully understood the brutal side of him. Hitting her in a fit of rage was one thing, but planning and executing a cruel joke involving their son required an unsettling lack of compassion.

When Gant told her to drive over to the jail and talk to Emil Wazenski, her first thought was that it was the prank she had been expecting, then when he told her Wazenski claimed he knew who killed Perry Stubbs, her *you-can't-fool-me antenna* really went up and she told him *nice try*.

"This is legitimate," he said. "At least my part of it is. I don't know what Wazenski has up his sleeve."

They had Wazenski handcuffed to a table in a room at the jail when she arrived. He looked broken and harmless, and she asked the jailer to remove the handcuffs.

"He's a killer," the big-bellied jailer said. "I think we'd better leave him secured."

"I'll take full responsibility," she said. She had read Wazenski's record. His only violent act had been to suffocate his wife with a

300

pillow. A desperate act, yes, but it had been a crime of passion. At any rate, she believed she could take him in a fair fight. The handcuffs came off.

"Thank you," Wazenski said after the jailer left them alone. He rubbed the red circles on his wrists. "They try to cut off your circulation with those things."

"They're not meant to be comfortable," Jackie said. "Now suppose you tell me why I'm here."

He looked at the video recorder on the table between them. "Are you going to turn that on?"

"Do you want me to?"

"No."

She would record their next conversation if this one proved worthy. People tend to be less forthcoming if they are being recorded.

"I have information regarding a murder," he said. "But first I have to know something."

"I'm listening," she said.

"Is Jonce Nash free?"

"Yes."

"Why?"

"First tell me why it matters," she said. "We're supposed to be talking about a murder."

"Because I need to be sure," Wazenski said. "Is he free because he turned over certain information?"

"Do you know something about that information?"

"So it's true," he said, stating the obvious instead of asking a question. "I was going to make that deal with the DA. Jonce cheated me. It was my idea."

She was glad the camera wasn't on. Anything Wazenski said implicating Nash now would be suspect, not that it meant it wouldn't be true. Lawyers are experts at taking a tiny seed of doubt and growing it into something big enough to sway a jury. Some are better at it than others, but they all have the ability at some level or they would have chosen another profession.

"Is what you are about to tell me true?"

"Yes, ma'am."

"Then stick to the facts. I've got a full schedule."

"Did he turn over a stack of papers about this thick?" He held his thumb and forefinger about a half inch apart. "Implicating Gain Prichard in some criminal activities?"

"You seem to know the answers to your own questions," she said.
"I know how he got them."

She waited for him to continue, wondering if she was going to have to drag the information he'd promised out of him word by word.

"I told Jonce I was going to see if I could get a deal. I thought we could both use that information to get our charges dropped. A parole officer for the two of us seemed a fair trade. Jonce told me to wait. Said he had a plan." He dropped his head like a pouting child. "His plan was to steal my idea and leave me in jail." He lifted his head and shook off the miseries and transformed himself into a different man right before her eyes. "Well, I'll show him," he said. His eyes were vibrant now. His face beamed.

"I think I'll turn this on now," Jackie said, reaching for the video recorder that was pointed at him. "If that's okay with you." Something told her whatever he was about to say may never be said again.

He nodded. Over the next several minutes he sat with his back straight and his eyes forward, and he delivered a damning account of the short time he had spent knowing Jonce Nash. Jackie listened patiently to details that had no impact on the case, slowly reaching the conclusion that the interview was a colossal waste of her time. Then, almost ten minutes in, he stopped abruptly and appeared to consider his next words very carefully.

"Tipton Palo paid Jonce Nash to kill that man."

"What man? Say his name."

"Stubbs. Perry Stubbs."

Jackie's heart almost leapt into her throat. "How do you know this?"

"I heard them arguing about it."

"You heard who arguing about it? State their names."

"Jonce Nash and Tipton Palo. We were at the motel, just before we surrendered.

"Exactly what did you hear them say?"

"Jonce asked me if I believed in the hereafter — forgiveness of sins and all that stuff. I said I did and he said maybe he would ask for a priest so he could confess to killing Stubbs and go to heaven. I told him I think you have to be Catholic to confess to a priest."

"How did he implicate Tipton Palo?"

"Jonce said to Palo maybe he wanted to confess to paying for the killing but Palo didn't want to confess."

"So Tipton Palo didn't actually say he paid Jonce Nash to kill Perry

Stubbs?"

"What he said was that he hired Jonce Nash but didn't pay him, so his soul was clear."

"Are you sure that's what he said? That he hired Jonce Nash to kill Perry Stubbs?"

"Yes. We all thought we were going to die."

"Is that all you have to say?"

He nodded. She switched off the recorder.

"When do I get out?"

"I'll talk to the DA." He had made the mistake of handing over his information before confirming a deal, but Jackie wasn't out to trick him. She would go to bat for him with Mosby and get him a deal. Keeping him in jail with Nash on the streets seemed cruel and unjust. "If Nash finds out about this you could be in danger," she said as she rose to leave.

"I am not afraid of Jonce Nash."

She felt the strange sensation of believing him.

"It's not enough," the DA said. Mosby had stopped by Jackie's office after lunch to hear what Wazenski had to offer. "I can't go after Nash on the hearsay testimony of a convicted murderer."

His reluctance surprised her. Every prosecutor she had ever known would jump at the chance to close a murder case, especially one that had triggered the most massive public corruption investigation in the city's history.

"The man smothered his wife with a pillow," he said, perhaps feeling the sudden silence of the room too uncomfortable. "Oh stop looking at me as though I've grown a second head!" He paced the tiny space like a cat angry for no reason, stopping every few passes to look down at her as though she had asked him to jump off a building.

"There's the statement Tipton Palo made to me," she said. "On the record. It corroborates —."

"He was trying to cut a deal of his own."

"So statements from criminals we make deals with are off the table now?" The notion was ludicrous. Big cases were cleared because of information harvested from criminals busted on some lesser charge. Justice hinged on deals. Joe Blow gets pinched for a bag of coke so he gives up his dealer. The dealer gives up his supplier and so it goes until every once in an infrequent while, someone untouchable gets touched.

Mosby stopped and looked at the empty chair at his knee as though he had seen it for the first time. He sat. His body seemed to melt inside his clothes. "Look, I know you mean well, but this is Mississippi, not Michigan.

"Is murder still legal in Mississippi?"

"Still?"

"There was a time —."

"You know very well what I mean."

"I'm afraid I don't."

"Why do you think Palo's not in jail right now?"

"He posted bond," she said.

"Besides that."

She shrugged.

"We had a nice little town here," he said. "Until the people of this town decided to elect that … that nobody mayor. Now everything's turned on its head and nobody knows who to trust or what to believe. He's made a mockery of justice."

"Wow," she said, not believing her ears. "Are you mixed up in it too?"

"Of course not!" He jerked straight in the chair then slowly melted again. "I'm not mixed up in anything. That's the problem."

"I don't understand."

"Why should you understand? You're new here. This isn't your town. These people going to jail aren't your friends."

"Did you know?"

"No, I didn't know. Maybe I suspected a few things but I didn't know."

"Does Palo have something on you?"

"You're not getting a confession out of *me* young lady," he said, then he produced some hybrid laugh that came out more high-pitched than he probably intended. "I'm too boring to be guilty of anything. If my life were a movie they'd have to wake the theater to go home."

"Then why the reluctance to move forward against Nash?"

"Palo's furious about the deal I made with Nash. If I let Wazenski out too he'll have my skin." He finally made eye contact. "He's still a very powerful man despite everything that's happened."

"He's a disgraced attorney," Jackie said. "There's already been one attempt on his life. His wife is divorcing him. He's sure to lose his law license any day now. Every friend he ever had is either in jail or running scared. They even kicked him out of church.''

Mosby smirked. "Is that what you think? You think Palo doesn't have any friends left? You think he spent all his money in Hayes?"

The revelation startled her. "What are you saying?"

"Nothing," he said. "I'm not saying anything. I don't know anything."

"But you just said —."

"I know what I just said. I'm rambling. I'm speaking out of turn. I'm telling you what I think, not what I know." He was beginning to sweat. He leaned forward the slightest bit. "Think about it. Palo spent so much money buying influence locally and not a dime where it really matters? He had his sights set on the governor's mansion. Do you really think he didn't cultivate a few fields in Jackson?"

"They don't seem to be helping him now."

"Don't they? Where is he right now? Do you think anyone else would be walking around free after what he's done?" He rubbed his balding head and threw his comb over out of place. "Tipton Palo won't spend one day in prison. Not one."

Jackie didn't know how to respond. The evidence against Palo was so overwhelming that it seemed impossible for him to avoid prison. The public wouldn't stand for it.

"If I try to use the statement Palo made against Nash, he'll retract it. It's that simple."

"But it's on the record," she said. "I'll testify that he made it."

"So what? He'll say he was plying you for a deal."

"But Jonce Nash really was shot in the arm," she said. "That corroborates the statement."

"Can you prove it?"

She frowned.

"Can you produce a doctor — any doctor — who'll admit to treating that bullet wound and not reporting it? No, you can't, because they'll lose their medical license. Besides, it's probably impossible to prove the wound came from a bullet. Sure, I can find a doctor who'll say with medical certainty that the wound in Jonce Nash's arm was caused by a bullet, but then the defense will call an equally qualified doctor who'll say it could've been caused by something else. Now suppose the jury believes my doctor and Nash says he shot himself in the arm? Can anybody prove he didn't?"

"Perhaps you're underestimating the jury," she said. Using his logic, no case would ever go to trial.

"That's another thing," he said. "The jury. Juries are made up of people. Common, ordinary people. The odds that at least one of them doesn't look at Perry Stubbs and decide he needed killing is … well, you know as well as I do what it is."

"Is that your position? That he needed killing?"

"My personal thoughts don't matter," he said. "I've never let my personal feelings interfere with my obligations. Not once. Bring me solid evidence against Jonce Nash and I'll nail his miserable hide to the wall, but don't bring me hearsay evidence from some wife-killer trying to beat a kidnapping rap."

"We have Palo's gun," Jackie said. "The gun he claims he used to shoot Nash."

"Which proves what? That Palo owns a gun. Do you know how many men in Hayes own a gun? Women too. And children." He took a breath and let it seep out. "Bring me the bullet," he said. "With Nash's DNA on it." He wagged his finger at her. "If it matches Palo's gun *then* I'll put them both away."

Jonce watched Bobbie leave for work through the window over the kitchen sink. It was Tuesday morning. Spring was in full bloom and so was she. Instead of tight jeans she wore shorts and a shirt that hung loose. Something about her got under his skin and he couldn't shake it. No woman had ever got to him the way she did. She had fire, like him, except hers came packaged in a female body. Being pregnant suited her. She looked better filled out, but soon the glow would become fat and she would be stuck with a kid. An idea had been kicking around in the back of his head that maybe he would take her away from Hayes. Maybe they would go away someplace and live off the grid. She'd have to get rid of the kid though. He wasn't going through that nightmare again.

It was too early for a beer but he had one anyway, then he had two more. Rules are society's way of hobbling people into submission. What difference did it make to a can of beer what time of day it was drank? He kicked the trash bag beside the refrigerator and a soup can rolled off the heap and dinged against the floor.

Maybe she had told Donnie something she shouldn't have and he had threatened to keep an eye on her. One of his friends, maybe, slinking around the parking lot to report back if she wore tight jeans and a halter top to work, or if she slipped out of her apartment and into another. Maybe Donnie didn't remember from Sunday to Friday night how she felt when he left. Maybe he didn't care.

Maybe, just maybe, they were planning on knocking him in the head and stealing what little money he had left. Had he told her about it? Had she snooped and found it? She definitely hadn't told Donnie about the sex. Donnie was a man's man and wouldn't sit still for news like that. He would've kicked Jonce's door open and reared up on his hind legs like a grizzly bear and took a loaded sock to the ear. No, it had to be something else. Maybe she told Donnie about the bullet in his arm.

He opened another beer and carried his loaded thoughts into the living room and plopped down on the sofa. Women baffled him, but so goes the human race. All she had to do was keep her mouth shut and she could have had the best of both worlds. Married on weekends and free during the week. What woman wouldn't want that?

She had to be dealt with. Donnie too. Him and her, her and him. First or last made no difference. John Brown's body lies a-smoldering in a grave. Be a shame, too. Her, not Donnie, not that he held anything special against him. A woman with her fire was a once-in-a-lifetime find. Like winning the lottery.

He decided to see Tipton Palo. It was a spur of the moment thing. They may as well have it out now or reach some sort of compromise. Money was off the table. Palo was too stingy to be reasonable in that regard, but he wasn't stupid. They had a mutual problem and that problem's name was Perry Stubbs. Killing Stubbs had been a mistake. It should have been the other way around — Palo dead and Stubbs still alive and calling the shots. Jonce didn't like being bossed around but at least Stubbs paid on time, and he had a good imagination. And he knew how to deal with cops.

It was hot for April. As Jonce left the shadow of the apartment building headed for his truck, he glanced over his shoulder toward the door where the woman cop lived. She hadn't been home in a while. Several days in fact. Maybe he would snoop around a little and find out where she was staying. He hadn't seen a moving truck come and take her stuff away, then of course he didn't recall one bringing her stuff when she moved in. Maybe she traveled light to keep ahead of her old man, or maybe she had moved out while he was in jail. Didn't matter. She had nothing on him.

The sign out front that used to say *Palo-West Attorneys At Law* now said *Palo Law Firm*. Rance West had abandoned ship. Good for him. Anything that made Palo's life a little harder to bear suited Jonce just fine. The pretty little thing planted at the front desk hadn't abandoned him, though. She looked up from her phone just long enough to tell Jonce that *Mister* Palo wasn't seeing anyone without an appointment. Jonce explored the cleavage left exposed by two unfastened buttons as he pondered the outcomes of barging in versus jumping through Palo's little hoop. He had nowhere he needed to be, and the view was nice. "Make me an appointment then," he said, glancing at the clock on the wall behind her. "Nine-thirty."

She tapped on her keyboard while he looked down her shirt.

"How about some coffee while I wait?"

She raked him waist-to-face with her eyes. "The cafe's down the street."

He had fifteen minutes to kill and her to look at, so he crossed the room and sat. Mouthy women held a special place in his heart, like wild horses to a cowboy. Maybe he had just met Bobbie's replacement.

The time for action had come. Kelton had been arrested and released and according to Jackie's contacts in Detroit, he was on the warpath. His knowing her location freed her to reach out to friends she would not have otherwise trusted. Most of her friends outside the police department were wives of his friends and had already been primed with his side of the story. The first person she called was their closest neighbor, and the phone call ended abruptly. Liddy Davenport was an entrepreneur with dozens of businesses spread across Detroit that she either owned outright or had a stake in. Her husband was a banker and one of Kelton's closest friends. They had both heard the story, she told Jackie, and they were appalled that she could do such a terrible thing. Liddy hung up without elaborating.

Her next call was to her old partner, Dillon Keys. He was the one she trusted, and they had maintained sporadic contact over the past two months. Dillon was the kind of man you would want beside you in a foxhole because he was as upbeat as he was tough. During the three years they had been partners, she had seen him lose his cool only once, and that was the first day she came to work with a shiner. He took one look at her and guessed the truth. No amount of lying on her part could change his mind. Eventually she confided in him, and from that day on he became her staunchest ally, ready to back whatever decision she made. It wasn't until later that she learned he had watched his mother get knocked around by the men in her life. First it was his father, then his step-father, then men he saw only coming at night or going in the morning.

"What are people saying about me, Dillon?"

"That you took off in the middle of the night with a man."

"That explains Liddy Davenport's reaction," she said. Dillon didn't know the Davenports because they didn't travel in the same circles. They talked shop for a few minutes, him catching her up on the cases she had abandoned and her painting small-town Mississippi in a favorable light.

"I'm filing for divorce," she said during a lull in the conversation.

"About time," he said. "Who's your lawyer?"

"I was thinking about Crenshaw."

"Oh, so you haven't done it yet."

"I'm really going to this time."

"You were really going to all those other times, too."

They chatted a while longer then said their goodbyes. Almost on cue Gant walked in.

"Timms arrested Brad Stovall about an hour ago," he said.

"Who's Brad Stovall?"

"One of Palo's cronies. He used to be an alderman until Mayor Pigg drove him out."

"What'd he do?"

"Crooked contracts with the city." He stepped in without closing the door.

"The look on your face tells me there's more."

"The mayor helped him get some contracts with the city a while back."

"I'm sorry," she said, thinking *so much for honest heroes*. "I know how much you like him."

"It's not like that," Gant said. Before he could elaborate the mayor appeared in the doorway.

"Someone forgot my advice about closing doors."

"You're always welcome in my office," Jackie said.

"Even though I'm a suspect now?"

"You're not a suspect," Gant said. "The contracts you helped Stovall get were all legal."

"Of course they were," Mayor Pigg said. "But try telling that to the state investigators." He looked at Jackie. "Brad Stovall operates a fleet of broken down dump trucks. Don't follow too close behind one of them because they all have signs on the back relieving him of responsibility for any windshields he might break."

She smiled. The mayor was more animated than she had ever seen him. More agitated than afraid. There was a story behind his last statement, she assumed, but she suspected it would be a long one so she didn't ask.

"Now this business about Stovall," he said to Gant. "You know I wouldn't ask you for any special treatment but this thing has my wife climbing the walls."

"Timms assured me you're not a target," Gant said.

"Do you believe him?"

"The indictments are for contracts that predate you."

"Indictments? As in more than one?"

"Three."

The mayor looked somewhat relieved. "Well, okay, if you say I'm in the clear. I don't recall seeing anything about Stovall in the documents I turned over, but I'll take you at your word."

"Palo rolled on him," Gant said. "He'd give up his own mother for a reduction in charges."

"You'd have to convince me he had a mother," the mayor said. The phone in his pocket rang. "Duty calls," he said after looking at the display then declining the call. He slapped Gant on the back. "Thanks for the information. I'll sleep better tonight." When he reached the doorway he stopped and turned. "I've started a rumor about you two. Don't make me out to be a liar." He closed the door on his way out.

Gant stared after him. "Pay no attention to that last thing he said. I'm sure he was joking."

"I'm not," she said. "Who's the best divorce lawyer you know?"

"Tipton Palo."

"Besides him."

"It's a pretty far drop after him."

"There has to be more than one decent lawyer in this town."

"Compared to Palo they're all third-rate," he said, "but if you pressed me I'd have to say Rance West."

"His partner?"

"Former partner."

"Can I trust him?"

"Well, he's a lawyer, but yeah, I think you can trust him. He's handled a lot of divorces."

"As many as Palo?"

"More. Palo's mostly a trial lawyer. His gift is how he handles a jury. Judges tend not to appreciate him as much so divorces never were his thing."

"I'll give West a call."

"Shouldn't you file in Detroit?"

"I have to."

"Shouldn't you hire a Detroit lawyer?"

"Yes, but I want someone here to keep an eye on things. There's no way to know who my husband has his hooks into."

Gant whistled. "Two lawyers on a detective's salary? That'll add to the rumor mill."

"Afraid people might think you're paying for one of them?"

"Maybe I will," he said. "Your husband's a wealthy man. You're an attractive woman. You're bound to come out of this with something." He winked to let her know he was joking.

"Are you proposing?"

He stood. "Not me. A man who can't afford a divorce shouldn't get married."

Chapter Twenty-Eight

J once awoke early Wednesday morning and waited outside his door for Bobbie to leave for work. As soon as she opened her door he pushed his way inside and locked it behind him.

"What —."

"Shut up and sit down!"

She recoiled. "I won't sit down! Get out now or I'll scream!"

Jonce backhanded her across the mouth and knocked her to the floor. She fell hard and stayed down, looking up at him with a sideways glare that showed spunk. Ellie had looked at him that same way the first few times. "What'd you tell him?"

"What did I tell who?"

"Donnie. Who do you think?"

She pushed herself up and sat with her back against the sofa and probed her busted lip with a fingertip. "He'll kill you for this when he gets home."

"Start talking or he won't recognize you when he gets home." He stepped on her fingers and made her cry out. More curse than scream. She was tougher than Ellie. Prettier, too, but that was a low bar for a woman to reach. Jonce had never sought out pretty women.

"I didn't tell him anything!"

"Then why was it so quiet over here all weekend?"

"We talked about other stuff. Married stuff."

"Like what?"

"None of your damned business!"

"You told him about me being hurt."

"You're crazy! Get away from me!"

Jonce glared down at her, not knowing what to think. "What about that abortion you're supposed to be getting?"

"I'll get it."

"You'd better because I don't need no kid running around."

"I wouldn't give birth to any kid of yours." She shot to her feet with a quickness that impressed him. "You're an animal! Get out before I call the cops and tell them you raped me!"

"I ain't through talking."

"Now!" She yanked her phone from the pocket of her shorts. "You've got three seconds."

"You'll be an accomplice after the fact."

"You're not holding that over me anymore. One!"

He raised his hands and backed away. "All right. Damn. Some women can't be talked sense to."

"Two!" She brought her finger to a hover over the screen.

"I'm going," he said. "But you ain't calling no cops. I'll swear you was in on it."

"Three!"

Jonce bolted out the door and down the stairs to his truck, then he tore away before the cops came.

Jackie found Rance West to be unprofessional and sloppy in posture and upkeep of his office, but Andrew Gant had recommended him, and the attorney in Detroit would manage the details. All West had to do was oversee the process and sound the alarm if the Detroit lawyer tried to slip something past her.

"So let me get this straight," West said, looking at her from his slouched position behind a desk that looked to have come from a second-hand office supply store. "You want me to handle the attorney who is handling your divorce?"

"I'm not sure *handle* is the word I would use," she said.

"Okay, you pick a word."

"I want you to deal with him and I'll deal with you."

"In other words, you don't trust him."

"In a manner of speaking, yes, I don't trust him."

"What makes you think you can trust me?"

"Chief Gant said I could."

West smiled. "Is that so? He said that?"

"Yes." She looked around herself. He clearly needed the money.

What she couldn't figure was why he was being so hesitant to take the case. "Will you take the case or not?"

"I'll need the particulars," he said. "Starting with the name and contact information of your attorney in Detroit."

She passed him a slip of paper. He perused it. "Is there money involved?"

"Yes."

"How much?"

"Does it change your fee?"

He smiled. "The more someone stands to lose, the harder they fight. The harder they fight, the longer it takes. My fee is based on billable hours. If I'm working on the case in any form or fashion, the meter's running. I charge two-hundred an hour, rounded to the nearest half hour. I'll —."

"That's too high."

He pushed back in the chair and studied her. "One-fifty, and that's as low as I go. This office may look like I'm desperate but I do all right."

"Is that why it's so easy to get an appointment with you?"

He laughed. "I like you. Tell you what ... I'll drop it another fifty since I'm not actually having to do the work, but if it turns out there's real money involved it goes up."

"Only if I approve the increase," she said.

"Okay, but if you don't approve the increase I stop working."

"And the increase won't be retroactive."

He nodded his agreement. They had struck a deal. "So the chief really said you can trust me, huh?"

"You sound surprised."

"Maybe you know my former partner."

"Quite well," she said.

"I wasn't involved in any of that stuff."

"I wouldn't be standing here if I thought you were."

"Fair enough," he said. "I'll need a small retainer of course."

"How small?"

"Five grand should get us started."

"I have three hundred," she said.

West frowned.

"There's money involved," she said. "If you get me half of our combined assets I'll agree to your first price."

"How much money?"

"Around three million that I know about."

He whistled. "Lady, you just hired yourself a lawyer."

Jonce hid out until dark, then he made a slow pass by the apartment complex. If Bobbie had called the cops they were either gone or laying for him. He wheeled his pickup around at the next corner and drove back and turned into the parking lot. Bobbie's front light was on, and her car was parked in the same spot with the right rear tire over the line, exactly as it had been when he left. Noticing things was second-nature to Jonce.

He parked and waited with the window down, taking in the sound and feel of the place. He possessed an uncanny ability to sense when a cop was nearby. The tiny hairs on the back of his neck would stand up and tingle. His talent had served him well in prison, earning him more cigarettes than he could smoke, and almost as many candy bars. Sometimes he demanded cash, but cash was hard to come by so he sold his services as lookout for whatever he could get. There was never a shortage of work.

His neck hairs remained still. The spot in front of the female cop's door was empty and her window still dark, same as it had been for several days. She and the chief had some kind of arrangement at his house, and right under the town's nose, too. He had snooped around and heard talk. Sometimes the straight and narrow takes a man smack through a pretty woman, and that lady detective sure was pretty.

The streetlight nearest Jonce had been out since he moved in, but it wasn't so dark that a man could approach the stairs and go up without being seen if someone happened to be looking. The parking lot appeared empty. Maybe too empty for so early in the evening. He waited another ten minutes, then swung open the door and hurried up. Bobbie's door tempted him but he opted for his instead. He bolted his door and stuck his eye to the peephole. Nothing moved. After sufficient time passed, he abandoned the door and put his ear to the wall he shared with the Booths. Her television was playing a sappy movie at a low volume. He tapped on the wall and got no answer, so he tapped harder.

"Go away."

He grinned. "I was thinking we might snuggle."

"Drop dead."

"Maybe watch one of them Lifetime movies you like so much."

"You belong in a Lifetime movie," she said. Judging from the direction of her voice, he guessed her to be on the couch. "Leave me alone or I'll call the cops."

"You wouldn't do that."

"I'm through playing with you, Jonce. I mean it."

"You won't call the cops because they might find them funny-looking little plants you got growing in that spare bedroom." He snickered. "Hows about we strip off our frillies and swap war stories. I bet you got some doozies."

She turned up the volume. A commercial for reverse mortgage blared through the wall. Some big name actor was trying to trick old people out of their homes. Everybody has an angle for getting their leg over somebody else.

He stood without moving until the commercial played out and the movie came back on. Eventually she turned the volume down again. "Be a shame if I suddenly had no use for you," he said just loud enough for his voice to reach her. "No telling what might happen if that were the circumstance."

She turned the volume up again.

Jackie was at her desk catching up on paperwork when Bobbie Booth walked in Thursday morning.

"The man out front told me to come on back," she said, standing in the doorway dressed in loose shorts and a baggy gray shirt with what appeared to be a monster truck on the front. Her eyes ricocheted off every object in the room before they settled intently on Jackie. Whatever she was afraid of had her ready to bolt. Jackie had seen that same look in the mirror not so long ago.

"Please, sit down," she said, gesturing toward the chair.

Bobbie closed the door without being asked to, meaning she needed privacy to steady her nerves. She sat. "I ... I, uh, have something," she said, unfolding the fingers of her right hand to reveal a wad of tissue paper. She probed at the paper with a finger then picked up something small. "It's a bullet. A piece of one anyway." She held it up and Jackie saw the fragment, then she dropped her eyes before speaking again. "I cut this out of his arm sixty-three days ago. It had just got dark and he knocked on my door but I didn't answer.

When I heard him go into his place I looked outside and there was blood on my door where I guess he had leaned against it. I could see his door wasn't shut good so I peeked inside and saw him on the floor. Dead I thought, then I saw his ribs move and knew he was breathing so I went inside and helped him into bed thinking how good it was for the both of us that he was so skinny." She looked up at Jackie. "He helped some but he didn't remember it later when he came around."

Jackie held out her hand. "Can I see that?"

Bobbie leaned forward and passed the fragment to Jackie. Her hands were trembling. "Am I in trouble for helping him?"

"That depends on what you helped him do."

"I just took out the bullet. I swear it. I'd never even spoken to him before that."

"Did he tell you how he got shot?"

"No."

"Weren't you curious?"

"I was too afraid to ask because I knew he was just out of prison." She wrung her hands together in her lap. Her face twitched. "I looked him up online when he moved in."

"You told me that once before," Jackie said. "When I came to your apartment."

"Oh, yeah, well, it was just curiosity. Staying alone as much as I do. Don says I'm nosy but I think it pays to know your neighbors, don't you? He's not the only convict living in our building but you probably know that, you being a cop and all. Leslie Kirkindal lives downstairs three doors from you and she did three years for drug possession. You already knew that didn't you? Don says I talk too much."

"You're nervous," Jackie said. "It's understandable."

"Don gets mad when he's trying to watch TV and I won't shut up. Jonce said I talk too much too." She made eye contact for a split second then back down. "He said I could talk the legs off a centipede. Should I shut up?"

"No," Jackie said. "Talk all you like." She had questions but they could wait.

Bobbie smiled. "I say I cut the bullet out of his arm but it wasn't exactly like that. It looked bad on the front side but then I felt this little knot on the back of his arm and it was that piece you're holding. I took a knife from his kitchen and cut a little slit and squeezed it right out, like popping a pimple." She blushed. "Sorry, I know that's gross but that's what it reminded me of." She looked up again. "You ever get pimples? Your skin's so smooth and pretty I bet you've never had a pimple in your life."

Jackie smiled. "I had plenty of pimples when I was a teenager."

"I still get one every now and then. Don says it's because I never grew all the way up."

"Lots of adults get them," Jackie said. "Does he know you still have it?"

"Lord no, I never told him about it. You won't tell him will you? He gets awfully jealous."

"I meant does Jonce Nash know you still have it," Jackie said.

"Oh, him. He asked me about it a while back and threatened me if I told anybody about that night. I told him I threw it away."

"Are you afraid of him?"

"He's been acting strange these past few days. Saying he might not need me around anymore. Stuff like that."

"Would you be willing to testify in court if it goes that far?"

Bobbie shrugged. "I guess he'll kill me either way," she said. "Me coming here like this."

"I'll do everything in my power to make sure that doesn't happen," Jackie said.

"You're probably wondering why I came this morning after holding onto it so long."

"It crossed my mind."

Bobbie adjusted herself from one hip to the other. "Well, after last night I … knew I had to."

"What happened last night?"

"Nothing you could arrest him for," Bobbie said. "He has a way of saying things and doing things that make you feel like the stuff he does is your fault. That it's you who done wrong and him who's done right. Like he's the victim and not you." She dropped her eyes again. "That probably doesn't make any sense to a woman like you."

"It makes perfect sense," Jackie said, though she wasn't willing to tell her why.

"I've never been afraid of men until him."

"Did he hurt you?"

Bobbie nodded without looking up.

"Physically?"

She nodded again.

"Did he rape you?"

Tears flooded Bobbie's eyes. "I won't testify to anything but the bullet."

"If he raped you we can put him away forever," Jackie said.

Her eyes flashed wild. "He's the devil," she said. "He'll kill me."

Jackie knew the chances of her being right were high. "When does your husband come home?"

"Tomorrow night."

"Do you have someplace you can stay until then? Maybe a relative?"

Bobbie froze. The nervous twitching stopped. "You're not going to arrest him?"

"We'll have to send this to the lab and test it," Jackie said. "It'll take a few days at least, maybe more."

Bobbie shot to her feet. "I shouldn't've come here. Forget about me testifying."

"You did the right thing," Jackie said, but it was too late. Bobbie was out the door and gone.

Chapter Twenty-Nine

It took five days for forensics to confirm that the bullet fragment from Jonce Nash's arm had been fired from Tipton Palo's gun, corroborating Emil Wazenski's claim that he heard the two men arguing about Palo shooting Nash to get out of paying him to murder Perry Stubbs. Suddenly Everett Mosby was eager to offer Wazenski the deal he wanted.

Jackie walked into the interview room with the DA and joined the inmate at the small table. Wazenski was handcuffed according to protocol. A small video recorder sat in the center of the table pointed at him but was not turned on. Mosby dropped into his chair and interlaced his fingers on the table. "My instinct is not to do this," he said, glaring at Wazenski as though he had slaughtered a convent of nuns instead of helping kidnap one corrupt attorney. "But my office is slammed with public corruption cases thanks to our overzealous mayor so today could be your lucky day."

Wazenski's face brightened. Jackie knew Mosby was feeding him a line. She glanced at her watch and wondered where Timms was. Stubbs was his case as much as it was hers.

Wazenski straightened his spine and spoke. "I heard Jonce Nash —."

"Not yet," Mosby snapped. "I'll tell you when to speak." He browsed some papers from a file he probably knew by heart. Lawyers live and breathe paperwork. Reputations may be made in the courtroom but legal fees are made generating paperwork. Tons and tons of paperwork. He raised his head abruptly and turned toward the door. "Where's that jackass Timms? I told him one o'clock."

Wazenski's hopeful face had diminished into confusion. His eyes bounced from district attorney to detective but he heeded Mosby's admonition and remained silent. Jackie's experience with Mosby was limited, so she didn't know how much of his behavior was an act and how much was real. Regardless, the effect his performance had on Wazenski was remarkable. The poor guy looked ready to jump at anything the DA put on the table.

"To hell with Timms," Mosby said, shuffling the papers he had been examining. "Let the state of Mississippi suck hind tit on this one if they can't send competent investigators." He zeroed his focus on the nervous man across the table and seemed to enjoy watching him squirm. "Now when I turn on this video recorder, everything you say will be under oath, which means it has to be the truth as you know it. Understand? No hearsay or half-truths."

"I understand," Wazenski said, nodding. "Truth, the whole truth, and nothing but the truth so help me God."

The door opened and everyone turned. "Sorry I'm late but I —."

"Save the buts," Mosby said. "Don't complain next time when you're not invited."

Timms eyed Jackie as he approached the trio, asking what was up with Mosby without uttering the words. She shrugged. Mosby reached across and hit a button on the camera, then he administered the oath to Wazenski for the record.

"State your full name."

"Emil Wazenski."

"Is that your full name?"

Wazenski nodded.

"Use words when you answer," Mosby said. "We can't hear your head shake."

"Yes," he said. "That is my full name. I have no middle."

"You are appearing here today to make your statement without an attorney present. Do you understand that you have the right to have an attorney present?"

"Yes."

"And you choose not to have an attorney present?"

"Yes. No attorney."

"Have you been coerced in any way, by any person, to appear here today?"

"No. I am here of myself."

"Okay," Mosby said. "Let's get started then. On Tuesday, March nineteenth, two-thousand-nineteen, you participated in an abduction that resulted in your subsequent arrest and present incarceration?"

"Yes."

"Can you name your accomplice?"

"Jonce Nash."

"And how did you come to meet Jonce Nash?"

"Through our parole officer."

"The deceased Gain Prichard?"

"Yes."

"Who did you and Jonce Nash abduct?"

"Tipton Palo."

"Why?"

"Jonce Nash said Tipton Palo owed him money for a job he did."

"Did he tell you the nature of that job?"

"No, but I heard him and Palo arguing about it later."

"When."

"Later that day … in the warehouse, then again at the motel. They talked about it both places."

"And in both places — the warehouse and the motel — Tipton Palo was being held against his will?"

"Yes, he was tied to a chair and he didn't like it very much."

Timms chuckled, netting himself a scowl from the DA.

"What was the nature of the argument?"

"Jonce Nash wanted Palo to create an offshore account for him and wire money into it."

"And he was going to share that money with you?"

"One million dollars," Wazenski said.

"Did either of the two men say what the money was for?"

"Yes, they argued about a job Jonce Nash did for him. He killed Perry Stubbs and Palo was supposed to pay him but instead he shot him."

"Did you hear Jonce Nash say he killed Perry Stubbs?"

"Yes."

"And did you hear Tipton Palo say he ordered that murder?"

"He didn't deny it," Wazenski said.

"But did he admit it? Did he say he ordered Jonce Nash to kill Perry Stubbs?"

"No." Wazenski's face darkened, then a flash of hope. "He said it was a mistake to shoot him instead of paying him."

"Who said it was a mistake to shoot who?"

"Palo — Tipton Palo — said it was a mistake to shoot Jonce Nash in the arm instead of paying him."

"In what context did he make that statement?"

Wazenski looked confused.

"What had Jonce Nash said prior to Tipton Palo saying it was a mistake to shoot him?"

"He told Palo he had picked the warehouse because that is where Palo had shot him in the arm instead of paying him to kill Perry Stubbs."

"Are you sure he said that last part? Just that way?"

"Yes."

"And Tipton Palo's response to that statement was what?"

"He said it was a mistake. Then he started begging Jonce not to cut off his ears."

Mosby sat back in his chair and crossed his arms with a look of triumph on his round face. Whatever his mood before turning on the camera, he had conducted himself with the utmost professionalism when it mattered. Jackie was somewhat impressed, but Mosby wasn't quite finished. "You spent time in prison for the murder of your wife. Did you kill your wife?"

"Yes."

"Was it murder? I mean, there were no extenuating circumstances that caused you to kill her?"

"Every day she torments me from the grave."

"Is everything you've told me today true?"

"Yes. Everything happened just the way I told you."

"What is it you hope to gain from your statement?"

"Freedom," Wazenski said. "I only want out of this place and I will never break the law again."

"Would you lie to gain your freedom?"

"No. I'm a good catholic."

Mosby leaned forward and turned off the camera. When Wazenski looked at Jackie she saw desperation in his eyes. The evidence against Nash was still weak, but Wazenski had held up his end of the bargain and deserved a break in her mind even if some of his story didn't align with his earlier statements. He seemed confused on what was said at the warehouse and what was said at the motel. A good defense attorney might rip him to shreds if it got that far. There was always a chance Nash would accept a plea deal to avoid the needle, but that chance was slim. Nash was too cocky to think they could pin him down.

Mosby drummed his fingers on the table and stared up at the ceiling for what seemed an incredible amount of time. "I'll withdraw the charges pending the outcome of Nash's trial," he said, then he leaned forward and pointed his finger at Wazenski. "But if he gets off you're going right back into the system. Got it?"

"Does this mean I'm free?"

Mosby pushed himself up and collected his documents and stuffed them into his briefcase. "Someone please explain to him what I just said." Without waiting for a response, he snapped his briefcase closed and made his exit.

Jonce was in a john boat with Bobbie in the middle of a pond and they had water around their ankles. She wore nothing but red underwear and he was completely naked. Don was there, but he wasn't in the boat. Jonce could hear his voice calling her. At first she ignored him, then she glanced back toward shore. Every time Don called her name she became less visible, as though she were evaporating before his very eyes. Jonce grabbed her arm and tried to hold her but Don kept calling and she kept vaporizing. The water rose halfway up their shins. Bobbie said she couldn't swim. Jonce told her not to worry because he could swim for both of them, then Bobbie pointed at the water and said *what about them?* The water was teeming with piranhas. The boat was sinking fast. When he looked back at Bobbie, she was gone. He searched the water but she was nowhere to be found. There was no blood. No screams. Then he saw her standing on the bank of the pond with Don. They were holding hands and looking across the water at him. Don waved. Suddenly the pond transformed into a raging river and Jonce found himself barreling downstream amid jagged rocks and enormous cottonwood stumps. The boat struck a rock and shattered like glass. Jonce went under and saw Gain Prichard standing at the bottom of the riverbed grinning at him like the Cheshire cat. Jonce jumped awake with the force of a hand grenade.

He looked about himself. He was sitting up in his bed with sweat beading his forehead, taking his air in gulps. The dim gray light through the curtain told him it was early morning. A quick accounting of the days told him it was Wednesday. He was alone.

He cocked his ear toward the wall and listened for evidence of Bobbie getting ready for work. Her apartment was deathly quiet. He looked at the clock on his nightstand. Seven-fourteen. She would already be at the factory doing whatever mundane job she did there. She rarely complained about working.

Jonce wiped the sweat from his forehead with a corner of the crumpled sheet, then he rolled out of bed and pulled on the pants he had worn the day before. Bobbie had looked good sitting in the boat. Red suited her. His brain clung to that image of her as the details of the dream began to vaporize. By the time he had brushed his teeth and washed his face, he couldn't remember the dream.

The living room was mostly dark and had a dank smell. The entire place needed a good cleaning. It needed a woman. Bobbie's apartment smelled like candles and burning rope. His smelled like ass and feet.

He fried two eggs and made coffee. He didn't know how to make coffee for one because it always turned out either too weak or too strong, so he made an entire pot. With Prichard dead the state would be sending a replacement soon and Jonce would have to get a job, gainful employment being a requirement of his parole such as it was. Too bad he had to trade Prichard for his freedom but a man has to pick and choose his comforts. Bobbie was a comfort he had no intention of trading away. Don would have to be dealt with sooner rather than later. Friday night, or Saturday. Sunday at the latest but probably Friday so he didn't have to spend another weekend listening to him go at her like a teenager in the back seat of Dodge Dart.

He ate his eggs with his fingers, sucking the fingertips clean after each transaction, thinking how he might look in the female section at Walmart picking out red underwear. Friday night was date certain for Donnie. As soon as he pulled into the parking lot and stopped, Jonce would slide into the passenger seat and put a knife to his ribs. They would drive someplace remote and Jonce would stick him, then he would set the truck on fire and hightail it back to town on foot and Bobbie would be unencumbered. His heart raced thinking about having her to himself. Life was about to get good again, even if he had to take a job doing backbreaking work. Parole wouldn't last forever, and when his time expired he and Bobbie would go away someplace and start fresh. Maybe Colorado, where the mountains reach the sky, or California, where taking from the rich would be like picking up seashells along the shore.

She was mad at him — Bobbie, but the red underwear and a few days of intense good behavior would bring her around. Women are suckers for gifts and smooth talk, especially after they've been knocked around a little.

He pushed his plate back and belched into his fist instead of declaring it to the room, practicing his manners for when Bobbie was around. Someone knocked at the door and his first thought was Bobbie, then he remembered she was working and he figured police. Who else could it be, but he was wrong. When he went to the door and put his eye to the peephole he saw Waz.

"So they finally let you out," he said as he pulled the door open. "I knowed they —."

"Move back inside Jonce Nash," Waz said with a revolver pointed at Jonce's belly.

"What is this? Where'd you get that old thing?"

"I mean it," Waz said. "Move back or I'll shoot."

Jonce stepped back like a spider being pushed back into its web by a fly. With all his thinking about Bobbie, he had forgot to think about Wazenski. "You sure do make things convenient," he said as the backs of his legs bumped against the table that stood against the wall. A lamp that had never worked teetered but didn't fall. Wazenski closed the door behind him without taking his eyes off Jonce. Whatever he had in mind, he seemed determined to do it. "Is that a thirty-eight? Looks old enough to go off by itself so you be careful if it's loaded."

Wazenski raised the revolver to eye level. "It's loaded, Jonce Nash."

"Well point it somewheres else then," Jonce said. "What's eating you anyway?"

"You double-crossed me."

"You mean that thing with Prichard?" Jonce laughed. "Now we both know them papers was mine. What right did you have to Prichard? Besides, you didn't know where I hid them papers. They wouldn't have let you out anyway. They would've still come to me and give me the deal. My papers my deal." He grinned. "Now put that gun down and let's be friends again. We're both out. What difference does all that other stuff make?" He turned toward the living room.

"Stay where you are, Jonce Nash."

"Stop calling me Jonce Nash. Call me one or the other but stop calling me both. You sound ridiculous."

"And put your hands up. Up!"

Jonce raised his hands. "Okay, easy does it. You're shaking like a dog shit'n a cocklebur. That old thing might go off and put a hole in me and we'll both be dead. Me from the bullet and you from the needle they'll put in your arm. They say that juice burns like fire ant piss. You ever heard that?"

"They won't put a needle in my arm for killing you," Wazenski said. "They'll probably pin a medal on my chest."

Jonce frowned. "I thought we was friends."

"Over there," Wazenski said, dipping his head toward the kitchen. "Sit at the table and put your hands behind the chair."

"You gonna tie me?"

"Yes."

"Maybe I don't wanna be tied. You ever think of what you'll do if —."

"Now!"

Jonce moved. The Polack was too fired up to be reasoned with. Jonce sat in the chair and allowed himself to be tied hand and foot like a hostage in a bad TV show, unafraid because there was nothing he couldn't talk himself out of. All Wazenski needed was a little time to cool off and come around to his senses.

"Stop smiling."

Jonce forced himself to frown. "I tried to include you in that deal I made but that little fat DA's a real hard case. It was all I could do to —."

"Shut up."

"Okay, but —."

"Shut up!"

Jonce watched Wazenski pull a roll of plastic wrap from somewhere inside the heavy coat he was wearing. It looked to be the ordinary kitchen variety minus the box. Wazenski placed it on the table opposite Jonce then sat.

"You've got one minute to make your peace with God, Jonce Nash."

A lump the size of a grapefruit formed in Jonce's throat. A minute wasn't much time to talk a Polack off a ledge. "Ain't no need in all this, Waz. Hell, you and me's buddies. If you're mad about the million dollars so am I. Palo's the one you oughta be mad at, not me. Turn me loose and we'll go get him and —."

"Forty-five seconds to save your soul from hellfire."

Jonce glanced between the brown cardboard tube of plastic film and Wazenski's eyes, suddenly remembering how the Polack had murdered his wife. Suffocation was a hard way to go. "You're bluffing."

"I can see the sweat on your forehead, Jonce Nash. Thirty-five seconds is not much time to pray away the sins on your soul."

Jonce forced a nervous laugh and pulled against the ropes. Easy at first, then hard. Prayer was for the weak and feeble-minded. "Do your damnedest you dumb Polack. My soul is fine."

Wazenski waited until the full sixty seconds had elapsed, then he stood and picked up the tube of plastic wrap.

"Now wait a minute," Jonce said. "I was joking about that dumb Polack stuff."

Wazenski stepped behind him. Jonce heard the whiz of plastic being pulled from the roll. Jonce twisted and jerked for all he was worth, then he felt the plastic press against his nose and mouth and forehead. At first he could breathe then he couldn't. He saw the cardboard tube circle past his eyes. One. Two. Three times. He sucked hard but couldn't get air. His lungs began to burn. His brain raced. The plastic film held his eyes open so he couldn't blink. Wazenski stepped into view and sat down across the table and watched with a blank face. Jonce tried to overturn his chair. It rocked backward but remained upright. His lungs hurt. He begged for mercy but Wazenski didn't hear. He thought of Jesus on the cross. All he had to do was ask. That was the teaching. He focused on Wazenski. On his face. On his hands that lay on the table with the fingers interlaced. He thought of the two thieves. One was saved, the other not. A violent shudder rocked his body. His heart pumped hard against his eardrums. Instead of asking Jesus for forgiveness he cursed him.

Presenting the case against Jonce Nash to the Grand Jury before arresting him for the murder of Perry Stubbs seemed an overly-cautious approach, but it was Mosby's call and the Grand Jury was already empaneled. The indictment should be a slam dunk. Waiting was the hard part. Jackie truly believed Jonce Nash was a monster capable of almost anything. Knowing he had been so close to her son sent chills up her spine. She feared him more than anything her husband might throw at her.

"Stop staring at your phone," Gant said from the door. "I just heard from Mosby."

"And?"

Gant stepped inside but didn't sit. "It's up to the Grand Jury now."

"Nash could be hurting someone right this very minute."

"He'll keep," Gant said. "It'll all be over soon."

"If the Grand Jury does its job."

"It will. Mosby may be slow to move but he's a pretty good prosecutor."

"Jordan really likes you," she said, then she felt herself blush. It was so easy to say things to him. Too easy. "I mean, in case you were wondering."

Gant nodded. "Good. I really like him too. You've got a fine boy on your hands."

"I should've put my foot down a long time ago about those video games. They're so violent these days."

"Not like when we were kids shooting at flying mushrooms," he said with a laugh.

"They're so graphic. It worries me."

"Afraid he'll turn into Jonce Nash?"

"Or worse," she said. "If there is anything worse."

"At least he's doing it on a game and not on the streets like some kids his age," Gant said.

Jackie saw the mayor in her doorway and wondered how long he had been standing there.

"How come I always know where to find my police chief?"

"Just keeping my best detective in line, Mayor," Gant said. "She's chewing her nails off waiting to put handcuffs on Jonce Nash."

"Whatever," Jackie said. She held up both hands and straightened her fingers. "My nails are perfect as always."

"I was thinking of giving Nash a key to the city," Mayor Pigg said.

"Just as long as you don't give him a key to the jail," Gant said. The men laughed.

"For services rendered humankind by your excellent dispatching of one Perry Stubbs," the mayor said as though addressing Nash in ceremony. "I present you with a key to our fair city."

"No one deserves to die," Jackie said as the two men laughed.

"Not true," said the mayor with a finger wag. "Not true at all." He frowned. "But, I see your point and have a higher opinion of you for it … you being sworn to uphold the law as written. It's a flawed system but it's the best one mankind has thus far devised, and all that other mumbo jumbo." He winked at the detective. "And if sometimes a Perry Stubbs comes along and makes a mockery of justice, well, may we always have a Jonce Nash to settle the score."

"I don't think —."

"And a fine detective such as yourself to put Nash where he belongs for his contribution."

"He's not where he belongs yet," she said. "Don't count your chickens. There's a big difference in running an illegal gambling operation and slitting a man's throat."

The mayor frowned. "Not as much of a difference as you might think. A ruined life is a ruined life."

Gant cleared his throat. "Were you needing something from me, Mayor?"

"Yes, I wanted to be sure you saw the article about us in this week's paper. I would've brought my copy but I didn't want to be seen carrying it on the street. People might take my possession of it as some kind of endorsement."

Jackie had forgotten it was Wednesday. Gant admitted he had not yet bothered to read the Hayes Beacon.

"Page four, bottom left, right next to an advertisement for pole barns," Mayor Pigg said. "A Dexter Mann original. A last hurrah for the great Tipton Palo."

"Sounds like something I'll skip," Gant said.

"No, don't skip it. Read it. You actually got more ink than I did this time."

"A glowing endorsement, no doubt."

"Persecution of a pillar of the community to help me win re-election."

"Is that what he said?"

"In a nutshell," Pigg said. "I didn't even know I was running for re-election."

"You better," Gant said. "You can't jump ship now."

Mayor Pigg slapped him on the shoulder and thanked him, then he winked at Jackie. "You take good care of this young man," he said. "And don't go dragging him off to Detroit or someplace far removed. Hayes needs him."

Jackie felt the heat in her cheeks.

"My mother thought I was going to be completely ruined by playing Frogger," the mayor said. "Jumping that little frog across all those logs while floating down a river was going to undo everything I learned in church on Sundays." He smiled. "Yes, I listened at the door again. It's a habit I intend to break."

Gant's cell phone rang and he stepped past the mayor and out into the hall.

"I'm sure my parents worried I'd never amount to anything," the mayor said. "Well, they were right."

"You're a mayor."

"Exactly my point," he said. "I'm glad my father's not around to see it. He had such high hopes for me."

Gant stuck his head through the doorway. "That was Mosby," he said to Jackie. "The Grand Jury came through."

She grabbed her purse and stood.

"Slow down," he told her. "I'll send Birch and Ramey to pick him up."

"I'd like to put the handcuffs on this bastard myself," she said. She looked at the mayor. "Pardon my language."

"I'm interfering with police business so I'll go," he said.

"I'd really like to do this," she said after he left.

"Pace yourself," Gant said. "He's not going anywhere."

Chapter Thirty

J once Nash was still warm when patrol officers Roy Birch and Kale Ramey kicked open his door to serve their warrant. They found him tied to a chair in his kitchen with three yards of plastic wrapped around his head. He wore jeans and nothing else. Blood dripped from both wrists and ankles and his eyes were open hard against the plastic film.

"He's been dead about half an hour," Jackie said. She and Gant arrived less than five minutes after Birch and Ramey made the frantic radio call. She had seen enough dead bodies to be accurate with her guesses. The coroner was en route and would confirm her estimate later.

One of the three paramedics still on the scene sidled up to the chief. He wore street clothes with no markings and Jackie guessed him to be in his early thirties. He was a head shorter than Gant and had a front tooth missing. Jackie remembered him being at the Prichard suicide, properly uniformed that time, and recalled his name being Keith, or Heath, or something similar. "I heard the call go out on my radio," he said with a thick southern accent, speaking as if every word weighed a pound. He hitched his thumb over his shoulder and said he lived on Sycamore. "When I seen it was a murder I told them boys not to disturb the body no more'n they had to. That's why his head's still wrapped. I hope it helps catch whoever did this." He looked around as though his next words held confidential information. "If this had been a normal call and his wife or somebody had been here we'd of made some little show of trying to resuscitate him, for their benefit, you know, but he was too dead to bring back and nobody was here so we left him wrapped."

"We appreciate the fine work," Gant said, patting the man on the back as he walked him toward the door. "Nothing like interdepartmental cooperation."

Jackie watched the paramedic leave. "He seems eager," she said.

"He's all right," Gant said. "At least we don't have a trampled crime scene."

"They might have resuscitated him," she said. "It's been done you know."

"We won't mention any of that in our report. Keith thought he was doing the right thing."

"I'm not glad he's dead in case you're wondering," she said.

"I wasn't."

"Now I've got two murder cases to solve."

"Job security," Gant said. "Makes it almost impossible for you to leave us now."

She looked into Nash's dead eyes and could almost feel the fear frozen in them. "He got off too easy."

"He died hard."

"A few minutes of panic hardly makes up for all he's done."

"His panic is just beginning," Gant said. "Where he's going is worse than any prison we could've put him in." He eyed her with his easy manner. "Or don't you believe in the Hereafter?"

"How do you know he didn't pray his way out of it at the last minute?"

Gant shrugged. "Even better. Another soul saved."

"And you think that's fair?"

"If he convinced God, then it's good enough for me."

"I didn't know you were so religious."

"I believe in the fundamentals," he said. "Just like I believe in the fundamentals of police work, like my detective taking photographs of the body before the coroner shows up and hauls it to the morgue."

Jackie retreated to her car and got the camera. She had only met the coroner once, at the Prichard suicide, and she hadn't seemed at all territorial. A fly landed on Nash's nose at the instant Jackie snapped the first picture. The next five shots tracked the fly as it navigated the victim's face. Nash seemed to be watching her as she moved this way and that to get every possible angle. His horrific expression at the moment of death was trapped by the plastic film, as though he were a photograph of himself. The pictures would be a goldmine for the DA, assuming she caught the killer. She pitied the jurors he would force to view them. They would be ordinary men and women who probably wouldn't sleep for weeks without seeing Jonce Nash's face. Some might see it for the rest of their lives, but it had to be done because justice spares no one, not even the innocent. Jackie's mind worked the case as she snapped photos of everything within sight of the body. Any number of people had reason to want Nash dead. Tipton Palo topped her list of suspects but he wasn't the murderer. She felt certain of that. He didn't have the stomach for it, but he had the money to hire it done and he certainly had motive. Bobbie Booth probably had motive, but this wasn't the work of a woman. Her husband, perhaps, but he worked out of town and his alibi would be easy to check. Gradually her thoughts turned to Emil Wazenski. Nash had double-crossed him, and Wazenski had smothered his wife with a pillow. Maybe suffocation was his thing. He couldn't overpower Nash with a pillow so he tied him to a chair. Now all she had to do was prove it.

Wazenski was in the wind. Over the past twenty-four hours Jackie had checked all known hangouts. He had moved three times in the ten months he had been out of prison. The last address — a tiny rent house two miles outside the city limits — still had unwashed dishes in the sink and clothes in the closet. His boss at Cluck's Wing Empire told her he had missed last night's shift.

"Damned good worker. I hired him back after he got out of jail no questions asked. Is he in some kind of trouble?"

"I just want to talk to him," Jackie said. "Call me if you see him."

After lunch she called her old partner in Detroit to get an update on her husband.

"He's moved this chick in with him. She can't be over twenty. Real looker."

"White or black?"

"Could break either way," he said. "I've only seen her from across the street."

Jackie didn't have to ask why he'd been watching from across the street.

"I appreciate you looking out for me," she said. "You know I'll do the same for you if you ever need me to."

"Speaking of which, when are you coming back? This new partner they've saddled me with couldn't solve a stick of gum out of its wrapper."

She laughed. "I think I recall you saying that about me when I first started."

"Yeah, well, maybe I did. So when are you coming back?"

"I think I like it here," she said. "It's hard to explain but I sort of fit in."

"Slow and easy, huh? Since when did you like busting jaywalkers?"

She laughed again. "For your information I've got two active murder cases on my hands, and I'm pretty sure jaywalking's legal here."

"How about Jordan?"

"He's adjusting."

"You've got his future to think about you know. Be careful or you'll have a first rate auto mechanic on your hands."

"At least I won't have to worry about getting my car repaired," she said. "And for your information there's a pretty good university less than an hour away."

"Jackie, Jackie, Jackie," he said with a tone of defeat. "What have they done to you?"

She told him about the sting they had pulled on Kelton. He approved. Hearing him say it, and knowing he meant it because he always shot straight with her, gave her the peace she had been searching for. When the call ended she knew she would never see him again.

Tipton Palo sat alone in the living room of a small house he had rented on a narrow shady street in a quiet neighborhood north of town. His cherry red Porsche looked out of place in the middle-class neighborhood, but Palo appeared unshaken by his fall in circumstance when Jackie let herself in at his request.

He opened the door wearing pajama bottoms and no shirt, waving a glass of something in his right hand as he invited her inside.

"I hope I'm not interrupting," she said as she followed him across the beige carpet to a long sofa with throw pillows and stained cushions. Empty glasses and bottles dotted every flat surface.

"Forgive the awful furniture," he said. "It came with the house. The mess I created myself." It was late afternoon and he was still wearing pajamas. "I asked you to come because I want to get this over with?"

He motioned for her to sit.

"I didn't kill Jonce Nash and I didn't pay to have him killed," he said. "I was not involved and I don't know anything."

"That should settle it then," Jackie said somewhat sarcastically. She no longer considered him a likely suspect but why let him off the hook?

"Don't get me wrong, I haven't lost any sleep over the fact that he's dead."

She couldn't help but glance at his attire.

"They finally got around to pulling my license to practice law," he said. "That doesn't stop me from defending myself though. In the unlikely event that I ever go to trial."

"You know what they say about lawyers who defend themselves."

"Fool for a client," he said, annoyed. "I'm still the best lawyer this town's ever seen. Maybe the best this state's ever seen."

"Why stop there? Why not the entire country?"

He laughed. "I'm not egotistical, detective. I'm honest."

"Are you?"

His mind seemed to drift someplace as the smile on his face slowly dissipated. Jackie noticed an almost empty bottle of scotch on the table at his elbow and wondered how long before he reduced himself to a drunk.

"You're still mad at me about that business with your husband," he said. "It wasn't personal."

"Wasn't it?"

"Do you play chess?"

"I've been known to."

"Justice is chess," he said. "You have to think beyond your opponent's next move."

"Is that how you justify it?"

He reached for the bottle and offered her a drink. She declined.

"I hate drinking alone," he said as he returned the bottle to the table unopened.

She looked around the cluttered room. "You seem to manage."

"The human animal is nothing if not adaptable," he said. He spread his arms to take in the room. "This is a temporary setback. Soon I'll have my law license back and my wife will be living on her teacher's salary again."

"How did Nash find out about my husband in Detroit?"

Palo laughed again. "He didn't know anything about that," he said. "As far as I know anyway."

It wasn't the answer Jackie expected. "How did you find out then?"

"Your boss told me."

"I don't believe you."

"You'll learn soon enough not to trust anyone in this town," Palo said. "He also told me about Nash intercepting your pizza and scaring you half to death, and how you went rogue and he had to restrict you to your desk." Palo was smiling and seemed to be enjoying himself very much, but Jackie wasn't buying it. Gant had proven his loyalty too many times.

"That's why I told you it was Nash who tipped me off," he said. "I knew you'd believe it."

"Anyone could have told you about that," she said. "It was no secret."

Palo spent the next five minutes relating details of private conversations between herself and Gant. Things only the two of them could know.

Jackie barged into her chief's office without knocking. He looked up from his paperwork with annoyance, then, seeing who it was, he smiled. She raised her finger to her lips and began searching his office while he sat stupefied. First she checked his bookshelf, pulling every book one at a time. Then she checked the lamp on his desk, and the coffee mug where he kept his pens and pencils and a miniature American flag on a tiny wooden pole.

He opened his mouth to ask for an explanation but stopped short of speaking. After searching all the obvious places, she looked around the room, then up at the ceiling, thinking the recessed fluorescent light would be the place only to dismiss it because lights go out and have to be replaced. She noticed the air conditioning vent in the ceiling, but the noise of rushing air would make it an unlikely place.

On the wall behind Gant's desk hung a large framed picture of Hayes in a bygone era. Horses were tied to hitching posts along Main Street and the courthouse was on the square instead of across the street. She motioned for him to grab one side while she grabbed the other. With a look of complete bewilderment, he helped her lift the heavy frame from the wall and lower it to the floor. The wall behind the picture was a brighter shade of beige than the surrounding wall but was otherwise unremarkable.

Gant grabbed a pad and pen from his desk and scribbled a word: BUG?

Jackie nodded. His office was bugged. She knew who but she didn't yet know where. Gant reacted quickly, rushing past her and pulling the large five-drawer filing cabinet away from the wall. Taped to the back was a tiny microphone with a short wire sticking upward. He pulled it free and dropped it into a glass of soda he had been drinking at his desk.

"Care to explain?" he said.

"Tipton Palo," she said. "He couldn't keep his mouth shut."

Chapter Thirty-One

It took four days for Emil Wazenski to walk into the station and turn himself in. Jackie found him sitting in the lobby when she returned from lunch. He looked incredibly small slumped forward with his elbows on his knees and his face in his hands.

"Refused to talk to anyone but you," the sergeant said.

Jackie invited him back to her office instead of taking him to an interrogation room. If he had come to confess she wanted him to feel comfortable. If he had come for any other reason she was prepared for that, too.

She closed her door for privacy and offered him a soda.

"No," he said. "I want to get this over with."

They sat in their respective places as though they were about to negotiate a bank loan. He appeared extremely calm. She recognized his behavior as that of a man about to unburden his soul. No rush. She had all afternoon.

"I killed Jonce Nash," he said without lifting his eyes from his knees.

"If you're confessing to a crime I need to read you your rights," she said. Technically he wasn't under arrest but she didn't want to risk having the confession thrown out by a sympathetic judge.

She Mirandized him.

"I killed Jonce Nash," he repeated, then he looked at her as though unsure of what to do next.

"Did you use a weapon?"

"I used a gun to get him into the chair. I used zip ties to bind him. I used Glad Cling Wrap to suffocate him. It was a three-hundred-square-foot roll for which I paid three dollars at Walmart. I checked out in lane four. I paid with a five. The lady's name was Kim." He reached into his pocket and produced a crumpled strip of paper. "I have the receipt."

As far as confessions go, he had just handed her a doozie. She second-guessed herself for not videoing the exchange but then he might not have been so forthcoming. Suspects sometimes get stage fright when the light on the camera goes red, but it was time. To proceed otherwise would be malpractice.

"Would you be willing to repeat what you just told me on camera?"
He nodded.

They moved from her office to the interrogation room with the two-way mirror. Shielding her phone, she texted Gant a heads up.

She turned on the camera and Mirandized him once more for the record, then at her signal he repeated his confession verbatim. He seemed relieved to have it off his chest.

"Is there anything else you'd like to add?"

"Twenty-five wraps," he said. "I counted them." He squirmed a little as though uncomfortable. "I count things. My first prison cell was ten steps long and five steps wide. It was three-hundred-and-fifty-two steps from my cell to the showers. Five-hundred-thirteen steps to the cafeteria. Twenty-one steps from the end of the serving line to the table where I ate my meals. One-thousand-twenty-eight steps —."

"I get the picture," she said, interrupting because she didn't want to give him leverage toward an insanity plea. There was one more question she needed to know. "Why did you do it?"

"Why did I kill Jonce Nash or why did I confess?"

"Both."

"I killed Jonce Nash because he double-crossed me. I confessed because I've become institutionalized."

"Why did you wait so long?"

"I killed him as soon as I could. I waited to confess because I was scared."

"Scared of what?"

"Hell."

Gant insisted on ordering pizza in celebration of Jackie closing her first major case. Jordan seconded the motion. She gladly accepted because it was her night to cook and the day had exhausted her. Since her tirade in his office they had become even closer. It's that way with friends sometimes.

Afterwards she went out to the back patio and found him sitting in his favorite deck chair staring out across his back yard as he did most evenings. "You've been very kind to us, Andrew," she said, causing him to twist his head around and up to see her over his left shoulder. He smiled and invited her to sit.

"I think it's time Jordan and I went back to our apartment."

"I see," he said after several seconds of silence. "You didn't enjoy the pizza?"

She laughed. "Of course I enjoyed the pizza."

"So it must be something else then."

"We've taken advantage of your hospitality long enough," she said. "Nash is dead and my husband's been quiet. My lawyer says he's not fighting the divorce. I think he'll leave us alone now."

"And if he doesn't?"

"Then we'll come running back for your protection."

"Do I detect a hint of sarcasm?

"Not on purpose."

"I think you should give it a little more time," he said. "A few days. Maybe another week."

"And then what? Another month? A year?"

He smiled. "A year sounds about right."

"If we don't leave now Jordan may start to think there's something between us," she said, touching the tail of the elephant in the room. She was certain he had feelings for her too, but the complications seemed insurmountable.

"Would he be wrong?"

His frankness surprised her. He reached over and took her hand and she felt the electricity of his touch.

"I don't think we should —."

"If you finish that sentence I'll be obligated to stop," he said. "I could lose my job if I don't."

"One of us would have to quit," she said.

"This ain't Detroit. The mayor likes me and you've just solved a murder."

"It practically solved itself," she said.

"Wazenski refused to confess to anyone but you. You have a way with people."

"I haven't solved the other murder."

"No one cares about Perry Stubbs. People are glad he's dead. Besides, we know Nash killed him and we know Palo paid him to do it."

"Knowing and proving —."

"Nash is dead and Palo's going to prison for a very long time."

"Do you think he will?"

"Unless justice is dead he will, and if he doesn't he'll never practice law again and he'll never hold political office. That's prison to a man with his ambition."

"Some people would say that's unfair," she said. "One set of rules for haves and another for the have nots."

"We all carry our own prison inside of us."

"Did you read that somewhere or make it up?"

"I don't know," he said. "I believe it though."

"What's your prison?"

"Loneliness."

"I'm married."

"Separated. Practically divorced."

"We barely know each other."

"I know enough."

"You haven't even kissed me."

He pulled her into his arms and kissed her, then he pulled back and stared into her eyes. Her insides felt like mush — like the way she had felt when she was fifteen and Billy Rakestraw kissed her underneath the bleachers at a high school football game.

"I still have things at the apartment."

"We'll go get them," he said. "Tonight. Right now."

It took all of thirty minutes to load the remainder of their belongings into Jackie's SUV. Jordan cleaned out his room while Jackie and Andrew carried out the rest. He was Andrew now, not Chief, or Gant. That would change in the morning, and every morning after that for as long as it lasted. No one can predict the future. The only thing she knew with certainty was that by morning they would be lovers. It had been such a long time since a man had touched her with tenderness.

As they loaded the last of her possessions into her car, she looked up and saw a light through the curtains of Bobbie Booth's apartment and decided to go up and let her know her neighbor's killer had been apprehended. Jonce Nash had been more than a neighbor to Bobbie, though in what fashion Jackie couldn't be certain. Lover or abuser. Only Bobbie knew. She had seemed both afraid of him and drawn to him, which is more common in relationships than most people realize.

Bobbie answered the door with a beer in her hand. The unmistakable stink of marijuana washed past her as she stepped across the threshold and into the artificial light of the overhead bulb. "I ain't done nothing," she said.

"I stopped by to tell you we caught Jonce's killer."

"Why tell me?"

"I thought you might sleep better knowing he's off the streets."

Bobbie's eyes were glazed. Half stoned or half drunk. Both, probably.

"He had a son in Texas," Jackie said. "We notified him but he refused to claim the body."

"Serves him right," Bobbie said. "So what happens to him now?"

"The county will cremate him," Jackie said. "They'll store his ashes for a while in case the son changes his mind."

Bobbie raised the beer to her lips and her shirt rode up. Jackie noticed the unmistakable bulge of motherhood. "Congratulations," she said, wondering who the father was but not daring to ask.

"Yeah, lucky me. Don's turning cartwheels."

"You should think about laying off the booze and pot."

"Spare me the lecture," Bobbie said as she backed across the threshold and reached to close the door. "I've had a bad few days."

Jackie struggled for something helpful to say, refusing to believe that the woman standing before her was a lost cause, but the door was closing and Bobbie was high.

"His name is Jay," Jackie said. "El Paso."

The door slammed.

Afterward

Jonce Nash is a fictional character first introduced in my debut novel, *The Night Train*. Over the years, readers have asked what happened to Jonce, so I decided to bring him back at the end of *The Reconstruction Of Walter Pigg* as a cameo appearance. The story needed a ne'er do-well and Jonce Nash was the perfect candidate. The reaction to his appearance left me little choice but to give him his own novel. If you want to know more about Jonce, I suggest you read *The Night Train*.

…. Carl Purdon

www.ingramcontent.com/pod-product-compliance
Lightning Source LLC
Chambersburg PA
CBHW020529020726
47494CB00006B/1685